ISLAND

E1GHT

01-26-23

Beautiful Bells,

Thank you so much
for your support. I
hope you enjoy the
adventure.

ISLAND E1GHT

BOOK ONE OF THE ATARAXIA SERIES

M.Z. MEDENCIY

atmosphere press

For those who loved and accepted this quirky,
eccentric human as she is.

You know who you are—Thank you.

PROLOGUE

This was the first and last time Leata was going to see her grandchild. The Queen's maid, Carla, opened the door and rushed in with a basket full of bloodied rags. She gave the two guards a stern look.

"Not one word," she said as she used her foot to close the door behind her.

She was surprised that the brutes had agreed not to interfere. Carla figured they knew their potential instant pass to the inferno if they allowed the murder of an infant and wanted to prevent it. Good on them.

"It's prolly going to die anyway," one of the guards called out.

Then again, maybe not.

Carla approached the grand bed where the Queen sat. She placed the basket down. Carla tucked loose strands of her wavy brown hair behind her ears, fully exposing her tan, freckled, beautiful face. She removed the rags in the basket to reveal a sleeping child. She looked up at her Queen and saw joy. Carla hadn't remembered the last time her Queen smiled, but finally there it was. The maid lifted the child and handed it to Leata.

"Your granddaughter, my Queen."

Leata embraced the child and began to sob. Even after years of captivity, Queen Leata still found the will to keep up her appearance. Her long blonde hair was kept high up, bound tight with a maroon ribbon. Her matching cashmere robes softly encompassed the sleeping child as Leata held her.

"Carla, what happened? Tell me of Anne and the other baby, are they okay?"

Carla hesitated, the shock of the recent events still fresh and coursing through her veins.

"Princess Anne gave birth to twins. One boy and one girl, but the male was stillborn. Kahel was so furious, he denied Anne medical attention." The maid choked back tears. "She died on the birthing bed. He stormed out and told us to dispose of both ba—"

"Enough."

Leata looked at the infant with eyes full of hope. Hope. Something else Carla hadn't seen in years. She continued to watch as Leata savored every second with her granddaughter. Carla smiled and for just a fraction of a moment allowed herself to believe that things would be all right. But in times like those, hope and happiness came with a price. Carla sensed a strange energy fill the room.

"My Queen?"

Leata slowly looked up at her.

"She is going to save us all."

Leata bent over and kissed her granddaughter on the forehead. A warming light began to emanate from Leata. The two guards mistook the child as the source of the energy, pulled out their blades, and rushed towards the Queen.

"No!" Carla tossed herself onto the infant.

Then, the world stopped. The world except for Leata and the child. The ribbons in her hair fell and her locks rolled into the air as a warm wind began to dance around her. The energy then multiplied in intensity, her hair gracefully fell down onto her back, and the energy burst through the small group, knocking them all to the ground, starting time again.

Carla was the first to regain consciousness. She turned to the guards, who were lying on the floor, groaning and stirring slowly. Leata was on her side, curled on the bed with the child peacefully sleeping in her arms. With one look, Carla knew her Queen was dead. She pulled herself onto the bed and gently brushed Leata's now-unbound hair from her face.

"Be at peace, my Queen."

Carla quickly removed Leata's robe and wrapped the baby. For a moment, she questioned her intentions, but a voice inside her reassured her that this was the right thing to do. Carla took one look back at the Queen then disappeared into the night.

PART 1

THE WORLD OF MANKIND

1

THE TOWN OF SALINAS

Sophia lay peacefully on the hill outside her town. She had been coming up here for over two decades now. Two decades seemed like forever to her. Since she was five, this spot gave her calm and peace. The leaves of the dogwood tree swayed to and fro and allowed the sun to peek through them. She closed her eyes and felt the wind greet her as it playfully tossed her long blonde hair across her face. She inhaled deeply, rolled onto her side, and started to twist the grass between her slender fingers. What now, dear friend? she thought.

As far back as she could remember, the wind had graced her with its presence. Like a childhood friend, she cherished the wind and viewed it as a tangible being. Growing up, she sang, danced, and raced with it. Sophia had mentioned her wind friend to schoolmates in her youth, but as children do they teased her relentlessly for it. Since then, she had kept it to herself. Sophia was excited today because today her husband Gabriel was to return from Tychi. He and several other townspeople were there performing. Her town, Salinas, was a unique, peaceful town. Their uniqueness stemmed from two factors. One, the town consisted mostly of entertainers from dancers to fire breathers, and, two, Salinas was very welcoming, they didn't expect its members to believe a singular belief, and didn't force its people to live a certain way. All they asked of you was to contribute to the town and not cause harm to one another. People would come from all corners to be enthralled by the sights, sounds, and sensations of Salinas.

Sophia, like her husband, Gabriel, danced. Oh, and how brilliant she was at it. It was what Gabriel had been doing the past week at Tychi. Sophia pursed her lips, thinking about Tychi. Tychi was southeast of Salinas, and it's where their King Kahel resided. The King's court, known as the "Elite," would occasionally call on Salinas to send its best entertainers to perform in Tychi. Lately, it had been more frequent. The Elite wanted to make the citizens look at the left hand while the right hand was up to no good, the right hand being King Kahel and his goons in the castle. Sophia didn't like being away from Gabriel, but she refused to set foot in Tychi; she knew staying off the King's radar was the only way to ensure happiness. At least she could fool herself into believing things were okay. They say ignorance is bliss and Sophia was perfectly content living like that to achieve her quiet life.

But things were definitely not okay.

King Kahel had been tearing apart towns to build metal monstrosities he promised would produce endless food and energy. But all he'd done is steal land from his people and destroy the Green. Taking property benefited Kahel and his Elite. In turn, it forced the now-homeless inhabitants to migrate to Tychi. Kahel addressed the growing population issue by dumping a family of five, who once had land and a good-sized house, in a small box he'd call a "dwelling" and then stack one atop the other and so on. Not everyone remained loyal to Kahel after he took their land. Many refused to move behind Tychi's walls.

Therefore, many people had been displaced. Those newly homeless became wanderers, thieves, and beggars. The roads weren't as safe as they use to be. Some of those people joined together, creating small factions of bandits. While bandits were seldom found near Salinas, Sophia had heard of some close to Crossings Forged and the scholar town of Vizzini. Most bandits tended to congregate in the south near the Stone Titans. There were abandoned villages past the Stone Titans and gods knew what else further, past the deserts. The Salinas Town Council didn't want their people to suffer the fate of being scattered throughout the land.

While Kahel was a force to reckon with, to the town of Salinas he was nothing more than a raving lunatic who was content destroying the Green to expand Tychi's borders. The Green was just about everything born of this land. The Green has Essence, and Essence is life. The trees have Essence, the fire has Essence, and all breathing beings have Essence. Once a tree dies, the fire fades, and breathing creatures go to their final resting place, their Essence is dispersed back to the Green.

Sophia remembered arguing with her mother as a child, "But, Mommy, I'm not green!"

"Yes, my love, you're not the COLOR green, but we are all a part of the Green."

This meant when Sophia's mother died, she became part of the Green. Another reason Sophia couldn't stand Kahel. When he destroyed the Green, he could potentially be destroying her mother. She didn't like the thought much. She also didn't like that Gabriel had begun to feel differently. His mother passed long ago, her Essence had also dispersed into the Green, but Gabriel didn't see Kahel as destroying his mother. He saw it as the people advancing and entering a new era of innovation. Sophia and the Town Council would do just about anything to prevent Tychi from coming to Salinas. So, for now, until they could figure out how to cloak her town from the greedy eye of Kahel, Salinas will go to Tychi. Sophia placed her arm over her eyes.

"Ugh. I feel so terrible, not going to Tychi with them, but he knows, he knows how much I hate there." A reassuring breeze.

"Maybe I can change my trade? I could do well at Weiya's House, and that way I'd never have to leave our town." Sophia tried to hold back a giggle.

One of the most visited houses in Salinas was that of the Courtesans and Chevaliers. While Houses existed throughout the land that focused on the needs of the flesh, they were nothing like the House in Salinas. No matter your chosen profession, all here in Salinas were masters in their field of work. Weiya's House of Courtesans and Chevaliers was no exception.

In other towns, people would toss a judgmental glance with their noses high, like the Elite of Tychi.

"It's naïveté that fuels those looks. So many have yet to understand that there is nothing wrong with what we do. This is natural; we fulfill a need the same way an apothecary fulfills a need," Weiya had once said to Sophia.

Weiya, a brilliant woman, held a chair in the Council and was Mother Courtesan. She ran the House and treated her members and clients with the utmost respect.

"This life isn't for everyone," she had continued, her long mahogany hair flowing unapologetically in the wind as she leaned back on the balcony. "But neither is being a scholar or a fisherman. For some people, it just fits." Sophia knew that she lacked the strength to not fall hopelessly in love with the ones she'd bed. The Courtesan life was not for her.

"We care deeply for all of them. That's the important part.

You really have to connect with your clients to give them the care and understanding they need. We just don't allow ourselves to fall in love with them."

It was truly magical how they worked. Every town member in their profession had their own kind of magic. Well, it wasn't magic, magic had been gone for many years now, but to Sophia, who had never seen magic, she believed that this is what it must have looked like. The ability to captivate others in such a way that it seemed hypnotic. That had to be magic. And it is what the town of Salinas had in spades.

Sophia sighed, stood, and brushed her white lace dress off.

"I can't believe I wore this." Her words faded as she examined her dress. The wind shot a large gust that blew Sophia's hair and clothing up.

"Eeeyah! That's a hell of a way to get my attention."

Another strong gust and up her dress went again. Sophia struggled to keep it down.

"Alright, alright, I'm going," she said as she grabbed the corners of her dress. Her mother would have been furious if she had seen her lay on the grass without a blanket. Stuff like that really didn't mean much to Sophia, but it had meant a lot to her mother. Like most of the people from her town, Sophia was quite active. Keeping things clean and wrinkle-free was tough. But, for her mother, Sophia always tried. The sun began to set, and she felt the wind gather on the small of her back, pushing her down the hill. She peered down at her beloved town from under the dogwood tree. Here on this hill was her favorite spot. From here, she could see the Nacunas, a mountain range north of Salinas, and the herd of wild painted horses across the Pyre River. The horses were native to just this area. They were a gentle herd that allowed select townspeople near them. Their distinctiveness brought admirers from miles away; the horses didn't even realize it, but they were helping tourism. The wind encompassed her, then urged her forward again.

"Where have you been?" she asked. "It's almost been three weeks; that's the longest you've ever left me." The wind apologetically circled around her.

"Missed me that much, I see," a deep voice said slyly from behind the dogwood tree. Sophia felt the wind instantly disperse. A tall man slowly emerged, his black hair slung across his shoulder in a braid.

"Gabriel!" Sophia threw her arms around his waist and slammed full force into him.

"Woah. I guess you really did," he said with a deep laugh.

"How did it go?" she asked.

"As well as expected; we performed, they cheered, I came home." Gabriel shrugged then looked at his wife. "That's a really nice dress."

"Oh, you like it?" Sophia said as she swayed to and fro.

"Sure, I'd like it better on the floor of our bedroom, though."

"Well, then," she said with a smile and went up on her toes to kiss Gabriel.

Gabriel slid his hand up her dress and on her rear. Sophia looked down, confused, then back up at her widely grinning husband. He raised his eyebrows. She quickly swatted his hand away.

"Fresh."

The wind returned.

"What?" he asked, "I had to see where the line was. So, if I stay five nights, can I get away with that?"

The wind began to push Sophia again, but she didn't need any help. She was leaving anyway. Gabriel began to follow after her.

"Six nights?"

No reply.

"Seven? Come on! I was just joking around, Soph, wait up!"

Sophia began to sprint down the hill towards the music coming from their town. She took a quick look behind her and saw Gabriel with a smile on his face, catching up.

If she could keep a small lead, she knew she could beat Gabriel home and lock him out again. Sophia covered her mouth as she giggled. She recalled the first time she and Gabriel raced down from the dogwood as children. At that time, she ran because she wanted to get away from his cootie-infested stinky face. However, somewhere between thirteen and sixteen, it all changed. The boy who used to tease her became her closest friend, then her lover, then her husband. Even after so many years, the child in her couldn't resist a race. Ignoring the sweat dripping down her sun-kissed caramel skin, she pushed forward towards the Courtesans' and Chevaliers' House. Several of them sat on their windowsills and watched Sophia's speedy approach.

"Incoming," one of the older Chevaliers called out.

Sophia launched herself onto the sidewall and climbed it.

"Don't step on me!" he yelled.

"Well, move out of the way then!"

As she ascended, Sophia was able to partially see through some of the silky blinds. Only for a moment, she couldn't resist watching the passionate kissing, the tender touching, and how the shadows flowed and crashed together like ocean waves.

"Dammit, Sophia, you're going to cause a commotion!" Weiya, the House Mother, hung out the window as she called out to Sophia who was already on the roof.

"What would your mother say," a Chevalier asked as he dramatically wrapped his deep violet robe around his body, "if she saw you climbing in that dress?"

"She wouldn't say anything," Gabriel boomed as he began

to climb the wall. "She'd just get that wooden spoon of hers."

Shit. He's getting faster, Sophia thought. "She'd wallop you for instigating!" Sophia screamed back.

"I'll whip you both in her name if I lose patrons because of your idiocy!" Weiya huffed and went back into her House.

Sophia's mother was like a parent to Gabriel, but then again the whole town was. It's how things were run in Salinas; if a child was orphaned, they became the town's child. Everyone then pitched in to raise and take care of them. It happened to Gabriel when he was two and Sophia when she was fifteen.

"Sorry!" Sophia called down to Weiya.

"Yeah, yeah," Weiya's distant voice echoed from in the building.

Sophia huffed and puffed as she leaned against the locked wooden door of her house. She knew that Gabriel must have been tired from the trip back to Salinas, so him indulging her hinted at ulterior motives. As of late, he had been talking a lot about Tychi. More than usual and all the talks were positive. A pit grew in her stomach, but before she could over-analyze any further Sophia heard footsteps creaking on her roof.

"How many pastries did you shove down your throat at those high-priced bakeries in Tychi? Because you are making quite a ruckus up there," Sophia called up to the ceiling as she rolled her eyes and opened the front door.

She was expecting to see Gabriel's defeated face, but all she saw was quiet dirt roads and the vine-entangled homes of her town. Empty. Her town was rarely this quiet. Generally, music echoed down these streets as street performers presented to the crowds. Bandits had been spotted on the Wanderers Trail between their town and Crossings Forged. Maybe they finally made it to Salinas, she thought. In a panic,

Sophia stepped out. She began to walk across the road to her neighbors' house. Three brothers lived there: twins, Domingo and Santiago, and their younger brother, Marcello, who was Sophia's age.

"Domingo!" she called out, then heard the distinct sound of her door slamming shut. She stopped in place, closed her eyes, and exhaled, knowing the novice mistake she made. Immediately after, she could hear the eldest brother, Domingo, yell across the street, "Marcello! Give me the guitar; we are late!" As if they all had been cued, the roads began to fill up, and the brothers walked out of their home. Domingo gave Sophia a puzzled look when he saw her cross face. He then looked at his younger brother, Marcello, who laughed to himself as he set up his percussion equipment.

"Gabriel and Marcello are up to something," Sophia called out to Domingo.

"When are they not?" Santiago, the middle brother said.

The brothers have always been significant figures in her life, and she adored them. They were her and Gabriel's neighbors for the past three years, and she and Marcello were childhood friends and shared the same birth year. The twins were twenty years her elders. When her mother passed, they took her in. Since her mother died when she was older, Sophia chose to stay with the brothers until she was ready to move out on her own. Santiago, the youngest twin, was born one minute after Domingo. He also was the shortest of the three, and his soft, neatly cut, light-brown hair and facial hair helped him look deceivingly younger than he really was.

On the other hand, Domingo's face showed its years. He was the tallest of the three and the tannest, with dark untamed facial hair and wavy locks that sat on his shoulders. Marcello had a face that women swooned for, which made Sophia roll her eyes. His facial hair was tame, blonde, and matched the hair on his head that he kept back in a short ponytail. The brothers actually looked nothing alike. They say that Domingo looked like his father; Marcello, like his mother; and Santiago, a mix of both.

"You deal with yours," Domingo pointed to Sophia's house, "and I'll deal with mine."

Sophia walked back to her house, opened the door, and walked right into her small humble living area where Gabriel worked to start the wood stove.

"What took you so long?" he said, his back towards her.

"Are you that sore that I am faster than you, that you had to rope in Marcello to this?"

"Yup."

"What?"

"I knew you would get all 'EEEE, bandits,'" he mocked in a high tone.

"Stuff it."

"If the brothers weren't out performing, you would go and check on them to make sure they were okay and if I was losing the race."

"You were."

"I could get you out of the house long enough to get in and lock you out." Gabriel flashed his signature smile. That smile. Gods, that smile did things to Sophia she could never admit to him.

"But how did you get them to agree?" she asked.

"Easy. You're cooking dinner."

"I'm what?" Sophia stormed out into the streets to face the brothers.

"Dinner at dusk, your place, tomorrow," Marcello sang as he tapped his congas. Marcello turned to a group of tourist women. He dashed them with a smoldering look, followed by a gentle head tilt and a grin. Sophia could see the women visibly swoon and sensually smile back.

"Marcello!" Sophia called out. "I swear you should work at Weiya's."

"I know, right? These guys, though," he gestured to his brothers, "won't let me. Something about my mother forbidding it," Marcello mocked.

"You'd ruin Weiya's trade," Domingo sniped.

"Disappoint too many customers," Santiago added as he strummed his guitar.

"Hey!" Marcello continued to drum, aghast.

Gabriel laughed as he put his arms around his wife. "Gods, it feels great to finally beat you, I haven't beat you in a race since—"

"Since I was eight, and I had twisted my ankle from landing funny on a leap."

"I don't care if I needed help."

"Cheated," she corrected.

"It was just nice to slam that door and have you on the other side of it for once."

Sophia turned to face her husband. "You're an idiot."

Gabriel shrugged and stared at Sophia. No one Sophia or anyone knew had eyes like Gabriel's. His piercing ice-blue eyes had more depth than a bottomless abyss; if you were brave enough to stare into them long enough, a chill would slowly start at the base of your spine then course its way through your body and settle in that space between your neck and the back of your head. Once the chill reached that spot, there was no turning away from him. Sophia had to be careful not to get too lost in them. Those eyes paired with his dark olive skin made for one handsome creature. She grabbed his hand and walked him back into their house.

"Ooooohoooo," Marcello teased from far behind.

"I'm going to burn your food!" She could hear the crowd's laughter as she closed her door. Sophia walked towards Gabriel and traced her fingers around the front of his bangs. She always loved how it parted perfectly in the center. Gabriel's dark hair fell past his shoulder blades and was often kept in a braid. His hair was longer than Sophia's, and while she was secretly jealous of it she understood he kept it long for his mother. One of the only memories he had of her was her braiding his hair and telling him how she loved its length. Sophia lifted his braid and placed it behind him, gently caressed his left shoulder, and leaned in to kiss his neck.

"Am I getting lucky tonight?" Gabriel asked.

Sophia took in a deep inhale and let the anticipation gather.

"Yes."

Then again, why wait; she wanted it as badly as he did.

Gabriel smiled and kissed his wife.

2
THE AWAKENING

In the void between physical existence and eternity, a being who had remained dormant without shifting for what seemed like millennia shifted. In its mind, it followed Gabriel and Sophia, and like those fleeting dreams that we wake up from, knowing in our hearts and sensing in the distant corners of our minds that we had learned something important but can't recall, the being didn't know why it began to follow Gabriel and Sophia. Something was different. Confused and weak, the being took an unnecessary breath and opened its eyes. Well, more like became aware. Gods really don't have eyes.

3

BREAKFAST IS
THE BEST BRIBERY

Sophia let out a whine of protest as Gabriel opened the shades to let the sun in.

"Good morning my love," he said as he kneeled beside the bed. "I made you breakfast." He kissed her forehead. Sophia, in turn, pulled the covers over her head.

"Too early," she managed to articulate and attempted to go back to sleep. She should have known better; Gabriel lifted the sheets off Sophia and scooped her out of bed. She could feel his bare warm chest against her cheek, and it was comforting to her. She snuggled against him and began to doze off again. Once downstairs, Gabriel placed Sophia down on a bench at the kitchen table. Their house was quaint. The front door led straight into a rectangular living space. One side held a fire stove and couches, while the other side had a bookshelf and two chairs. Parallel to that space was their white-tiled kitchen. An archway divided the two rooms, and across from that, through the kitchen, was a staircase that led up to their bedroom, their warm cozy bedroom that had their soft bed. It was Sophia's favorite room and the room she wished she was in right now. Instead, she was downstairs in the stupid, cold, tiled kitchen.

Sophia grumbled to herself then looked out the large window behind her. The sun had just risen. It WAS too early. She considered pouting, she considered kicking Gabriel, and she considered shoving him into the armoire upstairs. Sophia looked longingly at the stairs. She yawned and turned her attention to the right of the stairway as Gabriel clanked some plates in the sink. He was making a mess, and she was going to have to clean it up. She watched as Gabriel poured her a glass of milk. Her eyes wandered onto his body as he replaced the milk in the icebox. His back displayed a fantastic array of nicely toned muscles that led down to a perfectly formed bottom. She could imagine it through his sleep pants.

"Stop checking me out, Soph. I am not just a plaything created to give you the utmost satisfaction in bed. I am your husband," he said with a smile on his face.

"You're not? Darn. Someone should have informed me before we wed."

Gabriel placed the plate of scrambled eggs, bacon, and bread in front of Sophia then opened the window to the side of her. A soft morning breeze greeted her. Sophia cautiously stared at her plate; she knew better than to eat Gabriel's cooking. It wasn't his gift. But what talent he lacked in the kitchen couldn't overshadow the talent he had elsewhere. Gabriel was a skilled man. Not only was he a dancer, but he was also a carpenter, a hunter, a gardener, and so on. Sophia chose to overlook the only flaw her husband had. She gave him a weary smile and took a bite of the bacon. The salty flavor filled her mouth with joy. The food was good. Gabriel smiled at his wife. He sat by her and placed her legs on his lap. He began to rub her legs then her feet. With the taste of the delicious food and the relaxing massage, Sophia was in ecstasy.

"Mmm, bacon, and massage, oh, it doesn't get any better than this!" she said with her eyes closed. Something was off, she thought. Gabriel can't cook, and this tasted delicious, so he must have been at it for a while to get it to taste this good, and the only time he would ever massage her would be when he was after—

"Soph," he began in a gentle tone, "I need to ask you a favor."

Of course. She placed her hands on the table and leaned back.

"What is it, Gabriel?"

"The performances have been going great at Tychi. Huge crowds, lots of cheers, but many of the people there have seen you dance. They chant your name at the end of our sets. They are asking for you personally."

Sophia knocked Gabriel's hands off her feet and got out of her seat.

"No, Gabriel, no, no, no."

"But Soph, they will pay us seven visits' worth, just for you to be there. The people love you, and that one performance of yours lifted the spirits of many."

"That was a year ago, and before I knew what Tychi had become, what Kahel's 'leadership' had done to them."

"Sophia. This isn't for him, you know that. It's for the people who are suffering there. So many of them lost their homes and had to start again. It's a hard change for these people, and all the Elite ask us to do is to make that transition easier." Gabriel still sitting, reached out to Sophia and pulled her closer, he kissed her hand. "It's not for him."

Sophia looked into Gabriel's blue eyes.

"...for the people," she said.

"Yes."

Sophia thought for a bit.

"Okay," she caved, "but this is the last time, okay."

Gabriel brought her onto his lap and hugged her.

"I promise the moment we are done performing, we will head home."

Something deep and dormant within Sophia stirred; she exhaled slowly and decided it was just disappointment in her own defeat.

They discussed the details, bickered when Sophia realized they were going to perform in four days and came to a resolution. Even so, Sophia was frustrated. She began to walk upstairs. Gabriel remained seated. He grabbed her leftover milk and tossed it down his throat. As he placed the glass down, he saw a thin purple nightgown fall to the bottom of the steps. Now, it didn't matter what town you grew up in or what your beliefs were, this was a universal sign recognized by every man. Gabriel stood up and launched himself up the stairs. In no time, he and Sophia were repeating last night's events.

Eilith was an older woman, but you wouldn't know it by looking at her. Her gently toned body and a head full of unruly red curls masked her age well. Just like most mornings, Eilith worked the milk stand. She was placing milk back in the icebox when a familiar figure emerged from the curtain-like vines dividing the townhomes from the Town Square. Eilith watched as Sophia stepped from the dirt path onto the cobblestone road. She was about to call out to Sophia when she heard a tiny voice behind her speaking to a customer.

"Yes, the best goat's milk out there!" the little girl said. "And if you leave it out for a while, you can make stinky cheese! Everyone knows the stinkier, the better."

"Anna!" Eilith called as she lifted the brown-haired girl off the counter and placed her on the ground.

"I'm sorry, we advise you to put the milk in an icebox and drink it within a week, latest."

Anna tugged at Eilith's dress.

"But Gabriel said when it gets clumpy, it's cheese!" Anna said, pouting.

The customer laughed under the guise of a cough and walked away. Once they were out of earshot, the fiery redhead sat down and gave Anna a stern look.

"You can't keep telling people that bad milk means cheese. Bad milk is bad milk. Cheesemaking is a process that starts with the curdling of milk, but there are more steps than 'leave it out and wait till it gets stinky.'"

Anna said nothing; she let out a frustrated exhalation and placed her chin on the counter, looking out into the crowd. Eilith smiled and put a loose strand of Anna's short hair behind her ears.

"You weren't wrong, sweetie, just misinformed." Eilith knelt beside Anna. "Tell you what, how about I teach you how to make cheese, and when you are a Master Cheesemaker not only will you be able to school that Gabriel on cheese artistry, you will also be able to tell our customers how to make their own."

"Really?" The little girl's face beamed with joy.

"Really." Eilith kissed Anna on the head and stood up.

"Cheese again?" Sophia asked as she placed an empty milk bottle on the counter.

"Sophia!" Anna called out.

Sophia lowered down and embraced the little girl.

Eilith walked out from behind the cart and gave Sophia a welcoming nod.

"She's missed you. It's been some time since you've stopped in. The same?" Eilith said as she began to fill Sophia's bottle with light milk.

"Only half, thank you," Sophia said as she spun Anna around. "Gabriel's been gone for a week, and he's the big milk drinker."

Anna closed her eyes and held on tightly to Sophia. Anna was one of the many orphans in Salinas. Three years ago, her sick mother, who knew Salina's reputation with orphans, brought her to the town before she passed away. Sophia and Gabriel took her in and remained her keepers for eight months. She was only four then. After Anna became stable, she was allowed to move around from home to home like the other children. Still, she was attached to Sophia more than any other townsfolk, and Sophia to her. She knew Anna wasn't hers, but sometimes she dared to dream.

"Anna, come visit me after you are done here. You can help me cook dinner for Gabriel and the brothers." Sophia's eyes widened with the realization that she did not bring a big enough basket for the ingredients that a dinner for five would require. "But no leaving the cart early. Eilith needs your help. The whole town does, okay."

"Oh, okay," Anna said as she went back behind the cart. Eilith turned to Sophia.

"Cooking for the brothers?"

"Stupid Gabriel made a stupid promise I wish I didn't have to keep," Sophia said as she rolled her eyes.

"Make Gabriel cook then."

"No one deserves to be punished in such a cruel way."

Eilith's curls bounced as she laughed and said, "The poor man knows how bad he is; he came to my house this morning and begged me to make breakfast for you. He told me he was trying to convince you to go to Tychi," she said with a smile. "Was my breakfast intoxicating enough to convince you?"

"You have got to be kidding me." Sophia placed her hand on the counter and rubbed her temples. "I agreed only because I can't deny that much money to our town. But I hate that

Gabriel felt like he had to deceive me."

"Oh, Gabriel's intentions were harmless; he knows better than anyone that, once you become set in a decision, getting you to change your mind is like getting a mule to dance along to our music."

Sophia frowned. "Are you comparing me to a mule?"

"Just as stubborn."

"Fair enough." Sophia shrugged. She gathered her milk and placed it in her basket.

"Well, now I know that you will be joining, I will be sure to pack. I hear Ari and Carminda will be joining as well." Eilith leaned against the stand.

"Oh, wow, a show full of headliners, and Carminda? I haven't shared the stage with her in a long time."

Sophia and Carminda's friendship was best described as complicated. There was genuine love between the two, but at times it seemed as if Carminda resented Sophia, even though Sophia could find no reason why. They shared dolls, mud pies, cuts, and bruises as young children, but when Carminda turned seven years of age something changed in her general disposition. It was as if she wanted to hug and punch Sophia at the same time. It hurt Sophia for years to lose the closeness she had with her childhood friend. She knew, though, that such is life. Carminda eventually grew closer to Ari, her longtime boyfriend, as Sophia grew closer to and eventually married Gabriel.

"Headliners, you say?" Eilith laughed. "Well, if the occasion calls for it"—her tone turned gentle—"be mindful of your words when you are in Tychi. Many of Kahel's citizens blindly love and respect him."

"Oh, pfft, I'm not going to start a revolution or anything."

Eilith chuckled, "Of course not."

Later that night, Anna had come over to help peel the platanos and bread the fish. Once they were finished, Sophia kissed Anna on the forehead and gave her a pastry she wrapped in a napkin.

"Late night snack for you after dinner," Sophia said. Anna smiled and tucked it in her satchel as she hopped out the door and skipped back to Eilith's.

Sophia packed her and Gabriel's trunks and waited, unease growing, and that strange feeling she dismissed as nerves began ebbing its way back to her.

"We look out for one another. You and me. I will never let anything bad happen to you," Gabriel had said when he returned from working in the fields. "Don't worry; Tychi has become so much better since your last visit. You would be amazed at the innovative changes."

Before Sophia could explain to Gabriel for the thousandth time exactly how Kahel managed to achieve those "innovative changes," there was a knock on the door.

"Come in!" Gabriel called out.

Marcello peeked his head in and flashed a dashing smile.

"I could smell it from my house!" He rubbed his hands together. The three brothers filed in, greeted by Sophia and Gabriel. The dinner table was boisterous and full of love and laughter. Santiago and Sophia offered to wash dishes as the others sat by the wood stove and conversed loudly.

When the evening grew late, the brothers said their goodbyes and went to prepare for their trip. Sophia leaned on Gabriel as they looked out their door. The night lamps' little fires flickered, illuminating the streets. Gabriel put his arm around his wife and kissed her hair.

"All will be okay."

4

THE TOWN OF CROSSINGS FORGED

The morning sun had just crested the horizon when they all met at the edge of town. Weiya and Domingo discussed town matters and travel details. Weiya held the second Town Council seat and would care for the people in Domingo's absence.

"I stand with Eilith. This is a terrible idea," Weiya said to Domingo. She tossed her long hair behind her, giving way to her curvaceous body that was wrapped in a long, high-collared, lace dress. The indigo, sleeveless robe she wore for modesty had only three buttons at the waist and shouldn't have been enough to keep her warm, but Weiya did not complain.

"No worry, our people will be fine without your guidance yet again." She turned to walk away. "I am starting to think I should have run for first Town Council, being that I am constantly filling that seat."

"I wouldn't have even dared gone up against you," Domingo called out to her back.

Sophia tossed her trunk to Marcello, who was arranging the equipment in the first carriage of the caravan. Sophia bundled her arms under her alpaca wool wrap that she wore over her dress to keep warm. The harvest season was almost over, and the colder mornings were a cruel reminder that winter was on their heels. She snuggled with herself and watched everyone work out their seating arrangements. They were heading south, and it was going to get a bit warmer. She had hopes that the leg wraps she wore under her dress were thick enough to keep her warm till then. She wasn't worried about her feet. Her leather boots, a loving gift courtesy of Gabriel, had a thin lining that would do the trick. Sophia stopped shivering as a gentle warm breeze encompassed her. That wind was different; that wind was her friend. She smiled, knowing it would take the trip along with them. Sophia's reaction to the wind did not go without notice. Eilith's brows furrowed as she secretly watched Sophia. The dancers began to climb into carriages, all except for one. Carminda, another celebrated dancer in their town, was waiting for her partner, Ari. Sophia looked longingly at her old friend and wondered what caused the end of their friendship. Carminda grabbed her honey-brown hair and tied it with a ribbon then pulled the golden hooded cloak over her head. Apparently, she was cold too. Sophia yawned as Gabriel put his arms around her. Everyone squeezed into two carriages, some inside, some sitting on top. Eilith and Domingo sat in the front, steering the horses and leading the caravan. The trip to Tychi was as long and boring as Sophia remembered. They took the Wanderers Trail going west towards Crossings Forged, a small town that served as a hub in their region, which connected to the Southeast Trail then to the King's Road. The town was mostly blacksmiths, but it still had the usual amenities: pub, inn, and item shops. The last time Sophia visited Crossings Forged was a year ago, when she went to Tychi to perform. If there were any needs that Salinas could not provide for, Sophia would travel east to Jaru, not to Crossings Forged. The town of Jaru was closest to Salinas, not only in distance but also in views. It received weekly deliveries from Tavernport, a town further east and on the water, which backed King Kahel one hundred percent. Daily ships would load and unload goods from Tychi at the docks of Tavernport. Jaru would stock what came into Tavernport, allowing Sophia to have all she needed without setting foot in Tychi or a Kahel-supporting town. Granted, Jaru would inflate the prices, but it was downright worth it to Sophia.

The carriage was quiet for the majority of the ride, save for Ari instigating an argument with Sophia. Ari was easy on the eyes; his appealing facial features paired with a chiseled jaw and narrow eyes made for an attractive man. "So, Sophia, I am enjoying watching you," he said to her.

Gabriel's eyes remained closed, but his arms crossed as he raised an eyebrow, and Sophia gave him a puzzled look.

"How does it taste?" Ari leaned forward.

"How does what taste?"

"Your words, your pride. You've been antagonizing us for complying with the Elite's request, but the moment they up the pay you happily jump on the wagon."

Ari wasn't Sophia's favorite townsman; he didn't even break the top fifty. It's not that Ari was a bad person; he just fell far below the minimum level of finesse that makes people tolerable.

"My wife didn't join us out of greed, you dolt." Gabriel opened his eyes. "She did it for us, our town. She would never refuse such an offer, even when it required her to put her beliefs aside."

"Says the man who wrangled the deal that she couldn't refuse." Ari leaned back, content with his verbal jab. "And, honestly, we would have been just fine without the extra pay. There is no need to send her into the lion's den."

Carminda kicked Ari and shot him a look.

"Well, at least we agree on one thing, Ari." Sophia leaned forward a bit. "No matter how much the Elite tries to hide it, Tychi isn't safe."

Gabriel rolled his eyes. "You two need to lighten up," he huffed. "Tychi is actually a really cool place. You should see all of the new innovative things going on there. Makes Salinas look like we never made it past the dawn of the first day."

"You refer to Tychi as 'innovative' again, I will smother you in your sleep," Sophia said and leaned back as Gabriel smirked at her.

When they finally made it to Crossings Forged, the group set up camp outside of town. Everyone was removing tents and packs from the carriages when Sophia stopped in front of a large wooden marker with a faded script informing travelers that the trail that they had come from would lead them to Salinas, Jaru, and Tavernport. Sophia clutched the sleeping bags closer to her. All she wanted to do was avoid the conflict brewing around Tychi and Kahel. All she wanted was a peaceful existence, to remain blissfully ignorant, and now here she was heading in the direction that would most certainly deny it. As Ari put it, "going to the lion's den." A warm wind began to circle her. It gently pushed her back on the path home.

"I don't understand this anxiety," she said to her wind friend. Out of nowhere, Ari pulled the sleeping bags from her. "Are you going to help or not?" he said then walked away. "Oh, and talking to yourself. Not a good sign."

Sophia sighed then continued to help set up camp. When it came time to eat, they wandered into town, leaving Marcello and Ari behind to keep an eye on their belongings. Marcello protested at first but then surrendered to the group's decision after his older brothers promised him extra helpings of food. The gates of Crossings Forged were always open. If a wild animal or unstable person disrupted the peace, there were enough skilled men and women who had access to a disturbing amount of weapons that the situation would find a swift end. Steam from the workhouses filled the cobblestone roads, creating moisture that sat stubbornly on any object in its path.

"This is it," Gabriel said as they finally reached the pub.

Sophia turned to look and saw a small brick building with a sign that hung with two swords drawn between the words "Pub" and "Food."

"Right to the point, huh?" Eilith said.

She led Sophia through the door. Once in, the small building looked even smaller, putting into account how busy the place was. Gabriel held his hand up, and the group paused. He scanned the room then spotted the bartender who had just walked in from the back and handed a plate of food to a patron sitting at the bar.

"Old man!" Gabriel shouted in a severe tone.

Sophia's eyes bugged out. She never heard Gabriel speak obnoxiously to anyone besides Marcello. The room grew uncomfortably quiet.

The bartender lifted his aging head and looked at Gabriel.

"Bastard!" he retorted.

Smiles quickly decorated both their faces. The tension in the room dissipated, and chatter slowly began again.

"Sit where you want, Gabriel," he said as he walked out from the bar. The bartender looked around and realized there weren't many options. "Well, where you can." He wiped his hands with his apron and opened his arms out to give Gabriel a hug. As they embraced, the bartender caught a glimpse at

Sophia.

"My god, Gabriel, you weren't lying; she is a beauty."

He grabbed Sophia's hand and kissed it. For a split second, Sophia was enveloped with a sensation that could only be described as falling. To others, it seemed like she took a quick stuttered breath, but to Sophia it was as if the ground had instantaneously given out. The brothers Domingo and Santiago, who were standing beside her, stiffened as the wild-haired man looked up at Sophia.

"My name is Boris, and I own this shithole."

5

FOOD, PUB, BORIS

"Eat, drink, but it's not on the house, I'm not fricking rich." He laughed loudly as he walked back behind the dark wooden bar.

Gabriel led the group to the far left of the pub. They grabbed several open tables and moved them together. Then they proceeded to search for available chairs and brought them in close to one another. It wasn't the best seating arrangement, but anything was better than standing up.

"Chicken, rice, and beer?" Domingo asked the group.

With no signs of protest, he was off to put in the order. Gabriel relaxed in a corner seat with his arm around Sophia. The pub's main decor was dark wood except for the table and chairs, which were lighter. The colors reminded Sophia of what her hands looked like after gardening, fingers covered in dirt up to her cuticles with bright spots on her nails. The palette gave the illusion of a dirtier space. Above, five large, metal chandeliers evenly distributed light to the pub. On each end of the bar, two fireplaces stood, going full strength, making sure patrons would think twice before leaving the pub's warm comfort to brave whatever cold realities awaited them outside.

"Best food in town," Gabriel said in a matter-of-fact tone. "It's a bit of a walk, but you know this town always feels cold to me, the metal-making and the indifference of the townspeople, but Boris's pub is always warm."

"Has anyone else here met Boris? Or have you always picked up the meals on your own, Gabriel?" Eilith asked.

"A few of us have come to help Gabriel pick the food up, but Boris only cares to talk to Gabriel," a petite dark dancer said. "I mean he will say his 'hellos' and 'goodbyes'—"

"Let me guess," Santiago interrupted in a solemn tone, "but he is only interested in Gabriel and his conversations."

"What? Jealous, Santiago?" Gabriel teased. "I'm sure if you had anything interesting to talk about, he would converse with you."

Domingo returned with a large tray of yellow rice.

"I'll need an extra hand for the rest," Domingo said as he placed the silver platter down. Gabriel stood up and walked towards the kitchen. Sophia was about to follow suit when Carminda grabbed her hand. Sophia turned to face a silent Carminda.

"Eilith, why don't you help?" Carminda said. "I've wanted to catch up with Sophia for some time." Carminda tilted her head and looked towards the bar, a gesture completely missed by Sophia. Eilith gave Carminda a curious look then followed her gaze to Boris, who was staring intently at their table.

"Of course," Eilith said hesitantly.

Eilith followed the two dancers and Gabriel into the back of the kitchen. Boris walked to their tables with plates and silverware.

"So, Sophia, are you from Salinas?" He asked her.

"Well, yes."

"Any siblings?"

"No, it was just my mom and me."

"Oh? No father?" He smiled as he asked.

"No. He passed when I was young."

"Oh, so sorry, how young were you?" he pried.

"Well, um...I don't really know. I don't have any memories of him, so I figured I was pretty young."

"Why, your mother didn't tell you? What was her name again?"

"She didn't mention her mother's name, Boris," Santiago piped in. He tapped his fingers on the table while waiting for the kitchen door to open.

"Oh, well, it must be my aging mind. I forget a lot these days," Boris chuckled. "Well, what was your mother's name anyways? I've been here for a long time. I wonder if I knew her."

Carminda's brows furrowed. Boris shouldn't be talking about Sophia's mother in the past tense. How in the world this disheveled walking prune could know that Sophia's mother had passed? Before Sophia could reply, Carminda leaned into Sophia and nudged her.

"Hey, I was thinking we should take this time to talk about our lineup." Carminda smiled softly at Sophia and said, "I know that you are nervous about performing in Tychi, but I want you to know that I am by your side."

Sophia watched Carminda as she spoke. The last time she remembered Carminda saying more than one sentence to her was when Sophia and Gabriel wed. "Congratulations. I wish you both happiness," she had said, and even then that was the first time she had spoken to her since they were children. Overwhelming feelings of joy almost erupted, and Sophia had to work hard to keep them in check.

"Maybe, Eilith, you and I can sneak out at some point and poke fun at the latest 'fashion.'"

Sophia laughed.

If it was Carminda's mission to attain Sophia's full attention, the task was a success. Boris shot a nasty look at Carminda. She returned it with a pleasant smile. The kitchen door opened, and Eilith came out with two sizeable yellow rice platters, and the others followed, each with one platter of chicken.

Boris sat annoyed with his arms crossed as the two girls conversed.

"Enough talk, let's feast!" Gabriel boomed. "You going to join us, old man?"

Boris laughed.

"No, numbskull; someone has to run this place."

"Then get the hell out of here!" The two men laughed as Boris stood and patted Gabriel's back then returned to the bar.

They ate to their heart's content. Chicken bones and stray grains of rice decorated their plates. When they had their fill, the dancers returned to camp. Santiago, Eilith, Carminda had already left with their on-the-go food orders.

It was late, and only five other patrons remained in the pub. Boris finished wiping the tables down and made his way to Gabriel and Sophia. He pulled the seat out next to Domingo but paid no mind to him and began to chat with Gabriel.

"So, when do you perform? Who knows, maybe I can make my way to Tychi and see you."

"Boris, I could never ask you to close shop for a day."

"Boy, I haven't taken a day off in, well, let's see, sixty-two years, and I do not know how much longer this body has left."

Sophia studied Boris's face as he talked to Gabriel. He was a pale man; his lackluster skin made him look paler than he really was. His wrinkles were deep-set and heavy looking. He had short wild hair that, if it was red instead of grey, you'd think his head was on fire. But none of this caught her attention more than his eyes; they were a very light grey. No. Not light, dull. Almost devoid of life. She had never seen anyone with grey eyes before. After seeing Gabriel's shocking blue eyes, she never thought the sight of eyes could startle her again. These eyes not only caught her attention, but they also made her uneasy.

"Something on my face, darling?" Boris asked Sophia.

"Oh! No, not at all," she fumbled.

"It's my eyes, isn't it," he said.

Sophia nodded, embarrassed.

"Hmm, well, you aren't the only one to notice, sweetie. The greyness does take people by surprise. It's the town; we here are all exposed to metal, so in a way, we have steel running through our blood." He chuckled.

"I never knew exposure to metals could affect someone so drastically." Gabriel leaned close to Boris's face.

Boris leaned back, in turn, looking more puzzled than annoyed.

"What are you a fucking Vizzini scholar now?" Boris pushed Gabriel back as he sat upright. "These eyes are a trademark of life in Crossings Forged," he pointed out, "and many of the people here have them."

Domingo abruptly stood, kicking his seat back, alarming Sophia.

"It's late, and we need to get an early start," he said.

Sophia and Gabriel, confused at his quick change in temperament, slowly followed suit.

"He's correct, old man. Thank you for your hospitality as always. We perform in two nights. I'll be pissed to see you there, but also happy." Gabriel and Boris embraced and patted one another's backs.

"Always a pleasure," Boris said while he stared at Sophia.

6

RUN

The young goddess sensed how close to danger they were. Overwhelmed by a sense of urgency, she lifted herself from the bedlike chamber.

"Run. You have to run."

With what little energy she had, the goddess pushed herself up and out of the chamber and began the arduous search for Mother.

7

THE ROAD
TO TYCHI

Back at the campsite, the fire was still going, instruments were scattered, and snores could be heard from miles away. Domingo scoffed at the sight, his warm breath visible in the cold night. Sophia covered a small laugh.

"I think you two can handle this," she said, then kissed Gabriel and made her way to their tent. Gabriel and Domingo wasted no time and began to clear up the mess.

"It's like cleaning up after children," Gabriel said as he placed a set of bongos in the cart. Domingo picked up a few mugs from the ground.

"Gabriel, how well do you know Boris?"

"Well enough to know he's not an enemy," Gabriel said as he placed a pair of boots next to Marcello's tent. "Don't think I didn't notice the way you and the others were watching him. I mean, really."

"Did you notice his interest in Sophia?"

"Do you notice everyone's interest in Sophia? My wife is gorgeous," Gabriel said. "People will look, it's no reason for us to go up in arms." Gabriel, exasperated, turned to Domingo. He was about to tell Domingo off when he realized they had picked up numerous articles of clothing, most of it being Marcello's. "I'm pretty sure that's all of it,' Gabriel finally said. "I am also pretty sure Marcello lost some wager and was left in his trousers."

"No," Domingo said sternly. "His trousers are up there." He pointed up to the tree. Gabriel looked up and, lo and behold, saw Marcello's trousers along with his undergarments.

"He must have played cards with Ari again," Domingo said.

"By the look of the pile of Ari's clothes, it must have been quite a show. Unless you will have us retrieve those," Gabriel said and pointed to the tree, "I am off to bed."

Domingo snuffed out the fire. "Watch out for Sophia when we are in Tychi. It was the only condition I had when she agreed to come along. Remember that."

Gabriel smiled and put his hand on Domingo's shoulder.

"You worry too much, old friend. Are you channeling my Sophia?" He laughed and said, "things will be fine, you'll see." Gabriel walked to his tent. "Get some rest, Domingo," he called out. Gabriel lay down next to Sophia; he kissed her neck and fell into a deep sleep.

The following morning, hangovers and headaches reigned. Marcello stumbled out of his tent with nothing on but a confused look and a blanket around his waist. Domingo walked over to his little brother and slapped him upside the head then handed him his clothes. Marcello gave a goofy smile and went back inside to change. They packed up and headed out on the final half of their trip. It was as long and dull as the first half. After several hours, the caravan's speed began to decrease, and the slowing bumps shook Sophia awake. She reached her arms back for a quick stretch and followed the group as they disembarked. The sun was setting, reminding Sophia that she'd slept most of the day, her body aching from all the immobility. She stepped out and looked at her surroundings. They had stopped at the end of the Southeast Trail. Canopy trees intertwined above, giving the group an elegant green archway opening up on the King's Road, which leads to Tychi. Travelers passed by, shoving Sophia and the others out of the way.

"Hey, no need to be so rude," Sophia called out as a girl rushed past Sophia. The girl turned back to look at Sophia while pulling her dark green hood up. The young girl's pale blonde, almost-white hair, and caramel skin were so striking a combination to Sophia that she knew without a shred of doubt that the girl was the most beautiful person Sophia had ever seen. A tall man in a similar green hooded cloak grabbed the girl by the arm and urged her forward. Domingo, in a similar fashion, led Sophia away from the King's Road.

"Keep your words to yourself. You were told this back in Salinas."

Sophia stood her mouth, agape digesting the reprimand. She turned to face the outskirts of Tychi, which used to be lush farmlands with miles of vegetation and livestock. Kind families had tended to the lands, families who understood and respected The Green. Tears formed in Sophia's eyes, and shock began to settle in as she realized that all of it was gone. She took in the barren land that rose to the high Umbra Cliffs, on which Tychi rested. It was an abrupt change, farm to desert. In the distance, Sophia could discern three large ships at the marina.

"Battleships? Why?" she turned to ask Domingo, whose sympathetic look gave her the chills.

"Domingo, what happened here?" she asked. Domingo's look continued. Before he could even formulate a sentence,

Gabriel walked towards them with excitement upon his face. "Kahel moved all food production into the walls of Tychi, and most of it is being taken care of by the factories. You guys should see it; it's quite amazing. They have tours," Gabriel said. Sophia looked at her husband in disbelief.

"Tours? What happened to the farmers? What happened to this land? Why was it left to die?" she asked.

"The farmers work in the factory and the land provided all it could," he replied. It took Gabriel a moment to realize that Sophia had walked away from him. She continued forward to the caravan, recalling every blade of grass that had graced this formerly beautiful land. Sophia remembered the apple orchard and how the caretaker would chase children off his trees, treating them as if they were crows pecking at corn. She remembered the smelly cows, nippy goats, and spitting llamas. That wasn't so long ago, and she knew this land had many more years of life in it. Sophia knelt down and touched the dirt. She let her hand rest for a moment before she dug in deeper. She felt moist warmth between her fingers, but that wasn't the only thing she felt; it was there, obviously there, and something more. This land had life; this land had Essence.

"There is still life in this land, Gabriel, a toddler could sense it."

Marcello, Eilith, and the dancers knelt down and followed suit; they felt it too, the gentle tingling sensation of energy. This would be great land to harvest in, they all agreed. Sophia walked to Gabriel and Domingo with two fists full of dirt. She held it out to them.

"Come on, Soph." Gabriel pushed Sophia's outstretched arm and walked away, leaving her puzzled. Stubbornness set in. She didn't break her stance.

"Maybe he didn't hear me," she said, staring at Gabriel, her arms still out. "I think I should shove some in his face." Sophia began to walk towards Gabriel when Domingo gently touched her shoulder. She knew that touch; growing up without a father, she often received it from the three brothers' father and then Domingo after their father passed. It was the "Let it go, Sophia" touch. When she was younger, she wouldn't listen; heck even now, she still wouldn't listen, but this time, Sophia knew she had to.

"He sees a good future, Sophia," Domingo said as he walked to face her, "and stands behind Kahel's forward-thinking, but I know"—he paused then grabbed the dirt in her hands—"I know there is life in this dirt, but you must also sense that it is, in fact, dying." Sophia glanced at the group who were all preoccupied with other things and then leaned closer to Domingo.

"No. Not dying." Sophia had felt something more when she had touched the earth. Being teased as a child about her wind friend, Sophia rarely confided in anyone when she sensed something out of the ordinary. This time it was different; there was this sense of urgency pushing her to speak out. "Dying would mean it was returning to the Green in some way." She checked again to ensure no one else was listening in. "Domingo, it's just gone, like theft. I don't know how else to explain it"—her heart started racing—"but when I hold this dirt, I feel, I feel angered and wronged." Domingo let out a short, worried breath. He opened her hands and let the dirt fall.

"We all feel that way, Sophia." They watched as Gabriel boarded the caravan. "Well, most of us."

The dancers and Marcello entered the caravan as well.

"We'd better get going," Eilith said, then climbed into the front. Sophia entered the carriage and sat on Gabriel's lap.

"Well, hello," Gabriel elongated the last syllable.

"Shut up. I'm mad at you."

"I'll shut up as long as you stay on my lap."

"Get a room," a dancer said.

The group bickered in the back. Domingo sat down next to Eilith then pulled on the reins, and the horses began to move forward.

"You know I'm against this," Eilith said. "We are bringing her back to the place she fled from. I heard what she told you; she senses it, and she senses the threat."

Domingo remained silent.

"Is it really necessary to keep her completely in the dark? That's a bit dangerous," Eilith continued.

"If it comes to it, we can protect her." But as the words came out of his mouth, Eilith was sure that even he did not believe it.

The caravan wheeled onward, kicking up so much dust that it looked as if they were being followed by a sandstorm. Beyond the outskirts, lay the main gates to Tychi. Tychi had three entrances. The one to the far north was the marina. That entrance was seldom used by groups in wagons. It was a quarter mile of a zigzagging steep path along the flat end of the cliffside. So, unless you were on foot or horseback, you could forget it. It was a beautiful walk and one of the few things Sophia had looked forward to in the past. The other entrance was new and to the south. It led to the factory area, which looked like a giant silver mess. Sophia stuck her head out the window. The dust cut free around her, a comforting warm breeze that gently wiped the hair from her face. She knew that touch. Sophia closed her eyes.

"Thank you for being here," she whispered to the wind.

"Who are you talking to?" Marcello asked as he pushed Sophia and popped his head out the window. It was then he caught the sight of the factories.

"That's hideous," he said.

"Look how the sky is so dark above it," Sophia said.

"It's just smoke," Gabriel interrupted.

Sophia poked her head back into the carriage. " I thought

47

you were going to shut up." She began to move off his lap, but he quickly grabbed her hips and pushed her back down.

"No more out of this." He pointed to his mouth, then regally nodded to her.

Sophia poked her head back out of the window and saw a structure hidden behind the three factories. It reminded her of a spider. Five long pipes were protruding from the center dome. The pipes had a slight arch then went down into the ground. Sophia was puzzled at the design, and as if that wasn't strange enough the central dome had a watchtower shooting up from the middle of it.

"Marcello, look at that thing!" Sophia called out.

"Looks like a spider, ick. I hate spiders."

"...baby," Gabriel mumbled.

Marcello quickly slid his foot under Gabriel's crotch and kicked up.

"My baaaaalls!" Gabriel said as he fell over and clutched his man parts. The action tossed Sophia off him and on to Marcello. The scuffle that followed just about knocked the carriage over. As Marcello and Gabriel got into it, they managed to hit everyone, provoking them to jump in. Sophia laughed and thought this was all oh-so-funny till someone tugged a fistful of her hair.

"Ow! You rotten hobos!"

She grabbed the hand that held her hair and pulled it forward. When she saw flesh, Sophia bit down hard.

She recognized Marcello's screech through all the voices.

"I've had enough." Sophia climbed out the carriage window and sat next to Eilith and Domingo. The wind cleared around her, leaving her untouched by the dust the caravan was kicking up.

"Kids got a little too rowdy for you?" Eilith said as she naturally stabilized herself when the carriage violently shook. "One moment, darling." Eilith athletically grabbed the side of the moving caravan and leaped through the window. You could distinctly hear Gabriel and Marcello apologize then squeal like piglets. Domingo had a proud look on his face as he slowed the horses. The door swung open, and Gabriel, along with Marcello, went flying out.

"You CHILDREN can hop on the back of the caravan with the instruments," Eilith exclaimed. "Ten years of doing this, and you still haven't learned." Both men had boyish grins on their faces.

"It's because we like being handled by you!" Marcello exclaimed.

"And it's the only time you'll touch us!" Gabriel added.

They laughed and patted each other's back then leaped onto the last attached carriage.

When Eilith returned, Sophia lay her head on her shoulder. Sophia watched Tychi's main gates come closer and closer and reminded herself that this was her last trip here, ever. It was the only thing that kept her from screaming. She hated what happened to the surrounding lands, the land inside Tychi, and, most of all, its people. Sophia wondered if any town that Kahel leveled had fought back. If they had, then no one's spoken about it. Salinas was one of the lucky towns that hadn't been touched yet. Sophia knew it was only a matter of time, but she also learned to keep his Elite happy, so nobody would go skulking around their town with blueprints. The people of Tychi pride themselves on their technology, their clothing, and their way of living. This wasn't the type of pride that most towns have; this pride rivaled the utmost snobbery. Then there was the Elite: the Lords, Ladies, Barons, and Baronesses. And, well, you couldn't get any snobbier than them. The warm protective wind stopped suddenly at Tychi's gates, leaving Sophia unprotected from the smells of Tychi. She cringed her nose as the caravan crossed the threshold. The odor of the factories was too much for her senses; she turned quickly and hopped back into the carriage, only to find Gabriel and Marcello sitting with two giant smiles on their faces. She sighed and nodded in disbelief. She was hoping for some peace. Sophia turned to the dancers.

"Really? Dammit, Ari! You being the strongest, I figured you'd at least put up a fight, keep them out," Sophia said to the blonde-haired dancer.

"Meh" was all the reply she got.

Sophia squeezed herself between Gabriel and the window. She watched as the horseless vehicles putted past them on the cobblestone road. Gabriel enthusiastically began to point out anything and everything he could, describing the object from its concept to its in-depth engineering. Tychi was part steam, part metal, part stone and wood, and very little Green. She learned that most vehicles here were powered by steam and the fancier ones that puffed black smoke were powered by oil. Sophia saw the wonder in her husband's eyes and held her tongue, no need to start another fight. As he continued his guided tour, she looked beyond Tychi's technology and saw that the only Green here was hanging from baskets placed outside of the three-story-high dwellings' windows. The brick buildings were very close to one another, leaving only a narrow path to the back. Children played happily on the streets in front of their homes. The line of dwellings was endless. She wondered if these people missed their old towns. They must. Who would willingly give up the freedom of having their own home to live here?

"There aren't enough homes," she said. "All of those towns, those people. This only looks like half the population."

"The housing goes for miles, Soph, you just can't see it," Gabriel said, then continued to point out more sights to the group.

Tychi was the largest town of the land and had three Districts: a "Factory," a "Common," and an "Elite" District.

Common District started at the Main gates and ended at Tychi Center. The Capitol Road was the direct path to the castle; about half a mile of Common District, and then one mile of Elite District. They were separated by the Town Square. A giant, obnoxious water fountain with a marble statue of Kahel, his face looking regal into the distance while he held a staff, marked Tychi Center. Water spouted out from around him, making it look like an aura of sorts. It always made Sophia snort in laughter. The buildings around the fountain were Kahel's markets. That is where the products from his factories were distributed. This was where the Salinans were to perform, on the Elite side of the fountain. Sophia looked over the buildings and caught another glimpse of the factories far to the south. She couldn't explain it, but there was that feeling again like she was personally wronged.

It was a good twenty minutes before they cleared the Common District and began past the fountain; Sophia snickered along with Marcello, which in turn got Ari holding back laughter and the dancers into a giggle fit. Some Elites who were out near the fountain gave nasty looks to the caravan. The horses began to slow down, then came to a full stop.

"This is it!" Gabriel boomed.

The group exited the carriage and stood in awe as they looked at the Inn they were being housed in. Dwellings varied in size depending on the District you lived in. The Elite had landscaped yards and oversized houses where space was used for petty rooms such as a "sitting room" or a "tea parlor." Looking at this building, Sophia wondered how many sitting rooms it contained. The large yet welcoming three-story wooden structure was painted a muted yellow with intricate white trim in curving patterns that outlined its features. Tall windows that began two feet from the ground traversed the length of the first floor. The second and third floors also had massive windows. You could tell that each window was for a room. Nothing, though, stood out as much as the front door. It was dark blue with its center decorated with a beautiful, brushed-gold eagle head holding a door knocker.

While the group remained dumbfounded by the large Inn, Sophia sauntered towards the door and touched the eagle head. It was lifelike; she ran her fingers from the beak to the side of its face.

"Haast's Eagle," she said. "Mama used to tell me stories about these majestic creatures. And know what"—she turned to Domingo—"I've seen one. Flying high past the Northern Woods near the Nacunas." Sophia smiled.

Eilith turned her attention to Sophia and urgently squeezed Domingo's hand.

"Your mother spun some wondrous tales. And, because of her, every eagle is Haast's to you," Domingo said. "Me? I see just an eagle."

She examined the doorknocker more closely.

"Yeah? Well, it's still a Haast's to me," she said.

Gabriel stood in front of the Inn with his hands on his waist. "Well, what do you all think?" he said to the group, who were all still stunned by the sheer size of the establishment. Gabriel broke out in laughter. "I see you all approve."

"Approve? This is hands down the nicest place we have been housed," Marcello said as he pointed to the Inn. His face quickly turned sly. "How many Elite women did you have to bed to acquire this? Forty?"

Gabriel sighed and shook his head.

"Fifty? Or could it possibly be, fifty men?"

Gabriel's hand was swift as it met the top of Marcello's head.

"Honestly, though, who placed us here?" Marcello asked as he rubbed his newly sore spot

"An Elite who's"—Gabriel hesitated, knowing full well

what Marcello's response would be—"a friend of mine."

"Oh, so it was a sexual favor!"

"Marcello," Domingo reprimanded, "her name is Lady Yaren, and I wouldn't put it past him."

Sophia turned around. "Really," she said, giving Domingo a disapproving look. Domingo returned with a childish grin and shrugged his shoulders. Gabriel ignored the comments and escorted Sophia into the Inn.

8

THE INNKEEPER

Talbot, the Innkeeper, sat behind his desk. He pushed his spectacles back into place then scribbled some words down on a piece of paper. He was waiting on a large group; by the Elite's request, they were to be the only guests. They ordered him to turn anyone else away.

"Yaren better know what she is doing," he said to himself. They've been careful; they've been meticulous, till this point. Yaren urged him it was time. Just like that. Talbot rubbed his aging forehead. There was no going back at this point. He took in a deep breath and looked up at his Inn. He worked hard, so hard, to make this place what it was. The light that poured into the lobby windows lit the room as if it had a thousand candles. It illuminated all of the furniture, making everything look so warm and comfortable. Guests had mentioned that they would have been perfectly happy spending a night on one of his lobby couches. The colors inside resembled the outside, save for the delicately painted detailing within the molding. The artwork was scattered across the walls and told a story of far-off landscapes full of Green and free of Kahel's industrial advances. Talbot took a deep breath and resigned to the fact that he could never return to the only home he knew, and any place he tried to establish himself in he was doomed to flee from.

9

THE STAINED-GLASS WINDOW

Sophia watched as Gabriel walked confidently to the front desk and the rest of the group filed in behind them.

"Lady Yaren instructed us to come here."

"Yes," Talbot replied, "I am sure she did." His brown eyes were dark and accusatory. Talbot's demeanor took Sophia by surprise but left Gabriel unfazed. *Maybe he's experienced this type of behavior often here in Tychi*, she thought.

"Can you please escort us to our rooms? We have much to unload," Gabriel continued.

"I could," Talbot said as he turned to grab a key. "But it depends on the room you choose. You could have this room if you want"—he tossed the key on the desk—"or this one,"—he tossed another, his tone was unwelcoming and full of contempt. "Hell, you can have any room you want. Lady Yaren booked the whole Inn for your group." He looked under his spectacles at Gabriel. "So, what did you do for Lady Yaren to receive such a grand gift?"

"SEXUAL FAV—" Marcello's mouth was quickly covered by Eilith's hand.

Sophia was confused by the Innkeeper's attitude. She walked forward then placed her hands on the edge of the dark walnut desk.

"Did Lady Yaren pay accordingly? If not, please charge us what was denied."

"Actually, she paid double," he said, still focused on Gabriel. "I'm curious, though, what's so special about entertainers from Salinas?" His words trailed as he turned and took in Sophia. "Good gods." His elbow slipped, and he stumbled on his desk. Domingo took a step forward.

"I've got to inform Lady Yaren that, um, well, that you have all"—the Innkeeper searched for a word while maintaining eye contact with Sophia—"arrived." The last word ominously hung in the air, and for a few moments there was nothing but silence as he looked carefully at Sophia.

"Yes, ahem," he coughed. "So, the hall to your left splits in two. The right side leads to the dining area, and the left leads to the living quarters. Choose whichever room you please; you have two floors, and each room has dividers. So, you can expand the size of your room if you wish." He took another look at Sophia. "If you will excuse me." The Innkeeper walked through the door behind the desk and shut it. Domingo turned to Eilith; her jaw was clenched, and her eyes full of worry.

"I know," he mouthed to her. Everyone started to walk upstairs. Sophia lingered behind and began to observe the beautiful artwork displayed all over. She noticed the vases, trinkets, and knick-knacks placed on tables. Sophia wasn't a fan of having things clutter her home, but that didn't mean she didn't like them. She walked towards a small sewing box. It was a trivial little thing that was hand-painted. She traced it with her fingers then looked towards the paintings on the wall. The colors were so vivid and real that it felt like she was looking out a window. Three pictures, in particular, caught her attention. The center one was of snow-covered peaks; she knew these mountains very well. The Nacunas were eight evenly descending peaks that were split in the center by an icy river. In children's stories, The Nacunas were the home of a warrior people known as the Ibex. Graceful, agile people with hypnotic eyes, skin soft as feathers, and elegant ears that came to a point. The stories would tell of their battles with evil demons and the dark Essence that tried to consume the Green and destroy the land.

In reality, the Nacunas were a sight to be seen and another reason tourists visited Salinas. As Sophia took in the paintings, the door behind the desk opened, and the Innkeeper slowly emerged. She continued to examine, this time she focused specifically on two of the paintings. Those had lands she didn't recognize. Both were of a large valley surrounded by forests, and the Nacunas could be seen in the background. She had never seen that valley, which was strange because the Nacunas were north of Salinas and could be seen on its horizon. There was only one village that was that much closer to the mountains than Salinas, and it was—

"Atara," a voice said from behind Sophia. Startled, she jumped back. Sophia looked around and saw that the others had all left the lobby, leaving her and the Innkeeper alone.

"Of course, no one has been there and lived to tell the tale, but the artist who drew these just took the stories and put them on canvas," he said.

"That can't be Atara; it looks too serene," she added.

"Well, minus its inhabitants, the land is serene. Actually, if you think about it, take people out of the whole equation, and the world is serene."

Sophia looked at the Innkeeper and stared at his tired brown eyes. He was a bit shorter than her, which she attributed to his slight slouch. Though he was a man of great age, his hair maintained its youthful color, dashed gracefully with greys. She guessed him to be well past his eighth decade but dared not ask.

"Don't worry, my dear, the Atarans only stay to their lands and consume one another. They seem to prefer their own kind to others, probably taste better"—he let out a laugh—"good thing, since Salinas is the closest town to Atara."

"Heh." Sophia forced a chuckle. But the Innkeeper was well entertained by his jest. "I'm going to go fight for a room," she said as she pointed up.

"You do that, and if you have any questions about the art in my establishment please feel free to ask me. My name is Talbot."

"Thank you." Sophia sincerely smiled. She walked down the hall then took a sharp right and saw the eating area that resembled more of an oasis paradise than a dining room. Complete with indoor palm trees and a pond, the room spanned almost fifty cobblestoned feet to her left and thirty to her front. It was patio-style eating, with small and large bistro tables set up around the pond. Her favorite feature was that half of this area was ceiling-to-floor glass windows that gave her a view of the large garden. The excitement began to bubble; she turned around quickly and ran up the short spiral staircase to the second floor. It opened up into another hallway, the length of the dining room. There were several rooms, all with the doors open.

"If we open this divider, it makes the room larger," a dancer yelled, "and we can all be in one room together."

"Again, I see no gain in that idea," Ari's agitated voice echoed.

"Stop being such a social recluse, Ari!"

"I am not a social recluse; I just don't want to have to share a room with you two bumbling morons."

"Carminda, talk some sense into your man."

"He has sense; if I talk anymore into him, he'll end up permanently sealing these dividers." Carminda took in a breath. "What Ari means to express but can't, due to his obvious lack of polite sentence formation, is that we would like to have some alone time together on this trip."

"OOoooOOooO," the two girls said in unison.

"Dear gods," Ari said as he slapped his forehead. Sophia passed the rooms and the bickering faded as she reached the opposite end of the hall, where she found the last staircase. As Sophia climbed, she saw a variety of colors coming through the hall window. When she reached the top, she turned her attention to her left at the stained-glass window that had created a kaleidoscope of colors. The art on the stained glass showed a brunette woman in armor, holding a Haast Eagle above her. The eagle's majestic wings were outstretched and touched the sides of the window. There was an aura around it that kept demonic creatures at bay. She was taken away by the beauty of the art. Stained glass wasn't something that was found in any town except Tychi, and this was the first time in her life she had been this close to one. She felt so compelled to touch it. It was calling her. She became entranced, her hands instinctively reached up. The stained-glass eagle began to move, it slowly flapped its wings, and she felt a breeze, a very familiar breeze. Sophia went on her tippy-toes and placed her fingers on it. An eagle's cry echoed in her ears, her breath stopped short, her body stiffened, pain encompassed every inch of her, she couldn't cry, she couldn't breathe, and then the world went dark.

10

THEIR AWAKENING

She walked. One gentle step then another. Her exterior was a deep translucent onyx, her movements haunting and regal in the nebula-like space. When it felt as if she would never navigate her way through space and time, she found the star she had been searching for. Slowly, cautiously, she approached its center, where a creature with matching brilliant, translucent, onyx skin slept in a gold chamber.

"Mother. Someone's triggered the marker. The Apprentice has awakened."

11

AN ANCIENT MARKER

Eilith was resting on her bed, her back against the wall, when she was gripped with panic. She leaped to her feet, reached to her thighs, and removed a set of elegantly crafted sai that had been hidden under her skirt. Her eyes darted to the door, and her body followed. She peered out the doorway. Down at the end of the hallway, Eilith saw Sophia collapse on the floor.

"Oh, gods, no!" She cried out and raced towards Sophia. Before Eilith could reach her, a figure emerged from the door to her left. All of her very long existence, Eilith was taught never to take any chances. She threw out a quick jab; a palm block stopped it. She hooked her left arm, but the figure arched back. Her distraction was costing her. She was desperate to see if Sophia was breathing. The figure grabbed Eilith's left arm and spun her around. He locked her arms down.

"Stop it, Eilith! We need to move her before the others run

up here," Domingo pushed Eilith forward, giving himself room to defend if she blindly attacked again.

"I'm sorry," Eilith hastily turned back towards Sophia. She effortlessly lifted her and hurried back to her room with Domingo closely behind.

"She breathes, no blood, no wounds," Eilith said as she placed Sophia on her bed. "Where's Gabriel?" She hid her sai under the pillow and set her hands on Sophia's cheeks.

"I don't know, but the group is on their way," Domingo said. Eilith could hear hurried footsteps approaching. A gentle silver glow began to emit from Eilith's hands.

"It was a form of Essence that did this to her," Eilith said, "not dark, but"—she tried to think—"Essence that was left behind, a stray? No, that's not right, shit."

"Quickly, Eilith," Domingo urged, the voices were closer and closer. She concentrated.

"It was a Marker, an ancient one." Eilith opened her eyes. "Domingo, she set off a Marker. It must have been hidden in the stained-glass window. We must leave now."

The voices erupted in front of Eilith's room. Santiago was the first face to appear.

"Saaaaaantiiaaagoooooo, move out the way, you've been walking like a snail."

"What's going on in there?"

"Why did Eilith yell?"

Santiago calmly looked at Domingo. He stood in the doorway, blocking the group from seeing inside. Santiago saw Sophia on the bed and waited patiently for an explanation. The looks of both Eilith and Domingo were enough of an answer for him.

"Back off guys, Sophia isn't feeling well," Santiago said. "The trip must have exhausted her. It looks like she vomited on Eilith's bed. Smells rotten"—he cringed his nose—"but if you really want to see for yourself, go and ahead and look."

"Oh, gross! I've had enough of the stuff that comes out of that girl's mouth," Marcello's voice shouted from behind. "I'm out of here."

"Ewww, I can smell it!" Shoving could be seen behind a statuesque Santiago. When they had all returned down to the second floor, Santiago walked into the room.

"Explain."

"She touched a Marker, brother; Eilith believes it to be ancient. Markers themselves are old magic, so if this one is ancient there should be no danger. There would be no soul alive for it to call upon."

"There is no certainty of that," Santiago said. "Strange, don't you think, that an ancient Marker rests here in this Inn, and no one else has ever touched it?" Santiago questioned.

"It's over three hundred years old, that's all I can tell you, and its traces are leaving her quickly," Eilith said then removed her hands from Sophia's face. "She will wake soon. I suggest we reduce our risk and leave now." They all stopped and listened to the footsteps approaching. Eilith placed one hand under the pillow, ready to defend if need be.

"Oh, wow, that was one heck of a power nap," Gabriel yawned and rested one arm high on the door frame. His white shirt loose and pants unfastened, he asked, "What's up, guys? Sophia okay?" As he finished his sentence, Sophia stirred. She slowly lifted herself up. Eilith pushed her sai far behind the pillows before placing her hands on Sophia's shoulders.

"You fainted, sweetie." She looked at Domingo and Santiago. "I think the trip weakened you; maybe you should not perform tomorrow." That comment woke Gabriel up.

"No, no, no, no, she's fine. Sophia's had worse illnesses than fatigue. We've come all this way; it would be a shame for us to turn around. The people are really looking forward to seeing her dance."

There was a time when, if Sophia scraped her knee on a

64

fall, Gabriel would carry her everywhere or, if she had a slight cough, take her harvesting days. Not tonight. Tonight, the four of them saw a side of Gabriel no one knew existed, one that put others' wishes above his own wife's.

"It's okay, guys, thank you for your concern, but I'm sure I'm fine. Gabriel is right; this is, after all, my last performance here. I wouldn't want to disappoint." Sophia scooted herself to the edge of the bed and stood up.

"Let us walk the gardens, my love," Gabriel said. She walked towards him and wrapped her arms around his waist. Sophia felt safe and happy. Things were always right when she was holding Gabriel. The pair walked out of the room and headed downstairs to the garden.

Santiago paced to and fro in Eilith's room, listening to Sophia's and Gabriel's steps fade as they descended the stairs. He turned to Eilith and Domingo when he was content that no soul could hear their conversation.

"Do you think the Innkeeper is involved in this?" Santiago asked. "The way he reacted when he saw her was like he saw a ghost. Also, who has an ancient Marker in a public display like that? I believe he wanted her to see it."

"What if others have touched it?" Eilith said, still in thought.

"Obviously, no one has since Sophia set it off," Domingo snapped.

"No, what I mean is, what if that Marker was specifically set for her, so only she could set it off."

"There is no way someone predicted Sophia's presence here over three hundred years ago," Domingo said.

"Domingo, Eilith makes some sense," Santiago's brows furrowed. "You remember the stories Mother used to tell us? Of artifacts that could only be triggered by those born with specific gifts?"

"Of course I do. Every child wished that they would find

one and be called upon by the Majji, but the 'Majji' is a fictional character. And, let's say those stories were true, how is it an Innkeeper managed to get his hands on such an artifact?" Domingo chided.

"I don't know." Eilith grabbed her sai and began to strap them to her legs. "All I can tell you is that my senses tell me that the Marker was created by old magic. My instincts are telling me that the stained-glass window at the end of this hallway is a Majji relic, who by the by, is not fictional. Lastly, my gut is telling me that we need to get the hell out of here."

"I am with Eilith, brother; we don't know exactly who or what that relic called upon."

Domingo stood in silence and fussed with his beard for a bit.

"There is no magic left in this land," he said affirmatively, "The Marker called upon no one. We are fine."

"What?" Disbelief was all over Eilith's face. "It was triggered! That is evidence enough that magic still exists! She needs to be told..."

"It was the order of the Council that she lead a normal life," Domingo said, "and she will. Unless I see solid evidence that she is in imminent danger, we will not speak a word of this to her."

"Domingo, you are blind!" Eilith hissed.

"I have made my decision," Domingo said as he walked out the door. Santiago gave Eilith a sympathetic look and turned to follow his brother.

12

KING KAHEL

Ten guards and five specially trained men, known as Osprey, guarded the throne room as King Kahel paced, awaiting the return of his two personal guardsmen, Corentin and Sethos. Corentin and Sethos were the King's right and left hands, and he trusted those two with his life, this moment, was a glaring example of that. The two of them had left to investigate a situation that had the potential of being disastrous for the King. They left at dusk and now night had fallen. The stars could be seen from the large glass dome above Kahel's head. The throne room was as wide as it was impossibly tall, making the few chairs in the throne room look ridiculous. Kahel would use this room for entertaining. He'd have his servants place long tables on his left and right that spanned the entire room. He'd serve an obnoxious amount of food and drink to a pretentious group of people. If it was a really good night, he would present some whores, male and female, and all would get their choice and walk off to private rooms. Tonight was not a night to celebrate. He had fear in his gut. Fear.

Something he hadn't felt in over fifty years. A couple of hours ago, he was happily bedding two women. One woman had her blouse open with no undergarments on and was bouncing euphorically up and down on his lap while the other was completely naked behind him, kissing his neck. Even if he wasn't King, Kahel was sure to have many lovers. He was a natural in the art of seduction; add to that his reality-defying handsome looks, and you had every woman's fantasy and every man's nightmare. He turned around and placed the girl with the blouse on the bed. He continued with her while the other girl crawled and joined in. The three of them were in the most precarious position when Kahel sensed a presence, a presence that shot fear into him. He freed himself from the women and began to panic, which isn't very King-like. When he had gathered himself, he realized the two women had seen him in that weakened state. "Well, that was embarrassing," he said then grabbed the girls by the hair and pulled them to his door. It wasn't much of a struggle because Kahel's harem was all usually so doped up they didn't have much fight in them. He dropped the two women to the ground. "Stay." He then threw his robe on, tied his long blonde hair in a low ponytail, and called out for his left and right hands. Corentin appeared first; he was a tall, toned man, with light brown hair that came to his ears. His skin always had a perfect sun-kissed tone, and it glistened with a light glaze of sweat. One drop slowly ran down the side of his brown eyes. To Kahel, desire is desire, and he admired, respected, and desired Corentin. Though the two have had their intimate moments, Corentin preferred women. If Corentin allowed, Kahel would have had his way with him many times over.

Without saying one word, Corentin pulled Kahel out of his chambers and behind him. Kahel inched forward while grabbing his sides. Then, a large dark-haired man suddenly appeared and placed himself on the opposite side of Kahel.

Doing what they do best, both Corentin and Sethos were protecting their King.

"You sense anything in here?" Corentin asked the dark-haired Sethos.

"Nothing now, but that was definitely a Majji's Essence," Sethos replied. They slowly peered into the chambers.

"There is nothing inside there except those two, who unfortunately need their minds wiped," Kahel said. The women began to whimper. "Oh, shut up," he snapped.

Corentin's head shot up, and he raced to the window in Kahel's chambers, then leaped on the ledge.

"What the fuck is going on?" Kahel yelled, flailing his arms in the air, "The Majji's been dead for fifty years, he had no Apprentice, and we all know Majji can't reproduce, so why did I sense his Essence? Why did we all sense the Essence of the Majji?"

Corentin looked out into the darkening sky past the castle grounds and into Tychi. He closed his eyes then took in a short breath, "It was a Marker. Far older than Halcyon's reign as Majji, it's fading." He opened his eyes. "There"—he pointed—"Town Square, near the fountain. Sethos, we must leave now if I am to track it." He looked at Kahel. "With your permission."

"Go," Kahel commanded.

Sethos ran past Kahel and leaped out the window. Kahel rushed after them and stuck his head out the stone opening to see the two men scaling down the tower.

"Don't make a fucking scene!"

Sethos looked up and released a frightening grin. It never looked right whenever Sethos smiled. He was a large man, just as tall as Corentin, but he had a mass of muscles that gave him a huskier appearance. His hair was short and dark, complimenting his amber eyes, which grew to the size of saucers whenever he smiled. Kahel knew that the pair had the potential to make a real mess wherever they went. But that's what you get when you have bloodthirsty homicidal maniacs as your personal guards. Good for him, bad for everyone else. He chuckled.

"Fuck. Whatever." He watched as they leaped and continued on to the Town Square.

It was the last he had seen of them for hours. Waiting. He hated waiting; a king should never have to wait. He continued to pace the room, his guards eyeing him skeptically, unsure why they were there or what they were to do. The Osprey stood statuesque, staring into nothing. Their grey eyes were as ghostly and eerily empty as ever.

Sethos and Corentin opened the room's doors and stopped at the threshold. Kahel walked towards them. It was then he noticed the look in their eyes. Concern.

"All of you are dismissed," he told the guards and Osprey.

Sethos shut the massive doors once the last guard exited the throne room.

"I couldn't locate the Marker; by the time we got there, the square was full of citizens and the hired entertainment doing an impromptu performance," Corentin said. "But something else presented itself."

"A member within the group shows the traits of the Majji," Sethos added, "but whether they are aware of what the traits mean has yet to be determined. What we did find was that none of the citizens recognized it. The entertainer danced and pranced, and no one really knew what they were looking at. It seems that your citizens have all forgotten that time."

"An entertainer showed the traits?" Kahel burst into laughter. "An entertainer, a fucking entertainer. This I must see. Make arrangements. I will make an appearance at tomorrow's performance."

"Kahel, I find that unwise, what if it's a trap?" Sethos said.

"There can be NO trap; Halcyon the Majji has been dead for fifty years!" Kahel said arrogantly. "This entertainer is supposed to be his Apprentice, but they can't apprentice with a corpse, now, can they? The pathetic peaceful age of the Majji is over. This person's presence confirms it! I have nothing to fear. EVER! Halcyon the Majji, protector of the Green, is nothing but folklore and children's tales now!" Kahel's fear dissipated. "Tomorrow," he said laughing, "I shake their hands, and spit on the vengeful words of the dead. My reign will never end. I will never be challenged! All the Essence this world has to give is mine!" His voice had hit a delirious pitch. "We must celebrate tonight! Now I wish I didn't have my favorite whores' brains scrambled; maybe, they'll pick up the basic functions quicker than the others." He waved his hands. "If not, I'll just find more." He laughed. "You two are dismissed, celebrate any way you wish, just clean the mess up later," Kahel told the two men as he walked off. Acts of violence in Tychi had significantly escalated since Kahel started displacing his people. So, when Corentin and Sethos went out, they could have their way and dispose of anyone all while blaming it on the growing crime. That night, they did just that.

13

THE UNWANTED INVITATION

Last night's impromptu performance had Sophia invigorated. After her little fainting spell, she and Gabriel walked through the garden and then made their way out to the fountain. There, they were greeted with applause and cheers by Elites and citizens who recognized them. Eilith, Domingo, and Santiago burst out of the Inn to see what the commotion was about. Sophia wondered what had those three on edge, but their appearance added to the cheering, and so they appeased the crowd and performed two short songs. Sophia sat in the dining hall, stuffing her face with fruit then eggs. Gabriel sat chatting with the brothers. The dancers all scattered about, being as loud as ever. Far on the other side of the room, Eilith sat alone. Sophia grabbed her bread and milk and walked towards Eilith. She sat down, ready to speak, when Eilith cut her off.

"I'm fine, don't ask."

Sophia stopped with her mouth wide open, and she then turned to her food. Attempting to lighten the mood, she held up a slice of bread.

"Bread! The exciting food!" Eilith let out a quick laugh and smiled at Sophia.

"So, you are really okay?" Sophia leaned in. "I don't remember vomiting on your sheets yesterday."

Eilith's jaw stiffened as she said, "You didn't vomit on my sheets last night." Domingo stopped eating and looked over to Eilith. She gave him a challenging look then turned back to face Sophia. "You passed out in front of that stained glass because you set off a Majji's marker."

Sophia's brows furrowed.

"That's enough, Eilith!" Domingo boomed from the other side of the room. The dining hall went silent. Eilith took in a deep breath and closed her eyes. When she opened them, Sophia saw concern in Eilith's eyes. It put fear in her heart, more than she'd experienced since she was told her mother's illness could not be cured. For just a moment, Sophia was back there again, a teenager, scared, not knowing what to do. Realizing her error, Eilith reached out and put a reassuring hand on Sophia's wrist.

"I'm sorry." With that, Eilith stood up and walked away. Sophia took a bite of her bread then went after her.

"Leave it alone, Sophia," Domingo called out. Sophia ignored his words and continued past him. She didn't go far before she spotted Eilith sitting in the lobby, looking at the same three paintings Sophia examined the evening before. Sophia slowly continued forward, passing the main desk, taking a quick peek to see if Talbot was there, but the desk was empty. She approached Eilith and reached out for her hand.

"Do you remember the stories your mother and I used to tell you, Sophia?" Eilith asked.

"Of course, it was the only way you guys could get me to

bed. I looked forward to those stories, I wanted to follow the warriors in their crusades, fight the evil. I tell them to Anna now."

Eilith smiled and faced Sophia.

"They were great stories, weren't they?" Eilith's eyes glassed over. Sophia studied her face.

"Eilith, I am no fool. You are obviously bothered, so tell me what it is."

"There comes a time when no matter how hard you try to keep truth caged, it just manages to escape. This is out of my hands." Eilith turned back to the painting. "Forgive me," she said as she wiped a tear before it fell. "I sense soon though." Before another word could be said, the door opened and Talbot walked in, escorting a pale beauty with long golden locks and eyes greener than the Green itself. She was dressed in a long, soft, pink gown fitting like a second skin to her fantastic figure. Her hat was large, the same color as her dress with a few white feathers along its sides. It barely made it past the threshold.

"Oh, well, look who's right here," Talbot said. "Lady Yaren, may I please introduce you to your guests? This here are the entertainers Sophia and Eilith from the town of Salinas."

Yaren looked at both women. Her eyes lit up, she took in a breath, and Sophia swore she was about to run and embrace her. But Lady Yaren let out the breath and smiled sincerely.

"Eilith and Sophia? My, Gabriel was not exaggerating when he said you were a beauty, Sophia, and, Eilith, it's quite an honor to meet such a famous and well-known vocalist."

Eilith's eyes shot open with the sight of Lady Yaren. "Thank you. Let me call the group. Please sit, they will be more than honored to meet you here in the lobby."

As Eilith walked away, Lady Yaren walked towards Sophia, touched Sophia's hair, and gave her a soft smile.

Sophia, being unaccustomed to such forwardness, tensed up.

"Your mother was a beautiful woman; it is obvious now she passed that to you."

"Excuse me."

Lady Yaren let out a small laugh. "Sorry, what I meant is your mother must have been a beautiful woman. Which is evident through you and your flawless feminine features."

"Yes, she was," Sophia said slightly puzzled. "Many people said I looked nothing like her, so I figured I must have taken after my father who passed when I was just a baby."

"Of course." Lady Yaren pursed her lips. Talbot escorted Lady Yaren to the couch where she elegantly sat down.

"Talbot tells me you are interested in the paintings."

"Oh, yes, they are beautiful. I've seen the ones in all the bedrooms and in the halls but these three are amazing. How they captured such splendor and serenity. Amazing, I tell you."

"Did he tell you who painted them?"

Sophia looked at Talbot. "No, actually, he didn't."

"The late Queen Leata."

Sophia's heart stopped.

"Kahel's, I mean King Kahel's mother?"

"Yes, and just 'Kahel' is okay with me." She tilted her head towards Sophia, "He is no friend of mine or Talbot's here, so you don't have to worry what you say with us or in this house."

Sophia nodded. "Did Queen Leata also make that stained-glass window upstairs?"

Lady Yaren exhaled in relief and gave a gentle smile. "I am not entirely sure, but it was found in the same house that the paintings were in. I acquired the house years ago and wanted to find a safe place to display her art."

"There is a Haast Eagle in the stained glass and there is one on the front door too."

"Majestic creatures. It's been many years since one has

been sighted." Lady Yaren looked down at her folded hands. "I think they may be extinct."

"I thought so too," Sophia replied. "But I swear I've seen one. About five months ago, I was fishing on the Pyre River north of Salinas, and I saw a massive eagle flying out of the forest. I told my comrades here, but they always say, 'You see what you want to see,'" she mocked.

"Yes, the same goes for 'not seeing.'" Lady Yaren winked sweetly at Sophia. "I found many trinkets that had the Haast on it in the house I purchased. I figured she collected them as a child. Probably was her favorite animal."

Eilith walked into the lobby with Domingo.

"I am sorry to have kept you waiting; the others are just finishing up breakfast and will be out soon, please continue your conversation," he said.

Lady Yaren laughed. "Kept me waiting? Oh, please don't worry yourselves; it's very rare that I can sit and talk about things that interest me. Most of the women here only care about shoes and the latest trends. It is quite sickening."

"Lady Yaren, this here is Domingo," Eilith said. Domingo reached out and kissed Lady Yaren's hand, she nodded her head in approval.

"We overheard you on the way in. Can you tell us more about that stained-glass window?" Domingo said as he and Eilith sat across from Lady Yaren.

"Is there a reason why you are all so interested in the window? Did something," Lady Yaren wryly asked with a slight tilt of the head, "happen?"

"Lady Yaren!" Gabriel boomed, breaking the tense moment as he rushed towards her from the hallway. "I wasn't aware you were going to grace us with your presence. When Eilith told us we had guests, I figured it was some Tychi folk who wanted to thank us for our performance last night."

"Oh, that's humble of you," said Sophia, mildly disgusted

as she watched Marcello walked in behind Gabriel.

"Ha-ha, no, really I did." Gabriel grabbed Lady Yaren's hand and kissed it ever so gently. Sophia felt an uncomfortable emotion bubble up in her chest. Lady Yaren blushed, batted her long eyelashes, and gave Gabriel a look that had more desire behind it than Sophia was okay with. He smiled his signature smile at Lady Yaren. Marcello nudged Sophia then shielded the side of his mouth and with the other hand pointed at the little moment Lady Yaren and Gabriel were having.

"Sexual favors." His eyes were accusatory, and he nodded his head with confidence. Sophia rolled her eyes at him.

"It's sort of weird, don't you think?" Marcello whispered to Sophia.

"What do you mean?"

"She looks like you. Well, you in a couple of decades or so."

Sophia hadn't realized it, but it was quite obvious now that Marcello mentioned it.

"Well, I guess Gabriel is getting off with older women now. So, it's off to Weiya's for you when you want some"— Marcello's face grew cunning as he slowly mouthed—"sexual favors."

Sophia jabbed her elbow into his side.

He winced then put his arm around her, letting Sophia know it was all just a jest.

"To what do we owe the pleasure?" Gabriel asked as he sat next to Lady Yaren.

"Two reasons. One, I wanted to meet you all. And second, to inform you that Kahel requests your presence," she said to the group. "He will make an appearance this evening and shake all your hands at the finale. Then he will have a party in your honor tomorrow night at the castle."

"We will not attend," Eilith spoke. "We have a two-day trip home and must harvest with our people before the cold season comes."

Yaren remained unaffected by Eilith's words and coolly replied.

"There is no reasoning with him," Yaren spoke in a warning tone. "If you have been summoned you go. But"—she turned to Domingo—"if his couriers cannot reach you to deliver the invitation, you will be free to leave. Possibly a little earlier than planned, say hours before dawn." Her tone slightly changed as she turned to look at Domingo. "On a completely unrelated note, the stone walls that border this establishment have some remarkable features. Talbot's gardens are so lush that they hide paths well. You should all go for a walk around the back, you might find something interesting."

Domingo wasted no time processing her words. He turned and placed his hand on Santiago's shoulder. "Weren't you interested in the landscaping of the gardens, so why don't you and Talbot go talk about the structure in the office?" Santiago nodded and walked away with Talbot.

"I don't see what's the issue with us going to a party at the castle; it would be an honor, wouldn't it? The King himself invited us!" Gabriel said.

Sophia gave Gabriel an incredulous look. She had enough. She turned to Lady Yaren. "It has been a pleasure meeting you; you are the first Elite who hasn't made me lose my lunch or breakfast, whatever." She shook her head. "And thank you so much for keeping us informed. You truly are a kind woman. If you will excuse me, I'm not feeling too well. I am going to lay down."

Lady Yaren bowed her head a bit, and Sophia walked away. Instead of going upstairs, she made her way to the dining hall then through the back doors into the garden. Then began to run as fast as she could. *What the hell is going on?* she thought. Gabriel has never acted like this before. He has never disregarded her feelings, and, for all things, to go to a party hosted by Kahel. Gabriel knew how she felt about being here, about the King and his rule, and how badly she missed home. It was like he was trying to push Tychi on her. She wanted to see anything that wasn't Tychi. She had been here only here for one night, and it felt like she had been imprisoned for years. Why the hell was Gabriel acting like this? Why was he trying to make her see the "bright side?" Then it became clear to her; he wanted her to like Tychi so much because he planned to settle here.

"No, no, no." This was the opposite of what she wanted. "I never should have come here." Sophia made it to the wall bordering Talbot's property. She looked up and saw it would be an easy climb for her, so easy to get outside Tychi's borders. Before she even started, a hand gently rested on her shoulder. Growing up, Sophia knew Domingo's "let it go" touch, the shoulder nudge jest from Marcello, and this gentle touch, distinctively Santiago's, that emulated love, care, and understanding.

"Don't, Soph," Santiago spoke softly.

"I need to see outside these walls, I need something that is not Tychi."

"Kahel has Osprey watching on the rooftops. You climb up there, his men will spot you and ruin our exit strategy."

Sophia threw her arms around Santiago and began to sob.

"I don't know why I get like this here, Santiago, ever since I was a little girl. I just can't stand Tychi."

"Anyone with a connection to the Green would feel that way. But you have always had something more. All of us sense the Green, with you, though, she has lengthy conversations."

Sophia and Santiago sat down with their backs on the wall.

"It's leaving Gabriel you know," Santiago said looking up into the sky. "He can't sense the Green as much as before; he hasn't confronted Domingo about it yet, but we both know. It happens. When you stop listening, the Green stops speaking. It's why he is acting the way he does. He is more interested in the future Kahel has blinded his people with. It's against everything we were taught. This," he said, "is our true mother." Santiago spread his arms wide open to the garden. "It is what sustains us, it is what provides the necessities; nourish her, respect all her children, do not take more than you need and—"

"You will forever be a part of her," Sophia finished Santiago's sentence.

"Our Essence is old. There is no new; what is here is here, forever circulating," Santiago continued. "The reason you hate it here so much is that there is no circulating going on in Tychi. Those factories back there dig deep into our lands, though I don't know what it's doing just yet. But what I do know is that it's stopping the natural circulation of Essence. It's why you felt the way you did in the outskirts. Something is stopping the land from doing what it's meant to do."

Sophia sniffled.

"Come." Santiago held his hand out and helped Sophia up. They began to walk alongside the wall.

"I knew about Gabriel, you know," Sophia said as she wiped her nose. "I could sense it too, but I don't think he cares, which is okay. He doesn't necessarily have to believe in what I do or do what I do, just as long as he accepts me for me. But he knows the tech isn't for me; before he would never push, now though?"

Sophia stopped, not because she wanted to, but right in front of her was a massive oak tree growing into the side wall. It had to be at least thirty feet tall, with low-hanging branches.

"This will be our way out," Santiago said as he pulled open a hidden door. "It's made of wood; Talbot sanded it down and had it painted to look like the stone wall." With its low-hanging branches, the tree cleverly hid the door. The branches dropped on the inside and outside of the wall. People could quickly enter and exit Tychi with the coverage of the massive oak tree. Sophia stepped out a few feet, finally outside of Tychi and under the blanket of the oak, and she fell to her knees. She took in a deep breath, and the wind began to tease her hair. She crossed her arms across her chest.

"Sophia, you are not alone. Many of Tychi's people from both the Common District and the Elite feel trapped here. I've learned that Talbot and Lady Yaren give sanctuary and even a way out to the people here who ask for it," Santiago said, "but every day they lose allies. Either they join Kahel's movement or disappear; people are asking questions, snooping around, seeing through Kahel's facade. That's why we are here. Kahel feels that if you give the people festivities and toss enough confetti, they will forget what really is happening. A war is brewing, people are turning, and those battleships you saw at the harbor weren't for an outside war, it's to control the people here. Once he's done with Tychi, he'll sail to Tavernport and then march into Crossings Forged. I've even heard he's sent numerous ships into the Kalyptra, west of Tavernport."

"But why? There is nothing there but the Nacunas and, if you believe in them, Atarans; what is there for him to conquer?"

"Who knows? His desire for power and control has no limit," Santiago said.

"I have a feeling I am supposed to remain unaware, of these ongoings. So why are you telling me all of this?"

"You deserve to know, that's all. Let's return," Santiago said with his arm extended.

The wind gave Sophia's hair one last toss and blew heavily against her as she entered Talbot's garden.

14

IN 5, 6, 7, 8

The group voted on leaving one hour before dawn, with nine votes to go and three to remain, Gabriel, of course, was part of that three. Nighttime fell. You could hear the low hum of electricity as it kicked on. The Town Square was filling up with citizens; Gabriel even spotted Boris in the crowd.

The clock chimed, and it was time for the show to begin. The group made their entrance followed by cheers. After they had properly positioned themselves, the music started. Santiago and Domingo came in with the strings first, using their incredible skills to make the sounds echo and reverb; Marcello came in next with the percussion, again his talent shining through. The people in the back swore there were seven percussionists. The beat was fast. Ari leaped onto the stage the moment the brothers began singing. The girls came in next, their bodies fluidly flowing to the beat of the music. No one missed a step. The crowd cheered loudly. Then it was time for the next song.

15

EYE SPY

Kahel didn't care to see the whole show. He really didn't give a shit. All he wanted to do was mock her, the pathetic Green. As he slowly took what gave her life every day, he knew she cursed him, he knew she was planning something. Before he made his way to his balcony seat in Town Square, Kahel made sure he yelled a few profanities out the window, knowing she would hear it, he laughed. His seat was set high up on the roof of the highest building. He'd been there for a good hour and was bored out of his wits. Sethos had to nudge him awake a few times, which made no sense no one could see him all the way up there. The people cheered when he walked in, then they all bowed. He loved their obedience, their blindness, it all made him giddy. He laughed a bit again. Corentin was being his paranoid self and was out in the crowd staying as close to the people as possible. If yesterday's Marker had left any traces, he would be close enough to track it. Kahel was against it, more like he saw no point in it, but for obvious reasons, he allowed Corentin to do as he pleased. It was time for the final dance. Kahel sat with his fist on his chin when he saw him. There were two dancers on the stage. One female with blonde hair and beautiful skin the texture and color of light caramel, who had danced earlier, and he was impressed by her beauty, but now the one that caught his attention was the male. He was tall, with olive skin and long black hair that was tied in a braid slung over his shoulder. But his eyes, oh, his eyes were the traits of the Majji, ice blue.

16

THE DANCE

The group had been performing for over an hour and a half. Everyone had their moments to shine. There were instrumental segments that had the crowd swaying, then there was Ari and Carminda's duet. They performed an ancient dance form where most of it was spent on their toes, using special shoes. Eilith just finished her solo, belting out her swan song. The group saved the best for last. Sophia was tired, but this was the final song. It was a duet with her and Gabriel. The dance Tychi waited for. Santiago, Eilith, and Domingo chose a traditional song that was composed long before Salinas became a town. The crowd cheered as Marcello and Santiago walked on the stage and positioned themselves in front of their instruments. Before Domingo could appear on the stage, Eilith grabbed his hand.

"The energy tonight, while visually we see no Green, I sense her presence here. She is watching intently. We should have left," she said as she placed both hands on his cheeks and gently kissed his lips. "Something is about to end, and another begin."

Domingo grabbed her hands and returned the kiss. Deep in his heart, he knew she was right. Serves him right, going up against her kind. He let out an exhale and led her up to the stage. The crowd went wild. Gabriel and Sophia were in place. Santiago started the first chord on his violin. It gave the aura of mystery. Domingo came in next with his guitar slowly and gently, then Ari with his flute. Finally, Marcello brought in the percussion, slow shakers, and muted congas. The song's tempo was slow and became seductive the moment Eilith's voice joined the melody. Sophia and Gabriel began with slow a pace walking towards one another, her sway saying more than a love letter could ever. Gabriel walked towards her, his eyes passionate, they embraced into a quick lift, and he then lightly tossed and caught her into a pose, her legs wrapped around him. She pushed him away, and he grabbed her arm, their lips touched. The lyrics, the sounds, the dancing began to pulsate through Sophia; she felt at peace, everything vanished. It was just her and Gabriel, her heart felt full, her soul peaceful. In a trance, she continued the routine more connected to Gabriel than she had ever been.

17

HELL HATH NO FURY

Kahel repeatedly grasped at his chest. Sethos had fallen onto his knees, his body tense and immobile. Kahel looked at the dance, he couldn't call for Corentin, but Kahel was sure he had collapsed also. The light golden glow that started circling just the dancers had spread into the crowd. He should have heeded Corentin's warning. This was indeed a trap.

"Fuckfuckfuckfuckfuck..." He dropped the ground and began to crawl towards the balcony exit. The golden light kept spreading. "You fucking whore. You tricky fucking whore," Kahel called out to the sky. "That damn dancer already is Majji isn't he, and he's performing a healing right here in Tychi." Kahel vomited. "Oh, that's going to stain." A sharp pain came from his chest, and he let out a stifled yell.

18

IT BEGINS

In the star, the god held on tightly to the other god, the one she called Mother, who continued to lay dormant in the golden chamber. The space around them ruptured with light as powerful bursts of energy tore through their expanse. She enveloped Mother with her matter, attempting to protect the sleeping god.

"It has begun." She embraced Mother. "I promise to end this once and for all," she whispered. "I will not fall to the humans. I love you."

A sole luminous crystal-like tear fell to the ground from Mother's sleeping eye as the Daughter's energy dissipated.

19

THE HEALING

Back in Tychi, the song hit an instrumental solo. Ari's flute repeated a slow melody, and Santiago's violin was playing long harmonizing notes. Marcello's percussion picked up the tempo slightly. Sophia and Gabriel were side-to-side, their choreography in absolute synchronization. They both leaped into a spin, legs up and bent, and landed with one single sound. Sophia continued to spin away from Gabriel while he walked towards her. She blindly leaped backward into the air before Gabriel caught and lifted her slightly. Sophia gracefully arched herself over his shoulder. He then lowered his arms as she gently raised her legs up and then finally fully around him. She landed quietly, now back-to-back with Gabriel, and they both spun then embraced one another, arched back, and lowered themselves to the ground. Their performance was visually and emotionally compelling, Sophia didn't have to be in the audience to see that. She felt it, maybe because this was her last dance, but the energizing feeling she was getting from dancing was not like anything she had felt before.

20

THE WOMAN SCORNED

A pale green light began to emerge from where Kahel had clutched his chest. Essence. He fought to keep it within him. In a panic, he flailed his arms attempting to subdue it. It's been a long time since he's seen his dead wife. Most people would be scared, but not Kahel. He was furious.

"Nooo, Anne, don't you dareeee!" he hissed. The pain was unbearable. He bent to his side and punched the ground. The golden light growing from the performers had finally reached his balcony, and the glow that had exited his body merged with it. Sethos crawled to Kahel and flung him down the steps. Kahel's rolling body hit each step with authority. The glow was spreading quickly at this point. Kahel lifted his head and saw Corentin coming from the opposite direction.

"Take our King, I can make it on my own," Sethos called out as he rolled down the stairs.

"Beware, Sethos," Corentin said struggling for air. "I

chased two Atarans before I realized what was going on; there may be more." Corentin reached Kahel. He never thought he'd see his King in such a vulnerable state. Corentin wiped Kahel's face with his hand.

"It's okay I won't let anything happen to you." He cradled his King like a child and leaped down onto Capitol Road. He ran, his speed blurring, directly to the castle.

21

UNWELCOME
COMPANY

The crowd cheered and tossed flowers on the stage. Sophia
looked up at Kahel's balcony after the curtain call. Good, she
thought when she saw the empty throne. She didn't want to
shake his hand anyway. They bowed one last time then began
to pick up the flowers and wave at the crowd. Marcello was
gathering the instruments, and some entertainers walked off
the stage and made their way to the Inn. The brothers, along
with Eilith, entered to find Talbot and Lady Yaren standing by
the couches. She was wearing a long, high-collared, green
evening dress, just like her other gown, fitting her amazing
figure like a glove. Her hair was gracefully held up with a
diamond bird hairpin, the matching handbag clutched tightly
in front of her.

"You must leave." The urgency of her tone was shocking
and unexpected. "Immediately," she continued, "I know you
three understand more than what you reveal. You must have

sensed what happened out there. The strange energy that Gabriel and Sophia produced left Kahel unconscious. Once he comes to, he will demand your audience. And my people spotted five Atarans here in Tychi," she said to Eilith. "Two were chased away by Kahel's bodyguard, the other three they lost track of."

"Atarans? How did they get in?" Eilith asked.

"It seems that your performance created gaps in security. Many of the guards left their posts to watch. Tomorrow morning, I will spread the word that the Atarans were here and that your group left in the middle of the night in fear of them."

"The Atarans being here will work to your advantage," Talbot said as he led the brothers to the dining hall. "I've already sent three of your carriages with whatever belongings you had upstairs off to Crossings Forged, you can attach them all together there. Your last carriage is outside Tychi's borders under the cover of the oak tree. Cut through my garden, Santiago knows the way."

When the men seemed distracted enough, Lady Yaren opened her diamond-studded clutch, pulled out a small envelope, and handed it to Eilith.

"Read it alone. I can't reveal more. I have faith you will understand."

Eilith took the envelope and hid it in the top part of her dress.

Sophia's arms were full of flowers.

"I'm moving to Salinas, and when I grow up I'm going to be a dancer like Sophia!" A child said as they spun in circles.

"I want to be like Carminda and dance on my toes!"

"They were all so cool!"

It was worth it, all of it. Just to put smiles on their faces.

Sophia could sense so much love. It was hands-down magical. Sophia passed a flower to an older couple that was dancing to no music when someone tapped her on the shoulder. She turned to see a pair of grey eyes and short wild white hair.

"Amazing. Truly amazing, more than I anticipated," Boris said with a smile from ear to ear.

"Boris! You old hag! You made it!" Gabriel boomed from the stage. He dropped the instruments he was packing up and jumped down.

"Hey!" Marcello cried out as he picked up what Gabriel dropped. "No, it's okay; I can do it all myself."

Gabriel walked to Boris and embraced him. "I am so happy to see you here! My Sophia never disappoints, does she?"

"No. Not at all. I'm thinking the three of us should go out and celebrate your amazing performance, this being my first and last day off for a long time." Boris laughed. "I left my Tavern in the care of the chef. I'm sure I'll return to nothing but ash!" The two men laughed together.

"We need to bring the flowers in," Sophia said, "and Marcello needs help with the instruments, but I am sure when we are done"—she hesitated—"we can celebrate."

"I am surprised you weren't invited to meet with the King," Boris said. Sophia's heart began to race; she didn't like where this conversation was going.

"We were," Gabriel said as he handed flowers to Sophia, "but he left by the end of the performance. We all guessed he decided against it."

"Well then," Boris said slightly disgruntled. "Tomorrow night then? At the King's celebration!"

"We would," Gabriel muttered, "but the group wants to make an early exit tomorrow, and it's been decided to call it an early night."

"Oh, that's too bad, and not happening," Boris laughed. "A king's invitation isn't something you just ignore. If your group doesn't want to go, then let it just be the three of us. It's bound to be a great time!"

"I know," Gabriel agreed. "Let's see if we can convince the others"

Gabriel burst through the Inn door, startling the group. "Look who I found in the crowd!" he called out as he led Boris through the door. Talbot took a step back, and Lady Yaren grew stiff. Eilith slowly stood up and noticed the shocked look on Lady Yaren's face. Eilith walked towards her as the men exchanged hellos and welcomes.

"What is it?" Eilith whispered.

Lady Yaren gave a slight warning nod. "Can you please introduce me to the gentleman?"

"Oh, my goodness, forgive my rudeness!" Gabriel shouted from the doorway. He led Boris to where she stood. "Boris let me introduce you to Lady Yaren."

"Gabriel, you keep beautiful company," Boris said as he kissed Lady Yaren's hand.

Ari stumbled through the door with an armful of flowers. He and the other dancers pushed their way by dropping some flowers on the floor. Sophia tried to pick as many up before she closed the door behind her. Sophia followed the other dancers, who lined up near the front desk. The once-spacious lobby was now stifling. Boris gave Sophia a smile then turned to Lady Yaren.

"Always a pleasure to be introduced to an Elite."

"The pleasure is all mine," Lady Yaren responded. "Your reputation precedes you. Boris, owner of the best Tavern in Crossings Forged, former Master Blacksmith and the late King's personal confidant, what hard times you must have fallen upon when he was slain. So much so that you left Tychi to live at Crossings Forged. Not to say that your accomplishments there are to be belittled." Lady Yaren shook her head.

"Nonetheless, life at Crossings Forged cannot be compared to life here in Tychi. It's like putting ambrosia in the same category as stale bread." She laughed. "It's unheard of! And your eyes"—she placed her hand across her chest in shock—"how strange."

Boris laughed a laugh that rose the hairs on the back of Sophia's neck. He looked down and shook his head.

"An Elite, indeed," Boris said through his teeth. "The eyes, my lady, are a mark of the life in Crossings Forged. To comment on my 'hard times,' yes, it was hard but not as bad as Talbot here. From King's Steward to an Innkeeper," he said. The room grew silent and uncomfortable. "At least my Tavern is mine and not a gift of pity."

Unseen by anyone, Talbot's hands clenched into fists, then slowly released.

"Who said anything about the Innkeeper?" Yaren spoke as if Talbot was nothing more than an acquaintance to her. "I dare say, you need to refine your conversation skills. But I am interested in this 'mark' you mentioned. Do all of the people from Crossings Forged bear it?"

"No, my lady," Boris replied, obviously irritated, "mostly the workers."

"Well, then I guess many of Kahel's guards must be former workers from Crossings Forged, especially the Osprey, for they all carry this strange 'grey mark,'" Lady Yaren said as she turned to Eilith. Hint taken.

"Indeed, they must," Boris carefully replied.

"Boris asks us to join him and celebrate!" Gabriel interjected, attempting to lighten the mood. "Even maybe make it to the King's celebration, that's if we can change all your minds."

Talbot walked towards Sophia and the dancers.

"First, let's get these flowers put away, the best place would be my garden," Talbot said. "Santiago, Domingo, why don't you lighten their burden, and help them out. Also, someone should go outside and help Marcello." Talbot laughed. "I'm sure he will be upset if he got stuck with the entire cleanup while you all 'celebrate.'"

"I'll go help him," Eilith said. Soon, the only people left in the lobby were Gabriel, Lady Yaren, Boris, and Talbot.

"Lady Yaren, do you mingle with Kahel's guards often?" Boris asked. Lady Yaren gave Boris a sharp look. Elites never mingle with anyone, they socialize, and when they socialize they do so only with other Elites; this was common knowledge. "I mean you seem to mingle with everyday entertainers from Salinas, so I figured it was a daily practice of yours to befriend those 'beneath' you." Simple words were spoken by Boris but phrased perfectly to deliver three insults disguised as civilized conversation.

"No. I do not. But there are guards and Osprey stationed everywhere. These days, it's hard not to notice their cold, lifeless eyes," she coolly responded, "and these dancers from Salinas are entertainment that the Elite Council booked. I am one of the lead chairs. It is our practice to greet and dismiss those we hire. I befriend none unless they are Elite but keep civility at all times. If you would excuse me."

Gabriel kissed her hand. He had no idea what just went on between his two friends, all he knew was that Lady Yaren was very much upset.

"Thank you for your hospitality," Gabriel said.

Lady Yaren nodded as she walked out the door. Gabriel walked over to Boris, who had an annoyed look on his face.

"What just happened between the two of you?"

"An Elite, Gabriel?" Boris' tone was thick with frustration. "Ever wonder why someone so high-ranked would show any interest in you?"

"No."

"Of course, well..."

But before Boris could continue, Talbot cut between the two men.

"Why don't you go see what's taking your group so long," Talbot said.

"He's not going anywhere because we are talking," Boris added.

"I saw Marcello and Eilith dragging some instruments into my garden from the side gate," Talbot said ignoring Boris so hard that any person would question if he even existed. Talbot waved a reprimanding finger at Gabriel, "I will have to charge extra if you've ruined my landscape."

"Oh, I'll go check on that." Gabriel rubbed the back of his head as he spoke apologetically. When he was out of earshot, Talbot turned to face Boris.

"Now you, Boris, can get the hell out of my Inn. Why don't you wait for Gabriel and the others out front."

Boris exhaled.

"Ah. I was expecting that; after all, I took on an Elite."

"No," Talbot spat. "You took on me. This door to freedom"—he said with his arms open wide to the Inn—"was her dying wish. She knew what Kahel had become. How dare you reference the Queen's gift to me, you mindless drone."

Boris walked towards the door. "You chose the wrong side long ago, Talbot. The war has been over for years now, this new generation has forgotten it even happened. Whatever hope it is you are clinging on to, just let it go before innocent people get hurt."

Talbot closed his eyes and took a few calming breaths.

"You should leave; you don't want to keep the entertainers waiting."

"We are men of honor, lies are beneath us. We both know they will not be returning."

Talbot shrugged his shoulders and walked behind his desk. "I just saw them head upstairs, overheard them saying something about Atarans in Tychi." Talbot smiled "Atarans, here in Tychi. Strange, hmm." Talbot's eyes grew sly as his smile widened.

"Yes. Very." Boris, quite annoyed, now closed the door behind him.

Sophia expected a little more fight from Gabriel, but when she said there were Atarans in Tychi, he grabbed her and they both rushed to the oak tree at the end of Talbot's property. Eilith and Marcello were moving the last of the instruments into the carriage. Eilith held the door open.

"Is it true?" Gabriel asked Eilith. "Atarans? Here in Tychi?"

"Yes."

"Is it safe to go home?"

"It is. The Atarans may be savages, but we all know their enemy is not us. It's the King. Salinas has been untouched by them for centuries."

"You keep close to me," Gabriel said to Sophia as they walked through Talbot's secret door. The moment they crossed outside of Tychi's border, a large gust of wind picked up. With Sophia and Gabriel finally safe in the carriage, Eilith and Domingo got the horses going. The blasts of wind became stronger, creating a small sandstorm around Tychi. The curtain of sand and dust gave them the invisibility they needed to escape unseen.

22

KAHEL'S RAGE

Sethos and Corentin had exited their Regeneration Unit hours after they had entered and kneeled outside of Kahel's. They had waited for two days now, but his eyes remained closed. The Regeneration Unit sat upright against the wall of a small, circular brick room. The unit was the only source of light in the room. A green light could be seen coming through clear pipes that protruded from the ground and connected to the four corners of the chamber. The brightest light was the red light that emanated from the gel-like substance that held Kahel. The sound they had been waiting to hear finally came loudly from Kahel's unit. It was the sloshing, crackling noise made when their bodies detach from the inner lining. It is the sound of full regeneration.

"GET ME THAT MAN NOW!" Kahel shrieked.

"My lord, the dancers fled when they heard Atarans were in Tychi."

"Convenient. Oh, so convenient," a naked Kahel said as he stepped out of the unit. Corentin held out a blue silk robe.

Kahel stepped into it and tied the front in a loose knot. Which served no purpose, since he tied the knot so carelessly that his man parts were out in the open.

"How long was I out?"

Corentin looked awkwardly at Sethos as they both tried not to make any sort of smart comment as Kahel's manhood remained out.

"Well?" their King annoyingly screeched.

"Two nights." Corentin cleared his throat then guided Kahel up the stairwell.

"Atarans? How many."

"After some interrogations, we found that there was eight total in Tychi."

"You think Salinas harbors Atarans?" Kahel asked as he walked up a spiral stone staircase. At the top of the stairs was a keypad, where he punched in a code and the door opened into his bedroom chambers. Corentin and Sethos followed him out of the staircase and into his room. As they walked in, the room lit up. The door behind him slid shut.

"No. I do not believe Salinas as a town had anything to do with this attack," Corentin said.

"I believe the Atarans were here to back up the Majji if backup was needed," Sethos continued.

"We both have come to the conclusion that the Majji who goes by the name Gabriel has kept his people in the dark about his true identity. It seems not even his wife knows of it."

"How do you know for sure?"

"No one would foolishly bring the Majji here to Tychi, and we hear from our informant that his wife desires children. Any woman who wants a child knows not to mate with a Majji."

"I want you both to go to Salinas and get me Gabriel, no bloodshed. I don't want any rumors spreading through my precious lemmings. Snatch him in the dead of night, make his wife think he left her." Kahel laughed. "We don't want anyone looking for him."

"No," both Sethos and Corentin replied together. Kahel stood with a puzzled look on his face.

"Okay, I'm not sure if you remember, I'm King. ME, what I say fucking goes!"

Corentin and Sethos kneeled down.

"My lord, we will not leave your side again. What if this is what he wants? Us to go after him and to leave you vulnerable."

Kahel sat silent for a moment.

"Wait, wait, I changed my mind," Kahel said as if he didn't hear a word Corentin said. "What if this is what he wants, you two leave me here alone, then he attacked when I am at my most vulnerable, that plan will not do." Kahel fussed with the knot, finally tying it to cover his body. He turned to the kneeling Corentin and Sethos. "Send three of your best Osprey. Tell them quiet and clean."

Sethos looked up, "Yes, sir."

23

A SENSE OF UNEASE

It had been almost a week since they had arrived home. Their arrival had been met with confusion and joy. Sophia recalled Domingo leaping down from the carriage and greeting Weiya. Sophia knew whatever they were talking about must have been important. Domingo would have never left them all to unload the equipment if it wasn't something pressing. She decided that he was just updating her on the situation with the Atarans and was inquiring if there was any action on their side of the woods. Anna came barreling in around the corner and leaped higher than the most athletic Salinan right into Sophia's arms. The cold season was on its way, so everyone in Salinas doubled their efforts to store enough supplies to last them the next three to four months. When Sophia wrapped up her day's duties, she made her way out of Salinas' borders and walked up the hill to the lone dogwood tree, whose leaves had thinned out. She sat and admired her beautiful town as she watched one of the townsfolk light the street-lamps. The luxury of electricity was something only found in Tychi; though she hated technology, power was a convenience she would have liked very much to have in her town. From afar, she saw Gabriel and the others arriving with a carriage full of the hunt's prizes. The wind wrapped around her. Sophia felt uneasy; she couldn't explain it, but since they had returned her senses had been heightened. The littlest thing put her on alert. She sat down and faced the Northern Woods.

Those paintings in Talbot's Inn. How can a beautiful place be home to such awful people?

But were Atarans really all that horrible? she thought. They were there at Tychi and harmed no one. Apparently, they hated Kahel as much as she did. Maybe she should be a good neighbor and bring them some pie, but they would probably toss the pie at her face and proceed to gnaw at her arms. Sophia took a deep breath and headed back home. Anna was waiting for her right at the entrance.

"I'm staying at Eilith's tonight! But, don't worry, I'll be back to stay with you in three days," a bright-eyed Anna said to Sophia."

"Oh? Has Eilith asked you to help work on that piece of folklore Lady Yaren gave her?

Anna's brows furrowed. "She didn't. But I read it anyways. Then she took it out of my hands. Told me to mind my manners and my business."

"Sounds like Eilith."

Not even a day after they returned to Salinas, Eilith approached Sophia with a note that Lady Yaren had passed to her.

The note was of no consequence. Just a short story regarding the downfall of the Ibex Warrior clan. It's old folklore, and aside from some wording changes, which were expected, there was nothing that stood out. Still, Eilith read that note daily and swore up and down there was more to it. As it goes, the Ibex Warrior clan fought glorious battles to keep Mad Essence from dripping its evil into our realm. One day, a scouting group came across a man who possessed the ancient Mad Essence within him. He single-handedly wiped out the Ibex Warriors then was never seen again. Sophia shrugged to herself then scooped Anna up in her arms and gave her a big hug.

"Well, let me escort you then!"

Sophia loved the children of the town, but her connection with Anna was stronger than the others. She knew Anna was not her child, but she often felt like she was. Sophia still tried to conceive even though deep down she knew that she and Gabriel would never have a child of their own. Nonetheless, there were enough orphans in Salinas for everyone to take care of, so in a way, Sophia was a mother many times over. Sophia knocked on Eilith's door as she walked in. Eilith's house was much smaller than hers. There was only one room on the first floor; you walked directly into the kitchen/dining room/living room. The room was long. On the left side of the house were a sink and stove, and in the center was a small table that would sit two. Far in the back was one window and a door to her back garden. To the right was a staircase that led to her quaint bedroom and under the stairs was her pantry. Eilith was making soup when Sophia walked in with Anna.

"Here she is, Eilith, Anna banana!"

"I'm no banana! I'm a dancer in training!" Anna exclaimed.

"Oh?"

"Yess! Seeee." Anna then did a high leap into a small spin.

"Oh, brava, bravaaa!" Both Eilith and Sophia said as they clapped.

"Now go to my well in the back, Anna, and bring in some water," Eilith said.

"Okay, see you later, Sophia!"

"Bye-bye, Anna." Sophia smiled. "I'm going home to see what Gabriel's cooked; if it's crap, I am coming back here and having soup with you."

Eilith laughed and gave Sophia a hug. "You do that."

Sophia never returned. Gabriel's dinner was surprisingly quite delicious. Roasted chicken with vegetables. Sophia was sure he had Eilith cook this one too. Gabriel brought out a bottle.

"Wine!" Sophia gleefully looked at the red liquid in the bottle. "Oh, Gabriel, how did you get it?"

"At Tychi, I thought since we have two nights free from our town's children, maybe we could, you know...try again?"

"Gabriel," Sophia said softly. She knew how badly Gabriel wanted a child of their own; also, it wasn't fair for her to give up hope, not when he still had it. Sophia stood up and took the bottle of wine out of her husband's hand. She placed it gently on the table and walked him to the base of the steps. "I love you," she said and kissed him. While it was fruitless, deep in her soul, she really didn't want to give up. Sophia walked her husband upstairs. They disrobed and made love.

24

RUDE
AWAKENING

Sophia was barely awake. Even so, barely awake was more than she wanted to be. The past two hours with Gabriel, though amazing as always, had her exhausted. But again, she was feeling uneasy, and something inside was telling her to get the hell out of bed. Sophia quickly rolled to her left just as a sword stabbed through her side of the bed. Her eyes shot open, and she rolled off completely to see a man in dark maroon clothing.

"Osprey." The disbelief in her tone filled the room. The man was struggling to remove his blade from the bed when Sophia tossed the only thing she could find in her bedroom, the rocking chair. It distracted him enough to give her time to escape down the stairs. As she got down into the kitchen, she saw Gabriel trying to fight off two other Osprey.

"How is it I slept through this?"

"Sophia, run!" Gabriel yelled, blocking an attack and

kicking one of Osprey in the chest.

"I'm not leaving you!" Sophia grabbed a knife from the kitchen and started towards Gabriel, but before she made it to him the Osprey from upstairs raced down the steps, grabbed her hair, and slammed her down to the ground. The impact was strong enough that Sophia felt as if her head had split in two. Before her attacker could gain any more ground, Sophia quickly swept her leg and tripped the Osprey.

"Gabriel, how many?" She squeezed her eyes shut and quickly opened them trying to stabilize herself.

"Three, I think," he said as he dodged another attack.

Sophia turned around and tried to block as the Osprey jumped up and kicked her. She rolled into the small living room with the knife still in her hand. This was going to be an unfair battle. The Osprey stood over her, and she kicked her leg up and between his legs; the maroon-dressed man came falling down face to face with Sophia. She forcefully stabbed him between the eyes, his warm blood pouring out onto her.

"Two!" she called out to her husband, trying not to vomit. She fought the urge, got up, then grabbed another knife from the kitchen. She leaped on the back of an Osprey that was attacking Gabriel. The man was quick and moved to avoid her strike; instead of stabbing him in the neck, the knife cut into his lower arm. He threw Sophia off, ignored her, and continued on to Gabriel. Sophia realized then that they were only after her husband. She grabbed yet another knife and went back into the fight, but she watched as her husband fought. His arms and chest had cuts on them, and the only protection he wore was his sleep pants. Sophia charged again. This time, both Osprey pushed Gabriel hard against the floor, rendering him immobile, and went towards Sophia.

"Shit!" She bent down and pulled the knife out of the man she just stabbed in the face. She held both blades up and panicked. She tossed one knife that missed terribly; the other knife she slashed wildly as the two men attacked. She ducked and blocked, but it was no use.

When Gabriel came to, he saw Sophia trying to defend herself. One Osprey easily disarmed her and walked away while the other lifted his sword and cut her across her chest, blood seeping through her nightgown. Gabriel felt helpless as he watched his wife collapse; it was the opening the Osprey were looking for. They jumped towards Gabriel.

25

THE ATARAN

Lee fumbled in the outskirts of Salinas. The trek out of the Northern Woods was quicker than he anticipated. More often than not, he would find himself traveling down creeks and hiking through dense woods. The Green made him work on his entries and exits in the ever-shifting Northern Woods. It was the ingenious way the Green kept the Atarans safe. The swiftness of this exit only reinforced the urgency of his mission. He was still tired from the assignment in Tychi. He and the other Atarans were not anticipating being chased. He was grateful they all got out unscathed. As Lee approached Salinas, he became aware of the Green around him and in the town. It was strong here, and it was strongest around one house. Essence was being used. Lee pulled his fabric mask over his face and easily climbed the barrier wall. He was dressed head-to-toe in dark clothing that hugged his skin, revealing a lean and toned physique underneath. The material allowed movement, which Lee appreciated. Whether it was fighting or scaling this wall, the last thing he needed was something to restrict him. He was in Salinas for one reason and one reason only, a quick snatch-and-grab job. Well, not really snatch and grab; Lee didn't want to look like a common fugitive. He'd like to think they would talk, he would explain, and then walk back home with his new companion. Lee looked over the vine-covered rooftops of Salinas and focused on the house in the far left of the town. He could see Essence being drawn into that house, but it wasn't the normal path of Essence, and something was forcing it in. Lee raced across the rooftops. Once he got to the house, he cautiously lowered down and peered into a large window. The view was of a kitchen. He saw two Osprey fighting one man; he also spotted two dead bodies on the floor. Lee wasted no time and crashed through the window. He started for the living room when he was caught by a burst of air that projected him back into the kitchen. The gust of wind pushed him high up the wall and began to cut off his air supply. He felt pressure increasing around him. Lee struggled and managed to free one of his arms and push the entity back.

"Zephyr, it's me, Lee!"

Upon hearing its name, the wind entity stopped and dropped Lee. Lee unmasked himself and gasped for air. "What are you doing here?"

The invisible wind entity, Zephyr, grabbed Lee by the leg and tossed him into the ongoing fight in the living room. Lee crashed onto the backs of the Osprey.

"Save my wife!" Gabriel called out to him.

"Wait! What the hell is going on?" Instead of receiving a reply, Lee received a punch in the face by an Osprey.

"My nose!" Lee fought off the attacks with one hand and used the other to nurse his nose. "I think you broke it, you asshole!" He grabbed the Osprey arms and head-butted him. Lee saw a glowing red light coming from around the Osprey neck. He had wondered why Zephyr could not enter the living room, but that explained it. The talismans the Osprey were wearing were what caused the strange path of Essence he saw earlier. Those talismans were giving the Osprey strength by stealing Essence. If Zephyr were in the room, he'd be completely drained.

"Go for their talismans!" Lee yelled to Gabriel. The Osprey turned on Lee the way they turned on Sophia earlier, but this time they did not immobilize Gabriel first. Lee smiled at them and unsheathed a fine, thin blade. Once distracted, Gabriel took a small table to both the Osprey heads, they fell with one loud authoritative thud. Gabriel launched himself onto Lee. The force knocked Lee flat on his back, tossing his blade into the kitchen.

"Oh, this isn't my night."

Gabriel held a knife on Lee's neck and said, "I said to get her out of here! Do it, or I will kill you myself!" One of the Osprey jumped to his feet and pulled Gabriel off of Lee, while the other kicked Gabriel in the stomach. Gabriel, now on his knees, winded and exhausted, received a quick blow to the head. His body collapsed. Lee sat up, grabbed Sophia, ripped the talisman off the dead Osprey, and kicked himself back into the kitchen. Zephyr created a wind barrier in the doorway. Lee seized a small blade that he had strapped to his leg and stabbed the talisman. The two remaining Osprey flinched and became enraged. One touched the wind barrier with the palm of his hands. His skin was cleanly shaved off. The Osprey cupped his wounded hand.

"Return the talisman!" the Osprey ordered.

"Set that man free," Lee said as he stood up. Lee's height met 6'3" with grace and beauty, and his unkempt, short, sandy-brown hair swayed to and fro in the wind Zephyr was creating. Lee's amber eyes glared at the two Osprey on the other side of the barrier. Sweat dripped down his sun-kissed skin.

"You'll get yours soon enough, and I'll be the one that gives it to you," the taller Osprey said.

"Oh, yea?" Lee scoffed. "Just like your mother gave it to me last night?"

"What? Why you!"

Lee cradled Sophia and didn't flinch as the Osprey stabbed the wind barrier with his blade. He was easily disarmed, and Zephyr thrust the blade back at the Osprey. It caught him clear through his throat. Blood sprayed on the remaining attacker. He stepped back and allowed his dead comrade to fall. Lee knew his time was limited; Zephyr grew weaker by the second.

"If you want the talisman, leave the man," Lee said.

Blood had pooled between Sophia and Lee and began to drip on the floor. The Osprey tossed Gabriel over his shoulder.

"You have nothing. A broken necklace and a dying woman."

"Dying?" Lee looked down and realized Sophia was still alive.

"I have my objective," the Osprey said as he bent down and took the talisman off the other now-dead Osprey. It lightly rang like a wind chime when it touched his other necklace as he placed it around his neck. Lee cursed under his breath and watched the Osprey walk out the door with an unconscious Gabriel slung over his shoulder.

"Zephyr, we need to get the hell out of here, are you strong enough to cover me?"

Zephyr dropped his barrier and followed Lee out the door. The wind kicked up around Lee. Even under Zephyr's windstorm, Lee could hear the protests of a herd of horses. He turned his head as Zephyr dropped his protection. Zephyr's trajectory was clear, as dust and dirt rose and then a wall of water as he cut through the Pyre River. Lee had never seen such majestic creatures as the horses. Even from a distance, he could see their markings and was in awe at their fluid-like manner. Even as they whinnied and stomp, they looked as if they were ebbing and flowing like water. Whatever Zephyr did, the herd calmed and the horses stepped back. Zephyr then returned to Lee and covered him. Lee bolted north. Once he cleared Salinas, he raced up the hill and placed Sophia down under the dogwood tree. He removed Sophia's nightgown, leaving her only in her lower undergarment. He twisted her sleep dress up to mimic a cord. Lee then removed his top and placed it on Sophia's deep gash, which started at her breast and cut across her ribcage. He lifted Sophia and wrapped the twisted nightgown around her, holding his shirt in place. Sophia let out a stifled breath.

The path to Atara was impossible for anyone except Atarans to find. It's known to those who study history that these woods were full of Essence. The Green lived here, ruled here, and protected its people. The trees moved slowly, the rocks shifted, and the path of the creek fluctuated. The Northern Woods were always ever-changing, making it impossible to map out a route. Lee was Ataran; his people were the children of the Green. Feared by all, the Atarans have been depicted by folklore as part human and part monster, who consume one another and the dead. The stories were ridiculous to Lee, but they did have their benefits. Not many dared enter the Northern Woods, and for those who did the trees would just shift to lead them right back out.

"She won't stop bleeding. No medicine Salinas can provide will save her. We need to get her into the woods so she can heal." Lee lifted Sophia and ran into the Northern Woods.

"So, Zephyr, this is where you have been those days you've left us?"

A gentle breeze.

"Halcyon's been getting sicker, you know, and you being

gone had him pretty worried. All of us, actually. We thought Kahel got a hold of you."

Another soft breeze.

"Who is she?"

Nothing.

Lee groaned in frustration. "Zephyr, I didn't retrieve my target, I'm wounded, and I am, as that Osprey kindly informed me, going home with 'a broken necklace and a half-dead woman.' I can just see the Majji rejoice in my success here. Please give me something."

A soft breeze grazed across Sophia's face. Lee looked down and for the first time fully took in Sophia. Her full lips were the first thing he noticed, then her blonde hair that swung lifelessly down. He continued onto the perfectly formed face the color of caramel lying in his arms. Realization hit him.

"Oh, my gods. I touched her breasts..."

Zephyr pulled back a branch and used it to slap Lee in the face. Lee soon found himself in the middle of a tug-of-war battle with an unseen yet admirable opponent.

"Let her go, Zephyr; I'll carry her!"

The tug continued.

"Sorry! I didn't mean it in some skeeze-ball perverse way! I was just stating the obvious!"

The tugging became more and more aggressive. Sophia stirred and, just like that, Zephyr gave in.

Lee took a moment then continued to walk. "So, she is important to you?" He looked down at Sophia again. "I can see why," he said with restraint. "Her wound is closing, but she lost a lot of Essence. I am pretty sure that talisman had something to do with that. I hope Halcyon can tell us what it is."

Lee could feel the Green's eyes on him, protecting him, helping him heal, and allowing him, Zephyr, and Sophia passage to Atara.

26

EILITH'S FAILURE

Eilith woke as the sun began to rise. She looked to her side and saw Anna fast asleep. She quietly rolled out of bed and walked down the steps. Eilith opened her icebox and pulled out four eggs, bacon, milk, and orange juice. Her small home smelled of morning delights as she cooked away. Anna slowly walked down the stairs and sat at the table. The little girl rubbed her eyes and yawned. The back of Anna's hair stuck up like a bird's nest that was ravaged by an aggressive feline, while parts of the front of her hair were pasted to her cheek.

"I'm so tired, Eelee."

"Me too, Anna. I thought a good breakfast will help us snap out of it."

"I went to bed early, too, and I slept like a rock. A big fat one."

"Me too." Maybe her bed had one too many lumps, she thought as she put eggs and bacon on Anna's plate. She had just finished serving herself when someone knocked on the door. This early was strange. Eilith's gut tightened as she opened the door. It was Marcello and Santiago.

"Marcello, stay here with Anna; Eilith, come now," Santiago said.

Anna was oblivious to the severity in Santiago's tone, and Eilith looked at Marcello, who rocked back and forth on his heels as he tried to look casually over her shoulder at the food. Apparently, Anna wasn't the only one oblivious, and Eilith wanted to keep it that way.

"Feel free, Marcello."

She kissed Anna's cheek.

"I will return shortly."

Anna gave Eilith a full-mouthed smile.

Eilith followed Santiago to what she knew would be Gabriel and Sophia's house.

They lived in the far end of Salinas, whereas she lived in the northern point of it. The townsfolk that Eilith passed were all holding cups of coffee and yawning. The pair picked up the pace, enough to rouse suspicion. A light-blue aura had begun to surround Eilith, and the faster her heartbeat became the stronger the aura became. Frost spread in each of her footsteps. Santiago slowed as they arrived at the house. She saw Domingo, who leaped to his feet at the sight of her. With a swift movement, Domingo grabbed his brother and swung him into the house behind him. Santiago stumbled then caught Domingo for support.

"Eilith, do not cast! There is no danger here anymore."

Eilith placed her hand on the door jam. The wood beneath her hands began to crack and pop as it froze.

Eilith took a few calming breaths, and it was some time before she had successfully centered herself. The blue aura slowly seeped back into her. Santiago's face was that of shock and awe.

"Thank you, brother. I didn't realize," Santiago said. Domingo placed his hand on his brother's shoulder.

Eilith missed their exchange. Her attention was focused on the state of the house. The once-humble and welcoming living room was destroyed. Glass shards were scattered on the kitchen floor, and the blood, there was so much of it. She focused on three pools of blood. Bodies must have been there, she thought. The markings on the floor showed that one of the victims was pulled into the kitchen.

"Where are the bodies? Gods, please tell me none were Gabriel or Sophia."

Domingo walked to Eilith. "No, none were. One body is missing, though. Santiago and I disposed of the two dead that were here. They were Osprey, Eilith. Gabriel and Sophia put up quite a fight, but it looks like one of them may have fallen."

"Are you sure? Couldn't it have been another Osprey?"

"No. It could have not," Santiago's voice said behind her. "They were after Gabriel. Upstairs, there is a blade mark on Sophia's side of the bed. They wanted her out of the picture. There is no blood on the bed, so she must have woken and escaped her attacker." Santiago walked to the threshold of the kitchen. "Right here, an Osprey fell. I suspect Sophia must have done it when she came downstairs." Santiago continued into the kitchen. "Now, this is where I lose the fight. Someone crashed through the kitchen window, dragged a fallen body into the kitchen, and escaped with it. Since the Osprey left two of their own behind," he said and pointed to two blood pools, "I doubt the other fallen body," he continued as he pointed to where Sophia had fallen, "was an Osprey. So, it looks like there were two opposing intruders; one took Gabriel, the other took Sophia, and one of our dear friends is severely wounded."

Eilith covered her face with both of her hands.

"How did I sleep through this? How is it I slept through my only mission in life?" Anger and pain enveloped her. "I've failed my people."

"You've failed no one, Eilith. We all slept through this," Domingo said. It was at that point that Eilith took a deep hard look at Domingo. His face showed dark circles under his eyes and a kind of exhaustion that would be seen on a man who had spent the past month traveling.

"We were drained?" she looked between the brothers. "Our Essence was drained?"

"That seems to be the case."

"Kahel's closest Extricate Station is in Tychi." Eilith pointed out the door. "There is no way it could have reached us."

"You are right, it couldn't have, but here we are."

"We must go to Tychi."

"We are going to Tychi, Eilith, but you are staying here with Marcello," Santiago said.

"What?" Eilith's brows were set in a deep furrow.

"Our people need your protection, and two men traveling horseback together will attract less attention than one man and a fiery red-headed woman."

Eilith crossed her arms and looked away.

"We will seek an audience with Talbot and Lady Yaren. Ari and Carminda are already on their way to Crossings Forged to see if there is anything to learn there."

Eilith was about to protest them allowing Carminda out and not her, but Eilith knew that her unique features would always give her away.

"Speak to Weiya," Domingo said. "Inform her of what's happened. When our people wake, they will learn of this. Keep them calm, but you must stay alert." He and Santiago walked out the door and climbed onto their horses. "You were right, Eilith," Domingo said. "It has begun." Eilith watched as both brothers rode south.

27

LOOSE ENDS

Corentin was in his chambers when there was a knock.

"Enter," he said. The thick wood door opened, groaning as it reached its full potential. There before him, he saw one of his Osprey holding Gabriel over their shoulder. The Osprey kneeled and placed Gabriel on the ground.

"I have completed the objective." Apparently, he wasn't looking at Corentin because if he were he probably would have run in the other direction. Corentin's eyes looked strained, and his lips were tight.

"Yes. You have." What this Osprey didn't know was that Corentin had caught wind of recent events, including a fight that had ensued in Crossings Forged and the disappearance of the local Tavern's owner. But that wasn't what sent Corentin over the edge. "You also left both of your comrades behind, murdered the most prized and beloved dancer in Salinas, caused a scene in Crossings Forged, and, as I can see by the two chains on your neck, lost a fucking talisman!"

The Osprey kept his head low and remained quiet.

"You left a trail that leads straight to here, to the King!" The Osprey gulped.

"How is it that three Osprey couldn't handle this?" Corentin looked at the silent, highly trained guard.

The Osprey figured it was a rhetorical question and continued his silence.

"ANSWER ME!"

Maybe not rhetorical. "The female dancer took out one of my comrades, and an Ataran killed the other. The Ataran destroyed one talisman, that's why I only return with two."

"An Ataran? How many were there?"

"One."

"Only one to defend the Majji?" Corentin fussed with his hair. "Interesting. Is there anything else I should know?"

"The Ataran used magic, he cast wind."

"Did he die or was he weakened after the spell was cast?" Corentin asked, slightly intrigued.

"No."

"Damn," Corentin said with a smile. "I was getting bored; would have been nice to hunt again."

The Osprey dared a look, confused with the direction the conversation had taken.

"No matter, it couldn't be a casting spell, only the Ibex are known to cast. This Gabriel must have summoned his Elemental. That's the only explanation. But, to have no other protection, and for his Elemental not to follow you and attempt a rescue, this makes no sense." Corentin looked down at the Osprey. "You have no idea what I am talking about do you?" Corentin laughed to himself. "How quickly you lemmings forget your past," he sighed. "Gods, this is really turning into a fucking mess. Get up. Get up, you pathetic moron!" The Osprey reluctantly stood up. "Thank you, that makes this easier." Corentin lifted the man then tossed him out the window. He ordered the guards outside his door to shackle Gabriel in the throne room and to clean up what was left of the Osprey. Corentin then made his way to Kahel's chambers. On his way up, he met with Sethos and filled him in on the ongoings. Together, they entered Kahel's chambers. He was sleeping face down when the motion lights turned on. Three minimally dressed women slowly rose from Kahel's bed.

"My King," Corentin called out. "We seek your private audience."

"That's great," Kahel said with his eyes still closed and head on the pillow. "Whores. Leave."

The three women rose out of the bed, their dull grey eyes open and awake. They picked up their robes, covered themselves, and walked out.

Corentin's eyes followed the tallest one. A dark-skinned beauty slowly made her way past him. He gave her a smile that would be reason enough for any woman to give up her virtue. Both Sethos and Corentin approached Kahel.

"Gabriel is in the throne room restrained, and I've placed enough talismans around him to hold fifty Majji," Sethos said as Kahel slowly rose.

"I doubt that was necessary," Corentin added. "He bears the marks, but he is no Majji."

"I've had enough of this back and forth," Kahel said. He pulled his silky white trousers up and walked to Corentin. "Majji or not, this ends tonight." Kahel sped down his stairs and to the throne room. With each step, a light would illuminate in the hall. Barefoot, he approached the throne room. Eight talismans placed in a circular pattern lay on the floor around Gabriel. His arms and legs were bound to the ground by large iron cuffs, and he wore the same black sleep pants he was abducted in. His long black hair was loose and disheveled. The early morning sun bled its purple glow through the glass dome ceiling, exposing the sweat that was dripping down Gabriel's back. He had been struggling to free himself. As the lights turned on in the throne room, Gabriel wrenched his body around in an attempt to see who was entering.

"Where is she?" Gabriel called out.

Kahel was taken aback by Gabriel's mighty ice-blue eyes. It has been many years since Kahel's been this close to eyes like that, and the last time he barely came out with his life. A long-forgotten fear began to rise.

"Where is Sophia? What have you done to her!" Gabriel struggled.

Kahel turned to Corentin. "What in the hell is he blubbering about?" he asked quietly through the corner of his mouth.

"His wife, sir. She died while they were trying to acquire him."

"Are you fucking kidding me?" Kahel whispered loudly and surprised himself with how much he cared. "Do you guys have any clue what 'no mess' means?" Kahel dismissively waved his hand. Kahel walked around Gabriel and didn't sense anything out of the ordinary. He continued towards his throne and sat. Sethos and Corentin stood on either side of Gabriel.

"Now I find myself in an interesting situation," Kahel said. "I came down here determined to slit your throat and rid myself of a pesky issue. After all, you were either a nobody or the Majji; in either scenario, I'd prefer you dead."

"Majji?" Gabriel questioned.

"Yes, I know you are confused about what's going on so let me just clear things up." Kahel sat majestically on his throne, filling every inch of it. "You are going to love this story, it's quite the kick in the head. You see, the three of us swore you were the Majji." He leaned forward and gestured to both Sethos, Corentin. "I mean we were so convinced that we brought you here. Because, if you were the Majji; which don't worry because you aren't, there was this small possibility that people would follow you instead of me, splitting loyalties. It would lead to a rebellion, which I would squish, of course." He laughed and sat back. "Still, I just couldn't have that. So, I decided to nip the bud in the head. Unfortunately, on the way, we may have, well, killed your wife, which is another issue I'm going to have to deal with soon enough. Now, here is my predicament." He rose from his throne and walked to Gabriel, who had stopped struggling the moment he heard Sophia had passed. Kahel knelt face to face with him. "You are no Majji, but you are also not a nobody," Kahel grabbed Gabriel's chin. "You fought off three highly trained men, you have the traits of the Majji, and somehow performed a healing, but I can't sense anything more. For all we know, it may be buried deep, hiding from me. But you have potential." Kahel stood up and began to pace around Gabriel. "Let's see what I can get from you." He laughed again then took in a relaxing sigh. "Well, first things first, let's get him to a Regeneration Unit."

Corentin and Sethos loosened Gabriel's restraint and lifted him. Kahel looked at a defeated Gabriel.

"Why, no fight left in you?" he inquired. "Because of your dead wife?"

Gabriel stared blankly at Kahel.

"She is just a woman, a pathetic woman; they are useless and only good for one thing. There are more out there, trust me, you'll get over her."

Gabriel's heart raced, and his anger rose. Kahel sensed that.

"Don't worry," Kahel put his hand on Gabriel's shoulder. "She'll have company soon." He smiled. "I refuse to have your people talking about her murder and your kidnapping. So, I am just going to have to make your town disappear." He waved his fingers in the air.

Gabriel fought against Corentin's and Sethos' hold. "You can't do that! It will raise more questions; you wouldn't get away with it!"

"Oh, Gabriel, I've been doing this for years now. When a town thinks of a possible revolt, I 'relocate' them here and throw some fun little lies to the people that I needed to use their land for blah blah blah, doesn't fucking matter. Truth is, no town has actually been relocated, ever. Those people die for questioning my authority, just like all your people are going to die," he said with an evil smile.

Gabriel broke from Sethos' grasp first, then shot his free palm up at Corentin. He quickly turned around and kicked Sethos in the gut. Kahel's eyes widened, and his smile continued to grow. Gabriel grabbed Sethos' dagger and lunged at Kahel. Kahel caught Gabriel by the throat.

"Yes. Just as I thought. Such unique, strong Essence." Kahel's eyes were glowing red, and his nails began to grow out and pierce Gabriel's neck. Kahel squeezed a little tighter. His voice had grown deeper, then in a otherworldly tone said, "It's delicious." Gabriel struggled to no avail; he grew weaker, and his eyes closed. Kahel swung him across the room. Gabriel's back slammed against the wall, and he collapsed unconscious to the floor.

"We must move quickly. Throw some plans around, an Extricate Station over Salinas, I don't care. Kill anyone who asks questions, can't have any loose ends," Kahel ordered in his normal voice. "And, dammit, get him in a unit." Kahel walked out of the throne room.

Sethos walked to Gabriel and lifted him.

"Corentin, does he know of the Ataran?"

"No."

"Should we tell him?"

"No, not till we can figure out what their presence in all this means."

"Corentin, we know what it means," Sethos said as he carried Gabriel out of the throne room.

Corentin didn't want to admit it, but he knew as well as Sethos did that the Atarans being so active not only meant that they knew of Gabriel's existence, but they also knew of the Essence he possessed. While trying to prevent a rebellion and maintain the control he was intoxicated with, Kahel may have just started a war.

28

ATARA

Sophia stirred in Lee's arms. They had been walking in the Northern Woods for about an hour now, and at any moment the Green would open up and lead them straight into Atara. Zephyr kept close to Sophia, giving her a cool breeze when she began to sweat. Her wound had closed during the travel, but Lee knew she was not out of danger. Sophia not only needed medicine, but she also needed the Majji to draw Essence back into her. The trees began to thin, and Lee could see the tips of the Nacunas in the slowly brightening sky. Next, he saw the wind turbines, then he finally cleared the woods. This time, the woods opened up on the dead-center of the village. The townspeople were still asleep, and the sun was just about to rise, but one person stood waiting for him. The man's arms were crossed, and the vest he wore displayed a wonderfully toned upper body. His pants were fastened a little below the waist. Lee knew this man well. His name was Cyrus, Lee's best friend who had the knack of meeting up with Lee at the exact place the Green would open Atara up to him.

"How do you do that man?" Lee asked the tall, dark man. "It's starting to freak me out you know? Some people would think we've been bonded."

"Lee, what have you done?" Cyrus asked when he saw the woman in his arms. Cyrus reached out and took Sophia from Lee. Cyrus was about the height of Lee, but he had much more muscle tone to his body. He closed his eyes and placed his forehead on Sophia's. His full lips close to hers.

"She's dying," Cyrus said.

"I know. She needs your tonics."

Cyrus began to walk away.

"I didn't do this to her."

"Tell me then who did."

Lee filled his friend in on the ongoings of the night as they walked to Cyrus' home. Cyrus lived behind the bar he owned. When they entered, Cyrus placed Sophia on his bed and went into his pantry. Like Salinas, the houses in Atara were small. Cyrus' home was one room, and it was quaint. His bed was a few steps from the entryway and across from that was a large pantry. The top shelves were full of herbs and potions, and the bottom shelf held some clothes and bedsheets. There was a doorway that led to his kitchen covered by silver and purple curtains. The kitchen area was a passage to both his living space and the bar.

"So, you are saying that not only did you fail to acquire Gabriel, you lost him to Kahel's men?"

"Yes."

"And you came home with a wounded outsider."

"It would appear so."

"How did the Green allow her to pass?"

"Don't know," Lee said as he shrugged "But she kept me walking the woods for a while this time."

"Did anything go right?"

"Shut up."

"Do you have any wounds?"

"Just a broken nose, but it will heal."

Cyrus grabbed three bottles, two containing liquids and the other an herb. He hummed to himself as he mixed it all together. Lee leaned up against the doorway with his arms and legs crossed. Zephyr let out a quick burst, tossing Lee's hair wildly.

"Zephyr, welcome home," Cyrus said smiling as he continued to mix. "This will stop the infection inside. She will still need at least a week to heal internally." Zephyr blew past Lee and gently lifted Sophia up. Lee found the sight creepy. The wind pushed up behind Sophia, making her look like the living dead. Lee grimaced. Cyrus poured his tonic down Sophia's throat. "Call the Majji, she needs him to complete her healing." Cyrus then walked up to Lee.

"Now about your nose."

"What about it?"

Cyrus placed both hands on Lees' nose and quickly snapped it into place. Lee yelped and grabbed his nose then stumbled back out the doorway.

"It would have healed ugly," Cyrus laughed.

"Yeah, thanks, I think," Lee said.

"Now go get Halcyon."

"Do I have to..." Lee said reluctantly.

"He's going to hear of your epic failure eventually, best he hears it from you."

"Well, now that you put it that way." Lee then walked off. He practiced his speech and explanation numerous times on his way the Majji's home.

Atara was a large village; his people lived from the opening of the Northern Woods all the way to the base of the Nacunas. The woods encompassed Atara in a crescent shape. The only way in and out of Atara was through those woods. The Majji's house was built far from the main town, which was on the eastern point of the crescent. Halcyon loved his privacy, and the people respected that. It was a pleasant walk from Cyrus' bar, which was in the center of the village. Lee passed lush green trees that provided fruit and nuts, and he grabbed a pear on his walk. He wished the Majji lived closer to the waterfall, so he could grab a quick sip from the pool. There was always something to eat and drink in Atara, the Green made sure of it. In return, the Atarans nourished and respected the land. Atarans utilized wind turbines to power their village. Three large fans and five vine-suspended engines decorated their skies. This was technology unearthed in digs up in the Nacuna Mountains. Lee slowed his pace as he approached the Majji's home. He kicked the dirt path for a second before he entered.

Halcyon was an older man with long white hair braided and swung over his shoulder. He was nursing a cup of tea when Lee grudgingly entered the house. Halcyon sat at his table. He was in the center of a long bench when he turned to see Lee.

"Dear Gods!" Halcyon called out. He ran to Lee, placed both hands on his cheeks, then leaned his forehead to Lee's. Lee was a bit confused at first, then he realized he was still covered in the woman's blood. He grabbed Halcyon's hands and led them down. He looked into Halcyon's horrified ice-blue eyes. Lee always thought, for a man of two hundred and seventy-nine years, he looked terrific. Just a small amount of wrinkles were spread sparingly around his face, and soft bags were under his eyes.

"Halcyon, I am not wounded. This blood is of a woman who requires your healing."

"A woman? Who?"

"Gabriel's wife."

"Where is Gabriel?"

Lee looked at the ground.

"I see."

"I am so sorry, Halcyon. I tried, I really did, but the only chance I had to escape with Gabriel, he made me take his wife instead. He didn't care for his life. He just wanted her to live."

Halcyon let out a smile and shook his head. "Well, then lead me to her." Lee turned and headed back to Cyrus' bar.

When they arrived, Cyrus was sitting outside, and Zephyr was playfully puffing about.

"Nice of you to return to us, Zephyr," Halcyon said with a smile, "Lee tells me you've been spending your time away with this woman." He entered the room and looked at Sophia, and his look quickly turned into a gape. He raced to Sophia and brushed all the blood-caked hair from her face. He placed his hands on her cheeks and closed his eyes. A tender warmth surrounded Halcyon, and he felt calm and finally one with himself. Memories poured into Halcyon. The first one was over a century old, when he found himself wandering land after land, town after town, in search of his Apprentice. The memories sped forward. He was now in front of a cottage. He knew this cottage and cherished this memory. Unexpected tears began to fall. There was a beautiful young girl. She was only the tender age of ten. She had her arms out and was spinning happily in circles. Her hair, as golden as the sun, flowed freely, and her skin was soft and gentle as cotton, with her smile, her loving, serene smile that warmed all around her. This was the day he found his Apprentice, Leata.

"Impossible," Halcyon's voice called, barely a whisper.

"What is it?" Lee asked.

"I don't know how," Halcyon said as he sat up, "but she possesses my Essence."

Lee's brows furrowed. Halcyon continued, "the Essence that I passed on to my late Apprentice Leata seventy-nine years ago."

"Wait," Lee said, "You are telling me that she has Queen Leata's Essence?"

"Yes, all of it. This woman set off the marker, not Gabriel."

"That makes no sense. Gabriel has the eyes. Oh, my head is going to explode," Lee said. He placed his hand on his head. "So, Kahel has who he thinks has the traits of the Majji, when in fact he just has an everyday nobody?"

"Gabriel is not a nobody. There is a reason he was born and a reason he has the traits," Halcyon scolded.

Cyrus; who overheard the whole conversation, piped in.

"You both know the moment Kahel figures that Gabriel isn't the one with the Majji's Essence, he'll be infuriated. Gods know what he will do." Halcyon stopped for a moment and thought. Kahel had the potential to unearth mass destruction like anyone who lacks a conscience does. Kahel has destroyed Green, towns, villages, and the lives of many people, without an inch of remorse.

"Cyrus," Halcyon said, "find Garret. I want you two to go to Tychi. Keep your eyes and ears open. The moment you know what Kahel plans to do, report back to me. Zephyr, tag along; they may need your help."

"What are we going to do with her?" Lee asked.

"Heal her first. When she wakes, maybe she can explain to us what is going on."

29
A FATAL
DECISION

"I am so sorry," Talbot the Innkeeper had said as he quickly ushered Domingo and Santiago into his establishment "I sent word the second I heard of Gabriel's abduction. All Salinans that cross into Tychi are in danger." Talbot removed his glasses and rubbed his forehead. "The letters I sent told you not to attempt any sort of rescue."

"We left Salinas the morning the Osprey attacked. We wouldn't have been home to receive it," Domingo said.

"No, it should have reached you. There were three letter bearers, all on different paths, all on the lookout for you," Talbot said as he walked towards the paintings on his wall. "We knew there was a possibility of something like this happening. But it was a risk we had to take. I can't call for Lady Yaren. She is already under some scrutiny, thanks to your friend Boris. Kahel's people will be looking into her circles, acquaintances, and her history. They soon will uncover her connection to the late Queen."

Domingo and Santiago listened intently.

"Their situation, Leata's and Yaren's, was quite unique. Those two were inseparable. More attached than any siblings I have ever met." Talbot stood stoic for a moment. "When Halcyon the Majji found Leata, he knew without question that she was his Apprentice. And, so as it goes, the Apprentice studies with the Majji in Atara." Talbot looked up and saw the gaping looks on both Santiago and Domingo. He took in a breath and continued, "But Leata could not be separated from her little sister Yaren. So, the Majji took both girls to Atara."

"You are telling us that not only were Leata and Yaren sisters, you also expect us to believe that the legend of the Majji is true? And Queen Leata was to succeed him?" Domingo asked.

Talbot ignored his incredulous tone and sat down. He stared longingly at his paintings.

"Talbot! Do you speak the truth?"

"You know I haven't been home in eighty-eight years."

The brother sat confused at the strange turn in the conversation.

"You probably think my home is the castle, but it's not. Nor are any lands you may have seen. My home is there." Talbot pointed at his paintings. "Atara. That's where I met Yaren. A decade after the girls arrived, Leata was ready to enter the second part of her training. She was to travel the lands, but Yaren wanted to stay in Atara. Leata knew that in a few years she would return then finally settle in Atara for good, so she was okay leaving her sister behind. No one could have foreseen what happened next. Our True King, by chance, happened upon Leata as she swam in a lake. He hid behind a tree as she emerged to dry herself. Leata had been training for some time now, and she had sensed his presence. Not only had she physically bested him in a short duel, but her sharp wit and tongue also cut him down several levels. Our True King had instantly fallen in love. The Majji didn't stop their courtship; it was an amazing turn of events. Leata was going to be Queen of the lands and the Majji. She was destined to do great things. Leata continued to secretly apprentice even after she became Queen. But before she completed the training, she had become pregnant. I am not sure you are aware, but Majjis cannot spawn. Something like that had never happened. This is where I come in. I was sent from Atara to keep an eye on the situation. Leata had me appointed the King's Steward. Leata gave birth, and our Kingdom and lands were at peace. By the time Kahel was fifteen, Leata had slowed in her Apprenticeship, and the Majji was greying. A year later, Kahel took an expedition to the northern side of the Nacunas. He claimed to have successfully crossed the Kalyptra and returned a different man. He then slew the True King and had the King's personal guards, servants, dogs, cats, rats, you name it, all murdered. Many good men and women died that night. Some fled the castle, others switched allegiances, but I remained. I would never leave her side. There is this strange thing that happens when one becomes the Apprentice. People are compelled to keep them from harm's way. Kahel had no idea why he couldn't end his mother's life as easily as he did his fathers."

"Our Queen...was to be Majji," Santiago said to himself.

"How is it that you survived? If you chose to stay and weren't allied with Kahel, why is it that you lived?" Domingo asked.

"Kahel would have given his mother anything she wanted, and the only thing she ever asked for was my freedom. She gave me this establishment and told me in secret what I was to do with it, how I was to protect the citizens, give them asylum, and a way out. She knew what her son had become. When the letters stopped coming and Leata stopped showing up to her training, Halcyon came. He mercilessly attacked

Kahel, nearly killing him. All Kahel had to do was reach out and grab Halcyon. He dug his nails into Halcyon, and the Majji collapsed, but with his last bit of energy Halcyon burst into a blue flame and disappeared into thin air. Kahel was weakened and feared the Majji's return. So, instead of waiting for another surprise attack, Kahel hunted him."

"We were told as children the story of the Majji. But they were just that, stories." Santiago rubbed his temples.

"After years of living where no one can see you, people begin to question if you really exist."

"Talbot, what does this have to do with Gabriel and Sophia?" Domingo asked.

"Everything," he replied. "Halcyon never resurfaced after his battle with Kahel. I haven't seen another Ataran in decades. Both Yaren and I searched for Halcyon, and every person we sent out to the Northern Woods returned, never setting foot in Atara. It was then that we heard of Gabriel and his eyes. One of our men reported seeing a man that resembled Halcyon in his youth. We called upon Salinas, time after time. After Yaren finally met Gabriel, she knew something was off. He had the mark of the Majji, but that was it. According to Yaren, Gabriel spoke incessantly of Sophia; he never shut up about her. Yaren had a gut feeling; she had to meet Sophia, and her gut feeling proved to be right. While Sophia has features that her mother, the late Princess Anne, had, she also has an uncanny resemblance to her grand-mother. We thought Gabriel would set off the marker, but it was Sophia who did. That's when we knew what you have known all along, that she is Kahel's daughter. But she is not only that; did you know she possesses all of her grandmother's Essence? I sensed it the moment I lifted my eyes to her. I was told, that the day Leata died, a brilliant light surrounded her as she held her grandchild. When the light vanished, Leata lay dead, and the child was gone."

"So, Kahel is after Sophia? His own daughter?" Domingo inquired.

"No. Gods, no. He has no idea she lives; he was after Gabriel. A cruel decoy the Green must have provided. He bears the marks of the Majji, but he is not one. Kahel took the bait."

"Gabriel is here then?"

"Yes. Deep in the castle somewhere. Poor boy. There is no way you can get to him, and I'm sure Kahel is prepared for any sort of rescue."

"And Sophia?"

Talbot was caught off guard by this question.

"Sophia is missing too?" he asked.

Santiago told Talbot all they knew about the night Sophia and Gabriel were taken.

"Gods. Our people told us that only one Osprey returned with Gabriel. We can only hope that she was taken by an Ataran."

"I understand that Kahel has mistaken Gabriel for the Majji, but what I can't understand is why Kahel is so desperate to get rid of the Majji."

"There is an ongoing war that dates back before the dawn of the first day. It had been dormant for some time now. He's killing her, and it seems like the Green is ready to fight back."

Both Santiago and Domingo stared blankly at Talbot.

"The Green," he said again. "Kahel's Extricate machines, the machines that give him and his followers limitless energy, are killing her. Our world is dying, and the Majji is the only one who could stop him." Talbot rubbed his face and stood up. "Gods, there is so much more to tell, but you must leave; you've stayed too long, go through my garden."

"We cannot. We are to meet up with our comrades at the marina."

"No," Talbot said worry in his tone. "Kahel knows you are here, and soon he will learn Gabriel is no Majji. Your people are not safe. Go through the garden, save your town. Those you are meeting would gladly sacrifice themselves."

"Yes, but we are not willing to sacrifice them," Santiago said as he and Domingo stood up.

Talbot looked at both brothers and conceded. "Stay alive, my friends." Talbot embraced Domingo then Santiago. "May the gods be with you."

The brothers fled through the front door and mounted their horses. They slowed as they made their way down the curved hill path that led to the marina.

"Domingo, look!" Santiago pointed past the marina. In the distance, you could see two riders whose horses were giving them trouble as the ocean waves slowly made their way towards the horses. "It's Ari and Carminda."

"Something is wrong. It's not high tide," Domingo said as they reached the end of the winding path. But before they could get their horses to pick up speed, to Santiago's and Domingo's horror, they could see Kahel's archers rise from their hiding spot in the sand dunes and attack.

"No!" Santiago said then commanded his horse to race forward. They watched as Ari tossed his daggers and as Carminda gracefully pulled arrows from her quiver. Both their projectiles met their targets with sickening accuracy. For a moment there, the brothers believed things would be okay and they would make it back to Salinas alive. Then it all went horribly wrong. A docked battleship at the marina opened its rear hatch, and five riders came to the attack. Domingo looked behind him after hearing a thunderous thud.

"Gods, they are behind us, brother!"

In front of them, they could see Ari and Carminda racing to their aid. When the brothers saw Carminda rise out of her saddle and steady, they knew to duck. Arrows whizzed by them and caught two of the closest riders in their heart. A third rider caught up to Santiago. His blade was out and he slashed at Santiago. Blade met flesh as blood gushed from his arm. The shock sent Santiago off his horse. The rider then attempted to go after Domingo but didn't see Ari as he tossed his daggers. One met the man in his throat, the other on his shoulder. Blood oozed out and the man crashed to the ground. Domingo saw how close he was to Carminda, but she wasn't looking at him, which only meant she was after someone behind him. Their horses passed one another so closely he could feel the sweat off of her painted mare. He turned to see Carminda kiss the mare's neck as she leaped off of it, onto the rider's horse that was behind Domingo. She slew her opponent as Ari used his last dagger to kill the final rider. Sensing that the threat was over, Carminda turned her new horse around.

"Carminda!" Domingo yelled as a once-thought-dead archer shot a last bloody arrow into Carminda's chest. Ari was there to catch her as she fell to the ground. Domingo rushed to the archer and dispatched him quickly. He then jumped off his horse and found his brother.

"Santiago. Brother, you will be okay. We will get home through Darwin's Trail." Santiago was pale but conscious. Domingo turned to Ari as he wrapped fabric he ripped from his tunic on his brother's arm. "Ari. How is Carminda?" Ari's silence was all the answer Domingo needed.

"Her Essence," Ari choked. "I can't let her pass here." He looked lovingly at a dying Carminda. "You were brilliant, my love. Brilliant." He bent over to kiss her forehead.

Then more riders appeared on the horizon.

"Ari, you go. You take her back home. Warn our people," Domingo said. "Santiago and I will divert them."

They all knew this was the last time they would see one another. Ari mounted his horse, and Domingo handed him Carminda, but not before he and Santiago placed their foreheads on hers. Tears in their eyes, Ari looked one last time at the brothers and disappeared towards Darwin's Trail.

The brothers raced towards the Factory District, and just like they predicted Kahel's guards only followed them. The brothers were ready to sacrifice their lives for the Green, for their people, but they were running blind. Nothing made sense. Where was Sophia? Would Ari and Carminda make it home in time to protect their people? All the brothers could do was hope. They pushed their horses as hard as they could. The Factory District was visible. As they came closer to the entrance, they could see it was heavily guarded. The brothers rode close to one another; they patted each other's backs and held hands for a moment.

"It was a blessing having you as a brother. May our Essence pass peacefully to the Green."

"I love you, brother; pray for Marcello's survival."

"Yes, pray."

"May our Essence pass peacefully to the Green," Domingo said as he released Santiago's hand and picked up speed. They approached the Factory District with riders trailing. A golden aura began to surround them, and their hearts grew calm. The guard's swords, spears, and bows were at the ready. Santiago closed his eyes. He awaited death but instead was unexpectedly thrown from his horse. He landed hard on his side.

"Brother!" Domingo cried out. Santiago opened his eyes and found both he and Domingo on the opposite side of a massive sandstorm. Across from them, the guards were being violently tossed left and right, and their bloodcurdling screams could be heard for miles and miles.

30

NEW GROUND

Sophia held Gabriel in her arms. She sat staring at the dagger dug in his chest, blood languidly pooling beneath them. Tears fell. Her love was dead. Her cries came from deep within her soul; her body shook violently with her sobbing. She leaned in closer to him and held him tighter, but it wasn't close enough. She wanted to be dead too. She pulled the knife from Gabriel's chest and pointed it towards her own. Gabriel's eyes shot open, and he thrust the dagger into Sophia. She yelled. The pain, gods, the pain. Sophia struggled to reach for her chest to pull the knife out but was unable to move her arms. She closed her eyes and threw her head back in a howl. When she opened them, she found a strange man straddling her. Her ears were ringing loudly and couldn't make out what the man was yelling. He turned his head and began to scream at someone else. He turned back at her and began to yell at her again. She was able to make out a few words "tear, open...." Sophia lifted her head and saw that the amber-eyed man was not only straddling her, but he was also restraining her. He leaned in closer to her.

"Please," she could hear him say. "Please stop."

Why the hell is he asking me to stop?

But the gentleness of his voice relaxed her, and Sophia stopped struggling. A girl who seemed to be only fifteen put a hand on Sophia's face.

"There is no time to numb, I am going to have to sew." Sophia was shocked at the maturity in the girl's tone.

"Look at me," the amber-eyed man said. "Squeeze my hands as hard as you need and, if you need to, bite me, but you have to try to relax, okay," he said to her.

Sophia stared straight into his eyes. The girl started to sew. It all began to return to her, all of it, the Osprey attacking Gabriel, her being struck. That's what they were sewing. It made sense, sort of. Who were these people, and where was Gabriel? Tears began to fall.

"Jasira, hurry. It's hurting her bad," he said.

"Lee, don't rush me."

Jasira worked with efficient speed, putting her pale blonde hair behind her ears only once.

"There, done," Jasira said.

"I'm going to let your arms go now, okay," Lee said as he slowly lifted his hands up. "Promise not to dig at your chest like that again?"

Sophia nodded her head. Lee got off of her as Jasira walked away. He leaned his back against a wooden beam and crossed his arms. He waited patiently for Sophia to get acclimated.

"Where am I?"

"Atara," Lee coolly responded. In an instant, Sophia went from fear to being filled with confusion. Atara was a land of savages, but these two helped her. Savages rip people's arms off and beat them with it, kick the wounded, and piss on the dead, not plead with strangers to stop mutilating themselves.

"Why did you do that?" Lee asked his brows furrowed. "Dig into your chest like that?"

"I was dreaming there was a dagger," she thought of the look in Gabriel's eyes. "I was trying to pull it out."

"You've been out for several nights, immobile. Then out of nowhere, you start yelling and cutting into yourself," he said as he looked down. Sophia realized that he had been terrified. She recalled the look on his face when she woke: it was worry. She imagined what it looked like, an unconscious girl one second and the next a bloody screaming mess. It must have been quite a sight. Sophia couldn't see much of her dwelling, just that she was on a couch in front of a lit fireplace, and there was a chair tipped over on the floor. He must have been sitting when she decided to scare him. Guilt crept up her stomach as she looked at the man's untidy hair. It had light streaks of blood where he had run his hands through it.

"I'm sorry," Sophia said. Lee looked up from the ground and met Sophia's eyes.

"No, gods, don't be. I shouldn't have even asked you, gods, I just was trying to understand, after what you've been through. I just," Lee fumbled, " you, um,...don't be sorry."

His awkwardness caught Sophia by surprise. Jasira appeared in the nick of time with a shirt in her hands.

"Sit up," she said, and Sophia obeyed. Jasira placed a warm wet rag on Sophia's chest and began to clean the blood off of her. "I hope Lee hasn't been boring you." She scrunched her nose at Lee. "Well, let's not have you laying there with your breasts all out," she said smiling. Lee's face went beet-red, and he quickly turned around. Jasira popped a top over Sophia's head. Sophia winced and waited for pain to surge through her as she slipped her arms through the armholes. She was surprised when she didn't feel much of a sting.

"You just stitched me. Why is it that I am healing so quickly?"

"Because you are here in Atara; we all heal quickly here." She sat down on the couch next to Sophia. "I'm Jasira, and that's Lee. He's the one that saved you." Jasira looked towards Lee, who was still facing the wall.

"You can turn around now, Lee. I mean, really, it's not like you haven't seen her breasts before." Lee turned around with his hand over his face. He was so mortified the garbled high-pitched words "good gods" were barely audible. Sophia looked at the almost white-haired, tawny-skinned girl.

"I've seen you before. On the King's Road."

"Yes! I was with Cyrus," Jasira said cheerily.

"So, you were the Atarans at Tychi?"

Jasira nodded. "Mmhmm, along with Lee here and some others." Jasira turned to Lee, whose red face was now a more normal shade. "Halcyon will want to see her, now that she is awake."

"Who's Halcyon?" Sophia asked.

"Pffft, who's Halcyon?" Jasira scoffed. The blank look on Sophia's face was answer enough. "Jeez, you really don't know huh? He's the Ma—"

"Master in arms and also our village's leader," Lee interjected. He shot Jasira a stern look. "Hey, why don't you go grab Sophia here something to eat?" Without any protest, Jasira got up and walked out the door.

"Listen, I know you have a lot of questions, and the person best suited to answer them is Halcyon." Lee looked at Sophia. She noticed him stiffen a bit as he looked at her. "I'll go get him," he continued, "so please try not to dig your heart out again while I'm gone." Sophia felt another pang of guilt as she recalled their introduction and the terrified look on his face. For a moment, she thought to lighten the mood with a little quip about cannibalism and being Ataran but quickly discarded the idea. It was then she realized that she had been staring at Lee for a considerable amount of time. Her jaw loosed, prepared to speak, when she saw the look on his face. Sophia couldn't be sure, but it seemed like Lee didn't want to leave. Lee took some breaths as he looked at her, nodded, then walked out the door.

Sophia stared at the door confused by their exchange. She swung her legs over to touch the ground. She gave a halfhearted attempt to stand but quickly discerned that her legs were not going to cooperate. She looked around the home she was in; it resembled those of Salinas. A small round table was behind the couch with enough room for one, but you could squeeze two if you tried. The kitchen was flush against the wall, next to the front door. Sophia looked to her left and saw a small ladder that led up to a loft area, probably where Lee normally slept. The home was made of logs upon logs. It was beautiful. She was too weak to explore, and her courage was collapsing. She just wanted to see Gabriel and go home. Sophia turned to the fire and began to cry.

Lee was a quarter of a mile from his house before the tightness in his chest had become more than just uncomfortable. When he was halfway to Halcyon's, the urge to turn around had become unbearable.

"Go back, that's what your body is trying to tell you," Halcyon called out. Lee saw Halcyon heading in his direction with Jasira by his side, cradling fruit in her shirt. The night was beautiful and the moon new. Even without the moon's presence, each blade of grass sparkled from the light pouring down from the bright starry night.

"I'm so sorry, Lee. I didn't know we were keeping Halcyon's identity secret," Jasira said.

"Neither did I," Lee responded. "I just didn't want his existence to be known until we know who she really is."

"I know who she is, Lee; she is my Apprentice," Halcyon said as he coughed into his robe. Lee watched as Halcyon tried to hide the blood that he spat upon his shirt sleeve.

"We've been through this," Lee objected. "We don't know that. She could be some kind of super-Grey that Kahel created."

Both Jasira and Halcyon gave Lee a queer look.

"Oh, gods, fine. Fine! Just for now, until we know what the hell is going on," Lee said, "let's not reveal who Halcyon is."

"Agreed." Halcyon knelt down and grabbed some dirt. He then stood up, closed his eyes, and released the earth slowly in front of his face. When he was done, he looked at Lee, and his stunning blue eyes were now a soft brown.

As they approached the cabin, Lee could hear soft cries. He wasted no time and burst through the door. He placed the chair he had knocked over earlier upright and scooted it close to Sophia. She was laying on her side, sobbing.

"Are you hurting? Did one of the stitches tear?" He placed her hand between his, and Sophia locked eyes with him and began to calm down.

Halcyon lifted an eyebrow and turned to Jasira. She returned the look with a "don't ask me" gesture.

"The stitches are fine," Sophia said as she sat up. "I just want to go home. My people must be so worried, and Gabriel too." The name unexpectedly stung Lee. "Please tell me he is alive." Sophia pulled her hand from Lee and covered her face. "Please," she cried.

Halcyon walked to the front of the couch.

"Listen," Lee said to Sophia, his body language and tone a complete reversal from earlier. "I know that this situation is frightening, but crying isn't going to get us answers or help anyone," Lee said stoically. His quick change in demeanor caught Sophia by surprise.

"Lee!" Jasira scolded.

"What?" Whatever filter Lee had was gone, and he fought to keep what control he had left. He looked at Sophia, then Jasira, and then to Halcyon. Halcyon closed his eyes and took in a deep breath.

"We are in the dark about many things," Halcyon began. "I am Halcyon, and you are?"

"Sophia."

"Now, Sophia, what we do know is that the King wanted your husband, and he got him. Gabriel just about killed Lee, ordering him to take you out of the fight. Aided by your good friend Zephyr, Lee was able to bring you to us and save your life."

Sophia's brows furrowed as she stared at the graceful white-haired man. His braid was long and, like Gabriel's, slung across the front of his shoulder.

"Zephyr?"

"Zephyr is an Elemental; you may recognize him as the playful wind that was often around you."

"Yes! My gods, it has a name? Is he okay?"

"Yes. Out trying to see what we can do about your husband's situation," Halcyon said as he sat next to her. Sophia took in a deep breath and told her story, how she woke in fear and knew how to move, about the fight, and how they were just after just Gabriel.

"I don't understand, though. It makes no sense. We are simple people; we are a town of entertainers, and that's it. This all started in Tychi. When Lady Yaren and the Elite insisted we perform, they wanted,"—she corrected herself—"no, they demanded Gabriel and I perform."

"Yaren?" Halcyon asked. "Gods, that girl is still alive? Tell me, did she show you a painting of any sort? One with a woman and a Hast eagle?"

"No, she didn't. I did come across it at the Inn, but it wasn't a painting, though. It was a stained-glass window. The Innkeeper, Talbot, had an array of wonderful paintings. Many of Atara actually." Sophia turned to Halcyon ,and the small pieces began to click into place. "You wouldn't happen to know why?" she asked, slightly accusatory.

"Talbot is Ataran, Yaren is the late Queen's sister, and those two haven't just kicked a hornet's nest, they tossed it, shook it, and then for shits and giggles lit it on fire."

Sophia wrapped her arms around her waist. Whatever was going to come out of Halcyon's mouth next wasn't going to be good.

"They used you. They used Gabriel. They have their own agenda, and you and your husband's survival apparently wasn't on it."

"What do they want?"

"I don't know; bring down Tychi, maybe, start a war," Halcyon said. "They both have excellent reasons for wanting to see Kahel dead and Tychi fall." Halcyon took a deep breath and looked into the flickering fire. "It just doesn't make sense. Yaren wouldn't be so careless, even if she did lose her head for a minute, and Talbot would be the one to ground her, not to add fuel." Halcyon thought that, even if those two lost all sensibility, the moment they saw Gabriel, they would have protected him, not used him as a pawn in some sick game. And, to top it all off, even though Gabriel has all the traits, it was Sophia who touched the marker; it was Sophia who has Leata's Essence, not Gabriel. His mind swam left then right.

"I'm sorry, Sophia, I am lost in my head. Is there anything we can do to make you more comfortable?"

"I'd like to go home now. My people are probably worried sick about me, and I need to see if they know anything about Gabriel."

Lee sat back and crossed his arms. "You can't leave," he said in a very matter-of-fact tone. "The moment you step outside the forest, your wound will stop healing."

"So, I am your prisoner then?"

"If prisoners are allowed to walk around towns, live peacefully with its inhabitants, and are only asked to remain until their wounds are fully healed, then, yeah, sure, you're a prisoner," Lee said, agitated as he walked to his kitchen and poured himself a glass of water.

Jasira backhanded Lee across his shoulder.

"What the hell is wrong with you?" She quietly mouthed to him.

Lee turned away and drank his water.

"Sophia," Halcyon interjected, "you will need to remain till you have fully healed internally. You can stay here with Lee, or if you would like I can find some other accommodations for you. I will send word to your town that you are well and will return soon."

"Thank you, and it's okay. I can stay here. I wouldn't want to put anyone else out."

"Take your time getting up and adjusted," Jasira said, leaning forward from the back of the couch. Again, Sophia was thrown off by Jasira's youthful face and the mature tone, and she wondered how many decades this girl was. "I'll report to you any info I overhear those two yapping about," Jasira whispered as she pointed to both Halcyon and Lee. "I promise."

Sophia stared at Lee; she didn't understand why he was so put out with her. Maybe she may have been a tad bit churlish to say she was a "prisoner," but, really, how the hell was she supposed to know that her wounds would reopen if she left the boundaries of Atara? She was grateful that he saved her life, that he tended to her, and that he allowed her to stay at his home. Sophia didn't want him to think that she didn't appreciate all he had done. Before she could open her mouth to say thank you, Lee turned and walked out the door.

"Rest," Halcyon said. "Jasira picked some fruit for you, but I'll send her out to get you some fresh water and warm bread."

Jasira shot up, smiled at Sophia, and walked outside to find Lee sitting on the ground with his arm across his face as he leaned back on one of the many trees that decorated his property. Lee lived between Cyrus' bar and the Majji's home. His home was close to the forest, but whenever he returned from any journey, the forest would never open up here. He couldn't understand why and finally settled on the idea that the Green was having a bit of fun with him. After about three decades, he just got used to it.

"Um, I'm going to get that fresh water," Jasira said as she headed northwest to the river.

Halcyon emerged from the house and gently closed the door. He then walked to Lee, who he was struggling to keep it together.

"What the hell is wrong with me, Halcyon? I want to hold her and shake her at the same time."

"Nothing." Halcyon reached his hand out to Lee. Lee quickly slapped it away. "Stop being childish and get up," Halcyon scolded.

"I'm NOT being childish." Lee pursed his lips after the words slipped out. Halcyon kept his hand outstretched.

"It's not your fault," Halcyon said. "It's her Essence, that of the Apprentice. Anyone who gets close enough to her will feel compelled to protect her. Hell, look at Jasira; she ran into Cytrine's home, took a shirt, and ran all the way back." Lee grabbed Halcyon's hand. "You are a very strong-willed and intelligent man, Lee. Half of you is following the compulsion, while the other half is being YOU and trying to make sense of it."

"Heh, wait, gods, Jasira got that shirt from Cytrine? Man, I'm going to hear it later."

"Probably sooner than you want to since all that woman has been doing is interrogating anyone she can trick into talking to her about the stranger who kept your attention."

"I don't understand. Cytrine and I haven't been together for months now."

"Hell hath no fury, Lee."

Lee ran his hands through his hair and followed the Majji into town. Their walk was strangely quiet, which told Lee one thing, that something was on Halcyon's mind. How he looked down as they walked told him another thing, and it wasn't good.

"Are you going to let me in on what you know?" Lee asked.

"It's not what I know, it's what I sense." Halcyon looked up into the sky. "Why do you test me? You won't give me the time I need to see this through." All of Atara knew that Halcyon was sick. But only a select few knew he was dying. Halcyon was young for a Majji. From the moment they Apprentice till their death, a Majji's life spans five centuries. Halcyon hadn't even hit his 300th birthday, and his Essence was slowly returning to the Green. This isn't how it was supposed to be, and Halcyon knew that Lee knew that. His Essence was to slowly pass to his Apprentice, keeping them alive for centuries. When he relinquished the title Majji, he'd take the title of Master. Halcyon would live out his last fifty years or so in Atara, then be rested in the sacred Anadenanthera forest. It's what happened to his Master, and so on.

"I've been given my final mission. Lee. The Green is trying to tell me something, and all I have to do is figure out exactly what that is before it's too late."

31

THE CROWNING
CURTAIN CALL

It was the morning of the sixth day, and Eilith stared out into the paths west of Salinas. She ran her hand on Carminda's white-faced horse, which came galloping in, sans Carminda, a few hours ago. The impatient horse nudged Eilith several times. She tried to soothe the mare as best she could as she looked towards the trails. Either someone will come out of the Wanderers Trail or to the northeast from Darwin's Trail. Every inch of her ached with worry, and she had attempted to keep her cool but was failing. Weiya and Eilith had met with the townspeople to discuss potential outcomes and evacuations. The House of the Courtesans and Chevaliers was also a safe house with a hidden underground tunnel that led you out of the town, south of Darwin's trail. It was a long, tight walk with poor air quality and some questionable architecture, but an emergency out if they needed it. After a lengthy discussion, the town agreed to stay put and not move the children until they heard back from Domingo and Santiago. Even so, several of the new settlers packed up and left, which was fine by her. If a few wanted to go on their own accord, better for them. Salinas was a marked town now; even if they were to retrieve Sophia and Gabriel, their town would be under the watchful eye of the King, and they would have to flee, no matter what. Eilith saw movement coming from Darwin's Trail. Carminda's horse quickly left her side and raced towards a horse carrying two people that emerged from the path. It was struggling to continue on. Carminda's horse was then followed by the wild herd. They met up with Ari's horse, relieving him. Eilith then saw that it was Ari and Carminda, but Carminda wasn't moving. Ari switched horses and slid Carminda's limp body into his arms, and the white-faced mare began to gallop towards Salinas while the other horse collapsed. Eilith's heart sank as a blood-soaked Ari approached her. His tear-stained face told her all she needed to know.

"She passed the instant we stepped onto Salinas' soil."

"Where are Domingo and Santiago?"

Ari looked down. "They were the reason I was able to escape."

Eilith's face crumpled, and she covered a short sob. She looked away and wiped her tears.

"Domingo, Santiago, they wanted me to warn you all. Kahel plans to wipe our town out, we've got to move," he said.

"Ring the town bell and gather the citizens in the square; we must evacuate our people immediately." Eilith's voice trailed as she watched the horses. The connection between the Salinans and the wild horses was like none other. There was a mutual understanding built on a solid and respectful relationship. The horses were free to come and go as they pleased. Many of the wild herds were aggressive and hard to mount, but not these horses. So, when the horse next to her was whinnying uncontrollably, she knew the mare was trying to tell her something. Ari had just turned to run when Eilith caught his hand. She watched as two other horses helped the one that had collapsed across the river, then turned to the rest of the herd, who were bucking and neighing wildly. They were impatient, nervous. Carminda's horse put its nose against Eilith and nudged her. She caressed its face in return. Eilith's heart dropped harder than ever. Eilith's long life had been marked by violence and pain. She was grateful to have lived these last few decades peacefully, but that feeling she had when she was younger, before the massacres started, had returned. Back then, her people had known for centuries how to fight the darkness. But here, now, with her new people, they didn't have a fraction of that knowledge. Which equated to what sort of chance they had against an attack. The more lives she could spare from what was upon them the better. Eilith placed her forehead on Carminda's horse.

"Go, friend, run with the others, go." The horse let out a loud whinny in protest. "I will not leave my people, you must go." The elegant white-masked horse bowed her head then galloped off to meet the herd. They effortlessly crossed onto the western side of the river. She watched as they raced south towards Vizzini.

"Ari, Kahel's men are already here," Eilith said.

"What? How is that possible? No one was on the trail with me, and if they took the King's Road on to the Wanderers Trail, it would have taken them another full day."

"I don't know how, but the horses wouldn't normally come close to our town, so they sensed something." She turned to face Salinas. "Domingo has a telescope on his roof; we can check our borders from there. Do you have strength enough to carry Carminda?" Ari nodded. The two walked through the streets of Salinas, making their way to the brothers' home. It was early. In about ten minutes or so, the roosters would start to crow and people would begin their day. So, it was odd when there were already people walking in the streets. Eilith pulled Ari behind a house.

"Give me Carminda," she said as she took Carminda out of his arms. "Take your shirt off and wipe as much blood off of your body with it as you can." Ari did as he was told. When he was done, he threw the shirt on the ground and Eilith handed Carminda back. Eilith then removed her top, leaving her in only a thin sleeveless shirt that left nothing to the imagination. She placed her clean shirt over Carminda, concealing all the blood.

"Follow suit," she said. Eilith hooked Ari's arm, pushed him forward, and started giggling. She was walking erratically and waving her arm in the air.

"AaAAaaand it's in ttthhhieer eeyeesss," she sang and giggled some more. Ari, while carrying Carminda, began to walk in the same erratic way. They got closer and closer to the strange men in their town. Eilith looked into their grey eyes.

"Oh, he's a cute one, can he join us?" she said.

Ari laughed.

"No. I won't share." They continued to walk past the Greys as they eerily all stopped to watch them.

"Oh, won't you join?" She called out as they got further and further. The Greys continued to stare, said nothing, and turned away. The two Salinans encountered at least a dozen of them before they reached the brothers' house. When they entered the house, Ari placed Carminda's dead body on the couch, then raced to the roof, passing Marcello's bed and waking the sleeping man, who shot up and tried to steady himself on his legs.

"What's going on?"

"We have been invaded. Keep an eye on that door!" Eilith shouted back.

Ari and Eilith opened an overhead wooden trap door. The

metal door handle clanked loudly as the door fell open. They remained low as they climbed to the roof and crawled carefully towards the telescope. Eilith peered through it. It was then she spotted a line of men on top of the hill near the dogwood tree. Eilith knelt down and covered her face, and Ari took a quick look.

"Gods. They have archers north of us already. How is that possible?" Ari said.

"They must have been stationed at Jaru, and those men in our town are the Greys we saw at Crossings Forged. Ari, not only is our north covered, we can't escape through the main trail. We are surrounded," Eilith replied, still kneeling.

"Then go west. We've got to cross the river."

"Ari, the children. We can't move them quickly enough; we'd be sitting ducks."

"We ARE sitting ducks! There has got to be a way out!"

"If you can make it to Weiya's, you can take the tunnel to Darwin's Trail. Hide in the woods, disguise yourself as a traveler or a bandit."

"Weiya's doors are locked this early in the morning, and I will not leave without Carminda. To top it all off, that tunnel is bound to collapse if the whole town travels through it."

"No one said anything about the whole town."

"Eilith..." Ari's disbelieving tone reverberated in the air.

"There is a chance for you and some of the others to escape if you scatter, but not for me and not for the children. I will not have an arrow or blade touch them: I will not see their blood spilled. I need to get back to my home. I've got to make some tea." Eilith stood up and began to walk away.

"So, this is it?" Ari asked.

"Yes. I will not ask you to fight. You and Carminda have done so much already, now I ask that you try to survive. One last favor."

"Anything."

"Ring the distress signal before you leave," Eilith said.

"Of course."

Eilith embraced him.

"An honor, Ari, knowing you, training you. Be well, and may the gods be with you." She kissed his cheek and walked downstairs.

Ari stood looking out through the telescope, cursing under his breath. He ran downstairs where Marcello stood with a confused look on his face. Marcello looked at Carminda, then Ari, back to Carminda, then Ari again.

"I need to borrow some of your brothers' clothes," Ari said.

"She's dead. I walked to her, and she's covered in blood"— Marcello pointed to Carminda—"and dead."

"Never mind, I will get them myself." Ari changed his clothes and walked over to Marcello.

"Wait till you hear the distress signal, then go to Eilith's. The Greys will think it's just a normal town bell." Ari put his hand on Marcello's shoulder. "An honor, my friend." Ari walked to Carminda, ever so graceful that even in death he admired her. He placed a blanket around her, then lifted her. Ari walked out the door and headed for the church. He looked at Carminda's serene-looking face.

"You were amazing, you know that," he spoke to her, not paying attention to the Greys and the townspeople who were watching. "Your arrows flew and, like in practice, hit exactly where you wanted them to hit. Years of sparring, years of training; I swore I'd be the first to fall." Ari took a turn and saw the small church ahead of him.

"They are going to make the tea," he began to sob. "We are that fucked." He pushed the doors open to the church. "I'm going to try to get us out of here, okay."

There was only one church in Salinas, a simple limestone structure with large windows encompassing its sides. Ari's destination, the bell tower, was out back behind the church. Crossing through the church was the quickest way to access it. Ari stepped in and passed the pews that were arranged in a circle. In the center of it was a garden with a small dead branch of an Anadenanthera tree, a wooden dove, and many many flowers. The light poured in through the windows from the morning sun, giving Ari a false sense of peace. Here you were welcome to believe and worship who you wanted. Whether it was the Green or one of the gods, you were free to have faith. Ari walked to the back where the bell-rope was. He placed Carminda down for a moment to ring the bell three times, wait two seconds, ring twice, wait two more seconds, ring the bell one last time. Ari gathered Carminda and walked out the back of the church. He figured his best bet was to try to cross the river. He headed west, counting the Greys, but he quit after thirty. Ari stared out to the river.

The western town Vizzini swore fealty to Kahel, but Ari believed they only did that so Kahel would leave them alone. Which, now that he thought about it, was pretty smart. Why constantly spit in the face of your enemy when you could smile at them with pleasantries and spit on the floor as they leave? But Ari chose not to go to Vizzini; there were established micro-villages on the way to Vizzini, and he hoped he could find sanctuary in one of them. Once, long ago, there were Barons and Baronesses and Lords and Ladies of lands west of the river, but when the True King died Kahel took their lands, brought them into Tychi, and called them his "Elite." Besides the town of Vizzini, the villages of the west were always in need of something, whether it be food, heat, or clothing. Kahel would only give it to the towns if they turned in anyone who crossed the river in search of sanctuary. If they didn't have anyone to surrender, they would turn in one of their own. Given Ari's other option was staying here and fighting, heading west seemed the highest chance of survival.

"Here we go, my love." He sprinted to the river; an arrow zipped by him. He held on tightly to Carminda and was inches from the water when an arrow caught him in the leg.

"Shit." Ari limped forward into the water, grimacing in pain. He didn't dare look back but stopped when he saw a body float by in the river, then another. His hesitation cost him. He knew better, but seeing the bodies of his people float by took him by surprise. They really didn't have a chance. There had been too much planning on Kahel's end. Having the Greys already placed in Crossings Forged, it was apparent that Kahel had had his eyes on Salinas for a while now. Ari hoped Weiya had come to this realization by now and had begun evacuations.

"Gods, give them the time to serve the tea." He looked to the sky, defeated, as an arrow shot into his back. With Carminda still in his arms, Ari fell to his knees then to his side. His heart was filled with fear for his people.

May they all come to terms with their deaths and go peacefully into the Green, he thought. He reached out and touched Carminda's cold face. The river's current began to pick up the pace, and the water lapped over his and Carminda's body. It was soothing, refreshing. His vision began to fade then Ari let go.

32
NOT THE LAST

Marcello burst through Eilith's door. He did as Ari asked; he heard the distress bell then walked out the door. He was halfway there when one of the townspeople jumped from a window and cut the throat of a Grey. That's when Marcello decided to run. On his way, he encountered more fights all in the alleyways. His people would push the Greys into a dark corner, and, well, he didn't stick around to see what happened next.

"Eilith! Gods! Eilith, what's going on?"

Eilith sat quietly at her table, spinning an empty cup of tea.

"I was just, then, on my way, he, out the window, WITH A KNIFE!!" Marcello shrieked.

"Sit down, Marcello," Eilith said calmly. Marcello took a few breaths and realized how cold her house was. He pulled a seat back and sat in front of Eilith.

"Eilith, please, talk to me."

"Many years ago, I was ordered to travel from my home to Salinas. I was told that only when my mission was clear was

I to reveal myself to the town elders. Your grandfather was one of them." Eilith stopped spinning the teacup. Marcello stared at her with a confused look on his face. "I am from the Ibex Warrior Tribe of the Nacunas, and my mission was to protect Sophia."

"What, why?"

"Because she is Kahel's blood and, in the words of the dying Queen, 'she will save us all." There was a crash against Eilith's door, followed by panicked screaming. Marcello turned his head to the door.

"What's going...Why wasn't I told?"

"You were the unexpected third son, born so many years after the twin brothers. Your mother begged your father that he make you exempt and so you were. You brothers trained every morning and every night. They along with many from our town swore to protect Sophia." Eilith poured tea into the empty cup. "You didn't. This isn't your fight. Therefore, you have a choice. You can drink this tea and go to sleep peacefully, or you can join me and fight to the death."

Marcello looked at the cup. This wasn't what he anticipated his day was going to be when he went to sleep last night. He figured he'd hit the stand for a bit, flirt with the female customers, play with some of the children...the children.

"Anna," Marcello said softly.

"She went to sleep upstairs," Eilith's eyes watered up and began to frost. "After she finished her tea, she was tired, so I carried her upstairs. I lay her on the bed, kissed her, and sat with her till she was with the Green." Eilith wiped her eyes and found her strength. "The children that couldn't escape are with the Green now. We all knew what the distress bell meant, and the last thing we wanted for the children was for them to die frightened and in pain."

"Gods." Marcello lowered his face into his hand and began to weep. It was a mix of anger and sorrow. The decision to give the children tea without trying to escape infuriated him, but if Anna and the other children were ever to die then he wanted it to be peaceful, not violent.

"I get why you did it." His voice muffled, "I wish you had just told me." He lifted his head.

Eilith pushed the tea across the table to Marcello.

"Drink, Marcello, sleep; it's what your mother wanted."

Marcello rubbed his arms in an attempt to keep warm. It was then that he noticed his breath was visible.

"No," he said as he pushed the cup back to Eilith. "No one gave me a chance to choose what I wanted for myself. All of this was kept from me, and now, when the town needs as much help as it can get, I am useless." Marcello was absolute in his resolve. "I will do whatever you need me to do, but I want to die fighting."

Eilith stood up and opened her pantry. She moved some food to the side then reached into the back. A small clicking noise was heard as she began to remove the wooden back panel that the shelves were attached to.

"Help me," she told Marcello. He took the panel off her hands. The food came crashing down to the ground. He tossed the board. Eilith looked at Marcello in disbelief and with a little annoyance. In front of them was a compartment that was hidden behind the pantry, where he saw a pair of sai, brilliant curved blades, and an elegant silvery gown.

"Eilith... those, that's a—"

"A mage's gown," Eilith said while she lowered her skirt. "We may be dead in a few moments, but that doesn't mean I've lost all decency; turn your head." Eilith changed into the mage's gown then picked up a beautiful belt. It was made of dark silver circles that connected to one another. The center clip had a silver head of a ram on it. She wrapped it around her waist; it hung a bit loosely on her hips but did not slip down. Eilith grabbed a ribbon and tied her hair back, exposing the pointed ears that she had kept hidden underneath her long hair.

"Holy shit! You really are from the Warrior Tribe!"

"Why would I lie about that?" Eilith's house creaked with frost.

"We need to make it to the river. I'm going to cast, Marcello, and I am going to take down as many of those bastards as I can. But I need your Essence to complete this kind of cast."

Marcello turned around. Eilith was always a fierce woman, in every sense of the word, but now he saw a fierce warrior prepared to fall in battle.

"It is yours."

Marcello walked up the stairs and knelt by Anna, then he kissed her forehead. Eilith's house was now completely iced over, giving it a serene magical feel only told in fairytales. Small flakes of snow fell from the ceiling and landed on Anna's face.

"I'll see you in a bit," he said to her then walked downstairs and grabbed the blade.

"Ready?"

Eilith spun her sai then clasped them. "I'll charge, you follow. Kill whoever I miss."

The door swung open, and the town Marcello knew was no more. Homes were on fire, people lay dead on the ground, and others were fighting. He kept Eilith's fast pace. Whenever someone attempted to attack her, she quickly ended them. Marcello caught a few men coming from the sides. One Grey struck Eilith from the rooftop. He landed heavily on her. Marcello was occupied with a Grey who caught up from behind. Eilith was flat on her back, as the Grey attempted to lift her gown with one hand and loosen his pants with the other. She shot a knee up, hooked her right elbow across his face, and then kicked him off. The man stumbled back. He pulled two small blades out and began to laugh maliciously. The Grey lunged. She easily disarmed him and had him on his knees in moments. Eilith placed the tip of her sai under the man's chin and came close to his ear.

"How. Dare. You," she said between her teeth. Eilith tossed her free sai down into the Grey's manhood then slit his throat with the other. She turned to see Marcello struggling with his Grey. Eilith took one of the dead man's blades and flung it into the chest of the Grey that Marcello was fighting.

"Jeez!"

"Run!" Eilith yelled then gathered her sai. They reached the river and looked behind them. The Greys were no longer attacking Salinas; instead, they began towards Eilith and Marcello.

"Someone's changed the orders, Marcello! There is a commander here, instructing these men!"

"It could be any of them!"

"No, it couldn't; it has to be someone Kahel trusts. This is a big job, and I am sure he wouldn't want it botched up." It's been many years since Eilith needed the full use of her skills. She wasn't even sure she could accomplish her task. She needed to find out who their leader was. Eilith concentrated then shot her senses out. She could feel her energy traversing the town, touching tangible objects then spreading forward. Then, suddenly, like hitting a wall, she felt it. Dark, Mad Essence was blocking her. Eilith gasped. She was very familiar with that wall; it came fully equipped with soft, shoulder-length brown hair and looks that disguised the hideous creature hidden below.

"Corentin," she whispered.

"Who?"

Her heart raced. "He should be dead. He's over two-hundred- years old; he should be dead." The letter Lady Yaren had given her was cryptic. It told the story of the fall of the

Ibex Warrior Tribe. The story goes that, during a routine trip around the Nacunas, they encountered Dark Essence in the Western corner. They also encountered wild men led by a man named Corentin. It was a short, bloody battle. One of the Ibex escaped and managed to warn the tribe. Many of the women warriors were ordered to scatter with their children. The ones who stayed to fight died by Corentin's hands. But he wasn't satisfied, and he hunted every single warrior woman and child and, one by one, brutally murdered them until only a handful remained. Then, just like that, the murders stopped. She figured he had died; he would have been 155 years old then. Lady Yaren had written in a slightly darker ink, "and he was never seen again." She couldn't figure it out then, but now she knew. It was a warning; never being seen again doesn't mean he was dead.

"Holy shit, Eilith," Marcello exclaimed at the sight of the Greys. They leaped down from Salinas' town walls, filed through the sides, and walked through the archway. Fifty or so men against the two last Salinans.

"Back up into the river, Marcello," Eilith said with a protective arm across his chest. The moment both their legs were in the water, she instructed him to kneel. He knelt behind her then she slowly lowered down and counted the men.

"Sixty-seven," she said, facing the men as they inched forward. Including the archers, Eilith guessed Kahel had sent over a hundred, maybe one hundred and fifty, skilled men to massacre her new people. The townsfolk took out a pretty good chunk of them. Hell of a way to go, but she was elated with pride. Though some were well-trained, most of the people were just entertainers.

"Put your arms around me." Eilith placed her hands in the water as Marcello embraced her.

"Gods! You are like ice."

"Soon you will be too. Just close your eyes. I know this may sound stupid, but just try to sleep, okay."

Marcello nodded his head. He held Eilith tightly, and his face rested on her back, giving her slight warmth.

Eilith began to chant the old words from a time long before theirs and their ancestors'. She remembered her first home, the sound of the snow crunching under her feet, the smell of a cold morning. She loved the mountains. Her first village was located at the base of the northern side of the Nacunas. Her mind and spirit were home. The river beneath her froze. The ice crept up her body and Marcello's. Marcello's body suddenly went limp against hers. He was gone, but his Essence had fused with hers. Her body was now frozen up to her waist. Eilith closed her eyes and concentrated everything she had. Ice spread in front of her, racing across the ground like spilled milk. It reached the first Grey, who was an ice sculpture in seconds, then the next. It crawled up the walls then down into Salinas. It dashed through the Town Square and right out to the dogwood on the hill. It didn't stop till Salinas was covered entirely in ice.

Eilith clung to her Essence, not releasing her cast, not until he revealed himself. She knew he was still alive; she sensed the dark wall he carried with him. In moments, he walked through the archway.

"Well, what do you fucking know, an Ibex Warrior. Did you think your little parlor trick would kill me?" he proudly walked towards her. His hair was pulled back in a ponytail, and he barely wore any armor. His face had the same sickening beauty and arrogance that she remembered when she was eleven. She may have been hiding high up in an oak tree when he murdered her aunt, but she caught his features, sensed his Essence, and would never forget them. Corentin carried no weapons, but his hands were covered in blood. She knew what it meant, and the thought enraged her. Eilith's concentration was about to break.

"So many of your people tried that cast on me. The trick I learned?" he said proudly. "Stand on something that has no connection to the Green, something synthetic, and it won't harm you." He pointed to his boots. "Modified soles. A fine creation of mine. Kudos, though, on hiding out this long. We swore magic was gone, and now with you"—he walked closer—"it will be. The last of the Warrior Tribe." He glided towards her in oblivious superiority.

Eilith needed him just a little closer, and when the haughty bastard was in range she mustered a proud smile.

"Not the last, you asshole," she said out of her blue lips.

The ice crawled up her face and onto her now-pale hair. Corentin had no time to ponder her words. Eilith and Marcello's frozen bodies shattered into hundreds of deadly sharp icicles. The ice remained suspended in the air then shot towards Corentin with dizzying speed. There was nowhere for him to run. The ice shredded through his body and crashed into the wall behind him. He looked down in disbelief as his shirt quickly turned a bright shade red. Corentin fell back and lay staring at the sky. He took quick, short, shallow breaths, which began to slow and soon came to a complete stop. The iced town started to slowly defrost in the late autumn sun. The frozen Greys thawed, and their dead bodies fell in unison, letting out a tremendous eerie thud as they hit the ground. The river began to flow again, and a small breeze crossed through the now-silent town.

33

WE WERE PAWNS

Sophia held Anna tightly. She couldn't believe how much she had missed that sweet little girl; she also could not remember how long they had been apart. Sophia placed the smiling girl down and kissed her forehead. They began to walk around their vine-covered town.

"Well, what do you want to do today?" Sophia grabbed Anna's hand.

"Can we go to the river? I want to catch some wriggly fish!" Anna let the "sh" sound hang between her teeth as she smiled.

"Sounds like a great plan; let's get those fishhhhhhhhh."

Anna gave her signature pouty look. "Stop teasing, Sophia, it's not polite."

"Oh, sorry, can you ever forgive me?" Sophia smiled as she grabbed the fishing rods that appeared against a wall.

"Maybe." Anna smiled.

"Oh, who is teasing now?" They both laughed and walked to the river. The sun was rising, and Sophia wondered why they were up so early. Must have been Gabriel's doing. He always woke her on days she could have slept in. She recalled the one time he was in a very romantic mood and wanted to take her to the dogwood tree to see the sunrise. Even after her momentous meltdown, Gabriel still managed to drag her out of bed and up the hill, to watch the sunrise. They had sat there, and she would doze off on his shoulder. He shook her lightly as the sun gently peeked over the trees in the east. Sophia laughed a little at the memory. She and Anna reached the water. The river was calm, but an unfamiliar icy breeze came off the current. Sophia stood watching the river. Anna took the fishing poles out of Sophia's hands and placed them on the ground. She grabbed Sophia's hand and guided her towards the river. When her feet were submerged entirely, she looked down at Anna, whose hair had several flakes of snow on it.

"Sophia, can you hold me?"

Sophia lifted the child and embraced her.

"I love you, and I believe in you. Don't be scared, okay" Anna said nuzzled in Sophia's chest.

"Scared of what?" Sophia questioned.

Anna pushed herself back. Sophia looked into Anna's warm eyes. Anna closed them then fell asleep. Her body became cold to the touch, then limp. Sophia's heart started racing. She called out Anna's name, but no sound came out of her mouth. The cold breeze off the river blew strongly against Sophia. Anna's body turned into snow that danced away in the wind. Sophia continued calling her name as the snow got further and further from her. She turned from the river to see her town in flames. The fire traveled quickly and came closer to her. Sophia tried to run, but her legs wouldn't respond. The flames were upon her. She could feel her clothing and flesh catch on fire.

Sophia rolled off the couch and smacked hard onto the floor. She turned her head and saw Lee's fireplace. The sight of the fire sent her into a panicked frenzy. She screamed and scrambled away.

"Lee!" She turned her head, looking for him. "Lee!"

The man who sat by her side for the past few nights was nowhere to be found when she actually needed him. Well, that's not being fair; she did need him earlier that week, when she tried to dig her heart out. Sophia got to her feet as the door crept open. A beautiful dark haired woman wearing a half-sleeve blue tank and a long skirt walked through the door. Her body was slender, and she wielded breasts any woman could envy. Sophia inadvertently placed her hand on her scar. She looked at the woman and peered into her eyes.

"You keep calling him like that, you'll come off looking like a desperate woman," the woman said.

"What?" Sophia's confused tone trailed as she spoke again. "Where is Lee?"

The woman rolled her eyes and walked in. She closed the door behind her and placed the shawl she was carrying on the couch. She looked longingly around the house, then back to Sophia.

"You know he's been on 'take care of the mysterious woman' duty for a while now, and the first night he wanders out you conveniently lose it."

Sophia's brows furrowed. Who in all that is Green was this woman, and why was she upset? Sophia understood that she was imposing on Lee, but she thought they were maybe becoming friends. She must have guessed wrong.

"I'm sorry, who are you?" Sophia asked.

"No. The question is who are you? Coming into our land, expecting to be tended to at all times. It's ridiculous."

"I don't expect to be—"

"But I guess being a frail, imprudent woman who can't defend herself puts you in situations like these often." The woman crossed her arms.

Sophia's jaw dropped. She never had the urge to smack a complete stranger before, but if there were a time this would be it.

"Anyways, Lee asked me to keep an eye on you while he went to see Halcyon. You screamed; are you okay? Fire not hot enough? Splinter?"

Sophia took in a calming breath; there was no time, and she had to get to Lee.

"I have to go. Thank you for checking up on me. I am sorry for imposing; I promise you it was unintentional."

"You're not imposing on me. I hope you know Lee has other duties and obligations; we all do."

Sophia didn't know how to respond and walked past the woman. Then, she reluctantly turned around when she realized that she had no idea where she was going.

"How do I get to Halcyon's?"

The woman rolled her eyes and pointed east. Sophia wasted no time and began to sprint. It may have just been a dream, and it may have made absolutely no sense at all, but the visions had cut her so deeply. She wanted to go home; she needed to go home. Maybe there was a way an Ataran could go with her, monitor her health. If she deteriorated, she would return. Sophia knew that, once she held Anna in her arms, she would feel better. Sophia approached a small hut. Smoke puffed out the chimney in circular patterns, scattering into the night air. From her position, she could hear two voices arguing, then a third one attempting to diffuse the situation. The one diffusing tension was one she recognized as Halcyon's.

Then a fourth voice joined in. "It's too late. We couldn't save them, and we can't save him. It's done. Let's just drop this." This was Lee's voice.

"Lee, you don't get it, but she cast. I sensed magic, powerful and ancient magic; she was Warrior. And now they are going to burn the bodies then build an Extricate Station there. We can't let them do that. All of that Essence will be pulled into that machine," a warm voice responded.

"We can't fight them, either," the first voice added.

Sophia walked closer and closer as wind tossed her hair. It danced around her.

"Zephyr," she said quietly.

The wind picked up and became more brisk, tossing the grass, playing like a content child. Sophia giggled; she knew he was happy.

"Halcyon told me your name," Sophia said. "I'm so happy to meet you finally."

The voices in the house abruptly stopped. The door swung open, and Lee stepped out.

"Sophia," he said with restraint. He closed the door behind him and walked towards her. "You shouldn't be here. Come, I'll walk you back."

"No, Lee," Sophia said as she tried to turn around. "I need to talk to you and Halcyon. I had this terrible dream."

"Another time," Lee said and pushed her on against her will. Sophia tried to knock his hands off her shoulders, but Lee was adamant. Zephyr shot across the grass quickly and tripped Lee. He fell flat on his rear.

"What the hell, Zephyr!"

Sophia felt Zephyr gently push on the small of her back. She knew what that meant. She doubled back, dodged Lee, and ran towards the house. The moment Lee managed to get on his feet, Zephyr zipped across and knocked him over again.

Lee sat up and accepted defeat. "Ass."

Sophia burst through the door to find Halcyon sitting at his table and two other men standing. Both men were fit and could probably hold their own against a snow leopard. The darker-skinned man nodded his head as if he was saying "hello again" to her. The other man was olive-skinned with unkempt dark brown hair and a five-o'-clock shadow. He was tall and toned. They stared at her intently, but it was Halcyon's stare that caught her attention. Sophia stumbled back through the open doorway, only to be stopped by Lee. He led her back in and closed the door behind him. The whole time, Sophia didn't break contact with Halcyon.

"Your eyes...They are blue."

"Indeed, they are," Halcyon said.

"How is it possible? Only Gabriel. Ever. I've never seen..."

"The eyes of the Majji," he said.

"The what?"

"The eyes of the Majji, the color of the sky and sea. Sophia, I understand that your husband Gabriel had this trait. But not because he was Majji or was to be Majji"—Halcyon took a deep breath—"but because, by the will of the Green, he was born to a woman in Jaru that I used to bed." Halcyon looked into Sophia's wide eyes. "Sophia, Gabriel is my son."

Sophia stood, her mouth open. It seemed like this was common knowledge between the men because no one else had the gaping expression that was plastered across Sophia's face. Lee walked next to the darker man and leaned against the wall. He looked at Sophia with a sympathetic look. Why was he looking at her like that; so what if this man is her husband's father? Is it that bad? What else did these men know? Her mind raced.

"Oh, gods, is he okay?" she blurted.

"As far as we know, he is still alive. But Kahel will soon find out that there is no more to Gabriel but those eyes."

"And?"

Halcyon looked down.

"There is nothing we can do," he said.

"What? Is he going to kill him? No. You can't let that happen!"

The taller olive-skinned man stepped up to Sophia with

the same apologetic eyes as Lee. What the hell was up with the eyes?

"The technology Kahel possesses is far superior to any we have encountered, and he has security checks and systems that are unbreakable. Wherever Gabriel is in that castle, if he's still alive, there is no way we can get to him," he said to her.

Sophia covered her mouth and tried to hold back tears.

"Garret's right," Lee said. "Both he and Cyrus here are amazing at decoding and getting into anything unseen. But the further in they got, the more complicated the systems were."

"How long have you known"—Sophia turned to Halcyon, her voice barely a whisper—"that he is your son?"

"Twenty-five years," Halcyon replied.

Anger boiled in Sophia's belly, replacing the pain. "And in those twenty-five years, you had no reason to believe that Kahel would go after your son, who had 'the mark of the Majji?'"

"He had no skill, no power, nothing to threaten Kahel," Halcyon responded.

"Well. Obviously, something threatened him," Sophia said, irritated. "I've had enough of your indifference! I demand you give me passage to my home. I don't care if my stitches reopen or my wound stops healing. I'd rather risk that than spend another night here."

Lee took in a deep breath and looked down as the room grew silent. Even Zephyr stopped blowing outside. That's when Sophia's insides turned.

"Sophia," Halcyon said gently.

"Don't." Sophia's breath became labored as she worked hard not to fall apart. The conversation that she was not meant to hear earlier began to make sense. Then she recalled the dream.

"No. Oh, gods no." Her knees grew stiff; she clenched her

jaw and shook her head. It was all in vain, and at that moment she thought of Anna and the children. Sophia covered her mouth and held in her sobs. Her eyes betrayed her as tears fell freely down.

"We are so sorry," Cyrus responded as he approached her. She could feel the sincerity in his tone and see the pain in his eyes. "When we realized Kahel was going to attack your town, it was too late. He had troops positioned at Crossings Forged and Jaru. There was nothing we could do." He stopped and looked at Garret. "There is nothing we could have done then, but there is something we can do now."

"Drop it, Cyrus!" Garret yelled.

"What? What is it?" Sophia lightly questioned.

"Our informants tell us that Kahel is moving a lot of material up towards Salinas," Cyrus told Sophia, ignoring Garret.

Sophia wiped her face with her hands.

"He's going to put one of his horrid machines on top of my town, isn't he, on the graves of my people, isn't he?" Sophia turned to Halcyon, who stared at her with the same beautiful ice-blue eyes as Gabriel's.

"Yes." Halcyon looked down, ashamed.

"This you can stop. Right?"

"Possibly."

"But we won't do it," Garret interrupted, "no matter how fun it is to slap a sleeping bull on the butt." He gestured. "We refuse to put Atara at risk. Kahel has left us alone for years. We are not going to provoke him."

"We were pawns. For nothing," Sophia said in disbelief. "Haven't you put it together yet? Yaren and Talbot were trying to get your attention, and now they got it. Why did they want it? Only you have the answer to that." She looked at the men. "What is the point to have such highly skilled men if you choose to sit here like cowards! You failed to protect your son, you refuse to stop Kahel's minions from creating a station at Salinas, and worst of all you know, you know what Kahel is capable of! I've seen what he's done to the people whose lands he's taken; I've seen the warships at his marina. This is bigger than my people and me and bigger than you and your people. No one else has an army to stand against him. No one. That leaves just you here, and yet you sit and fester like rotting flesh, ripe for the crows' picking." She turned to look at Lee, who had his arms crossed and was looking at the ground. She then opened the door and left. Zephyr blew a cautious burst across her face.

"Leave me be," she whispered and continued walking.

Lee strode out and watched Sophia walk off.

"She's not really mad at you, Zephyr," he said, "but she should be left alone for now."

Zephyr swirled around Lee then dispersed high into the sky. Lee continued to watch as the darkness of night enveloped Sophia as she wandered out of sight. She was right, he thought; whatever it was that Talbot and Yaren planned was going to be for nothing. They weren't going to declare war.

"Keep a close eye on her, Lee, I'm serious," Cyrus said as he stepped out of Halcyon's hut. "That woman has more heart than our world combined, and it's what she follows. I bet her heart is telling her to do something foolish right now."

"You mean 'go' somewhere foolish right now," Lee responded, "but the Green would have to let her out of the Northern Woods first."

"Still." Cyrus looked into the darkness. "Keep an eye on her."

34

THE ESCAPE

Sophia approached Lee's home, her heart pounding in her chest. She had to find a way out; that part was clear, but the question was how. She examined her surroundings. Lee's home was surrounded by trees. The main village was close enough for Sophia to see, but that was not the direction she wanted to go in. She turned to see the Northern Woods, where only Atarans were free to come and go as they pleased. She didn't care what the villagers told her; she would find a way out tonight. Sophia knew the only hope for escape was if Lee was not guarding her. Accomplishing that would prove tricky. This was his house, after all. There was no chance of her sneaking out if he was up on his loft bed. Sophia rested her head on the door.

"Did it work?" Sophia jumped back as the woman from earlier spoke. "The damsel in distress bit. Is that all you have to offer? If so, it is a pathetic way to get his attention." The blue-tanked woman walked out from the side of the house. "I thought Lee would be escorting you back," she said, attempting to explain her presence. With everything that was happening, the last thing Sophia needed was more disdain and pettiness.

"No," Sophia responded, walking past the woman then stopping. "He should be on his way soon." She turned and watched the woman curiously. Sophia's mind worked quickly and saw an opportunity. "I know I asked this before, but who are you?"

The woman looked blankly at Sophia then exhaled, "Cytrine."

In the distance, Sophia could see Lee walking towards them.

"Hello, Cytrine, I'm Sophia. I'm sorry about this, but honestly, it can't be a surprise that you had this coming."

"Had what co..."

With a loud crack, Sophia's fist came in contact with Cytrine's face. Cytrine lost her balance and fell over.

"Two birds, one stone," Sophia said as she shook the pain out of her hand.

"Oh, my gods, you crazy whore!" Cytrine nursed the side of her face.

"Funny you mention that because you would have been so coveted in our town. I mean"—Sophia gestured towards Cytrine—"wow. Weiya would have loved to have had you in her House. We don't call them whores, nor do we really use that word because that's in bad taste. We call them Courtesans. Artists in their trade, let me tell you." Sophia winced as she rubbed her knuckles. "Honestly," she whispered angrily, "you aren't angry at me, and you know that, whatever that is, you are projecting all that shit on me. I am not your enemy, and, yes, I just hit you. I really am sorry, but I get that you have your reasons for being awful, and right now I have mine."

Cytrine watched in disbelief.

Sophia looked over to Lee, who was now running. This

was her chance to sell it.

"How's that for 'a pathetic damsel in distress!'" Sophia flailed her arms erratically, her tone spiking on all sorts of levels. Acting was not her trade; she knew that. Cytrine, on the other hand, was more confused than ever and began to back further and further away from Sophia, who continued to yell.

"Get out of my face. I want to be left alone! ALONE!" Sophia called out loudly, hoping Lee could hear her. "I can't stand the sight of any of you!" She turned into Lee's home and slammed the door shut behind her. It wasn't hard to make her act believable; Sophia really wanted nothing to do with the Atarans. Through the shut door, she could hear Cytrine yelling at Lee and him apologizing for Sophia's actions. She pressed her ear against the door.

"You don't understand what's going on, Cytrine."

"Well, why don't you tell me? You've been so busy lately, dodging me, and it got worse when she arrived. We don't talk anymore, Lee; 'friends' talk."

"I know, Cytrine; I'm sorry, but not now. Just go home, okay? I'll send Cyrus over to check your face when I see him."

"What are you going to do?"

"I don't know, wait till she cools down."

"Are you going to stay here? Why don't you come to my place? Just for tonight," Cytrine said in a vulnerable tone. It was clear that Cytrine and Lee were involved, and she had lingering feelings for Lee. Whatever it was that ended between those two definitely was not Cytrine's idea. Sophia felt a pang of guilt. Cytrine was heartbroken and possibly a little face-broken now.

"No, it's okay," Lee said gently, "I'll just sit out here till she's asleep, then I'll go to bed."

"If you so choose, but I'm here. If you need me."

That was the end of the conversation. She could hear

Cytrine walk away and Lee slide down the door. Dammit; if he was guarding the entrance, she had to find another way out. Lee's house had one window, which was over the sink that was next to the door; therefore, that exit was out of the question. Then there was the skylight in the loft area. Sophia climbed the stairs. The small loft area was simple, with a soft bed on the ground, big enough to sleep two, a stack of books in the corner, and an interesting, plaid-upholstered chair. Sophia pulled the chair to the skylight and pushed against the glass. It shifted slightly to the left, letting in fresh air. She waited an hour before she lifted herself through the skylight. Sophia quietly crawled on the roof to the front of the house. She peered over and saw Lee sitting against the door fast asleep. She went down the back of the house, cautious not to make a single noise on her descent. She turned to the woods and made a run for it. Sophia was only a few steps into the Northern Woods when Atara disappeared behind her. With her guard up, she continued forward. The woods became denser and denser. Sophia regretted not bringing a knife. Gabriel always carried one strapped to his calf, and it often came in handy. She really wished she planned this better. Sophia felt a prickling sensation on the back of her neck. She placed her hand there then turned around. To her shock, she saw that the woods had opened up behind her. She turned forward to see that it had also opened up in front of her. Sophia was in a small clearing that was thickly surrounded by trees. She could climb, but Sophia knew it was no use. The Green wasn't going to let her out.

"Please," she pleaded to trees around her, "please let me pass. They are my people, my family; I can't just stand by and watch their final resting place be defiled. I can't let him do it. Please, let me through."

Even if the Green decided to let her through, Sophia couldn't think of what her next move would be. She didn't know how to stop Kahel's will. She was one woman against gods-knew-how-many armed men. But underneath her doubt there was this pull coming from deep within, telling her that none of that mattered. She had to go to her people, and that was the end of it. Sophia covered her face and bent over. An aroma not associated with forests unless they were on fire filled the air. Sophia looked up from her hands and saw that the forest had opened up at the very base of the woods. It was a couple miles down, but the origin of the scent was fully visible. The town puffed black smoke where the homes had been. Some spots still held flames; others crumbled down into ash. Sophia raced down the hill to the dogwood tree and leaned forward in disbelief.

35

THE SEARCH

Lee shifted where he sat, his back rubbing against the door. He groggily opened one eye then the next, and he rolled his head back and listened for Sophia. When he was satisfied with the amount of silence in the house, he got up and entered. The fire had died out, and he would have restarted it, but it was late, and he was sure if she were cold she would be complaining. Lee quietly climbed up to the loft and plopped himself down. The cool breeze from the skylight was unwelcome. He grabbed the blanket to the side of him and pulled it over his body as he rolled to his side. It was cold. Why in the world would he have left the skylight open and lit a fire? He marveled at his stupidity and closed his eyes.

"SHIT!" Lee jumped down and checked the couch. "SHITSHITSHIT!"

He was halfway to Halcyon's when Zephyr caught up with him

"She's gone; she's either trapped in the woods, or she somehow got out." Zephyr flew past him. Within moments, he was face to face with Halcyon.

"You must retrieve her, Lee."

"Well, I figured that."

"No harm must come to her."

"Well, I figured that," Lee responded seeing the fear in Halcyon's eyes. "Halcyon, what haven't you told me yet?"

Halcyon hesitated for a moment. "Bring her back, Lee. Zephyr, old friend, please lend us your strength."

It was as if a large animal landed beside Lee. The ground let out a groan and dust kicked up. Golden, translucent wings appeared, then a beak, as Zephyr let out a loud cry and his true form materialized. He was large and he was magnificent. Lee walked forward in a trance, to touch what he saw, but Zephyr quickly snapped at Lee's hands.

"Hey, watch it, you pocket of hot air!"

Zephyr shrieked and started towards Lee.

"He's HUGE!" Lee exclaimed, looking up.

"Oh, jeez," Halcyon said under his breath. "Zephyr, let Lee ride with you; we need to get through the woods as quickly as possible. Sophia is in danger."

Zephyr let out a defeated cry and lowered his head. Lee looked perplexed.

"How am I supposed to ride him? He's just air!" Lee said as he poked into the creature. Zephyr swung his head, catching Lee right on the chest.

"You are not riding on him; you are going to ride WITH him."

"Eh?"

"Gods, Lee, you are wasting time," Exasperated, Halcyon shoved Lee into Zephyr. As quickly as he fell in, his body rose. Lee was sitting on top of Zephyr, his legs and rear submerged. "He's bonding; it's the only way to ride together. This is an honor, Lee. He's only bonded once before this, so wrap your arms around his neck."

Lee did as he was told.

"Go."

The speed was supernatural; though Lee could maneuver, he let Zephyr take the reins. They blazed through the forest in moments and were only a few miles away from Salinas. Lee was shocked when he sensed Zephyr's fear, and it made his more desperate. Their emotions merged, and Lee could feel the love Zephyr had for Sophia. Zephyr let out a whimper, and they continued on to Salinas.

Sophia had not stopped running until she reached Salinas. The moment her body stopped, she bent over and vomited. The combination of exhaustion, the smell, and the sight of the town made her retch again. The beautiful green rooftops, the trader's market, the music, the laughter—it was no more. Sophia walked on the cobblestone path while some wood still cracked as a small fire made its way through it. Sophia could see where each house used to be. She also saw blood. Everywhere. She would have thrown up again, but there was nothing left in her stomach. She felt like she was floating through and that this was a dream. It had to be a dream; no way was this her reality. In a daze, she continued to the end of town where her home used to be. Something caught her attention. In the outskirts towards the trails, she saw a large mound of dirt.

"That wasn't there before." Sophia hesitated but then wandered closer. It was then she noticed that in front of the mound was a ditch. At this point, Sophia wasn't controlling much of what she was doing. She motioned towards it, knowing exactly what she was going to see. Then there, right before her eyes, was proof that they were all gone. It was the final straw. Sophia, now emotionally and physically exhausted, collapsed. She fell hard to the ground overlooking the bodies of her people.

Lee and Zephyr reached the dogwood tree. It was here they separated. Lee met the earth with a large thump. He grabbed his head in an attempt to stop the spinning but to no avail. Lee leaned to the side of the dogwood and gagged. Zephyr's form was dissipating, but he nudged Lee with his beak before he completely disappeared into wind.

"I'm okay," Lee said as he stood up. "It took a lot out of me."

Zephyr blew against Lee's hair.

"You too, I gather."

Lee looked down at what once was Salinas.

"Oh, gods." Lee's eyes scanned the town.

"I think we should start towards Sophia's and Gabriel's former dwelling." Zephyr flipped Lee's hair. That was enough of an agreement for Lee, and they began towards the town. The closer they got to the town, the faster their pace became. In no time, they were both in a full sprint. Lee sensed when Zephyr, who was at his side, come to a stop.

"What is it?"

Zephyr shot a gust to the west. Lee could feel him move.

"The river? She's in the river?"

Zephyr zipped away, and Lee followed. The fire hissed and popped while it consumed what was left of the wood. Lee stepped in a puddle as he pursued Zephyr.

"There hasn't been any rains, Zephyr, and still this town looks as if it had flooded." The wind stopped. Lee watched as Zephyr inspected the stagnant water, and he sensed his desperation as Zephyr raced towards the river. They approached a brick wall and passed through the archway that opened up to the river. Zephyr pushed air against Lee, forcing him to turn around. There, he saw splattered on the brick wall a large amount of blood.

"Cyrus was right, someone cast here, and it was one hell of a spell," Lee said. He continued to investigate the area. "Whoever cast it needed a lot of Essence and the aid of the Water Elemental." The puddles made sense now. As Lee attempted to piece together what went on in that specific area, a bright sparkling object caught his eye. It was submerged at the base of the river. Zephyr hesitated then slowly glided beside Lee. They approached the object. Zephyr shot out an angry gust that slammed into the ground, kicking up dirt and water. The connection between Lee and Zephyr hadn't entirely been severed, and Lee began to experience a feeling of deep sorrow. He walked towards the object, which he realized were two objects and instantly recognized them. They were a pair of sai. Lee reached into the water and lifted them. He was quite familiar with this style of craftsmanship.

"These belong to the Ibex Warrior Tribe. Why are you so heartbroken, Zephyr?" Lee clutched his chest. "Did you know their owner?" Lee felt Zephyr's heartbreak increase exponentially. Zephyr shot up high into the sky and disappeared.

Lee's eyes opened wide as he scanned the sky.

"Oh, great! We haven't found Sophia yet, you know!" he shouted up. Lee tucked the sai in his belt. He walked along the outskirts of the town, heading towards the main road. It was then that he spotted Sophia; she was far ahead and laying on the ground. He began to run and found that his legs hadn't recovered from his earlier sprint. Lee could only manage a slow jog as he slammed his fists on his thighs, attempting to loosen up his muscles.

"Sophia!"

She lifted her head. Relief swept over Lee and he slowed his pace. Sophia turned to look at Lee then turned to look forward again. Lee stopped, leaned forwards, and grabbed his knees. He took in a few good breaths and shook his legs out. By the time he turned to look back at Sophia, he had begun to worry again. Sophia was scrambling backward. He watched the panic in her body as she struggled to get to her feet, but something had caught her attention. A large green entity arose from every inch of the ditch.

"Run, Sophia!" Lee tried to sprint again. He watched as her legs kept giving out. Lee pushed himself with every last inch of energy he had.

"Lee!"

The green entity crept towards Sophia. Lee pulled out his blade and prepared to fight whatever the hell that thing was as it moved closer to Sophia. Seemingly from nowhere, Zephyr burst up in front of Lee and materialized. This time, Zephyr wasn't translucent. He was flesh and bone. Massive muscles rippled throughout his torso, and his eyes stared down at Lee. He stood with his wings outstretched, blocking Lee's path.

Sophia was on her feet, and the green mass came to a dead stop in front of her. The entity began to stretch out, and Lee could see the ribbons of green that it was composed of. It was Essence. Some wrapped around Zephyr, allowing him to keep his solid form, and some reached out to Sophia.

"Zephyr, this is too much Essence; even split between the three of us, we'd all go mad."

Zephyr did not move.

"It'll kill her," he pleaded. When that didn't work, Lee pointed his blade at Zephyr. "You leave me no choice." He started to swing his blade when Zephyr swung his massive head and caught Lee right in the chest again. This time, the blow sent him flying back.

Lee watched in horror as Sophia reached out and touched a green ribbon of Essence. It merged with her. That was the catalyst. The monstrous green entity fused together into a long pillar then hooked down and shot into Sophia's chest. Lee remained helpless as it encompassed her body.

36

WATCHING

Alone in her vast expanse, the goddess clenched her fists. She lacked the strength to get up, to move, to do anything that would stop this chain of events. In another time, no other god would dare defy her. But now, in this condition, there was nothing she could do but watch. She didn't understand what her last child's motives were, but Daughter was out there and any god that walks the mortal plane was in grave danger.

37

WHAT JUST HAPPENED

Within seconds, it was over. Sophia's body lay sprawled on the ground. Zephyr faded to wind, and Lee was allowed passage. He knelt by Sophia and cleared the hair from her face. He placed his head on her chest and waited for a heartbeat. He never got one. It was then that Lee lifted Sophia's dead body.

"Look what you have done!" he yelled as he cradled her body close to himself. "Look, you self-righteous freak!" So much had happened within the past few days, but amid all the confusion one thing was clear: whenever he was with Sophia, he felt like he was home. It was a strange sensation, one that was most likely the effect of her having Leata's Essence, but it didn't matter to him. He had begun to welcome the feeling. It was nice to have. Lee rested his cheek on Sophia's forehead and started the familiar walk back to Atara.

Sophia took in a sizeable, desperate breath, followed by normal ones. Lee fumbled her in his arms, nearly dropping her fragile body on the ground. Zephyr blew a defiant gust at Lee. Once the shock passed, Lee watched Sophia breathe to make sure he wasn't hallucinating. When he was satisfied, he cautiously continued towards the Northern Woods. Zephyr brushed the hair out of her face.

"Eventually, you are going to have to explain to me what the hell just happened."

38

A KING'S FURY

Kahel paced outside a large Regeneration Unit. Sethos sat on the floor with his head between his knees.

"Don't worry, Sethos, he'll be okay, he is the great Corentin; he's been through worse. There is no way a peasant from a small town could have killed him." Nothing but feelings of doubt followed Kahel's words. Corentin was found dead, they told him, but Kahel refused to believe it. When they retrieved the body, Kahel put him in the chamber. He needed to figure out what the hell happened in that town, but he wasn't about to risk any more men. So, he ordered them to clear the area and head back to Crossings Forged. It had been days, and Corentin hadn't emerged from the chamber. Sethos knew he was gone, but Kahel refused to admit it. Sethos stood up and placed his hand on his King's shoulder. Kahel stopped pacing and stared at the chamber.

"This can't be possible; he can't be gone," Kahel said. "It makes no sense, the man was two-hundred-years old, so how is it that he was taken down by a town of entertainers?"

"Kahel," Sethos said, still unsure if he should reveal Corentin's secret. "Corentin kept something from you, and I am afraid it was sheer arrogance that led to his death. When the Osprey delivered Gabriel, he told a different story. Gabriel and his wife did fight back, but an Ataran accompanied by an Elemental was the reason the amulet was left behind and that the others died."

"An Elemental?" Kahel turned to the chamber and slammed his fists on the metal structure. "Dammit, Corentin! You know I wouldn't have let you go if I knew an Elemental was present in that area!" He grabbed the sides of the chamber and began to kick it fiercely. "You arrogant fuck!!! It was suicide to go there! You thought you could take on that much magic?" He stepped back then pushed the chamber. "Well, you couldn't, and now you're dead! Fucking happy?" Kahel ran his hands through his blonde hair. "Fuck!" He looked at Sethos. "An Elemental? Gods, well, at least we fucking know for sure that Halcyon is still alive. If that much magic still exists in our world, he must be getting stronger." He looked at Sethos. "You think this means Ibex Warriors have returned?"

"From the dead? No. But just maybe Corentin didn't slay them all."

"Hundreds of years and they've just been in hiding." Kahel stood, pensive for a moment. "We need to have some Osprey sent to the Pass and another battleship into the Kalyptra. We don't want anything or anyone coming in or out. Secure Tychi; we set our plans in motion today." Kahel looked at Corentin's chamber and took in a deep breath. He gritted his teeth. In all of his long existence, the unrequited emotions he felt for Corentin were the closest he's ever come to being in love while simultaneously being in lust. Whatever existed in the cavity where there should be a heart, broke. He choked back a sob and allowed a single, private tear to escape down his cheek and onto Corentin's unit. It was all he could give him, all he could give the man that he adored. Out of respect, Sethos stepped back and turned around. Kahel took another moment to gather himself.

GUARDS!" Two men walked into the room. "Take Corentin, bury him in the family crypt, and make sure you bring his favorite whores and belongings to keep him company." Both Sethos and Kahel placed one hand on the Regeneration Unit then leaned their foreheads to it.

"Goodbye, my friend. You will be missed." Kahel turned to Sethos. "Destroy what's left of that fucking town. I want those people's ashes delivered to me so I can piss all over them. Let's get moving on the Extricate Station, have it heavily guarded." He began to walk away then turned around. "Oh, and burn the Atarans' forest."

"Where are you going, my King?" Sethos asked Kahel's back.

"I'm going to have a nice ol' chat with our friend Gabriel." Kahel grabbed a blade from one of the guards as he left.

39

THEIR STORY

The Northern Woods allowed Lee quick passage and opened up at the bar. He held Sophia in his arms and walked towards Cyrus, Halcyon, and Garret, who stood still, watching him. The trio remained silent as Lee approached. The only sound audible was of the fans powering their town. Cyrus was the first to break their silence.

"It's not that I don't like her or anything, but she brings darkness to our home, Halcyon, I feel it."

"Fear clouds your judgment, Cyrus; it's not darkness, it's change," Halcyon replied.

"Change can bring darkness." Garret shrugged. "I'm just saying."

Lee closed in on the group and handed Sophia over to Halcyon. Lee looked into his fading blue eyes.

"Do you not trust me?" Lee asked.

"I do trust you," Halcyon replied.

"Then why keep so much from me?"

"It was for your own good, Leonardo."

Lee winced at the sound of his full name. "How is it for my own good? Explain to me how keeping me in the dark about what the hell she is; because she is not human, no human could still be breathing after what just happened to her."

Halcyon cocked his head.

"Oh, you don't know?" Lee said, all patience and manners gone. "Wait, maybe I shouldn't tell you, could be for your own good," he mocked.

"Lee." Halcyon's authoritative tone echoed in the night.

Lee ignored the reprimand and turned to Garret and Cyrus. "Do you know what she is? Any clue? Well, I'm going to let you in on something: she died. Then came back to life."

"What?" Halcyon exclaimed.

Lee turned back to him. "Oh, yeah, that woman there was chosen by a large mass of combined Essence, which shot right into her and killed her, only to bring her back to life moments later. Some more news for the three of you: she is also a pain-in-the-ass brat who doesn't listen and apparently needs me to save her and deliver her to you"—he looked down at Sophia—"unconscious. Twice!" He turned to where he knew Zephyr was standing and pointed. "Oh, and Zephyr materialized into a solid form and knocked me back half a mile, so she could be assaulted by the Mad Essence." Satisfied with himself, Lee then walked away.

"He did what?" Halcyon hissed as Zephyr zipped away.

Cyrus took in a deep breath. He patted Halcyon's shoulder and ran after Lee. Garret stood there with his arms crossed, shaking his head.

"The Green allows her passage in and out of Atara, and she is not Ataran; Zephyr protects her, and she is neither Majji nor Apprentice, yet she lives after being attacked by Mad Essence. Halcyon, what are you keeping from us?"

"Nothing that can't wait."

Garret uncrossed his arms and walked away. The Majji

just stood there alone in the night with an unconscious Sophia in his arms, and then he began towards his home. "You know, Lee got one thing right: you really are a pain in the ass"—he took in a deep breath—"must run in the family."

It was a few hours morning, and the Majji had remained awake. He sat alone at his table. The evidence was there: the uncanny resemblance, the facts that Garret pointed out, and how Essence willingly chose her.

"It chose her, without her calling it, the Essence chose her." He sipped his tea then sat back on his seat. He needed more time, he thought to himself, he just needed more time,

"The Green knows what she is doing." He took another sip of his tea. "Gods, she'd better." Sophia stirred in his bed. Halcyon turned to look at her, then poured a cup of hot tea for her. He walked into his room with both cups and placed one on the nightstand; he would offer it to her when she woke up. Halcyon sat down in a rocking chair that was next to the bed. He then lifted the other cup to his lips. Sophia shot up, screaming louder than any harpy Halcyon had ever heard. The shock sent him upright and his teacup across the room. He leaped towards the bed as she began to claw at herself. He tightly held her arms down and called her name out, but Sophia continued screaming. In a matter of seconds, Lee was in the room.

"Camped outside my house, I see," Halcyon called out over Sophia's screams.

Lee ignored the comment. "What's wrong with her?" he yelled.

"The Essence, it was too much, Lee; she's going mad!"

Lee walked over to a frantic Sophia. Halcyon struggled to keep her arms down. Lee looked at Sophia then slapped her straight across the face. He held his hand in disbelief then stepped back. Sophia's eyes opened and turned to Lee. The screaming stopped, then the struggling stopped. Halcyon cautiously loosened his grip. Sophia placed her hand on her cheek.

"Thank you, Lee, I think."

"I don't know whether to say 'please forgive me' or 'you're welcome,'" Lee said in a guilty tone.

"Both work." She smiled.

Lee gave Sophia a lighthearted smile before he backed away. Halcyon handed Sophia the cup of tea. She shakily accepted it and took a small sip, then sank down into the bed. Lee leaned up against the wall with his arms and legs crossed and waited for her to speak.

"I heard them all. I felt their pain, their anger. I saw their deaths, and I died each time they did; it was horrible." Sophia covered her eyes and began to cry. Lee wanted to reach out and hold her. But he knew there was nothing he could do that would help. The thought tore at him.

"Sophia, how about now?" Halcyon asked, "Can you feel them?"

"Somewhat."

"How do they feel?"

"Calm, now, at peace."

"Why is that?" He asked even though it was evident that he knew the answer. Sophia thought for a moment.

"Because they are with me," she said, surprising herself.

"Yes. Exactly."

"Halcyon, why are they with me?"

"Sophia, there is something that I must tell you, and it may be hard for you to take in, but it explains everything that is happening." Halcyon rubbed his forehead. "You are my Apprentice. You hold all of her Essence, all of the Essence she gained from me during her training."

Sophia sat puzzled and was about to say something but

was cut off by Halcyon.

"My Apprentice was the Queen Leata, but she died before we were able to finish her training."

Sophia looked at Halcyon in disbelief.

"The late Queen was in line to be a Majji?"

Halcyon nodded his head.

"Wha...How in the world is it that I have her Essence?"

"Her best friend and lady-in-waiting was a woman named Carla."

"Carla..." Sophia said. "Carla was my mother's name." Her mother, who Sophia was told repeatedly she looked nothing like and who died when she was young.

Lee's brows furrowed. Halcyon turned to Lee finally "I kept all of this from you because I wasn't certain, but now I am. It is said that the night Leata died, a bright light came from her room, killing her, Carla, and a newborn girl."

"Oh shit..." Lee knew the story; just about everyone knew a version of the story, or at least they thought they did.

"But rumors arose that Carla escaped with the child, even though the guards swore the light took them all. The rumors continued, saying Carla lived and raised the child as her own. I now know these rumors are true." He turned to Sophia. "You, Sophia are the daughter of Kahel and Anne, Princess of the Kingdom, granddaughter of the great Queen Leata, and the last living creature that can carry Essence of the Majji."

Whatever was left of her already-shattered world disintegrated before her. There she sat, realizing who she thought she was was a lie. She wrapped her arms around herself, but arms couldn't keep her together. Her father was Kahel. Her father murdered her friends, her family, her grandfather, her grandmother, and, she was pretty sure by now, her husband. The Green was dying, and people were suffering because of her father.

"Sophia," Halcyon called. "Try to hear them, your people."

Sophia was hyperventilating. "I don't want to," she said as she shook her head and began to rock herself. "I don't want to."

"Halcyon, maybe you should give her a moment. You just gave her a lot to process," Lee said cautiously.

"We don't have a moment," Halcyon said. "This is what Yaren and Talbot were trying to tell me. They didn't use you as pawns; in the end, they were the pawns. Kahel's retaliation will be swift. Yaren and Talbot were willing to risk their lives to tell me that you lived. Sophia, what are your people trying to tell you?"

Sophia stopped rocking and looked up at Halcyon. She didn't want it all to be in vain. Sophia centered herself and took some calming breaths. "Okay, I'll try."

She closed her eyes. Halcyon touched her shoulder and paced with her breathing pattern. In moments, a very dim green light emerged from Sophia. The Essence within her had no spoken language. Sophia realized that she wouldn't hear words but more like sense intentions, emotions.

"They want me to breathe. I feel their warmth, their love. Many of them knew all along who I was. They were my guardians." Sophia took several breaths as the Essence within her voiced another story. "They are trying to tell me something more. I sense someone familiar." Sophia looked up at Halcyon. "Mom." Silver, smoke-like ribbons exited Sophia, filling the area. Luminous human figures with their features blurred started walking through the room. In a matter of moments, the only things that remained from Halcyon's bedroom were Halcyon himself, Lee, Sophia, and the bed she sat on. Lee reached for his blade.

"No," Halcyon whispered "It's okay. They are communicating; they want her to know their story."

The room was foggy and the people translucent, but it was clear enough for them to make sense of what was happening.

"Mom!" Sophia crawled to the edge of the bed and reached for Carla as she crossed in front of Sophia.

"Mama!" Her voice was desperate, like a child's.

"I don't think she can see you, Sophia." Halcyon walked to Sophia and placed a reassuring hand on her shoulder. Carla walked in, covered in dirt and grass stains. The blurred figures were curiously turning towards her. She was in tears, carrying a small bundle. You could see the helplessness in her face as an elder came to her and brushed the side of her face. He knew her.

"Father, I did not want to bring danger to our town. I tried so hard to get into Atara. But the trees refused me."

He looked at his daughter, puzzled. "It's common knowledge that the Northern Woods do not allow passage to anyone except Atarans, and why should you want to go there unless it's death you seek?"

Carla unwrapped the bundle to reveal a sleeping child. "She needs to eat."

His face lit up with joy. "Is this why you ran from the castle? You had a child outside of wedlock? A child poses no threat to our town."

Carla's face crumpled. "She is not mine; she is Princess Anne's."

Her father took a step back.

"I did not take her for money, or for jealousy," Carla clarified. "Kahel ordered her death. I snuck her to the Queen, so she could meet her granddaughter, maybe talk her son out of a senseless killing." Carla's eyes grew desperate. "Father, then there was a light, a brilliant light, and when I woke Leata was dead, but I heard her in my heart, clear as day. She told me to take the child to Atara, to run, that the wind would cover my tracks, and it did, Father. The wind protected me, engulfing Tychi in an incredible windstorm." The man fell to his knees to console his daughter. The fog shifted, and then they were in the center of town during a town meeting.

"The decision has been made." An elder spoke. "We will raise her as our own, here. Queen Leata wanted the child to live; she wanted the child to go to Atara for a reason, a reason we need not know. All we need to know is that our Queen sacrificed herself for this child, and so this child needs to be protected. We will fulfill that for our Queen."

Sophia looked at the gathered people and recognized several faces. The father of the three brothers was the lead town elder; he had two children to the side, both well into their teens. It was Santiago and Domingo. She also saw Eilith and her fiery red hair in the back, leaning up against a tree. Carla's figure stepped back and remained as the silvery smoke thickened. Sophia reached out again. "Mom? Mom, can you hear me?" Carla turned to face Sophia and walked towards her. Carla put her arms around Sophia and Sophia cried as she held her mother for the first time in almost a decade. They were able to have several moments before the scenery shifted again. They were now in Tychi, just a few weeks ago, at the performance. The angle was different from their view during the performance. They were looking from above, from Kahel's booth. They saw Gabriel and Sophia dancing below, but they could also see Kahel. They watched as a glow emanated from Gabriel and Sophia and how Kahel fell to the ground, clutching his chest.

"What's going on?" Sophia released her mother from their embrace. "I didn't see anything remotely similar to that light when we were performing."

"It's Essence and powerful magic combined," Halcyon said with an astonished smile. Sophia thought there was some-thing more behind that smile but decided not to pursue it. They watched as the golden glow created by Sophia and Gabriel's performance grew larger and larger. Halcyon stepped back in shock as a pair of arms formed in the light, reaching out towards Kahel. Soon, a golden translucent head emerged from the glow. The features of a beautiful woman came through, long hair flailing as it continued on towards Kahel.

"Leata..." Halcyon called out.

Kahel, in turn, had a gentle green light emerge from him. That light also grew a pair of arms, and then a head appeared, that of a young girl in her late teens. She reached out for Leata's golden arms, her body struggling to come out of Kahel. They saw more green arms form that began to push the girl, helping her as she tried to escape. Tears fell rapidly down the young girl's cheeks as the golden figure of Leata came closer. Kahel became panicked and attempted to subdue the green light.

"Nooo, Anne, don't you dareeee!" he hissed.

The girls' arms finally reached Leata's, and she was pulled free from Kahel's chest. Leata embraced the girl as she cried. They both became one with the golden glow. The fog in the room shifted again. The figures of Leata and the girl stepped out while Carla remained seated on the bed next to Sophia. When the fog formed again, they were now in Salinas, while fire encompassed the town, and they watched as Eilith and Marcello raced through the brick archway and into the river.

Sophia was wiping her tears as she sobbed. Carla soothingly rubbed her back. Halcyon held his hand on his chest, and Lee had slumped down to the ground; they were watching the fall of Sophia's people. A strong, silver, shimmering glow grew around Eilith. Her body began to freeze, and so did the bodies of the men who were after her. A tall man walked through the archway, his glow a dark red. They said a few words before Eilith finished her casting. The man fell dead. Green light emerged from the dead bodies; some dispersed into the air, but others joined together. The dark red glow that once encompassed the man shot out of him and was quickly controlled and subdued by Eilith's silver glow.

Eilith's Essence pushed the red glow down into the ground until the dark-red light was finally gone. The figures of Eilith and Marcello, who was carrying Anna, stepped out of the fog. The fog slowly disappeared. Halcyon raced to the transparent figure of Leata and fell to his knees.

"I failed you, Leata. I was supposed to protect you, I, the Master to the next Majji. I was a coward; I should have returned a second time. I should have kept attacking Kahel. I shouldn't have given up."

"You couldn't have known what my son had become," she replied in a tone only a Queen could use. "But you should have returned after that first battle. The Master and the Apprentice were never to be separated in the first place. I know I was a stubborn child blinded by love, but you were also a headstrong man blinded by power. Having me as Queen and Majji was an irrational plan, and now that we are finally together again, I am dead and you are dying. Your gifts being taken back by the Green."

"What?" Sophia called out. "He's dying?"

Leata walked towards Sophia.

"My darling child, you were magnificent; you followed your heart as I needed you to." Leata motioned to the teenage girl to come over. "This is your birth mother, Princess Anne; you saved her. Kahel had her Essence trapped inside him for over two decades."

Sophia found it strange that a woman younger than her was her birth mother. But she knew how Kahel took a young girl for his wife, hoping to turn her into some sort of breeding factory.

Carla squeezed Sophia's hand. "Sophia, I am so proud of you, you grew to be so strong."

"Halcyon," Leata said, "did you see that Mad Essence that came from the man they call Corentin?"

"Yes."

"It originated in the west."

"How is that possible it was destroyed? The First Majji is said to have destroyed it all."

"Not all," Eilith piped in. "I was able to extinguish the bit that Corentin carried, but only with the help of the Water Elemental, Shiva."

"Shiva came to your aid?" The news stunned Halcyon.

"Halcyon," Leata started speaking again, saying, "I know the second you realized that you were dying, you began to worry about how the Atarans might survive without a Majji and if it was even possible. So, I understand that you've spent years building up Atara, so it can flourish without you, but while you were focusing on these people our world was dying. She calls to you for your help. If you do not respond, she will go silent, like before the World's End, but this time she won't have the strength to birth herself again. Everything and everyone will die," Leata said.

"You must stop Kahel," Eilith continued, "and train Sophia. With us by her side, she will be one of your strongest warriors." She nodded in certainty. "Lee, I believe you retrieved my sai. Please give those to Sophia."

Lee agreed and bowed his head.

"Can I say bye?" little Anna added.

She hopped out of Marcello's arms and ran to Sophia. Sophia was able to hold her. She ran her fingers through Anna's hair. Sophia held back her sobs.

"I'm so sorry. Anna, I'm so sorry this happened to all of you. This is my fault; I should have never gone to Tychi."

"No, Sophia, all this HAD to happen. I get it now; this all happened because she needs you. I'm with mama, Carminda, Ari, and everyone, and I'm happy. We are okay, just like your mom told you; we are going back to the Green. I love you forever and ever," she said as she nuzzled Sophia's neck.

"Forever and ever, Anna." Sophia embraced the child. Her

light grew bright as they held, then Anna was gone.

"Only a few of us choose to stay with you; others wish to join the Green peacefully," Eilith said.

"Sophia," Marcello began to say, "my brothers, they are not with us. I learned they charged into Tychi's Factory District. Their Essence is most likely there; please, retrieve them, bring them to the Green before they are taken in by Kahel."

"How is Kahel stealing people's Essence?" Sophia turned to Leata.

"Kahel has grown dark," Leata said. "He left as my son, years ago, and returned a different man. We believe he was infected by Mad Essence during his expedition west. He managed to bypass the Kalyptra somehow. Since his return, he's been able to control the Essence of the dead and will it to become a part of him. He's also built these contraptions he calls—"

"Regeneration Units," Lee interrupted.

"Yes. Those. I grow weak, but I will say this before leaving: those machines, large and small, siphon the Essence directly from the center of our world. They give him and whoever he puts in them power, but it comes with a price."

"He controls them," Lee added again.

"I leave this all to you, Halcyon," Leata said, "goodbye, friend, granddaughter, Master."

"Mom, stay longer." Sophia held her mother's arm.

"Oh, my darling. I love you, you know that, but you don't need me anymore."

"I always needed you around, mama, please, I miss you so much!"

"I have the utmost faith in you, Sophia, and that you are safe in Atara, and it's time I rest. Be strong, my darling girl." Carla embraced her. Sophia held her mother for the last time. Carla kissed her then dissipated.

"Thank you for saving me, daughter," Anne said as she merged with Leata.

"We will be by your side," Leata said.

"As will I," said Eilith.

"And I," added Marcello.

The room became bright with a golden light, and then they were all gone.

"Holy shit," Lee said. "Well, Garret's going to be excited because I guess we are going to war. All or nothing with that guy."

"So, it seems," Halcyon said. "Sophia, are you up for this?"

"Anything," she said eagerly, "for my people."

"I was afraid you'd say that," Lee said under his breath.

"Lee, you are my best; you will be her trainer. She needs a home, and till one is built she will continue to stay with you."

Lee walked to Halcyon then pulled him out of the room. "I don't think that's a good idea," he said in a hushed tone. "Maybe you should have Garret or Cyrus train her. You saw how I reacted to being around her before. If I'm with her every day, won't it get worse?"

"Lee, you should only feel protective over her, nothing more. That's what we all feel because she is partly Majji." Halcyon gave Lee a queer look. "You don't feel anything more, right?"

Lee flustered and turned away. "No of course not." He scratched the back of his head, saying, "but maybe she should stay here tonight, you know, don't really want to move her."

Halcyon watched Lee pensively, then smiled. "It seems now you are the one keeping something from me."

"Heh, I'm going to see Cyrus and Garret, fill them in, and then have a chat with Cytrine. She's already fifty shades of crazy. Telling her that the woman who sucker-punched her will remain here in Atara is going to send her over the edge."

Lee was out the door when Sophia wearily stepped out of bed. At first, her body resisted the standing position, but Sophia willed herself to walk forward.

"I can't sleep," Sophia said as she wandered out of the bedroom. "May I go for a walk?"

"Atara is your home now, Sophia. You don't have to ask permission," Halcyon replied.

Sophia walked to the door then turned to Halcyon, asking "Why does Lee hate me?"

Halcyon's face softened. "Sweet child, I don't think he hates you. You need to understand you have the Essence of the Apprentice, which makes you half-Majji. That comes with benefits. One is that people around you, unless they are there to harm you intentionally, will feel compelled to protect you. A gift from the Green; you also can communicate with Elementals," Halcyon paused before adding, "well, at least we know you can communicate with Zephyr. Whether you can call the other Elementals has yet to be seen. The Elemental Shiva responded to your friend Eilith's call, but she was Ibex." He took a sip of tea. "I digress; the point is, Lee has always been cautious of his emotions and actions. He doesn't like being compelled."

"But I am not doing it on purpose."

"He knows that."

Sophia sighed in defeat. She turned the knob and walked outside. Just like before, she had no idea where she was going, so she headed towards Lee's. The walk was pleasant enough, the sky was black and speckled with stars, and the air was dry and cool. Her bare feet enjoyed the soft grass underneath. Halfway to Lee's, she decided to turn right, towards the Nacunas. From what she knew, no home had been established between Lee and the Majji, and most Atarans had their homes near the bar, which was on the western side of the crescent. She was heavily drawn to this area and the Nacunas. She walked closer and closer, then was hit with a calming sensation. Sophia sat down in the grass. "Here. This is where my home will be." She was on a small hill and could see several more massive hills, miles and miles ahead of her at the base of the Nacunas. It was quiet, and the only sounds that could be heard were the night insects and the closest wind turbine. But even that was in the distance.

"Sophia," a strong male voice called. The sound was strange and seemed as if it came through a pipe. It had a slight echo that faded quickly into the air. Sophia stood up and examined her surroundings.

"Who's there?"

A gust of air brushed by and landed beside her. Zephyr materialized and bowed his head.

"Zephyr?! I can hear you now?"

"Yes, Leata's Essence has been awakened within you."

"Can anyone else hear you?"

"Yes, Halcyon," he said as he raised his head. Sophia examined her bird friend. "Hast eagle. I've always loved your kind." She reached out and caressed his beak. "You were Leata's Elemental, weren't you?"

"Yes. She was not what I expected when I met her. From birth, our kind is taught that humans are a selfish and cruel race. But we answer to a higher calling. Once one of yours becomes Majji, one of ours will join their side. I was afraid at first, but Leata treated me with respect, not like a servant or a pet but as a friend. Not since the Ibex Warriors have we been treated with such respect."

"Did you know them? The Warriors?"

"No, not personally, but my ancestors co-existed with them for years." He rested on the grass. "I knew Eilith was one of them. She was an incredible human—so much power. I'm saddened by her death but happy that it was she who put an end to that monster, Corentin."

"She used to tell me stories when I was a child about the Warrior people, who'd of thought those weren't stories, but her memories?"

"I know the tales if you ever would like to hear them again."

Sophia smiled and kissed Zephyr's beak. "Do you mind if I sleep here with you?" she asked.

"It would be an honor."

Sophia lay down and nudged herself up against Zephyr; she could feel his warmth enveloping her. It was satisfying to know that she wasn't crazy, and all the times she was teased as a child because she swore the wind was alive were worth it. Zephyr was the last connection, though loose, that she had to Salinas. Sophia closed her eyes and, in seconds, was fast asleep.

40

AN ATARAN'S
PURPOSE

Sophia had no idea what time it was when she woke up, but
the sun was mid-sky, and during any season that meant only
one thing: she had overslept. She kicked her legs out in a long
stretch and then sat up. Zephyr was awake and blowing at the
grass with his beak.

"It's been a long time since I've slept that well."

He let out a small kaw in sympathy.

"No, no, it's okay, I'm not looking for a shoulder to cry on,
just wanted to say 'thank you.'"

Zephyr's head shot up and looked towards the town, then
he dissipated into the air. Sophia fell through him and landed
hard on the ground behind her.

"Eyah!"

"Sorry."

Sophia heard footsteps and voices approaching. It made
sense why Zephyr changed form so quickly. She guessed no

one had seen his true form.

"She's here! She's here!" Jasira called out, her pale blonde hair swaying as she ran towards Sophia. She was flanked by two other Atarans, both women. The three wore protective leather gear and looked tired.

"Are you okay?" Jasira called out.

Sophia stood up and brushed off her bottom. "Yes. Just needed to be alone, that's all."

"Oh, man, Lee had a fit when he couldn't find you this morning! He was all like 'that stubborn pain in my ass, where is she' blah blah blah, and Cytrine, goodness, that woman, she doesn't like that someone else has his attention." Jasira said as she caught her breath. "But, hey, who cares!" she said cheerily. "You're okay; all's well."

"Why is Cytrine so angry?" Sophia rubbed her forehead and began to follow Jasira and the two women back into town.

"Don't take anything she does personally." Jasira waved at Sophia dismissively. "She has 'dreams,' and Atara isn't enough for her. Well, if it isn't enough, then get the hell out, I say, but she's tried, and she can't. That's why she's so mad. Halcyon won't let her go out alone." Jasira leaned in to say, "you know, without a partner or being bonded."

"So, she's trapped here?" It made even more sense now to Sophia why Cytrine was bent out of shape over her and Lee being bunkmates. He was Cytrine's only chance out of here.

"Hyah, she was hoping that Lee would be 'the one,' you know. But, nope. No bond, no nothing; Lee ended it after a few years."

"Years?" Sophia asked.

"Those two had nothing in common. Lee is low-key and content here, but she wanted out. I never knew what he saw in her anyways," Jasira said.

One of the female Atarans turned to face Jasira. "Really?" the woman asked. "Her body alone made me consider leaving my husband."

Sophia thought of Gabriel and how there was no news of him. She slowed her pace and let the others walk ahead of her. She noticed Jasira slowed down with her. Sophia centered herself; she didn't want to panic. There was no evidence that Gabriel was dead or alive. She quietly reassured herself. Gabriel never gave up hope, and so now neither would she.

"Did I say something to upset you?" Jasira asked.

"No, no, it's okay. But I do have a question, what is 'bonding?' I've heard it mentioned a few times and can't seem to figure it out."

"Well, it's one of our gifts from the Green." Jasira leaned in to say, "Everyone in these lands can sense Essence and even have some magic the further northwest we go, but our 'bonding,' only happens to Atarans. At some point in our life, whether it be birth or when we are a hundred and twenty years, another Ataran comes along, boy or girl, who we are meant to be with. When I say 'be with,' I mean friendship. But what makes it different is that you are forever connected with them. You sense their sadness, their anger, their pain, and if you are bonded with them, just by being around them, you can ease whatever it is that ails them."

"Wow."

"I know!" Jasira said excitedly. "But that's not the coolest part. Bonding dates back hundreds of years, and its main purpose was healing. Say the person you are bonded with is injured in battle, some of that injury is transferred to you, so you both share the wound. That way you both can carry on, and as long as you get your butt back to our woods, any mortal wound that is shared won't lead to death."

"That's amazing. I remember hearing tales of the cannibalistic Atarans eating one another to steal Essence to regenerate and live forever."

"Well, we do that too. Only if you break our laws though; it's why I was looking for you. Don't worry, I'm sure they will only take a leg, maybe some fingers."

Sophia stopped short.

"I'm kidding." Jasira elongated the words, mocking Sophia's naïveté. They had walked past Cyrus' bar and into the center of the town. It was packed full of Atarans, and Sophia spotted Lee. He was sitting on the lip of a water fountain. Next to him were two people Sophia recognized: Garret with his olive skin was still brandishing his five o'clock shadow, and Cyrus stood with his arms crossed, accentuating his dark muscles. The fountain was simple enough, ornamented with a winged man holding a tipped pot. Water flowed out of the pot and into the pool below. Halcyon stood in front, waiting and looking through the crowd. Jasira ushered Sophia through the people and stopped when they were next to Halcyon.

"She was sleeping northeast of here, Zephyr was with her," Jasira reported. Halcyon nodded and opened his arm towards Cyrus. Jasira reluctantly walked towards Cyrus, and they both sat near Lee.

"Friends, family," Halcyon boomed. "We have gathered today to welcome a new member and to inform you of our soon-to-be-troubled future." He began to talk about Sophia's hometown, about her past, and finally who she really was. Daughter of Kahel; there were a few gasps, oohs, and ahhs. Sophia felt like she was the main feature of a carnival show, and the way Cytrine was looking at her Sophia wondered if there was a "stone the freak" family event that followed.

"We must protect the land that Salinas used to reside on; we will not allow another Extricate Station to go up. We will also destroy as many of those stations as we can. But this is just the first of many burdens we must take upon ourselves. I've lived in silence too long, and our land suffers from it."

"She brought this upon us," Cytrine called out. "We've lived in peace for years, Tychi hasn't declared war, so why do we have to get involved in this mess!" Some Atarans nodded in agreement. Sophia thought, if she pulled her shirt over her head and curled in a little ball, then maybe she could disappear.

"We are Atarans. We must protect the Green when she is in danger. There will be no world to pass on to our children if we continue our silence. It is true Kahel has left us alone, but only because he feared the outcome of poking a bear. Instead, he plundered and murdered around us. I'm sure our silence only added to his belief that I was dead and the Atarans would stand idly by while he continued his tyranny."

"Why now?" asked a male Ataran.

"Mad Essence lives."

The crowd began to speak above one another in multiple roars. Words such as "impossible" and "has to be lies" were the few Sophia could pick up.

"It lives and grows stronger. Every day. Not only must we stop the Mad Essence, but we must also stop Kahel. For good."

The group grew silent.

"I require my fighters to resume their training and my gatherers to stock food and supplies. We will all meet every week, from here on, to discuss where we stand. Thank you for hearing me." The people bowed their heads, all except Cytrine, whose eyes shot daggers at Sophia. The people began to converse among one another and slowly dispersed.

"Garret, anything to report?" Halcyon asked.

"Yes, but I'm not sure she should be here to hear this."

"She is training under Lee now, so she is going to need to be informed."

"Fine," Garret said and took a quick glimpse at Sophia, then turned back to Halcyon. "Kahel lost it after he couldn't resurrect Corentin. I saw him slaughter his own men as he walked to the lower jail cells. I couldn't get past the security system there. The grid is too advanced. Anyone who talked to the entertainers when they were in town was interrogated, then killed, women, men, and children." Sophia was pale and barely keeping it together. Jasira made her way to Sophia and held her hand.

"Garret. You should stop," Jasira said.

"I told you guys that she shouldn't be here."

"Continue," Halcyon instructed.

Garret looked apologetically at Jasira and continued. "Even if the entertainers stroked a cat, that cat was killed too."

"What the hell, Garret!" Jasira yelled.

Garret shrugged. "Yaren and Talbot escaped to Tavernport and then took a boat east towards the Kalyptra. Kahel's Osprey are on their heels, though they are still out at sea. It's only a matter of time before they catch up. Plans for an Extricate Station are underway. I figure, in a month, we will have visitors."

"Okay, we have a lot of work ahead of us then," Halcyon said. "Jasira, blueprint Sophia's new home; Garret, keep watch on the forest outskirts; Cyrus, organize training for the fighters; and Lee"—Halcyon gestured his head towards Sophia—"get her ready."

41

TRAINING

The next few weeks were an absolute whirlwind, and it all started the morning after she was introduced as a new member of Atara. Sophia had been exhausted and was hoping to get a little more shuteye. Heck, she deserved it, she thought the night before. Sophia had snuggled into the corner of the couch when Lee tipped it forward. Sophia rolled flat onto her face. Before she could let out an expletive or push herself up, Lee grabbed her feet and flipped her over onto her back. The motion knocked the wind out of her.

"You failed your first test. If I were an intruder, you'd be dead." Lee put the pair of Eilith's sai on her chest. "These are yours. Become familiar with them and always keep them close. Let me say this"—he tapped the sai—"these are one hell of a weapon. The quantity of magic it took to forge those doesn't exist anymore. Neither do the beings or the metal."

Sophia examined the sai that had belonged to Eilith. Sophia held on tightly to them, then crossed her arms across her face. She began to weep.

"No. Sophia. No more crying. It won't help them, and it won't help you. This is the last time I will allow you to cry for them, so let it all out now."

Sophia let out a loud wail of pain.

"Turn that pain into what drives you. Make it your determination." Lee watched as Sophia was overcome by her grief. *This isn't what a warrior looked like*, he thought to himself. "I think Eilith may have been wrong about you," Lee said and turned to walk away. Sophia flipped to her side and, with the couch as support, pushed hard. Her body slid across the floor towards Lee. She hooked her leg around his, and he came tumbling down. Sophia got to her feet and looked down at Lee. Her tear-stained red face turned hard.

"Hey," Lee called out, impressed. "That was good." The last word became caught in his throat as he saw the flurry of tears falling down her cheeks. She was hurt, she was angry, and he felt like a jerk.

"You're an asshole!" Sophia said as she walked away.

Well, at least they agreed on one thing, he thought.

Every morning, it was the same thing: Lee rolling her off the couch, and no matter how early she'd try to wake up he would be seconds ahead of her. Sophia had once managed to swing at Lee as he approached, but it was all for naught. The couch would still be tilted, she'd still roll onto the floor, she'd still lose her sai, and he'd still flip her over and say, "You're dead." After that, their training would be over for the day. She'd be deflated but would secretly enjoy the free time.

The Atarans had already broken ground and started building Sophia's home. Jasira, who was apparently a math and drafting wiz, had everything calculated and ready, not even a day later. Jasira had chosen the area where Sophia had fallen asleep with Zephyr for the build. Her home, like the others in Atara, was simple save for one modification: Sophia requested as many windows as possible. To accommodate that, Jasira added a large, sliding, glass wall. The plans showed a doorway on the southern side of the house. Upon entrance, to your right was the sliding glass wall, and to the left was a wood-burning stove with an expanded cooktop. They planned to put a table with benches on the western side of the home. A ladder would start near the end of the sliding wall and lead up to a sleep loft area situated above the northern side of her home. Under the ladder was where you could find the icebox and pantry. Sophia loved walking to the build site and helping out. She would have nothing to do after Lee tossed her off the couch. Some mornings, she would be able to catch Cyrus during a break from training. She learned through him that he and Jasira were bonded and that there was a five-year difference between the two. Jasira was eight years old when the bond appeared.

"A group of us traveled to the far east on a fishing trip," Cyrus had told Sophia. "Jasira was filleting a fish when a bear attacked. The group fought off the bear, but she had sustained severe wounds. I was applying pressure to one of her injuries when cuts began to appear on me. I knew what it meant; I also knew I could heal quicker than Jasira."

"So, what happened?" Sophia leaned in, absorbed by his tale.

"I held her tightly and begged the Green to give me her wounds. Which she did, and Jasira was able to walk home."

Before Jasira and Cyrus, the youngest pair to bond was eighteen years of age. It turns out Jasira didn't take too well to being bonded so early in her life. That was thirteen years ago. After their chats, Sophia would follow him back to the training area and watch. She saw Cyrus move his blade swiftly and precisely. He'd easily dodge his opponent's attacks. One man lunged, and Cyrus turned quickly, grabbed the man's arm, and stole his sword.

"Remember any weapon they use can be a weapon you use."

The words stuck with Sophia. The next morning when she felt the couch tilting, she held on tightly and took a ride with it. When the couch was on its side, Sophia pushed up against it and towards Lee, knocking him back and off-balance. She grabbed her sai and leaped over the couch. Lee picked up a chair and easily dodged her attacks. He dropped the chair on her foot, then grabbed her arm and twisted it behind her. Lee pulled her back and against his chest. She tried to attack with her free hand, but he grabbed it and slammed her hand on the table. Sophia dropped the sai.

"Good job, Sophia, you lived thirty seconds longer than you did the past twenty-one days. Want breakfast?" Lee said as he held Sophia's body tightly against him.

"Sure," she replied. "You mind letting me go first?"

Lee released Sophia and walked to his pantry. He pulled out bread, eggs, and butter.

"You've been storming out all those mornings, meaning that you never stuck around for food. So, now that you understand anticipation, we can start your training."

Sophia looked at Lee incredulously. "I thought we were already training."

"You're kidding me, right?" Lee cracked an egg open. "Your heart may have been in it, but you were not mentally prepared. You need to understand; in battle, the other person will not play fair. There is no 'let's wait till our opponent is ready.' If they can get you when you are sleeping, they will."

"Do you need help with that?" Sophia asked, pointing to the eggs.

"No, no, I got it. But grab the kettle so we can have tea."

Sophia got up, filled the kettle with water, and brought it to Lee.

"Your mind needs always to be open to the possibility that

any situation can potentially be a fight, you need to assess wherever you are at all times and see what you can use to your advantage. In this particular situation, the couch was what I was using against you, and it was also the quickest thing for you to use to defend yourself." Lee picked up some hot coals from his fireplace with a pair of tongs and walked them to his kitchenette. He placed the coals under the stove and began to cook the eggs and heat the water.

"You couldn't have told me this earlier?"

"Some things can't be told, Sophia. You need to feel it. It has to come naturally to you."

Sophia thought to herself as Lee poured tea. She remembered when the Osprey attacked. She was fast asleep, but something told her to move. Instinct. It began to make sense to her; Lee was trying to get Sophia to tap into her natural instinct of survival. She nodded her head in realization. Lee noticed. He let a smile escape as he placed the food on her plate.

"You know your home will be done soon. You won't have to worry about me rolling your ass out of my couch every morning, mooch."

"Ha. Funny." Sophia shoveled a forkful of eggs into her mouth.

"It's a really nice place, far away from the town, though." Lee tried to stop what came next, but it was too late. "If you get lonely out there, you are more than welcome to stay here." He stared at his plate as he sat and then began to eat.

Sophia stopped in the middle of chewing and looked at Lee.

"I thought you hay'ed haffin me around."

Lee's mind scrambled for an explanation that didn't involve him enjoying her company, her outbursts, which he found cute as hell, or just the comfort of having her there when he woke.

"It's just nice, to have, um, someone to fill this huge home."

"Oh," Sophia said as she swallowed. "Why is this so big anyway?" Sophia asked while she waved her fork in the air.

"I lived here with my parents before they died. They were much much older, and, well, couldn't keep their damn hands off each other. With that said, I was born. They died twenty years ago. I was eight; they were close to a century old." He laughed. "Goodness, did they love each other, though I was their only child. They tried for many years, but it didn't happen. Not till me." He pointed to himself with his fork. "So they implored Halcyon to build a larger home for the three of us and decided to leave it to me when they passed. Halcyon agreed. Of course, I didn't sleep here for a long time. It was too empty without them. But I dealt with it, months later."

"My mother died when I was fifteen," Sophia said, "she was young though."

Lee tilted back on his seat.

"I'm sorry."

"Mm, it happens."

"Well, this is a terrible conversation."

He and Sophia laughed.

The next morning when Lee attempted to tilt the couch, Sophia repeated her actions from the day before. This time, she continued to flip the sofa entirely around and back on its feet. She grabbed her sai and rolled over the couch. The first thought that crossed her mind was that Lee was better than her, so instead she waited for him to move. He gave her a smile that she returned. Then he went towards her, and in seconds she was disarmed and pinned to the floor.

Lee could feel his blood flowing hot and knew that he wasn't only just feeling 'protective' over her. He gathered himself and let her go.

"Good job. So that you know, I will attack you whenever, wherever, on top of weapons training that we start this afternoon." Lee got up and went to his pantry, where he grabbed bread and eggs. "Can you bring me the kettle?"

Sophia rolled to her side then stood up. She grabbed the kettle and was about to hand it to Lee when he went after her with the coal tongs. Sophia yelped and used the kettle to defend herself. Her sai were on the floor and out of reach, so she focused on defense and figuring out how to disarm Lee. Sophia flung the kettle at him. As he dodged it, Sophia stepped in close and kneed him in the crotch. Lee went down, and she grabbed the tongs and pointed them at Lee.

"You know that will only work on a man," he said with a pained look. Sophia gave him a quirky smile and shrugged her shoulders.

42

BREAKFAST AND A BRAWL

When Sophia moved into her new home, she found it to be a relief to be away from Lee. It wasn't that she didn't appreciate everything he had done; it was that being around Lee was mentally and physically taxing. Lee was a fantastic fighter and well-rounded in literature, mathematics, and history. All topics Sophia didn't retain from her youth, during her school days. She would become embarrassed when he would start a conversation, and she would have to ask him to explain. Weapons training that afternoon was more like a weapons lecture. They spent the afternoon learning this history of the sai, and the names of each and every part of the sai. The sai had seven parts to it, each with its own name and purpose. The names were from a lost dialect, and Sophia had a hard time trying to memorize and say them. Sophia's sai were created during the reign of the First Majji. The rare metal used to create them had been enchanted and then blessed. Lee had asked her to get reacquainted with her sai and, by tomorrow, to know every part of them and what each was used for. Walking into her home that night was beyond refreshing. Her head ached with all the information she had taken in. The first thing Sophia did when she arrived in her new home was pour herself a hot cup of tea. She then climbed the ladder to her loft, spilling some of the tea on the way up. Sophia lay back on her bed and closed her eyes. That night, knowing Lee wasn't there to roll her out of her bed, she slept soundly.

When morning came, Sophia shifted out of bed. She wiped her face where she had been drooling then stretched. A heavenly scent caught her nose. She climbed down the ladder to find an incredible breakfast spread laid out for her: pancakes, eggs, fruits, toast, butter, milk, and, good gods, bacon. She served herself then walked outside hoping to thank the person who made the food, but no one was in sight. Sophia picked up a pancake and took a bite, then she stepped out again, but whoever it was that created the delightful morning feast wanted to make themselves scarce. Sophia shrugged her shoulders then turned back to find Lee sitting at the table. Startled at his sudden appearance, Sophia gaged a bit on her food.

"Sit, Sophia."

Not good. Sophia hesitantly sat down next to Lee. She turned to him, hoping to gauge his mood. With her back to the wall, she cautiously scooped some eggs.

"You didn't poison the food, did you? Because that would suck," she said with a mouthful. Lee let out a smile, as a small laugh escaped him.

"Woman. You never learn. First off, is this normal?"

"To have my friend poison my food? No. I'm going to have to say that this is a first."

"I didn't poison your food."

"Fantastic!" Sophia stuffed her face.

"Sophia, waking up to a full breakfast spread, does this happen often?"

"No, but it's awesome! You should do it more," she said with a smile ear to ear.

"Gods," Lee said as he rolled his eyes. "When something is out of the normal, you need to become alert. Where are your sai?"

"Upstairs," Sophia said like a scolded child. "What did you want me to do? Attack the plates? Stab the fruit to death? 'Cause, gods know, it had it coming."

"Next time, I will poison it."

"Funny."

"What do I tell you at the end of training?" Lee asked.

Sophia leaned up against the wall and looked up. He told her a lot yesterday, but nothing about rewarding her with a delicious breakfast. Crap, that was something else she needed to add to the list of accomplishments Lee had: he was apparently a good cook too. Ugh. Sophia was feeling stupid again. She grabbed a piece of bacon and took a bite. Then it came to her. She turned her head to the side and looked at Lee.

"That you would attack me anytime...anywhere?"

"Yup."

Lee rolled over the table and onto the opposite bench, then he kicked the table, pinning Sophia against the wall. She yelped in pain. He picked up a fork and stabbed towards her. Sophia blocked the attack with her hand. She tried to squeeze out from between the wall and the table, but Lee's strength was more than she could take. Sophia grabbed the plate and defended against Lee's attacks. She grabbed another and flung it at him. She then focused all of her efforts on distracting him so she could push the table back. Sophia grabbed plates, cups, food, whatever she could get her hands on and began tossing them at him. Lee used both hands to deflect the projectiles. When he knew he lost the advantage, he jumped on the bench and over the table, when Sophia kicked it upward, freeing herself. Her sai were upstairs, so she grabbed her kettle. Lee laughed.

"Shut up!" she snapped.

Again, they fought, he disarmed her, and she ran outside, knowing her home was too small of a space to fight. The outdoors gave Sophia more room to move. They sparred all the way into town. Sophia had connected a few punches and a beautiful side kick to Lee's kidneys. Being in Atara, her knuckles healed quickly, but that didn't mean the initial pain wasn't there. The fight ended just outside of Cyrus' bar, where Sophia again swung at Lee. He caught her arm, pulled her in, tripped her, and landed on top of her with an arm across her throat. They panted heavily for a moment, then smiled.

"You are getting much better," Lee said proudly. He looked into her eyes for what became an uncomfortable amount of time, then forced himself to get up. "This afternoon, training circle, bring your sai." Lee walked away.

Sophia sat up and brushed herself off. The area was full of townsfolk who stopped their daily routine to see what the commotion was about. She spotted Cytrine, who began to walk after Lee, and Jasira, who had a quizzical look on her face. Sophia remained seated for a moment with her tousled hair, a mess embedded with leaf and grass, then looked down at her sleepwear that was newly decorated with bloodstains and rips. She examined herself and chuckled. Man, was she happy they weren't cannibalistic. She would have been screwed. Jasira walked up to her and held a hand out. The girls walked into Cyrus' bar. They found a spot in the far corner and sat down.

"Well, that was interesting," Jasira said as they sat down.

"Yeah, well, we have to spar, and Lee is trying to get me

to realize that any situation can lead to a fight. I'm getting really good at having my ass handed to me."

"Um, no...not that."

Sophia waited for an explanation and didn't get one.

"Listen," Jasira said, quickly changing the topic, "Garret reported this morning that Kahel moves towards Salinas, but he has more men than he needs for establishing an Extricate Station." Jasira looked left and right, then leaned in closer to Sophia. "I think he plans to attack," she whispered.

"Attack Atara?" Sophia whispered back.

Jasira nodded.

"It hasn't been confirmed," Cyrus' voice boomed from behind the bar, "so we are trying to keep it as silent as possible."

Jasira's face flushed twelve shades of red before it settled on a hue. "Jasira and I are going to do some recon. See what information we turn up," Cyrus told Sophia. He walked towards the girls, then turned to Jasira with a coy smile. "Till then, can you please keep the gossip to a minimum?" He walked back behind his bar and grabbed his blade. "Time to whip the boys into shape." Cyrus walked out the door. Jasira's face followed him, and when he was out of sight she lowered her head down on the table and groaned.

"Ughhhh..."

"Now *that* was interesting."

"How fair is it that you are bonded to the guy you have a crush on?" Jasira said with her head still on the table "You know, before the bond, I didn't have a crush on him, but then again I was eight and what do eight-year-olds know? Now I don't know if the pull I feel to him is the bond or my actual feelings."

Sophia looked over to where Cyrus had disappeared.

"Jasira, that is one handsome man, anyone could easily crush on him, bond or no bond."

Jasira lifted her head up and gave Sophia a smile.

"I know, huh."

"So, you are going on recon with Cyrus?"

"Yeah, a bunch of us are. Lee is going too. We have to check our perimeter and see exactly where Kahel is going to put all these men."

Sophia sunk in her chair. This girl was younger than her, and the heightened risk of attack and going out on recon didn't raise any sort of emotions in her.

"Aren't you scared?"

"No, I've gone on recon hundreds of times. Remember, I was even there the day you danced at Tychi. Though at first Cyrus and I were only there to pick up some rare tonics, but when Lee and the others showed up plans changed. They stationed me at Tychi's borders. Make sure the gates remained open, you know. Lee and Garret went in further to check out the Majji's son." Jasira bit her lip when she realized that she just brought up Sophia's dead husband. "Sorry. I didn't mean to—"

"Don't," Sophia said, "don't feel bad. But listen, I've got to go, I need to clean up my home." Sophia was ready to leave when a thought occurred to her. "Hey, if you want to help out, I've got a crapload of food all over the place. I'm sure some is still edible."

"Who cooked it?"

"Lee, right before he tried to stab me in the face with a fork."

"Huh. Lee's cooking is awesome, I'd eat that off the floor!"

"Good, because that's where most of it is."

They got up and headed out of the bar.

Jasira was Sophia's first guest, well, first invited guest. It was nice to have her around to help clean her home. Unfortunately, the food was tossed everywhere and inedible. They were very excited when they found that a stack of pancakes had survived, teetering on the corner of the wood stove. Sophia also found a bowl of eggs that landed in the loft area. The afternoon sun began to come around, so Sophia said goodbye to Jasira, grabbed her sai, and headed to weapons training. When Lee quizzed her on the parts of the sai, she answered correctly; when Lee asked her the history of the sai and origin of her sai, she answered correctly; when Lee asked her what the proper way to hold the sai was, she replied with, "Stabby part forward?"

Lee palmed his forehead. This wasn't fair at all; they didn't cover that yesterday. But it's obvious that the stabby part goes forward. Why the heck did he slap his head?

"Tsume and saki forward," Sophia corrected, hoping that identifying the correct names for the ends was what he was looking for.

Lee grabbed his own pair of sai and flipped them into his hand. The blunt end forward in his palms and pronged ends against his forearm.

"Saigashira forward?"

"Yes, the end, the saigashira, forward. Grab yours, hold in like this, make sure there is no space between the center prong and your forearm. Sophia, what's the name of the center prong?"

"Monouchi."

"Good."

Sophia did as she was told. The sensation of the monouchi against her forearm felt right, fit right; it was like these sai were explicitly made for her. Which was strange, since they had belonged to Eilith.

"I want you to understand that choosing a weapon is a big deal; the weapon becomes a part of you, so treat it that way. It's not some strange object you are holding. It is an extension of you. So, when you punch, go for it with your sai; when you block, block with your sai. Make sense?"

"Perfect."

Lee lunged. Sophia used the sai to block, and it came naturally to her. She could defend against him so easily. Sophia spun, dodging an attack, then began to charge Lee. Sure-footed, she hooked a few punches and landed a rib shot. Lee stumbled back. Sophia kept coming. He flipped his sai, so the prongs were faced forward, and disarmed Sophia.

"Hey! I thought you said the correct way to hold them was saigashira forward!"

"It is, I just flipped mine. This is the other way to use them. Try to flip them."

Sophia picked her sai up from the ground and tried to flip from one end to the other. She was successful. But she had a few issues with hand positioning. Lee instructed her that her fingers were never to go between the prongs. Once she had the grips correct, he started to teach her how to disarm an opponent by catching their weapon between the prongs. By the end of their lesson, Sophia had several cuts that were healing and had some serious practicing to do.

Lee and the others had left that night on recon. Sophia, now home, sat outside her open sliding wall, looking up into the sky.

"Magnificent, isn't it," Zephyr said. He materialized in front of her and lay down on the grass.

"It is. So much we don't understand, so much to learn."

"This is true, but you must first come to understand the land you live in before you go off dreaming of new ones."

"Hm. Where have you been lately?"

"Nacunas. It is my home."

"Are there others like you living there?"

"Yes and no." Sophia waited for more, but Zephyr remained silent. He looked wistfully at the sky then turned to face Sophia. "You should rest. I overheard Lee saying something about sneaking in tonight for more training when they return."

"Awesome," Sophia said glumly. She left the sliding door open and climbed into bed.

43

BORIS IN
CONFLICT

Boris crouched as far to the ground as possible. The soldiers hadn't seen him, but he couldn't move from his spot. He knew better than anyone that the Greys and the Osprey could spot movement almost a mile away. Boris was trapped. He flattened his body and slowly crawled back down a grassy mound. He cursed his conscience for surfacing at the worst possible moment. He didn't expect to grow fond of the Salinan boy; nonetheless, Gabriel had managed to awaken endearing feelings that Boris thought to be long dead. Weeks back, he recalled hearing the news of the Osprey crossing through his town with Gabriel in tow. He slammed his knife clear through the fish he was filleting, then walked out the back door. He had no clue what he was going to do, just that he couldn't allow Kahel to have Gabriel.

When no one was in sight, he walked towards the unoccupied Osprey horse. In the distance, he saw a body wrapped and tied to the back of the horse. Boris ran to it and uncovered it. Gabriel lay there, still breathing but completely unconscious. Boris started to work on the rope, trying to free Gabriel. Why in the world didn't he take the damn knife? He knew the consequences of what he was doing and couldn't explain to himself why he was still doing it. He was a Grey now, so why wasn't he robotic like the others? It would make his life easier. The knots were tight, and no matter how hard Boris tried he couldn't undo them. A door opened, Boris worked harder, and when he realized that he wasn't going to free Gabriel in time, he chose just to release the horse. Maybe this way, Boris thought, he would get a head start and make it to Tychi before the Osprey. There, he could tail the man and find where they intended to keep Gabriel. Boris looked at his young friend; he placed his forehead on Gabriel's.

"I am so sorry, my child, I will make this right." Boris looked at Gabriel's unconscious face. "I promise you."

Stupid promise, Boris thought to himself as he reminisced while he tried to get comfortable behind the mound. He recalled tailing the Osprey without any difficulty. After all, Boris had access to the castle. Moments after he had seen the Osprey enter the castle, he saw the Osprey fall out a window. It was then that he learned that Gabriel was not Majji. After Kahel's whole scene, Boris snuck down to the dungeons and waited till they brought Gabriel down. When only one cell guard was left, Boris walked towards the man.

He mustered all the Grey that was left in him and spoke. "I hear you have the Salinan down here."

"This area is restricted; you should not be here." The pompous guard puffed his chest when he spoke.

"Save it. You all know I was critical to this boy's acquisition, and I just want to make sure that Osprey who took a nosedive out the window didn't bumble up and snatch the wrong man."

"Fine, make it quick." The jail guard stepped aside and allowed Boris to walk down the moisture-filled stone hallway. He passed two depressing, empty cells, then arrived at Gabriel's. Boris wrapped his fingers around the bars and laid his head on the cell door. He had no idea how to pull off Gabriel's escape; he only knew that he had to. Gabriel was a pawn, and Boris knew that the moment he first saw Sophia. After their performance, he had tried to get the pair into the castle; if he had succeeded, maybe at least Gabriel would come out of this alive. There was a stirring in the cell. Boris looked up and saw Gabriel sitting, rubbing his head. It was then the two made eye contact.

"They were all right not to trust you," Gabriel said as he leaned against the wall.

"Yes."

"Did you do this?"

"No. But regrettably, I was part of it."

"Why?"

"I had no choice."

"Bullshit! Everyone has a choice, Boris!"

"I haven't been Boris for years now."

"What are you talking about?" Gabriel's brows furrowed and he placed his hands on his head again.

"They took him when he was sleeping. The Boris you speak of had so much knowledge, and Kahel wanted that knowledge. Boris refused to speak, so they killed him."

Gabriel's eyes widened.

"When he was dead as a doornail, they tossed him into a Regeneration Unit, and I emerged with all of Boris' knowledge. I am a Grey. A mindless slave, destined to serve Kahel for eternity or until he decides not to allow me to regenerate anymore. So, while they all still call me Boris, his body is just the shell that I live in."

Gabriel was on his feet in seconds. He pulled Boris through

the bars and repeatedly slammed him back and forth into the cell bars.

"You fucking asshole! I trusted you, I trusted you!"

The cell guard came running in and pulled out a small metal rod. He clicked a button at its base, and the rod tripled in size. The guard jammed the rod through the bars as blue electric sparks had begun to encompass it. He caught Gabriel directly in the chest. Gabriel cried out and released Boris. The guard then grabbed Boris and tried to usher him away.

"I'm fine. Give me a moment," Boris said as he broke free from the guard.

"You've had long enough. Is that the man or not?"

"Yes."

"Then it's time to go."

"Okay," Boris said then nonchalantly grabbed the guard's weapon, flipped it, activated it, and poked the guard with it. The guard let out a short high-pitched yelp as the blue sparks spread across his body. He went down instantly.

"What a wuss," Boris said as he tossed the weapon to the ground and walked to Gabriel's cell. "You took double that hit and there you are, awake and standing."

"Hurt like hell, though," Gabriel responded.

"I can't free you," Boris said. "That guard doesn't have the key, and if he did there is no way I can get you out of this castle unseen. A rescue would require an act of the gods."

Gabriel sighed in defeat.

"I will find a way, and I will return."

"How am I to trust you after all of this?"

"Understand that Greys usually have no free will and no conscience, but I do. Part of Boris has returned, and his thought process makes sense to me." Boris then began to walk away. "When the guard wakes up feel free to mess with him."

Gabriel smiled.

"Something along the lines of, 'Boris? He was never here,'"

Gabriel said. "'What are you talking about?'"

"Yeah, just like that. Later, bastard."

"Old man."

Boris had walked out of the castle with no problem. Not wanting to have any attention drawn to him, he took a ship to Tavernport, then made his way to the outskirts of Jaru. There he remained hidden, trying to work out another way to get Gabriel out. But there was none. His only answer was to head west to Eurija, break the treaty, and start a war with its inhabitants. This would cause a big enough distraction that, with Kahel looking west, Boris could easily sneak in and pull Gabriel out. The only problem was making it west without getting killed. During his short stay at Jaru, he had noticed a suspicious amount of Greys in town, and this made the people of Jaru nervous. Many of its citizens spent the days indoors, avoiding the Greys, making it hard for him to get supplies. It was during his stay at Jaru that he heard that Salinas had been "relocated." His heart sunk. He knew exactly what that meant. He decided now was the time to move. The trail to Salinas was going to be heavily guarded, so he disguised himself as a homeless drunk who hitched a ride on a cart to Crossings Forged. When they arrived where Salinas used to be, Boris looked around in shock. There was nothing left of the beautiful town.

"Did you hear?" said a man in the cart. "They relocated Salinas, going to put an Extricate Station here?"

"That's great news!" piped a woman. "Hopefully, when we get back, construction will be underway," she said excitedly. "King Kahel said that it will produce endless energy; imagine all we can do with it."

"I'm sure they will break ground soon. The Wanderer's Trail, from here all the way to Crossings Forged, is full of his workers camping out."

That was Boris' cue to hop off the cart. He knew those weren't workers. Kahel was up to something, and it wasn't good.

"Where are you going?" yelled the man.

"Your constant chatter was enough for one to consider flinging themselves off this carriage. But I decided to forgo ending my life and just take Darwin's Trail. Far from you and that harpy," Boris said rudely.

"Drunk."

"Bah!" Boris said as waved his hand and walked away. When the carriage was out of sight, he raced towards the Pyre River. He wasted no time crossing it. When he felt that he was safe, Boris collapsed and gasped for air. He set up camp and was careful with his fire. Attracting attention by having a fire was a fool's move. After his food was cooked and rocks heated, he put the fire out. He placed the warm stones around him, then covered himself with his cloak. He was asleep in moments.

The ground shook. Boris didn't know what time it was, but he jumped up, frightened, with a bow knife in hand. Nothing was around him except the massive fire to the east, towards Jaru. Several people leaped down from the trees, one was carrying another, and they quickly made their way into the Northern Woods. It didn't take long for Boris to connect the dots.

"Atarans. Kahel is going to attack Atara."

Boris quickly tossed the rocks around and made sure no one would know that someone had set up camp in that space. He ran towards a small area full of grassy mounds. Boris lowered down and covered himself with his cloak as troops came in from the King's Trail. There he remained, cursing himself, reliving his actions, then cursing himself again.

44

CARDINAL MOVE

Sophia shot up, startled. The high-pitched shriek that woke her echoed into the night. She slid down the ladder, skipping steps, before checking the kettle that she thought was left on. As she snapped out of her dreamlike state, she realized the sound that woke her was more bird-like. While she hoped Zephyr had caught Lee trying to surprise attack her and had him pinned underneath his terrifyingly sharp talons, her gut told her something was wrong. Sophia climbed back up that ladder to grab her sai, then continued outside. Zephyr stood tall with his neck stretched long and high, turning his head left then right. Sophia looked down at his claws. No Lee. Damn.

"What is it?" She placed a hand on Zephyr's side.

"Darkness approaches. The Ataran soldiers have mobilized." He twitched his head again like he was listening to an invisible creature. "Someone one is returning, wounded. They are rushing in through the woods. The wind tells me the forest has opened up at Cyrus' bar. I must go." Zephyr dispersed into

240

the air and was gone. Sophia turned back into her home and speedily climbed her ladder. She removed her nightgown and pulled a plain shirt over her head, then heaved a leather-laced vest over it. She struggled into her pants, then boots, and finally tied her hair back. She placed her sai in her side holsters and raced to Cyrus' bar. One foot in front of the other, concentrating on her breathing, as Lee had taught her. With his training, Sophia's speed had increased. Even from afar, she could see blood on the ground in front of the bar. Sophia ran through the back to find Jasira lying on the same bed that Sophia herself had once occupied. Jasira's face was ashen and bloody, her hair full of soot. She was clutching her chest and coughing up blood.

"Oh, gods!" Sophia rushed to her as Cyrus stumbled in, carrying herbs. Sophia saw the trail of blood he was leaving and hurried towards him to offer support.

"Cyrus, you are wounded too; let me be your hands, tell me what to do." Cyrus gratefully handed over the herbs and told Sophia what to mix and how to mix it. When she was done, she had a blue paste in a bowl.

Cyrus sat at the foot of the bed and pointed to Jasira. "Put it on her wound, now." Sophia walked over to Jasira and opened her shirt; Jasira had a hole the size of a fist in her lower abdomen. Sophia filled the gap with the paste and almost with her own vomit.

"Why isn't she healing?"

"We are; that looks so much better than what it was. Now, please put the rest of that paste here." Cyrus opened his shirt to reveal an identical wound. Sophia did as he asked. Cyrus closed his shirt and leaned his head back. Sweat dripped down his face.

"What happened?"

"Jasira and I headed towards Jaru to see if Kahel had any troops camped out there." He turned to Sophia and said, "he did, and they had traps in the trees. They were expecting us. Which meant they were coming after us." He could see the fear in Sophia's face, "Don't worry, we've already sent out our soldiers. They are setting up a perimeter. We will be fine. Just shocking, after so many years Kahel makes his move," Cyrus said.

Sophia grabbed her sai and walked out the door.

"Where do you think you are going?" Cyrus called out with his eyes closed.

"To help."

"I can easily stop you, but I won't. I'm not leaving Jasira." Sweat beaded down Cyrus' face as he took in deep breaths. "Just tell Lee I put up a good fight, okay."

Sophia nodded.

Sophia wasn't there when Salinas was first attacked, but she would be there now. She stepped into the woods and in seconds was outside the Northern Woods, facing the backs of hundreds of Atarans. She could see Zephyr and a giant cat whose tail and mane were flames waving in the air. Halcyon was under the dogwood tree with Lee, Garret, and six other Atarans. His generals, she presumed. Sophia wandered down, attempting to blend in with the Ataran soldiers. Some recognized her, so she let out a little whistle as she turned away from them. She looked upon the land that once was Salinas.

There was nothing there now. No structures remained. There were no vine-covered rooftops, all the cobblestone roads were gone, the ditch had been filled, no music, no dancing, no anything. It was as if it never existed. She took in a deep breath, then wandered further down, eavesdropping on as many conversations as she could, hoping to get some information as she approached the dogwood. After about twenty minutes, she learned that Kahel's troops were moving fast, just like they did on Salinas, and he was using new weapons, but they had Halcyon and the Green, so no one seemed too worried. Sophia looked down at the dogwood tree; she was close. A breeze seemingly lingered around, then tossed her ponytail in the direction of the dogwood. Zephyr shot his head up.

"Shit." Sophia stood there, immobile.

Zephyr looked directly at her. It was like she was eight again and was caught picking the cherries out of the fresh pie her mother just had baked; she shrank down. Zephyr zipped quickly towards her and materialized.

"What in the name of all the gods are you doing here?" he boomed.

"Helping," she said innocently.

"No. You are turning around and heading back to Atara."

"No. I am helping."

"You have no fighting skills yet. Go back."

"No."

"You are as stubborn as your grandmother!"

"Thank you."

"That wasn't meant as a compliment."

As Sophia and Zephyr continued their argument, the Atarans around her began to clear away. In Sophia's eyes, she was arguing with Zephyr, the massive Haast Eagle Elemental, but Sophia was the only one who could see and hear him. To the Atarans, she was having a bizarre argument with herself. This continued for a few more moments before it caught the unwelcome attention of Lee and Halcyon. She was arguing quite spiritedly when Lee and Halcyon approached.

Sophia crossed her arms.

"I'm not leaving; I'm fighting, and that's that!"

"Like hell you are," Lee called out.

Sophia turned her head to protest but was distracted by a bright light in the sky. She examined it curiously, then quickly realized that it was coming closer. Fast. The ball turned into a blazing circle in the sky. It came closer and closer, Sophia covered her head and knelt down. The ball of fire made contact with the ground, then exploded, sending the land around it high into the sky. The Atarans began to scramble in confusion. Lee pushed Sophia back

"You stay back here; if anyone comes close to our forest, you kill them."

Sophia nodded. Zephyr shot high into the sky and zipped far to the south. The lion raced into the hole made by the explosion. Lee and the other generals began to separate their troops. Lee was in the front with Garret, with three other generals and their soldiers behind them. One general and his force spread out and stationed themselves in front of the forest. The other two ran east and west. Everything was moving quickly; Sophia turned her head left, then right, trying to make sense of it all. A frightening roar emerged from where the lion had disappeared to.

"BRACE YOURSELVES!" Lee yelled. Every man and woman knelt down and held on to the earth. Sophia did the same. The ground began to rumble and shook violently. Waves of land rolled towards where Kahel's troops were hidden. Trees collapsed as the rolling earth passed it. More and more trees fell; you could hear the screams of Kahel's men as their hiding place was exposed. There were hundreds of them, almost a thousand. Another roar erupted from the hole, followed by the lion, except this time he was completely engulfed in flames. With a broken staff in hand, Halcyon walked up to the lion. He placed his free hand on the back of the lion. Flames flickered off the lion's body, but Halcyon did not catch on fire. This was when Sophia realized that the lion was his Elemental. Halcyon raised the staff, and a blue light encompassed him. Immediately after, the lion's fire turned shades of blue. The regal flame that demanded respect engulfed them both. It was beautiful and hypnotic. Sophia had never seen anything like it before. Halcyon and the lion controlled the growing flame, then shot it forward. It traversed the space between the opposing troops and speedily reached the fallen tree line. The leaves violently shook as the flame charged through them, but not even one leaf caught fire. When the blue flames touched Kahel's front lines, it was like blowing the ashes out of a wood stove. The men just disintegrated. The blaze wiped out over three-quarters of Kahel's army, making it a fair fight. Halcyon fell onto his knees. The lion lowered down. Halcyon proceeded to get on the creature's back. The lion then turned and headed back to Atara. Sophia heard Lee call out a command. She stood up and watched the opposing troops charge towards each other. Sophia raced down to the dogwood for a better view. The lion slowed down as it approached Sophia. It padded slowly by with Halcyon hunched over it. The lion stared Sophia down.

"Child. You should not be out here," he said with a deep voice. "I know you can hear me; return with us."

"Don't bother, Mahes," Halcyon weakly said, "she won't listen. Stubbornness is a trait passed down in her family." Mahes let out an irritated growl and moved towards the forest.

"Don't get yourself killed, Sophia," Halcyon said in the distance.

The fight was underway, and the Atarans were uncanny. Even though most of them hand the underhand, fighting two to one, they still managed to dance around Kahel's men. Swords, axes, bo staffs, and spears clashed loudly, and punches and kicks connected. Garret was laughing through the whole fight; he and Lee seemed to be having a conversation while fighting.

"Arrogant," Sophia said to herself. She saw how Lee fought. His katana flowing freely through the air, it was as if there were no worries in the world. He was just doing what must be done, fighting with no emotions. Sophia couldn't take her eyes off of him. For his age, it was a wonder that he was such an accomplished fighter. Sophia leaned forward on the tree. They were winning. How could you possibly defeat people who heal one another? You couldn't. Then, as Sophia was getting comfortable with the idea of winning, a tremendous blast to her left sent her flying. The first blast was followed by another and another. She was disoriented. Her ears were ringing, her vision blurred, and she walked like a child taking their first steps. Black smoke was her only surroundings. The explosions came from the east, where Jasira and Cyrus had been wounded. Sophia grabbed her sai and slowly walked into the smoke. She tripped over some rubble and landed on her hands and knees. Sophia pushed herself up and noticed her hands were covered in blood. She saw some cuts on her legs and arms but nothing that would produce that much blood. The smoke began to clear, and Sophia saw where the blood had originated. Body parts were scattered around her. Sophia bent over and vomited. She really could never stomach blood, let alone gore. It was apparent that the troops that went east were no longer living. They must have gotten caught in some giant trap. So, that answered her question: how do you kill an Ataran? You blow them up. Sophia saw about fifty of Kahel's men headed towards her, pushing a giant catapult. The troop of Atarans that was stationed north of the dogwood headed further north to protect the woods. This left her alone with the charging men. She dropped to the ground with all the bloodied bodies and waited, praying that someone would make it to her before Kahel's men did. But no one arrived. The men passed right by her, thinking she was dead like the others. They began to head north to the forest. Sophia caught the last man in the foot with her sai. She jumped up, covered in blood, and right-hooked the soldier across the face with the end of her sai. Sophia picked up her other sai and caught the next soldier from behind. She slashed his heel and kicked him in the back of the head as he went down. This finally caught the attention of the remaining forty-eight men.

"You all keep pushing the catapult to the forest," The leader called out. "The rest of you, after her."

Shit shit shit shit shit.

The men turned and took a few steps towards her, then stopped. They seemed a bit terrified which Sophia found funny. Granted, she was covered in blood, so maybe they thought she had come back from the dead, but she was still one woman against all those trained men. That's when she heard steps behind her, running like a herd of horses, and Sophia turned to see Garret and his troops running up the hill behind her.

"Told you it's fun to slap a sleeping bull in the ass," he said, widely smiling as he passed Sophia and examined her blood-soaked clothing. "Apparently, you like it too, you little psycho."

"Wait, no, this isn't." Before Sophia could finish, weapons met and another fight began. Two men came after Sophia. She fought the first one off easily but was shaken by the dull look in his grey eyes. The next one came after her; at this point, she was having trouble. These were the same grey eyes as the Osprey, the same grey eyes as Boris. She had lost focus, allowing the soldier to disarm her. She stepped back, then he grabbed her by her neck and began to raise her. Sophia's feet scraped the grass, then were in the air. She tried to pull the man's hands off her neck. In the distance, she could see Lee fighting three men, then turning his attention to her.

"Sophia!" he cried out.

Lee kicked one man in the stomach, then rolled over his hunched back. He pulled the soldier's blade from his hand and stabbed another attacker who lunged at him, leaving two soldiers now. Lee hooked his arm around the hunched man's neck, lifted him back up, and turned him around. He used the man's body as a shield when the third soldier came at him, blade forward. The soldier caught his comrade in the belly. Blood gushed from the man's abdomen. Lee pushed the newly dead man into his remaining opponent. The weight of the dead man made the soldier stumble. Lee walked up to him and slit his throat. He then turned around and raced to Sophia. She could feel the bones in her neck start to give. Lee came from behind, and he hooked his arm around the soldier's neck and squeezed. Sophia fell to the ground, coughing. She didn't have much time to gather herself before she was being attacked again. Sophia rolled back to avoid being stabbed. She couldn't find her sai; if she made it through this, Lee was going to kill her. The soldier lunged, so she turned and shot her elbow down on his hands. He dropped his blade, and she caught it, then set it on him. The weapon, being more cumbersome than she anticipated, felt wrong in her hands. She clumsily tried to wield it. The soldier grabbed her arm and head-butted her, and she heard a crack and fell to the ground. Her head was spinning. She couldn't open her eyes, let alone move. She waited for the final blow but felt nothing. She saw the blurred body of the soldier fall beside her.

"Hey, hey, look at me are you okay?" Lee asked as he examined her.

"I can't see."

"Oh, gods, you've got a river of blood coming from your head."

Lee scooped her up.

"No, leave me down here, you have got to fight." Sophia tried to stabilize her wavering body unsuccessfully.

"It's okay, we've won. The troops here are falling, and Zephyr blocked the southern passages. No one is coming in, and no one is coming out. Hang in there. I'm taking you home."

Home. The word was foreign to her now, but it did send waves of calmness through her body.

Sophia leaned into Lee's chest and passed out.

Lee looked down at the now-unconscious Sophia. He smiled and let out a short laugh.

"That's three."

45

MORE THAN ENOUGH

Lee decided against requesting help from Cyrus when he saw Sophia's wound had begun to heal. Instead, he brought her to her house and laid her down on her bed. Lee stared at Sophia for a moment. The fear he felt on the field was the first time he'd felt any emotion while fighting. But seeing those men attack her had affected him, and he was scared of losing her. Lee cleared strands of hair from her face, and then placed her hand on his cheek. He turned in and kissed it. That's when he knew that what he felt was more than protection. Lee left a now-healing and fast-asleep Sophia alone in her home. He turned and walked towards Halcyon's.

The battle was successful, to an extent; they lost seventy men and women in the eastern explosion. When Mahes shook the earth, he made sure to keep the trees' root structures intact, which allowed Garret and his men to raise the trees that fell. Lee arrived at the Majji's hut to find Cyrus was planting gladiolus. Several near the front entrance, and a few in a newly dug garden. Since the dawn of the Majji, each Majji has had their bloom. Whenever the bloom would appear, it would be a sign from the Green for the Majji to pay attention to their surroundings. It also signified a Majji's beginning and their end. Halcyon's bloom was the gladiolus.

"What happened?" Lee walked to Cyrus with a worried look.

"He's not healing anymore. I'm unsure whether or not he knew that before he used magic. His little stunt saved us all but at a price. He's lost a good three years of life."

"Three years? He didn't even have one."

"I know. Halcyon's Essence leaves him every day; the Green is calling him. Lee, we need to prepare." Cyrus placed his hand on Lee's shoulder. Lee shrugged it off and walked into the small hut. There he found Halcyon, looking pale, drinking a cup of tea at his table.

"Hey, you're alive! How's our little spitfire?" Halcyon said.

"She's good, had a nasty head wound, but she's healing at an incredible rate."

"The Green likes that one; training going well?"

"Yes."

Halcyon motioned Lee to sit. Lee did so and looked down at his hands. They sat in ominous silence for a bit.

Halcyon then took a breath and spoke. "Listen, I know that it comes to no surprise to you that I'm dying, but now it's going to come much sooner than planned."

Lee shifted uncomfortably. "What do you need me to do?"

"We need to unite the staff." Halcyon placed his broken staff on the table. Lee's listless expression quickly turned into a gape. He looked between Halcyon and the staff for several moments.

"What? That's impossible; the other half is high up in the Graveland, not to mention is there for a reason. Neith, our

First Majji, used it to trap the Mad Essence. We can't remove it; that would be...blasphemous."

"Lee, I will always respect our beliefs, but you need to understand Mad Essence is free. Corentin was possessed by it, and I'm pretty damn certain so is Kahel. It's escaped."

Lee sat, looking incredulous; he opened his mouth to say something, but when nothing came out he closed it. Lee stood up and paced for a moment, then turned again to face Halcyon.

"We just survived our first battle in what I am sure will be many to come," Lee stated. "My head is still spinning from hearing that someone set off a Majji marker, from rescuing Sophia from the Osprey and watching them take Gabriel, and most of all from the fact that there is a person here in Atara who has the Essence of our late Queen and others co-existing within her. So, excuse me for asking, but can we just stop for now. Because, quite frankly, all of that is more than enough."

Halcyon exhaled, his face full of guilt and sorrow. "I have no Apprentice; therefore, I am the last Majji. It is up to me to choose the next leader, and I will give that leader as much magic and power as I can. So, I need to unite the staff." Halcyon's desperate tone caught Lee by surprise. Halcyon rubbed his brow and began in a much calmer tone. "I mean Neith no disrespect, but her efforts were in vain. As a Majji herself, if she were presented with our dilemma, she wouldn't hesitate. Neith would attempt to unite the staff. We will always make the ultimate sacrifice for our people. So, no, Lee, we can't just stop for now."

Lee ran his hands through his hair and crumpled back down into his seat.

"Fuck."

Not only was he about to agree to something that would certainly send him to the far depths of Hades, but he would also potentially be condemning those he would have to take with him. Just the expedition alone was dangerous, and that was not putting into account the creatures they were bound to encounter. Knowledge of Eurija, the lands far west, and its inhabitants had been passed down from generation to generation; no one had traveled into those lands in over a century. To top it all off, the Graveland, where the other half of staff resided was considered sacred, and setting foot there is forbidden.

"There has to be another way. Couldn't we fabricate another staff?"

"This staff is made from the Anadenanthera tree. That tree is extinct."

"Gods, be merciful, even if we cross Iceway unscathed, we still have to..."

"Leave that to me. I'll get you through the Iceway alive, but you'll be on your own after that."

"They won't be happy to see us."

"I know, but what other choice do we have?"

Lee remained silent for a moment, then accepted his fate. "I'll need a small team with me."

Halcyon exhaled, but whether it was a sigh of relief or an exhale of fear Lee never figured out.

"Granted, just make sure one of your members is Sophia. She needs to see," Halcyon said.

"I don't think that's a good idea."

"It's not, but it's also not our choice. She was chosen by the Green; she has to go." Halcyon saw the look on Lee's face. "I know how you feel about her, Lee, you have to try not to let it cloud your mind."

Lee stood up and walked towards the door.

"How? How can I not let it cloud my mind? I let the Osprey seize Gabriel, it was my fault he was taken to the castle and killed, and now I covet his wife?"

"You also saved her life, and isn't that what Gabriel's asked of you?"

"Yes. I just don't understand how I let this happen."

"Lee, the heart does as it wants; no matter how many times you tell it who to love and how to feel, it will do as it will. Don't beat yourself up about this. Gabriel's death is not your fault, and your feelings for her, well, it's not for you to decide. Don't fight it, accept it, come to terms with it, and you will find peace."

He always hated when Halcyon made sense.

"This expedition will take a little over a months' time." Lee said, "You better be alive when we return."

Halcyon laughed.

Outside, Cyrus was finishing up planting the gladiolas when blood seeped through his bandaging. Lee walked towards him and took the rest of the flowers.

"Sit," Lee demanded. "You need to rest."

Cyrus didn't argue and sat down. "I overheard. Crossing the Iceway undetected is nearly impossible. The further west we go, the stronger our gifts become, but even so it's still a dangerous journey."

Lee lowered himself next to Cyrus and exhaled. He knew quite well that keeping everyone alive was going to be impossible. The pair sat in silence.

The peaceful moment was ended by the sounds of rapidly moving steps heading in their direction. Garret, still covered in dirt and blood, came running towards Lee and Cyrus. "Solider, trapped in the woods. Two of them." He gasped for air between words. "Don't know how they got in, and why the forest hasn't let them out yet. Cytrine found them. She ran back into Atara, she was pale as a ghost. Frightened."

"So, there really is no stopping from now on," Lee said to himself. He shook his head at the ground, then pushed himself up. "Did the soldiers see her or attempt to attack her?"

"Don't know, she didn't say."

"Okay. You two are with me. The three of us are overkill, but I'd rather be safe. We don't know if the Green has Osprey trapped in our woods."

Lee walked through the town, heading to Cytrine's house. If they were trapped in the forest, they must be in the holding field. When Cyrus, Garret, and he arrived, Lee knocked on her door. Cytrine opened up to three men peering at her.

"Did they harm you?" Lee asked.

"No, but they did see me," she said. "Be careful." Cytrine grabbed Lee's hand. "Are you healed from the battle?"

"Not fully, but enough."

"Maybe you shouldn't go; those two have bond partners." She gestured to Cyrus and Garret. "So, if something happens to them, they will recover easily. You, Lee—"

Lee clenched his jaw; he always tried to avoid the topic of not having a bond partner yet. It was unnerving because, besides him and Cytrine, all the other unbound Atarans were much younger. It made Lee wonder if he and Cytrine were destined in some way. She was a beautiful woman, but for years he had tried with her only to come to realize that she wasn't someone he could see himself spending the rest of his life with. The thought was depressing to Lee.

"I'm well aware of my situation and Cyrus"—Lee pointed—"has a hole in his stomach. I only have superficial cuts. I appreciate your concern. Anything you can tell us about the soldiers?"

Cytrine walked up closer to Lee, saying "They must have been Kahel's sentries, trapped in there for a few days, they looked haggard." She then pressed close to Lee's ear so the other two wouldn't hear. Cyrus and Garret took the cue and stepped back.

"When this is done, come over. I can make you dinner, you can relax." Lee could use some relaxation, but he knew the kind of relaxation Cytrine meant, and that came with more strings than any scholar could count.

"Thanks, Cytrine." Lee turned back to Cyrus and Garret as she closed her door.

They were silent the entire trek to the Northern Woods when Lee held his hand up and stopped the trio.

"This makes no sense. None at all. Why would the forest keep two of Kahel's men prisoner?" Lee stared into the woods.

"Maybe so they could provide information, and having them alive was more beneficial for us," Garret said.

"Or maybe they turned, and wanted to aid us," Cyrus added.

"Or maybe it's a trap." Lee faced his friends.

"You underestimate the Green. She would never let anyone into Atara that wasn't Ataran or would cause us harm," Cyrus said.

"Nonetheless, something is not right. Whether or not they are there to harm us, Garret is right; they will have information. I think we should bring water and some bread. Whoever they are, maybe we can talk to them."

"Water, bread, knives, check," Garret said with a smile. After gathering some supplies, the three wandered into the woods. The three Atarans held out their weapons as they sauntered. It wasn't guaranteed the woods would open them up into the holding field, but it did. And there they were, just as Cytrine has said, two of Kahel's sentries. One was wounded and laying across the other's lap, breathing heavily. The one sitting up was holding the other tightly and became protective the moment he had spotted Lee and the others. The three Atarans examined the sentries from a distance.

"Lee, those are not soldiers," Cyrus said. "Look at their clothes, look at their eyes,"

Even from afar, it was apparent that those were not the dull grey eyes of a soldier; they were brown, full of life. Lee lowered his katana to the ground and slowly approached the two men. When he saw the healthier-looking man grow stiff, Lee lifted both hands up and stepped back, signaling his benevolence. When the man understood, he slowly relaxed.

"Please help us," Domingo said, "my brother's fever runs high, and his wound is infected. I have to keep tearing at it so it won't heal with the infection inside."

"I know those faces, Lee," Garret said as he raced to the two men with some water. He knelt down and opened his canteen. "These two were part of the group of entertainers that performed in Tychi. Don't you remember?"

The familiarity of their faces soon turned to recognition, which meant they were survivors from Salinas. Cyrus and Lee walked over to them. Cyrus looked over Santiago's wound.

"I can heal this. Worry no longer, your brother will be fine. Please, come with me," he said, holding out his hand.

"Go where?" Domingo retorted. "We have been trapped in here for the past four days. Every time we tried to leave, we would be sent right back here."

"That's because the forest was protecting us Atarans." Garret closed his canteen. "And probably wasn't sure of your intentions." He put Santiago's arm around his neck. "Is this okay? I can carry you if you need."

"Thank you, this is fine." Santiago groaned as he, with the aid of Garret, got to his feet.

"I think after she figured you weren't going to harm us, she decided to trap you here for safekeeping," Garret said as they walked towards the woods.

"Do you need healing?" Lee asked Domingo.

"No, I only had superficial wounds, which healed the moment we stepped into this surreal place."

The group of men walked through the woods and into

Atara. The townspeople stood still, then began to back away. Lee gestured that everything was okay, but that didn't stop the gapes and stares that they received. Jasira went up to Garret and took Santiago off his arms.

"Thanks, kid," Garret said. "I'm still pretty beat up from the battle. I thought I was going to get some shut-eye then the shrew shrieked."

Jasira let out a short laugh then nudged Garret with her elbow as they recalled the dramatic fit Cytrine threw over the men in the woods.

"Come with us," Jasira gestured at Garret. "If you need healing, I'm sure we can make room."

Garret looked at Cyrus, who clenched his jaw and gave Garret a look that was enough to stop a stampede of wild buffalo.

"Yeah, I'd better not. You have patients. I'll just get back home. I'm sure my sisters are worried." Garret returned a challenging look to Cyrus, then leaned close to Jasira "Take your own advice and rest, so you can heal." And with that, he walked away. Jasira and Cyrus walked to the back of the bar, supporting Santiago. Domingo and Lee followed.

Cyrus and Jasira were putting together herbs and oils.

Lee knew these men had questions but also knew they needed rest.

"My name is Leonardo, but everyone here calls me Lee," he said as he put his hand on Domingo's shoulder.

"Domingo, and that is my brother, Santiago. We are from the town of Salinas." Domingo paused for a moment. "Were from the town of Salinas."

"I'm sorry for you and your people," Lee said. "What Kahel did is unforgivable. There is much to tell, but I think it's more important that you both have a good night's rest, and I am sure what I am about to tell you next is going to help you sleep. A few weeks back, I rescued a woman by the name of Sophia from being killed during the kidnapping of her husband, Gabriel."

Tears fell down Santiago's eyes. He grabbed his brother's arm.

"She has been living here with us," Lee continued. "She has a home, as will you. I know you have questions, but they all can wait till tomorrow. She is safe, and you are safe."

"Gods have been merciful! Sophia lives!" Domingo hugged his brother, then Lee. "Our little Sophia lives."

Lee was taken aback by the affection he just received but returned the hug and patted Domingo on the back.

"I have a home that is large enough to house two. It is yours." Lee said. Domingo stood, dumbfounded by the grand gesture.

"We couldn't possibly take your home."

"Trust me, it's okay," Lee nodded reassuringly. "It really hasn't felt like my home in a very long time, and it's too big for one person. It feels empty."

Jasira turned and gave Cyrus a troubled look. Cyrus gestured for her not to worry about it as they applied the ointment to Santiago's wounds. When the brothers were healed, Lee walked them to their new home and made sure they were comfortable before he left. Lee reported back to Halcyon, where he learned that his expedition west would begin in two weeks' time. After his chat with Halcyon, Lee stood outside with no real home to go to, but still he walked. He knew exactly where he was going, not sure why, but his legs brought him there. He could have questioned it, then doubled back somewhere, anywhere, but he didn't. He just went to her home. Lee knocked twice, and Cytrine opened up. Just as she had promised, food was prepared. A nice stew, rice, and chicken, all ready and set up on the table. It had been a while since Lee had eaten a good meal, well, that's if you don't count all the food he ate while he was preparing Sophia's breakfast. He remembered the look on her face when she thought he poisoned her food. Lee let out a short laugh.

"What?" Cytrine smiled. "What is it?"

"It's nothing," he replied.

"So, I can't believe you gave your home to those men. I mean, yes, it's a big house, but it was your big house."

"Yes, mine and mine to give away. It was just too much space for one person."

"Here, yes, but you know how big the houses are outside of Atara?"

"Hmm, you and your dreams," Lee said as he finished his rice.

"I just want more than this." Cytrine opened her arms to her home. "I feel like a prisoner here." She got up and walked towards Lee. She pulled his chair back. "It would be nice to have someone to be a prisoner with." Cytrine placed her arms around his neck and then straddled him. Lee leaned back and took in the woman who was willingly offering herself to him. Cytrine was hands-down the most beautiful Ataran; beauty wasn't everything, though, physical appearances change throughout the years. Lee wanted a connection, and they just didn't have it. No amount of beauty could make him forget that. Cytrine wanted out of Atara; she wanted physical, material things that Elite had in Tychi. Lee wanted what his parents had; he wanted to find a partner he could grow old with.

"What are you thinking about?" Cytrine asked in a sensual tone.

"My parents."

"Well, that's a mood killer."

Lee let out a laugh. His thoughts grew slightly fuzzy, and he became tired. Even though this is a situation most men would be glad to be in, it was wrong for him to be here with her when he cared for another. Sophia still loved Gabriel, that was glaringly obvious. To add to that, Lee couldn't forgive himself for letting the Osprey take Gabriel. Now, Sophia had two men from her hometown to fill in any emotional gaps left by the loss of Gabriel. Lee wasn't accustomed to questioning himself. Things were so much easier when he didn't factor in what his heart wanted. He leaned forward and kissed Cytrine. He was tired of being a slave to his emotions. She pressed up against him and began to kiss him more passionately. Lee returned the kiss but didn't move his body. He felt sluggish and groggy.

"Cytrine, I don't feel right."

"I can fix that," she whispered into his ear. Cytrine got up, grabbed his hand, and led him to the back of the house where her bed was. She stripped off her clothes, revealing an incredible body and a set of absolutely perfect breasts. Lee stood there, knowing that this wasn't the greatest of his ideas, then again the fog filling his head made it hard for him to remember any of his ideas at all. Cytrine pushed Lee back onto her bed, then began to unfasten his belt.

Almost thirty minutes later, they lay on her bed, both covered in sweat. He pushed himself up and shifted away from her. He sat on the side of the bed and put his hands in his hair.

"What's wrong, Lee?" Cytrine asked as she held him from behind.

"I shouldn't have come here,"

"Yes, you should have. We are good together, you know that."

"Cytrine, I don't love you."

"That's fine, Lee, we don't need love. We can be companions. The timing is perfect actually. You don't have a home anymore, and with you by my side Halcyon will be okay with us leaving."

"What? I don't want to leave Atara, you know that."

Cytrine, now exasperated, let Lee go and dropped to the bed.

"Because she's here," Cytrine said under her breath. "Just lay down. Go to sleep. I have a delicious breakfast planned for tomorrow morning. We can talk about how we won't work out then."

He was confused at her calmness. After all, he just told her flat out that he didn't love her, right after they had sex. He was too tired to analyze it. Processing his thoughts grew more and more difficult. Lee barely managed to slip his pants back on before he collapsed on the bed next to Cytrine. She smiled wryly, turned around, and went to sleep.

46

TWO BIRDS, ONE STONE

Sophia grudgingly woke and braced herself as she checked for a head wound, finding nothing. She rubbed her face. As her eyes came into focus, Sophia noticed that she was in the same clothes she wore the day before. Head to toe, Sophia was covered in dirt and blood. Thoroughly disgusted, she raced down the ladder, stripped her clothes, and ran out back towards her bathing pool. The sun had barely crested the horizon, and a light fog settled above the dew-covered grass. Sophia turned behind her house and jumped in, not paying any mind to the coldness of the water. She grabbed some dried moss and started scrubbing her skin, she picked up a bottle of hair wash Jasira gave her that was made out of lemongrass and lathered it into her hair. The clumped-up knots fell apart as the dried blood washed out. Her lips were blue and her teeth chattering, but she still dunked her body deep into the pool. Sophia held her breath and remained under for a little while, letting go of everything that happened out on the battlefield. She knew she had to, that holding on to all of her grief would destroy her. A sense of calm flushed through her, and Sophia wondered why the courage to continue on had been nonexistent before this moment. She had been through a lot in the past few weeks, and she was surprisingly holding it together well. Sophia counted to five, then lifted herself out of the water and walked, stark naked, back into her home. Living far from the townspeople was nice. She liked the privacy. Sophia lit the wood stove and wrapped a blanket around her. She sat and held her hair out, so it would dry. It was early morning and usually by this time Lee would have thrown her off a couch, lured her in with a poisoned breakfast, or just flat out punched her in the gut. Instead, her home was quiet and peaceful. Sophia dressed in a tank top and skirt. She tossed a shawl around her shoulders and was about to head to Lee's when she saw a letter on her table. It was addressed to Sophia and written in elegant handwriting. Sophia opened the letter and read its contents. It was an invitation from Cytrine to join her for a victory breakfast. She never thought of Cytrine as the type to hold a breakfast, but who was she to question it. It was food.

"She had better have fruit...and eggs...and bacon..." Sophia said as she took the trail closest to the Nacunas to get into town. The trail's scenery made it easy for Sophia to get lost in thought. She contemplated her former home and how she wanted Salinas to become a sacred place, a place of peace and reflection, not a land fought over. Already two battles have been fought on that land, gallons of blood spilled, and countless deaths. She was getting a late start, but this is something she knew she had to do. Sophia followed the path right into town and almost into a chicken coop.

"Hey, Sophia!" Jasira called out cheerfully.

Sophia looked up and realized her trajectory. She was

about two steps away from becoming friendly with a group of cluckers. Her eyes darted left and then right. She hoped Jasira was the only one who was in the area. When Sophia was satisfied, she turned to Jasira with a toothy grin.

"Oh, hey! Hi, what are you doing up? Shouldn't you be healing?"

"Were you about to walk into the chicken coop?"

"What, no, I was just"—Sophia fumbled in her mind—"counting the chickens, just in case, one...um, escaped?"

Jasira let out a laugh. "You were, weren't you!!"

"Shut up."

Jasira continued to laugh, then grabbed her abdomen. Sophia remembered that's where her wound was. Sophia walked over to Jasira.

"Are you okay enough to be walking around? I saw that wound, Jasira."

"I'm okay, it's just sore, that's all."

"I'd say." Sophia said, "So where are you heading?"

"Cytrine's. You?"

"Me too. Victory breakfast, right?"

"Yep. She probably invited all of the generals and the Majji too."

The girls chatted the rest of the way. Cytrine lived in the center of the village, just a few minutes from Cyrus bar. They could already hear people in the small house. Jasira knocked on the door, and Garret opened up.

"Hey, Sophia!" Garret said, and then turned to a cheery-faced Jasira. "Are you feeling alright enough to be here?" he asked with concern in his eyes.

"I'm fine." Jasira said, "Like I told Sophia, I'm just sore."

Garret shrugged. "Alright then, in that case, come on in; Cytrine has quite a spread."

There were six men in the house including Halcyon, Cyrus, and Garret. Cytrine's house was larger than most homes in Atara, save for Lee's. She had a large, rectangular table with two benches that could hold about ten people. Her house was long, with the kitchen on one side, the table on the other, a sitting area followed by a wall, and a doorway covered by a tapestry. Sophia figured that was her bedroom. Cytrine was hard at work, scrambling more eggs as the men gobbled their food and laughed like hyenas. Sophia walked to the kitchen area.

"Can I help you with anything?" she asked Cytrine.

"Nope, just sit and eat before there is nothing left."

Sophia wasn't going to argue, and Jasira wasted no time finding a spot at the table. She elbowed Garret as she reached for the bread. He playfully pulled her back by her shirt as she struggled for a roll. The two bickered for a moment. Then Cyrus placed some bread in front of Jasira. She stuck her tongue out at Garret. He smiled and continued to eat his food.

"Sit, sit, Sophia," Halcyon said. She sat next to him and grabbed some fruit. No bacon. Damn. She popped a grape in her mouth.

"Where is Lee?" Sophia asked Halcyon.

"Not sure. I figured he'd be here. Cytrine invited all of my generals."

As if he was cued, Lee pushed the tapestry over and appeared in the room, shirtless and groggy.

"What the hell was in that food last night, Cytrine?" Lee said with one hand on his head the other holding up his unfastened pants.

Then it went silent.

Dead silent.

Eerie silent.

Your ears could pop because it was so silent, silent.

Everyone was looking at Lee, except Cytrine, who continued cooking.

Lee's eyes widened as he took in his company. Cyrus,

Jasira, Garret, Halcyon, and Sophia with her eyes the size of saucers.

Garret was the first to break the silence with a high-pitched wail of laughter. He shook his head and continued to eat, and one by one people turned away from Lee and their conversations began again. Sophia looked at her folded hands, then her lap, then over to Lee. Halcyon placed his hand on Sophia's arm. She was breathing quickly, and her mind was a haze. Lee was her friend, her trainer. This shouldn't be affecting her the way it was. She should be laughing with Garret, but something deep down inside her was trying to pitch a hissy fit, and it was taking all of Sophia's self-control not to give in to it. She turned back to her hands with her brows furrowed. Jasira finished her cheese and walked up to Cytrine.

"Real nice, Cytrine," she whispered, "what the hell is wrong with you?"

"I have no idea what you mean."

"Seriously? That's the response I get? You're better than this." Jasira's voice rose with every word. "This breakfast had nothing to do with our victory, or to raise the spirits of our officers. It was to prove a petty point, wasn't it? You know we lost a lot of people yesterday, and this, this is what's on your mind."

"Don't care what this breakfast had to do with"—Garret swallowed a large mouthful of eggs—"its food and it's good."

"Oh, put a cork in it, Garret!" Jasira's hair whipped as she turned to face Garret.

Garret shrugged his shoulders and ate some more eggs. Sophia, not being able to make sense of anything, stood up and walked to the door.

"Thank you so much for the food, Cytrine."

Cytrine turned to Sophia. "I'm glad you liked it. Oh, and,"—she gestured her head towards Lee while keeping eye contact with Sophia—"that's for the nose." Each word was dripping with animosity.

Sophia turned out the door, and Jasira followed. Lee disappeared into Cytrine's sleeping area, then reappeared as he put on a shirt, then started after the two girls. He stopped short and stood beside Cytrine.

"Good gods, Cytrine, in what reality did you see our friendship surviving after this? What part of this did you see working out?"

"We worked out just fine last night, and I'd say you sure enjoyed working out with me."

Garret choked on his eggs as he tried to hold back a laugh.

"That's just great. You just informed your guests how easy it is to bed you."

"No. I just showed everyone how easy it is to use sex as a weapon. A very powerful and fun weapon."

Lee gritted his teeth. "Oh, go on, tell them more." Lee pointed to the table of people.

"Yes, please go on!" Garret raised his fork in the air and continued, "food and a show, this is so entertaining!"

Cytrine's eyes bore deep into Lee. "You keep saying you want 'Atara,' you want 'normal.' Not me because I want more, because I am 'different.' But guess what, Lee? She. Is. Different"—Cytrine pointed at his chest—"and she doesn't want to stay here either. Especially with the man who handed her husband over to certain death."

"That's enough, Cytrine!" Plates and cups rattled as Halcyon slammed his hands on the table. "Hand over your herbs and tinctures, all of them!" He stood up and maneuvered his way towards her. "Drugging a fellow Ataran for personal gain, I've never heard of such a thing. Our people are in mourning. Not only have we lost brothers and sisters, but we also lost the peace that was graciously bestowed upon us. We now have enemies outside of Atara, and I refuse to have my people become enemies within Atara."

"Enemy? Banish me then," she scoffed. "I've asked. I've pleaded, and you won't let me go!"

"So, you resort to this?"

Cytrine crossed her arms. "Sophia once told me, 'two birds, one stone.' Smart cookie, that one."

Halcyon looked up and let out a long exhale. "It's not up to me. You've tried to go on your own and the Green won't let you out of Atara. She doesn't trust you."

Cytrine's lip began to tremble and eyes water. She looked at Lee.

"You could have been happy. We could have gone to any town, away from here. Away from the poison that is slowly making its way here, away from war. But you didn't even want to try. You treated me awfully and still I held hope for you, for us. But I've had enough. You are a fool, Lee." With that, Cytrine walked into her room.

Cyrus stood up and searched through her pantry. He pulled several vials out, then examined a nearly empty jar.

"Vervain." He poured what was left of the herb out of the jar. "Used for relaxation, but a heavier dose can knock a man out."

Lee stood there, embarrassed. The men had finished eating and were clearing the table. Lee's gaze met with Halcyon's disapproving eyes. He didn't need those eyes; Lee already disapproved of himself and all the crappy decisions he made last night. He was going to get an earful, he knew it, but right now he had to go after Sophia. Lee walked out the door, slamming it behind him.

"Well, that was excessive," Garret said as he picked some fruit from a plate Cyrus was clearing.

When Lee caught up with Sophia, a small argument ensued. Jasira, who was with Sophia when Lee made it to them, stood to the side and watched it all unfold. It was then Sophia felt something happen within her. She loved Gabriel, she loved and missed him, but seeing Lee at Cytrine's like that woke something deep within her. She tried to suppress it, but Sophia couldn't control it anymore. It rose quickly from deep within, and in moments it took over her body.

"Not what it looked like, Leonardo?"

"Well, I—"

"Spent the night at Cytrine's, which meant at some point last night you made the conscious decision to go there."

Sophia struggled to gather herself; she heard everything that came out of her mouth but had no control of it. Panic shot through her. Sophia centered herself the way Lee taught her to and pushed down whatever it was that made her lose it. She felt it yield and retract back into her. Sophia took in a deep breath of relief, then covered her mouth. The drastic change in her body language was noticed by both Jasira and Lee, who looked at one another, searching for an explanation.

"I'll see you at weapons training," Sophia managed to say as she faced Lee and Jasira. "Jasira, please don't follow me. I'm not in the mood to have company." She then turned in time for her tears to fall unseen.

Jasira stood there with a perplexed look on her face. "What was that?" She pointed to where Sophia had walked off to. "For about a minute, she was an entirely different person. Tell me you saw that."

"Yeah. She must have been really upset about what happened at Cytrine's."

"I think you should steer clear from Cytrine for a while."

"Easier said than done."

"You haven't told her about the two survivors from her village, huh?"

"Didn't have much of a chance, now did I?" Lee said, staring into the distance.

"Cyrus stopped in to see them before he came to breakfast. He gave them some more healing herbs and relaxation tea. They went back to sleep after that. I'm heading there right now to check in on them." Jasira began to walk.

"I'll join you; I'm going to need to fill them in on what's been happening," Lee said.

47

A SOMBER REUNION

It was late afternoon, and Lee hadn't arrived at the training facility. Sophia didn't waste any time waiting for him. She flipped her sai from one position to the next, then took quick jabs into the air, followed by elbow hooks. She gracefully moved on the floor, dodging her imaginary foes. Her movements resembled dancing more than fighting. Her eyes closed, she slid from one position to the next. Carminda's face flashed in her mind. Her elegance and strength, Carminda must have been a fantastic warrior, Sophia thought as she continued her fluid motions, was this her? Was this Carminda? She could clearly envision how Carminda would have fought. Sophia then opened her eyes. She let out a soft laugh then jabbed forward.

"That's good, Sophia," Lee said as he entered the training circle. Sophia turned to face him. Almost immediately, she regretted everything that she said earlier. There was never going to be a right time to address this; it's best she got it out of the way now. Sophia felt terrible for acting childish. More important things were happening, and she refused to let something so trivial hinder her progress.

"I am so sorry," Still holding her sai, she dropped her arms. "It wasn't my place to say those things to you. You've been nothing but kind to me, and I completely lost it. You are a good friend. I shouldn't have treated you that way."

There was some restraint in Lee's face that Sophia caught. He motioned as if he was about to say something but then thought better of it.

"Sophia, when you were healing from your wounds, Cytrine came across two strangers in our woods. They had been trapped there for a while." Lee waved at the doorway as he continued to speak to her. "One was wounded and both emaciated, they've been healing and staying at my place." Both Domingo and Santiago walked through the doorway. "They claim to be from Salinas, and we are all pretty sure we saw them performing that day in Tychi."

Sophia's sai made a clinking sound as they hit the ground. Her chest began to rise and fall rapidly, then she was running before she knew it and flung herself into the brothers, each arm wrapped around a neck. The brothers closed the circle and embraced her. Together, the trio fell to the ground. There they shared a bittersweet welcome.

"Sophia, our little Sophia, your ability to cheat death continues to amaze us," Domingo said as he kissed her forehead. Sophia grabbed Domingo's hand and placed it on her cheek as she cried.

"We are so sorry we weren't there." Santiago brushed Sophia's hair off her face. "We are so sorry. Your friend Lee told us everything." He kissed her hair. "We should have told you."

Sophia continued to cry.

"We thought if nothing were to come of what Carla had told us, you would at least have lived a normal life," Domingo said. Sophia turned up and looked at him. He wiped her eyes with his thumb, then continued, "and if the worst were to happen, we would protect you. Everything happened so quickly, we had no idea we were walking into a trap. Please forgive us."

Sophia's sobs slowed.

"None of it matters"—she looked at the brothers—"you are here." After a few good minutes, Sophia let the brothers go and sat back, she wiped tears from her eyes, took some breaths, and gathered herself. She felt a powerful stirring inside her. The feeling was similar to when she confronted Lee this morning but differed because she knew it was the Essence within her. It was speaking, and she needed to relay the messages without being so fervently out of control. Sophia took another moment before she spoke.

"She loved you so much," Sophia said to Domingo, referring to Eilith. "When all of that Essence entered me, hopes and dreams, intentions, emotions, all of it intertwined, it was all so confusing. I was consumed and lost. I could feel the struggling and fighting; however, some of the Essence was trying to gain order within itself. Getting through it all was hard. But, of all the Essence, four rose stronger than the rest, sending a sense of familiarity towards me. Like pillars they stood. I lay in the center and saw them surround me and hold the other Essence at bay. They gave me the strength to hang on, to come back from the darkness."

Lee listened intently and recognized that moment; it was back in Salinas, right after she was attacked by the Essence when Sophia lay dead in his arms.

"It was Ari, Carminda, Marcello, and Eilith," Sophia continued. "They told me their story, and I could feel them. The love Eilith had for you, Domingo, cannot be compared to anything I've ever experienced. Ari and Carminda are happy now; so are our people. It's how I've found peace, and you must too."

Domingo's face crumpled and he leaned on his brother's shoulder. Lee understood that this was a personal moment for the three and that he should take his leave. Without saying a word, he took a few steps back towards the door. They could train a little longer tomorrow afternoon. Sophia looked up and shook her head 'no' and mouthed, "Stay, please." Lee looked into her eyes. It was then, at that exact moment, that Lee finally accepted that whatever that woman wanted from him he was going to give. He leaned back against the wall and crossed his arms and gave Sophia an acknowledging nod. Sophia then closed her eyes and grimaced. Lee walked towards her. She clutched at her chest, then folded over. Domingo reached towards her as bright green Essence escaped her body. It came out of her and encompassed both Domingo and Santiago. Sophia shook slightly as her body began to sway and her sight darkened. Just in time, Lee's warm arms wrapped around her. He was on his knees, holding her.

"Thank you," She whispered.

"Anytime," Lee said as he helped her stabilize. Sophia sat back on her legs. Lee cautiously let her go, making sure she could support herself. Still shaking, Sophia touched Domingo's hand. His eyes were wide with confusion.

"Marcello stayed with me, but when he realized you both lived he wanted to join with you," she said. Sophia smiled. "He was so happy you were alive. It's been a while since I sensed anyone. Usually, once Essence merges, it's merged for good. But the link between the three of you is abnormally strong."

"Our brother lives within us now?"

"No, not live. He's long since passed, but he will always be a part of you, giving you strength when you need it. I've learned that the deceased can share their Essence with a loved one, but it's only possible if that person is near them when they pass and with the help of a Majji. If not, they just join the Green. I served as a vessel in this case. Helping the Essence that's been close to each other for decades finally join as one. Atara is a magical place; Essence lives and breathes freely here. I'm sure you'll sense his energy within you both soon. The more you remain here, the more you stay together, the more you will sense him."

It had been several weeks since the brothers had seen Sophia, but the change they were witnessing was drastic. They both looked intently at her, and the eyes that looked back at them were not the eyes of the young woman they knew in her twenties but of a wise woman with hundreds of years of knowledge. Domingo put his hand on his brother's shoulder. Santiago gave a slight nod. The acknowledgment was made that there was more going on than they understood, and now was not the time to address it.

"How did our brother fall?" Santiago asked.

"Marcello was brave," she said with a peaceful smile. "He sacrificed himself to aid Eilith. She was a powerful mage, Domingo. If the Ibex Warrior Tribe flourished, she'd be one of the strongest among them. Her cast took down an entire army and Corentin."

"Corentin?" Domingo said. "Now I believe you when you say she's at peace. That bastard hunted her people, even killed her aunt while she hid high in a tree." Domingo sighed. "It's good to know they are at peace. All of them."

Sophia smiled and with Lee's assistance stood up. They

shared what knowledge they knew, and Sophia gaped when she learned that Lee gave his home away to the brothers. Then it was Lee's turn to gape when Sophia offered her house to him.

"What?"

"You have nowhere to stay. You kept me safe at your house when I had nowhere to go. Please let me return the favor."

They had a few drinks at Sophia's, and the brothers admired her home's location. Zephyr zipped by for a quick welcome and had Sophia formerly introduce them. Of course, she had exclaimed, "I told you he was real!" several times before they left the house. They went to Cyrus' bar and caught up with Jasira, Garret, and Cyrus.

All in all, it turned out to be a good night. It was nice to put the battle and that morning's debacle behind them. Lee sat and watched as Sophia laughed along with her fellow townspeople. He kept a smile on his face, but deep down inside he was full of worry and concern. His mentor, the man he looked up to as a father, was dying, and in two weeks he, Sophia, and other Atarans were going to embark on a perilous journey to a place that even he wasn't ready to see. Atarans knew of the World's End; it was a very dark time of their history. They were taught as children about their horrible past and the wars that came from it. The rest of the towns and even Tychi deny it ever happened; after a few years of not teaching or speaking of it, the knowledge of it just ceased to exist. It was one of the many things that fueled Lee's hatred of Tychi and towns like it. Ignorance drove him mad. Lee sipped his agave and nodded to Cyrus.

Sophia examined Lee and contemplated what was that feeling she had earlier. Why did it feel as if she was sharing her body with the Essence of the Apprentice and another entity? But is that how it was supposed to feel like? Is this what it was like for her grandmother, Leata? At some point, Lee noticed Sophia as she stared at him. He laughed gently and mouthed, "are you okay?" Sophia snapped back, turned red, and held her drink to her cheek. Lee smiled and shook his head.

"Oh, one day I'll beat him at Kings!" Jasira said then hiccupped. "Cyrus has been teaching me!" She pointed to Cyrus with an empty cup in her hand. Garret returned with two glasses full of beer. He swapped the empty cup out of Jasira's hand. He sat down next to her, and she gave him a smile.

"This dagger in my spine hurts, Cyrus," Lee said with a laugh.

"Don't put me in the same category as a common turncoat," Cyrus said as he poured a drink behind the bar and handed it to a patron. "You are a master at that game, and when you play Jasira you don't teach her, you destroy her. It's about time you have a rival. With her mind and proper instruction, she'll have you running for the hills." Cyrus said.

"Obviously. Why do you think I never taught her?" Lee nudged Jasira. "I'm not ready to relinquish my title as, what is it you called it? Oh, yes. MASTER!" Lee's voice dropped a few octaves as the last word came out of his mouth. The group laughed.

"Kings?" Sophia said, "Isn't that an old man's game?"

Jasira furiously waved her arms, trying to get Sophia's attention. By the time Sophia noticed, Jasira's palms were already covering her face.

"Old man's?" Lee called out. "No way, it's all about strategy and wits!"

"Oh." Sophia said, "It's just I only saw elders play that game."

"It's an ancient game, dates back further than you can possibly imagine."

"Oh, hell, here we go," Jasira said as she got up. "I'm going to call it a night; if you all were smart, you'd do the same too. He's about to go on a tangent."

Everyone pondered their options, then one by one started fake yawning and stretching. Cyrus began to laugh again.

"Hey, guys, come on. It's really a great story," Lee insisted.

"Yeah, I'm a bit tired, it's been a long night, maybe some other time," Santiago said.

"I agree. I'm wiped," Sophia added.

"I don't want to hear your stupid story," Garret said, then patted Lee's shoulder and left. He waved his hand to the group as he walked off.

"Why couldn't we just do that?" Domingo whispered to Santiago as he pointed to Garret. Jasira overheard and unsuccessfully covered her mouth to prevent her drink from spraying out when she chuckled. They all started to laugh again.

"Yeah, real freaking funny." Lee rolled his eyes.

They said their goodnights and began walking out the door. Sophia told Lee she would have blankets set out for him when he got in. He had almost forgotten that she had invited him to stay at her place. It would be nice to be close to her again, but his confusion grew. At some points, he swore she returned his feelings, like the outburst this morning. Then he thought it was all in his head, like when she apologized to him this afternoon. Lee walked to the bar and sat.

"I'm not giving you a free drink," Cyrus said.

"I'd never take advantage of our friendship like that," Lee said with a smile. "Listen, Cyrus, you already know about the mission Halcyon has tasked me with."

"Yes."

"I want you in my party when I go west. But I don't want Jasira. She's too young, this journey is going to be rough, maybe too much for her."

"She only looks young; Jasira is two years over two decades. She goes," Cyrus said adamantly.

"Well, when you say it like that, she sounds like an elder. She still hasn't been training as long as we have. Please don't fight me on this. I already have to deal with the fact that I have to take Sophia, I can't handle having to worry about Jasira."

"You don't have to worry about her. Leave that to me."

"Gods, you are thick."

"No, Lee, I am bonded, and when it happens to you then you will understand. Where I go, she goes; where she goes, I go. Always."

Lee was now thoroughly frustrated. Only the experienced should go on this journey. He understood they were bonded, but for crying out loud why would Cyrus put his partner in danger like that?

"Oh, really? Where she goes you go? Well, she went out the door. Why don't you follow?" Lee mocked while he gestured towards the door.

Cyrus gave Lee a flat look

Lee sighed. He would poke fun at Cyrus for his devotion to Jasira, but in all honesty he was jealous.

"How do you know, man? That what you feel for her isn't just the bond trying to keep you closer?" Lee asked.

"The bond made me want to protect her, to fight alongside her, always to put her safety above others. She was the one that made me fall in love with her. When we bonded, I didn't instantly fall in love with her. It came years later."

"And she?"

"Still needs to figure things out," Cyrus said as he pushed back from the bar and towards the divider that led to his room. "But this isn't about Jasira and me, is it?"

"Am I that transparent?"

Cyrus chuckled. "Come, I'll make some tea, we can talk before you go to Sophia's."

48

THE SECRET
SALINAN SURVIVORS

It was nighttime and Weiya, the former Mother Courtesan of Salinas, hid her long mahogany hair under her brown hooded cloak. She looked like a commoner in Vizzini, which was exactly what she was trying to do. Weiya had sent out one of her Chevaliers to meet with an informant. He was to return tonight. The informant, an Elite man with ties to the Osprey, was a customer of hers who had frequented the House in Salinas. In all actuality, several men of high standing in Tychi had visited the Courtesan House. She thought it was best to keep that information from Domingo. The Elite man in question had fallen head over knickers for Weiya, and she used that to her advantage. Hours before the attack on Salinas, he had warned her. She had no time to go across town to ring the bell or to inform Eilith. Weiya needed to protect her people. She evacuated the members of her House first, then with the night as her ally she warned many citizens of Salinas. When the dawn began to crest the horizon, Weiya knew she did the best she could. She was the last to emerge from the tunnel and was faced with dozens of bleak faces looking to her for direction.

"We must split up. All of us," Weiya had said, weeks ago to the dirt-covered Salinans. "Jaru, Tavernport, and Crossings Forged. Do not go to Vizzini. Exercise as much caution as possible and keep an eye out for factions of bandits and thieves. Know that some of them will do you harm but keep an eye out for those you can join. Never tell anyone that you were from Salinas." The people nodded. "Those of you with children, Jaru will be the safest town. If any of you have strong, trusting connections, now is the time to contact them." Weiya motioned to one of the Chevaliers from her House. "We brought through all of our rations. We've also been keeping a good stock of dry rice on the other side of this tunnel here." She pointed to a dead tree stump, where a female member of her House pulled out a handful of small handbags. "There is enough for all of us and our journey. All of you be safe. And may the gods be with you." She watched as, one by one, the Salinan citizens grabbed rations and disappeared into the woods. A tall, slender, chiseled-jawed, attractive Chevalier walked up to her.

"Weiya. Where are we to go now?"

She looked at his tan skin which accentuated his light amber eyes. She ran her hands through his blonde hair with a strong parental love that she shared for all of her Chevaliers and Courtesans.

"Alejandro," she said with such caring gentleness. "You all," she addressed the members of her House, "have a choice." Her Courtesans and Chevaliers all assembled around her. "We have made some strong connections in doing what we do. If you chose to seek refuge with someone who has offered it to you and that you trust, then seek them out, and if they ask, you must marry them. Change your look, change your name,

283

and find a new trade."

"What if that is not what we want?" a mesmerizing female beauty asked.

"Then you can come with me to Vizzini. Vizzini is my former home and where I was raised. My family owns a tea trade there. We can continue our business behind a tea storefront. I've retained many strong allies there. I'm sure the planned attack on Salinas has been spoken of there, so I will be expected." She smiled at them.

"What if that is not enough?" Alejandro asked as he placed his forehead on Weiya. Tears fell from his eyes. "What if we want vengeance for the lives we couldn't save?"

Weiya pushed him away.

"We cannot take on Kahel. Our combat training is not at the level of his Greys and Osprey. I will not start a fight we cannot win." She looked at her people. "Those of you who want to leave to find those who have offered you sanctuary, please go now, and may the god be with you."

No one moved.

"Then Vizzini it is."

No one moved.

"Don't be fools," she snapped, "I am offering you a chance to start again, doing what we do."

Alejandro looked at the horizon, the sun was high up. "By now, Salinas will be nothing but ash. It may not have been your home, but it was ours, Weiya. We were never fully accepted anywhere else, but there at Salinas we were family, and Kahel has just taken all that away. The children that we couldn't save, there were so many. I would rather die in pain, covered in blood, doing something to thwart Kahel than wrapped in silk, living in luxury, doing 'what we do.'"

This was hard for Weiya to process. She had always lived her life with survival as her main goal. She'd gone where she had to go, do what she had to do, and at times betray who she had to betray, just to survive. But that was until Salinas, that was before her Courtesans and Chevaliers, that was before she had anything to lose. Weiya looked at her people.

No.

Weiya looked at her family, who loved and accepted her for who she was.

"Gods dammit! Do you all feel this way?"

The Courtesans and Chevaliers nodded. Weiya exhaled and conceded.

"Alright." She sat on her heels and ran her hands through her hair. "We need to establish ourselves in Vizzini first. There's a little over a dozen of us. We can't all go in at once, especially dressed like this." Weiya stood up and gestured her clothing. She had a point. All of the Courtesans and Chevaliers wore dirtied lavish fabrics that enveloped their bodies most proactively. "Crossings Forged has everything we need, and their gates are open all night. Let's, each of us, call in some favors."

They had spent several nights in Crossings Forged, each of them attaining different attire and new identities, all of it paid for by the skills of their trade and a promise to welcome their patrons with open arms once a new House was erected in Vizzini.

Vizzini, the town of scholars was sprinkled with Elites and commoners. But the ratio of scholars far outnumbered the latter two. The town was heavily funded by Kahel, therefore it had backed him unequivocally. That was until the attack on Salinas. While they swore fealty, they secretly despised their King. This profoundly played in Weiya's favor. The visual layout of Vizzini was much like that of Tychi. Just abundantly smaller. You had your houses made of stone and wood, painted in yellows, whites, and muted greens, some even splashed with a faded rouge. Smaller steam-powered machines hobbled along the clean cobblestone road. Weiya had to jump clear from a comically miniature vehicle that putted steam and rode low to the ground. It carried two people in a long, metal cylinder that moved around on eight, metal, squat legs. The passengers wore thick, black goggles and sat so low their heads barely met her hips.

"Out of the way, tech-testing!" The irritated voice was sharp and staccato.

"Scholars." Weiya rolled her eyes. When Weiya had first arrived at the three-story teahouse, she had noticed that the foundation was sturdy, but the aesthetics were in rough shape. The once-vibrant, turquoise, wooden double doors now were dull and lifeless. Two of the glass panes in the door grill were cracked. The black paint on the first story was chipped and peeling, and glass on the windows that matched the grilling on the door was in dire need of washing. The shutters on the second- and third-floor windows were shut, and the white paint that had once seemed so welcoming on the exterior of those two floors had faded to a murky grey. Weiya had stormed into the shop and dropped her bags. The interior of the teashop was well-kept, a surprising change from what she had just seen.

The manager she had employed walked out from the back. He wiped his hands on his apron. Then smiled widely when he saw her face.

"Weiya," the jet-black-haired man said as he placed his hands on his hips. His smile made his gently sun-kissed skin glow. "I knew I didn't have to worry about you."

Weiya smirked and harumphed playfully. "It takes more than a wayward army to take me down." She looked at her establishment. "So, what happened out there?"

"Can't find any help here in Vizzini. Scholars and Elites want their elixirs and teas and to tinker with their toys, read scrolls or just do nothing. They do not care to make extra coin doing hard labor."

"So," Weiya thought out loud. "It wouldn't be too suspicious if we bring in 'workers' from outside to help with some renovations."

"Always something up your sleeve." The man leaned forward on the counter. His muscles almost busted through his shirt. "What's the plan?"

"Pour me some black tea, and pour yourself a mug too."

The manager raised an eyebrow and laughed as he turned to prepare the tea.

During the day, the manager and Weiya restored the shop, and during the night they would secretly escort the Courtesans and Chevaliers through the town and into the shop under the guise of workers. The more people Weiya brought in, the faster the restoration had become. In less than one moon's cycle, the work was complete. Weiya watched as the Courtesans and Chevaliers put the final touches to the first-floor teashop, adding brilliantly colored pillows on the floor around the low, dark, wooden tables. The sheer, colored fabrics that were hung from the ceiling gave the tables against the walls some privacy while also adding to the aesthetics of the shop. She had already assigned out the upstairs rooms, and each Courtesan and Chevalier arranged their space to whichever way they pleased. An old storage room in the back of the first floor was cleared out and renovated into exceptional living quarters for the manager. He would run the teashop portion of the House until dusk, then would retire to his room. It wasn't kindness on Weiya's part at all. She knew to take great care of those who held her secrets, but most importantly she knew to keep them close.

Weiya adjusted the brown hooded cloak as she closed her eyes to the night sky. Everything that happened had happened so quickly. And now here she was waiting patiently for Alejandro, who was due to return from Tychi tonight. The visit was risky, to say the least, but there was no talking him out of it. He had promised her that his clients would ensure his safety and met with Weiya's informant.

Alejandro appeared in the outskirts of Vizzini. She rushed over and swung her cloak off, then around him. With the cover of darkness, the pair maneuvered their way to the teahouse undetected.

"You okay?" Weiya asked as she prepared herbal tea for Alejandro. She watched as he flopped down, seemingly weighted by the information. She walked over and handed him the hot cup. Two things, Weiya knew: one the others were upstairs listening in, and two she was not going to like what Alejandro had to say.

"The people of Tychi are all prisoners. The Elite are allowed passage through Tychi only after stating what their business outside Tychi is."

Weiya gathered her skirt from under her and sat down.

"Domingo and Santiago survived the ambush in Tychi. Carminda was mortally wounded during the strike and died with Ari in the attack on Salinas. Domingo was spotted assisting an injured Santiago into the Northern Woods. They never reemerged."

"Do you think?" Weiya interrupted.

"No, not yet, Weiya. I haven't gotten to the crazy part yet."

Weiya sat back, befuddled for a moment, then let him continue.

"Eilith cast. She cast an incredible spell with the help of Marcello." Alejandro finally looked up at Weiya. "Your Elite told me that they called her 'Ibex Warrior,' and she took down the whole army and killed Kahel's number one, Corentin."

Weiya's mouth opened but no words came out.

"Gabriel's in the dungeons of Tychi's castle"—Alejandro

placed his hand on Weiya's shoulder—"and Sophia, no one knows anything about Sophia. She's gone missing. But—"

Weiya looked up at Alejandro hopeful of receiving a speck of good news.

"But I think that she is in Atara. There would be no other reason for Domingo and Santiago to wander into those woods. We should investigate that. After all, we are here in Vizzini, the town of scholars. Let's read up all we can on the history of Atara. I doubt they are monsters like we've been told. All the years that Salinas was an established town, they never attacked."

"Yes," Weiya said with life finally back in her body. "Yes, we will do our research. Texts, scrolls, maps, everything we can get our hands on. When we are fully armed with knowledge, we'll lead a group into the Northern Woods." The moment she finished her sentence, she heard light pitter-patters down the steps. The Chevaliers and Courtesans all appeared, insisting on their participation.

49

HARROWING
MISSION

Zephyr stood uneasy. The cold season had arrived, and nights were darker and the air cooler. Sophia sat outside her small wooden deck with an alpaca-wool blanket wrapped around her.

"I cannot join you in this journey," Zephyr said "I tried to plead with Halcyon to let you stay, but he refused. The Majji said it's 'the Green's will for you to go.' He is a foolish old man who thinks you are the answer to the questions left after Leata's death." Zephyr clicked his beak in annoyance. "Lee will tell you to join his group, but refuse him. You think you've seen evil in the eyes of Kahel, yet that is nothing compared to what you are about to face there. Your destination is a dark place, and the path there is full of Mad Essence and creatures you have yet to understand."

"Why can't you go with me? I feel so safe when you are around," Sophia asked as she pulled her legs under the blanket.

Zephyr lowered his head and closed his eyes.

"I am forbidden to cross the Iceway, and even if I flew across it I'd cease to exist the moment I enter the Graveland."

"Because you are composed of Essence?"

"Correct."

"And Mad Essence absorbs all good Essence." Sophia thought for a moment, then looked up at her winged friend. "Am I going to go mad?"

"Humans have a better chance of survival than creatures like me."

"So, the chances of us returning from this mission are slim?"

Zephyr nodded his head.

"Why?"

Silence.

"Zephyr, he wouldn't put me in any kind of danger unless there was a reason. Right?" His silence wasn't comforting at all.

"They aren't going there just to contain the Mad Essence, are they? What aren't you telling me?"

Sophia heard steps coming her way, she looked over to see Lee walking in their direction. His breath could be seen in the cold night.

"What I'm guessing Zephyr hasn't told you is that we are going there possibly to release it," Lee interrupted. "I don't want you to go either, but the Majji has his reasons. We don't question them," he said pointedly.

Zephyr shrieked and shot a gust of wind at Lee, knocking him to the ground. Lee got up with his blade in hand.

"I've just about had it with you."

Zephyr puffed his chest and spread his wings.

"Stop!" Sophia demanded. They obliged, leaving her at a loss for words. She wasn't too sure what to make of their sudden obedience. Sophia walked towards Zephyr, he bowed, and she rubbed his beak.

"I'll be okay."

He let out a small cry and nuzzled her chest.

"Perv," Lee said under his breath. Zephyr snapped his head towards Lee.

"No," Sophia gently whispered. Zephyr relaxed and lowered his body to the ground. "You are my closest friend, and you are one of my first memories. I know you have my best interest in mind, but I feel like this is something I have to do. Promise to be here to wish me farewell."

"Of course."

Sophia kissed Zephyr's beak. Zephyr gave Sophia's hair one last toss before he dissipated into the air. Sophia turned to Lee, as he reached her deck and sat down across from her.

"We have to retrieve the other half of Halcyon's staff," he said. "Hundreds of years ago, Neith, the First Majji, and her people fought a long, grueling war. She was able to trick Mad Essence into her. She then stabbed herself with her staff, trapping it inside her. With her last breath, she snapped her staff in half and handed it to her second in command. He then became the Second Majji. Since then, when an Apprentice becomes a Majji, half of the staff is handed down to them. The staff is made from Anadenanthera and cannot be recreated."

"Anadenanthera, isn't that the Tree of Life?"

"The one and only," Lee replied as he reached inside the house and grabbed a blanket. He opened it up and placed it on his lap. "Halcyon has no Apprentice, no heir. So, he wants to give us all as much of a chance of surviving as possible. He wants to reunite the staff."

"Let's say that we make it back from this apparent suicide quest, is that even going to work?"

Lee leaned back on a post and looked up into the night sky "I don't know, Sophia."

They sat outside in silence for a while before heading

inside and going to sleep. Lee slept on the floor near the wood stove while Sophia stayed in the small loft area.

The next two weeks went by quickly. Sophia continued her training, rapidly improving her combat skills. Jasira and Cyrus traveled to Jaru and Crossings Forged to collect equipment, rations, and the necessities for the group. Lee worked fervently, mapping out their projected path and gaining as much information as he could. Along with the research, he took time to choose his travel party carefully. Cyrus, Jasira, and Sophia were a given. The brothers refused to take no for an answer when offering to join the party.

"Not only is Sophia family, but we were also tasked to protect her. We will never leave her side again." Looking into Domingo's face that was full of resolve, Lee conceded. Lee had also asked Garret and his bond partner, Raja, to join. Raja, a tan man whose height and muscular build would make a dire wolf piss itself, was a gentle soul that balanced out Garret's abrasive personality. Garret and Raja had fought alongside one another since they were seventeen. Finally, Lee added two experienced navigators, Quentin and Suresh. Best friends and bond partners for over five decades, Quentin and Suresh were the oldest in the party. While Quentin had dark skin and dark hair pulled back in a short, neat ponytail, Suresh had lighter skin and white hair separated in two braids. Both men kept facial hair, which made them look older than they really were. The pair possessed the most knowledge of the Iceway and the lands past it. They would often return from reconnaissance missions with healing injuries and harrowing stories from the frozen Iceway.

50

TALBOT
AND YAREN

Far out in the eastern ocean, Talbot tilted Yaren's head back and poured several drops of fresh water into her mouth. Their rations were running low, and he had no clue how much longer they were going to be out to sea. The last few days had been tough on their spirits. After barely escaping Tychi and taking refuge in Darwin's Trail, they cut north to Jaru. There, Yaren had discreetly sold some jewelry to obtain lodging, new supplies, and clothing. Talbot had connections in Jaru, which helped keep them hidden in the town. It was there they learned of the massacre of the Salinans. It was as if the wind had been taken out of their sails. The Atarans had not come to help, and for all they knew the Kalyptra was still up.

The Kalyptra was a magic barrier in the form of a thick fog that began east of Tavernport, a great distance out into the ocean, and traveled north to the Nacunas. Ships that dared to venture east could get lost, and those that went north would disappear. If they did return, it would be in the form of debris and driftwood.

The room they hid in while in Jaru was small and glum. The walls were a dark wood that remained undecorated. There were two small beds and a pan for everyday bodily needs. While it reminded Talbot more of a holding cell, he was happy that he was able to keep Yaren safe thus far. But still, he wanted to go back to his Inn, and back in time to talk Yaren out of her crazy idea. Sure, he'd still be in Tychi, but at least Yaren would still have her home in the Elite District and he would have his Inn.

"We have to go to them," Yaren said as she sat cross-legged on her bed.

"Them? The Ibex Warrior Tribe? You can't be serious. Those are myths. No one knows if they are still alive."

"If the Kalyptra is still up, they still live. You know this. Kahel is destroying our world. They must know that the treaty has been broken." Yaren said.

"Yes, yes. But you forget, I am not willing to travel to Tavernport. And, say we did, we don't even have a boat."

"Get a boat and have it meet us south of Tavernport," Yaren added stubbornly.

Naturally, Yaren had gotten her way, because here they were, out at sea. The boat rocked back and forth as the waves gently patted it. The fog was so dense that if you cupped your hand and opened it, you would find a small cloud inside. Talbot dropped the anchor, and it hit bottom quickly. Still, they couldn't see past their noses. He had a keen sense of direction, but it meant nothing here, where even if he were on the right course he would never find land. This far from Kahel, magic is strong. And the inhabitants past the Kalyptra preferred not to be found.

"They haven't dropped the Kalyptra," Talbot said to Yaren.

"It will happen; we may not be alive when it does," she

said with a gentle smile, "but our efforts will not have been in vain. They know who we are and know we're here. Everything has been set in motion."

"We are dangerously low on supplies. We need to go back to land." Talbot knelt by Yaren.

"Kahel will be waiting for us."

"I know." Talbot exhaled.

"I'd rather die here on this boat than give him the satisfaction."

"Yaren," Talbot said softly. "I will not watch you die." A tear broke free from his disheveled face. "I stood idly by and let your sister die. I can't, not again, not if there is a chance you will survive. I'm taking the boat back to shore. To Tavernport."

Yaren shifted on Talbot's lap and snuggled towards his abdomen.

"No."

"Yaren."

"I said no."

"Dammit, you are as stubborn as your sister."

"Runs in the family," she said with a smile. "We will retrace our steps. Touch land south of Tavernport, get as many supplies as possible, return the boat, then head far south.

"Kahel's armada is out at sea searching for us, and you want us to head towards them?"

"Don't you remember? His armada is docked. With Salinas mysteriously gone and his citizens asking questions, he's going to need many men at Tychi to control them, and that includes his armada."

"Not all, some will be out at sea between Tavernport and Tychi."

"Then this wonderful steamboat of yours will have to be very quiet." Yaren smiled.

"Okay, let's say we land without getting caught, get enough supplies, and head west without getting caught, what then?"

"Dock at Carion and pray the Kalyptra is dropped."

"Carion? It's a ghost town." Talbot, now visibly exasperated, put a free hand on his temple.

"Exactly. No one will search for us in a place where there are no resources ready. Me, an Elite Lady who is accustomed to servants doing everything for her, and you a simple Innkeeper, Carion would mean death to us." Yaren pushed herself away from Talbot and looked at him with hope in her eyes. "But we've lived off the land for years. It is a perfect place for us to hide."

"Yes," Talbot said resignedly, "it is." He gently placed Yaren down and stood up. His boat was a modest size, with an under cabin that slept four. Yaren refused to go down there; she wanted to breathe the free fresh air as long as possible. Talbot left her on the bench and walked to the deck. He raised anchor and looked into the fog.

"Cowards! This is your fight too!" He yelled into the dense fog. "What good does it do, hiding? When the time comes, there will be nothing left to claim!" His voice echoed, with no response. Talbot started the boat engine. It sputtered, then putted, and the gears began moving. Steam billowed from a tall pipe, and Talbot turned the boat around.

51

THE ICEWAY

The morning of their departure came. The air was crisp, and the sun's light began to creep across the land. As promised, Zephyr was there to say goodbye to Sophia. She leaned up against her friend and rubbed her arms in anticipation. Garret's seven sisters fussed over him, then exchanged playful punches then hugs. Jasira's parents were holding her and getting in as many kisses as possible. Tears fell from her father's face; he, like his daughter, had pale hair that came down to his chin and dark skin. Her mother was tall and slender with dark brown hair tied in braids. She sniffled and wiped a tear from her caramel face. The parents didn't want to release Jasira.

But eventually, they relinquished their daughter. One by one, the families said goodbye and walked off, leaving the group and Halcyon in silence. Sophia kissed Zephyr's beak, and he walked away, then dispersed into the air.

Halcyon stood up. The group went down on their knees, all except Sophia, Domingo, and Santiago.

"Guys," Lee said, "down." The three looked around, slightly confused as they kneeled like the others. Halcyon let out a smile and shook his head. He began to chant. He held his broken staff directly in front of him, then pointed it up towards the sky. The air around them began to vibrate, and Sophia saw Jasira's hair lift for a moment, then go back down to her shoulders. Sophia felt invigorated, her heart elated, her mind focused, and most importantly she felt determined. She looked up at Halcyon.

"May the gods be with you," he said. Halcyon placed a hand on his forehead and stumbled back. Garret and Lee shot up to support Halcyon. They sat him down on the lip of a well.

"Sophia, come." Halcyon waved her over. Sophia rubbed her arms and walked to Halcyon. "As you travel into the Iceway, gifts will awaken within you. You carry the Essence of the Apprentice, so the further you proceed into the Iceway the stronger our bond will become. Don't fight it; in dire situations being able to connect with me hundreds of miles away can come in handy." Halcyon gently laughed. He closed his eyes and attempted to steady his weakened body. "We don't have much time." He then lowered his head between his knees. Halcyon sat there for a moment, catching his breath. When he looked up, he saw ten pairs of eyes on him.

"Well, what are you waiting for? Get the hell out of here!"

Sophia had never been to the Western point of the crescent-shaped forest that was the Northern Woods. She knew it was safe, but in this situation fear was more potent than her curiosity. All those horror stories she was told as a child were enough to subconsciously keep her from wandering into the western point of anyplace. Just like the stories told about the Atarans, the people who lived in the west were also considered immoral and dangerous. They wouldn't eat you alive, which gave her hope; however, they would bludgeon you to a bloody pulp if they spotted you, which took her recently acquired hope away. At least the Atarans knew how to be resourceful, she thought to herself. If the stories about the Atarans were all false, maybe the stories about the people of the west were too. Once the group entered the western tip of the forest, the trees quickly thinned and led to a trail between the Nacunas. They all stood just outside the path and marveled at this natural wonder. The mountain walls towered above them like ice giants competing in height. Sophia nearly strained her neck attempting to capture their full altitude. The group took a collective breath and then wandered in. Sophia watched curiously as Quentin, Suresh, and Raja placed their hands on their holsters. Sophia had never spoken with Quentin and Suresh, but their skins were both covered in scars, telling stories of numerous battles. She had also seen them that awful morning at Cytrine's. They had been helping Lee during the planning, but at most her interaction with them has been a slight head bow in her direction.

The path was wide enough for the group to walk side by side with some room to spare. It wasn't wide enough for Sophia, though; she felt her heart rate jump and panic grow deep within her. She had never been claustrophobic in her life, not even that time she hid under her house for hours from her mother because she tied Marcello high up on a tree for dipping her hair in the ink well. But, these walls, they terrified her. The invigoration she felt earlier began to fade. She could see fog ahead of them, obscuring their vision.

"Something more," she mumbled to herself, "there is something more." The sensation that there was a piece of valuable information that she should know was making her uneasy. Sophia rubbed her arms in frustration. Rubbing her arms together had become a coping mechanism for her. Santiago saw her and held his hand out, and she accepted the invitation. Sophia walked close to the brothers. Their presence made her feel a little better, but she still felt as if there was more to this journey. Lee looked back and noticed Sophia's body language.

"On the other side of the mountain is the Pyre River and Salinas." Lee's voice broke the silence. "This trail leads us far west. The Nacunas offer us cover and protection."

Quentin looked back and scoffed. His dark skin strangely glistened with sweat on the cold path.

They had been walking for a good hour when Sophia's instincts were about to explode. The Majji said her gifts would awaken, and with her senses heightened she thought that this had to be it. Something was coming. Something terrible, and it seemed like the Atarans knew it. She felt an inexplicable anger boil inside of her. Just as she was about to demand answers, Suresh held a hand up and stopped the group.

"Weapons out," he said, "slow now, be on alert." They all followed his instructions.

"Lee?" Sophia asked and waited for a response, but when she received none she continued. "The moment I saw those walls, I felt threatened. Anything you should tell me?"

The group came to a dead stop, and all the Atarans turned to look at Lee.

"You didn't tell them?" Jasira said while holding out a small blade.

"Didn't tell us what?" Domingo asked.

"Gods, Lee, what the hell, you needed to prepare them!" Jasira called out.

"I was hoping I wouldn't have to." Lee shrugged.

The group started to walk cautiously into the fog.

Lee took a defeated breath. "You feared the Atarans because of the stories you were told right?" he said. "'Don't go north to Atara because they are savages, they will begin their feast while you cry for mercy."

"Yes? And?" Sophia replied.

"Well, us Atarans had our own stories as children, but ours were true." Lee looked wearily at Sophia, then turned to face the fog. "Don't go to the far west, the Fae will massacre you."

"FAE?!" both brothers called out.

"DOWN!" Suresh yelled.

Sophia felt the brothers push her down to the cold ground; she looked up and saw only Suresh standing. He pulled a glass orb out of his coat and tossed it into the air. He sliced the sphere in half with his blade. The two segments burst into flames, creating a massive fireball. Suresh winced and shielded his face with his arm. He took a few steps back and watched. Just as quickly as the fireball appeared, giant shards of ice flew in from ahead of them. The fireball caught the shards and stopped them from coming any closer to the group. It rapidly grew in size, melting every single ice shard that had come their way. When the fire evaporated, they stood up. Domingo walked to Lee and punched him in the stomach. Lee let out a grunt and bent over in pain.

"Fae?! Is this the truth you speak? You are taking us to the Fae?"

"No, not taking you TO the Fae," Lee responded in obvious discomfort. "Taking us THROUGH Fae territory."

"Territory? What the hell? The Fae should all be dead; they died hundreds of years ago when magic died."

Lee placed his hand against the ice wall, trying to catch his breath. This was the first time Sophia ever saw anyone knock the wind out of Lee. The group stood still and watched.

"You've got quite a punch there, Domingo," he managed to say before he turned and placed his back against the ice wall. "Magic didn't die," he said and took in a deep breath.

"It thrives in the west," Raja, Garret's bond partner,

added. "Where Kahel hasn't touched, he is still trying every day. The town of Hokai is full of his lackeys, and they established a checkpoint at the Pass just outside of Fae borders."

"We are aware of Hokai," Domingo said, "it's full of liars, backstabbers, and thieves. They would turn on any foreigner who set foot in their town."

"Yes, and no," Quentin said. "There are all sorts of hooligans living there, but there are also families who were unfortunate enough to be relocated there. They have to turn in anyone who wanders into their town to Kahel's guards. If they don't turn in at least five people a month, Kahel stops sending rations," Quentin said. "We all know that no one travels west anymore, so those towns have started a lottery. They turn in their own people now. It's the only way they can survive. Kahel believes that anyone who travels west is only there for one purpose, to cross into the new territory. He has those towns heavily guarded, but the Fae are smart. When they attack, they do not let themselves be seen, so Kahel still has no idea what he is up against."

"The Fae do not like humans at all," Jasira said, "and won't think twice about killing us, but we do have a trick up our sleeves." She beamed. "We Atarans have the potential to wield magic just like the Fae. Our gifts awaken the further we travel into their territory, on top of that Halcyon cast shell, barrier, and intuition spells on us. It's what helped Suresh detect their attack," Jasira said.

"So, you see, magic is still alive and well. I thought you would know this, Domingo," Lee said. "I mean, Eilith had the skills to cast, that was magic."

Domingo shot Lee an irritated look. "I knew she could cast," he hissed. "I knew she was part of the Warrior Tribe, which gave her casting abilities, but I also knew it would kill her, because she used her Essence to cast, not magic."

"The ability to use your Essence to cast IS magic; instead of drawing energy from around her, she drew it from within her. The Warriors were amazing people, and no other human creature in history ever possessed that ability. "

Domingo closed his eyes and took a deep breath. It was apparent to everyone except Lee that talking about Eilith was making him upset. Santiago placed a hand on his brother's shoulder. Sophia stood with an annoyed look on her face, and she examined each person, then threw her arms up.

"What the hell are Fae?" Sophia called out.

The group continued forward.

"Fae are just about everything alive, conscious, and natural. Quentin and I have learned from ancestors and our own personal research that they can be trees, creatures, or even invisible, like the wind," Suresh said.

"Did you know of them?" she asked the brothers.

"Our grandfather told us tales," Santiago began, "and we told you those same tales of the woodland folk that roamed with the Ibex. But, just like the latter, we were told they ceased to exist many, many years ago."

"Why do they hate humans?" she asked.

"Who cares," Garret grumbled. "If they attack, we kill them, and that should be the end of it."

"Garret," Jasira scolded.

"Jasira," he mocked.

"You can be such a brute sometimes."

"Oh, don't get your undergarments in a wad."

Jasira's jaw dropped, and she gaped at Garret. The group ignored the bickering and continued forward.

Sophia turned to Cyrus. "Are they okay?"

"Unfortunately, this happens more often than not," he replied. "You learn to ignore it."

Quentin and Suresh led the group, followed by Jasira and Garret, who were still yapping at one another. Raja and Cyrus were beside them, rolling their eyes. Domingo, Santiago, and Lee were a little further back from the group, and Sophia was bringing up the rear. She marveled at the height of the walls, the opacity of the ice. If it was a fraction thinner, she was sure you could see right through to the other side. It was all so impossibly beautiful to her. She looked even higher up and caught a quick shadow hovering high in the sky above the walls. It flapped its wings and then was gone.

"Zephyr?" She said to herself, knowing very well it couldn't be. She heard footsteps racing towards her, and Sophia then looked down from the sky. As her eyes adjusted to the lower light, she caught a glimpse of Lee before he tackled her to the ground. She flew back and fell hard onto her back. She just about had it with being tackled.

"Stay low and cover your ears, Sophia!"

Lee rolled off of her and positioned her on her stomach. She faced forward and saw that everyone, save for Suresh and Quentin, were already down and braced for another attack. She must have really spaced out back there. Both Suresh and Quentin pulled their blades out and jammed them into Iceway. They began to chant. It got colder, much colder. The loud crackling sound of ice forming echoed as the ice grew out from each side of the wall. In front of Quentin and Suresh, a new ice wall started to form, blocking the path directly ahead of them. When the sides of the ice wall connected to a whole, Quentin and Suresh kneeled down and covered their ears. Sophia could see the ice wall had begun to crack. It shattered, and a loud piercing howl echoed into the air. The group writhed in agony while keeping their ears covered. Sophia felt as if her brain was swelling, pain shot to all corners of her head. She wanted to scream but could barely breathe. When the howl dissipated, gasps were heard. Jasira clumsily made her way up, then used the side wall to brace herself, where she threw up. Domingo helped his brother up, who was having a hard time gathering himself. Sophia felt Lee's much warmer hand touch hers while she was laying on her side, taking calculated breaths. She looked up and saw Lee standing above her.

"Are you okay?" he asked.

Sophia grabbed his hand and lifted herself up.

"What was that?"

"A Fae," Lee said while moving a strand of hair from her face and tucking it behind her ear. "Are you sure you're okay?"

"Yeah, I'm better than Jasira there." Sophia tilted her head towards Jasira, who was now dry heaving.

"Then why are you crying?" Lee wiped the tears off of Sophia's face with his thumb. It was then that Sophia felt her heartbreak. The feeling grew from that same place deep within her; in the same place she had felt sadness over Lee spending the night at Cytrine's, she now felt a painful betrayal that she couldn't explain. It was like the people you love the most just told you they never wanted to see you again. Two sobs escaped her chest before she was in Lee's arms. Her watery eyes peeked over Lee's shoulder, and she could see Cyrus holding Jasira's hair back. Lee caressed the back of Sophia's hair and tilted his head closer to hers. Being close to him felt nice, she closed her eyes. It also felt right, like she was home again. Home...Gabriel's face flashed in her mind. She gained control of the emotions emanating from deep within and shut them down. Sophia pushed away from Lee. She took a deep breath. It looked like no one noticed their little moment; everyone was preoccupied with either themselves or their partners.

"I'm okay, I swear."

Suresh explained to the group, while they recuperated, that history calls the kind of Fae that attacked them a Banshee. He also told them that this is the last attack they would experience until they reach the end of the trail. Both he and

Quentin have had these same attacks every time they wandered into Fae lands. They also explained that inexperienced travelers would have either been impaled or had the veins in their heads burst. That did not make Sophia feel any better. Sophia traced her hand along the wall as they walked. It was getting dark, and they were going to have to set up camp soon.

"Beautiful, isn't it?" Jasira said, "Long ago, the Fae, Atarans, and the Warrior Tribe created this passage. They lived harmoniously."

"What happened?"

"No one truly knows," said a steady, gentle voice. Sophia turned to look at Raja, Garret's bond partner, who said, "Suresh, this is a good enough spot. We should stop here and rest." Raja placed his hand on the ground.

"What is it, my friend?" Garret asked.

"Darkness is upon us. I feel we should rest up so we can be prepared if there is another attack."

"They never attack more than twice," Quentin said.

"You said that, but you also have never traveled in a group more than two." Raja looked up. "I feel them backing away, but still they watch." He turned to Suresh, asking, "do you sense it?" Suresh took a few deep breaths and closed his eyes, then he gave Raja a nod of approval. They set up small tents enough for two, and in this cold it was smart to share heat. A fire was lit, and Jasira and Cyrus made food. They quietly ate a small feast of brown rice, red beans, and warmed caramelized peaches. After dinner concluded, they sat around the fire, continuing the earlier conversation.

"The Warrior Tribe and Atarans started expanding further and further out, and the Fae, well, they retreated back," Quentin said.

"But that couldn't be the reason behind all this hostility," Jasira added, "there has to be more to it than that."

"She's right," Raja's said in his deep, comforting voice. "A whole race of creatures do not decide on a whim to attack any human they see."

"They don't, but all you children are young; the stories told to your parents stopped with them." Quentin said, "My great grandfather told me that, just like us, they are organized, have complex hierarchies, civil wars even. So, the decision to retreat back and sentence any wandering human to death was a thoroughly discussed decision." He placed his hands behind him and looked up into the starry night above. "Then there are the stories, which are just that, 'stories;' we do not know which ones hold validity. There are ones about land battles, where we pushed the Fae back because they tried to take over our lands, then others about a difference in opinion on how we should live. You see, some Fae are mammals like horses, pigs, goats, and, well, we eat those. Then there are the stories of cross-breeding."

"Wait, what? Cross-breeding?" Domingo asked.

"It was forbidden for Fae and humans to copulate, but apparently that didn't stop some lovers from consummating their relationship. I guess the Fae feared a half-breed." He tossed a small piece of wood into the fire. "We all know it's impossible. Just as the Majji cannot have a child with a human, the Fae cannot have a child with humans. Our genetic makeup"—Quentin looked up to see Lee glaring a hole into him—"I mean, what makes us human isn't compatible with what makes them Fae. No matter how long any of them could have tried. A child would have never come out of such a union."

Sophia clenched her fists. "Why?" she asked. "Why couldn't they? Two people in love should be able to start a family if they want to. It's not fair. Being in love is all that matters."

Sophia and Gabriel had tried to have children for years and were unsuccessful. They were given special tea, milk, meals, and potions to promote fertility in both men and women. Still, no baby came to them. Santiago, who was sitting next to Sophia, placed his hand on hers. The brothers knew this was a sensitive topic for her. She let her body fall onto his. Santiago then wrapped his arm around her. Lee took in a short breath and watched as Sophia grabbed Santiago's hand.

"If you think about it, though, Leata gave birth to Kahel," Sophia continued, "and Halcyon fathered Gabriel. They were Majji, and they had children."

"Leata was still just an Apprentice," Lee said, looking intently at Sophia, "and Gabriel"—the name was like acid coming out of his mouth—"well"—he thought for a moment then turned and looked at the fire—"he remains a mystery."

"But you must understand, Sophia," Suresh said. "That wasn't cross-breeding. They were still part human; it's the only explanation we have. Some Fae may look human but never were."

"Like the story of the bird and fish that fell in love." Domingo motioned one hand up in the air and the other to the ground "Both couldn't survive in air or water; their love just could never be."

"This is just too depressing for me," Jasira said. "I'm going to bed."

"I will join you." Cyrus stood up and walked with Jasira to their tent.

"We all should rest," Raja said.

They agreed. Suresh added some more wood to their fire and gave each person a wake-up shift to keep a lookout and the fire going. Sophia walked over to the tents, realizing she never made any arrangements for which was hers and who she would be sharing with. But she knew all along, it made sense, partners would tent together. Closeness always helped with healing, physically, spiritually, mentally, and emotionally. The brothers would probably tent together, which would leave her and Lee. Her stomach turned. She'd shared a roof with him, but these tents were small. They were designed to allow their occupants to share one another's heat.

"If you would be more comfortable, you could always stay with me," Santiago said from her side, "and my brother can stay with Lee."

"I would never ask that of you," Sophia said staring at her tent. "You may not be Ataran, but you have to admit since you've been here the bond to your brother has grown stronger."

"You sense it too then?" Santiago leaned closer to Sophia.

"Yes. Just like so many things, I don't know how I sense it, I just do."

"Well then. Sophia," Santiago said as he kissed her cheek. "I will see you in the morning." He gave her a short hug then walked away. Sophia turned to look at Lee. He had just finished his rounds and patted Garret on the back, who had drawn the short straw and had to take the first shift. Lee walked to their tent and opened it up.

"I need to get some rest. After Garret's shift is Raja, then you, and then I. I can take your shift if you want."

"Thank you." Sophia happily accepted, there was no point in being modest. She was exhausted and wanted to get as much sleep as possible.

Lee opened the tent and crawled in. Sophia followed. There was a large sheep wool blanket laid down and two other blankets made of alpaca wool. The quarters were so close, she could already feel his heat. Lee took his shirt off, and for the first time Sophia saw the tone of his body. She'd seen him topless numerous times, but most of those times they were sparing and she was dodging an attack of his. Her eyes focused on his necklace. She had never noticed it before. Sophia assumed he removed it during training and wore it under his shirt at all other times. The chain hung low on his collar bone, made of a white braided string and two rings knotted together in the center. After he folded his shirt, their eyes met. Her face grew red.

"I never noticed that necklace."

"Halcyon had it made for me after my parents died. It's their wedding bands."

"Oh. It's beautiful," she said, looking to the ground.

They sat in silence for a moment.

"Listen," Lee started. "It's going to get cold tonight; it's better we stay close and share the blankets."

"I know."

"It's also better that we have as little clothing on as possible." Lee gulped, then turned his head and fussed with his hair. "I mean, we don't have to. but it will be a rough night if we don't. I promise I won't look."

"It's okay, Lee," Sophia said as she removed her shirt. "I trust you." She pulled the blankets over herself. "I'm covered now, you can turn around." She lay on her side and felt the cold air enter under the blankets as Lee positioned himself. He was hesitant to place his arms around her, so Sophia guided him. His arm radiated warmth across her scar, and it was an unexpected and yet calming feeling to her. She let out a small sigh.

"Does it hurt at all?" Lee asked, regarding her scar.

"Yes, and no. I don't feel any physical pain from it, but it's a constant reminder of everything that I have lost and how powerless I am to the horrible things that are happening now. That knowledge causes more pain than having this wound cut open a thousand times over."

Lee took in a breath, searching for something consoling to say, but he was at a loss.

"And yet," she continued, "this scar also ensures that I will never forget them or him."

Lee held her tightly and kissed her hair. She let him.

Sophia knew it was wrong of her to accept any intimacy, but the emptiness she felt from all the loss she's experienced was somewhat filled by Lee, and it was nice to be held again. With her body warm and calm, she fell into a deep sleep.

w." Boris sat down and eyed the Regeneration Unit. He let
head fall back and wondered what would have happened
he had just stayed in Vizzini. He could have easily remained
ere peacefully. It wouldn't take much to alter his
pearance. Cut or dye his hair, speak with a different accent.
e Elite there would pay him no mind, too busy with their
ssip and designs. He felt bad that he thought to betray his
rd to Gabriel, but the chances of Boris getting to his final
stination were slim. Boris took a bite of the bar and leaned
rd back into the wall. He sat on the floor and waited for the
her base to check in. Several hours later, it happened. Boris
a groan escape as he ignored his body's objections and
od up.

"S.T Extricate Station, Hokai Station checking in." The
und emanated from both Regeneration Units. Boris placed
e gauntlet on the side of the unit, and the comm unlocked.
e began to cough loudly.

"Hokai Station, this is S.T Station," he said in a hoarse
ne.

"Is everything alright there? You didn't initiate check-in."

Of course, he was at the lead station. Made sense, since
is one was closer to Tychi.

"Apologies." He coughed loudly. "On my way back, I
countered a large dust devil. I need to regenerate."

"Understood. Check in at zero-hundred. Hokai station,
ver and out."

Zero-hundred, he thought. That was four hours away, and
e needed to be here to initiate check-in. The check-in after
at would be at dawn, giving him time to traverse the desert
t night. His Grey eyes could see several times better than
ormal human eyes during the dark. But they would see much
etter if he regenerated. Again, he looked at the Regeneration
Unit. He popped the last piece of a supplement bar in his
houth. He recalled the comforting feeling of stepping into a

52

BORIS AND
THE GREY

Boris dragged one of the sentries' bodies behind the Stone
Titans. His travels after being nearly detected in Salinas had
been long and exhausting. Still, he had managed to disarm and
disable both guards that stood outside the massive monu-
ments. The entire trek south, the hot sun had beat on him
relentlessly, so Boris sat in the shade of a Stone Titan without
an ounce of guilt for wasting time. He took several long
breaths, allowing himself to cool before moving the last body.
Questioning for only a moment the morality of robbing the
dead, Boris proceeded to search their bodies for money,
weapons, and supplies. This was no time for ethics. Boris was
able to procure a little cash, two attack rods, and the guard's
gauntlet keys. This meant somewhere around here was a
small base, probably with food. His provisions had run out,
and he had only been drinking two sips of water a day for the
past two days. Boris pulled his cloak hood up and walked out

of the shade. He knew he was lucky, back in Salinas. He had remained unnoticed when the booby trap was set off. It was all still fresh in his memory. He had huddled low, and when it was evident that the soldiers were not going to cross the Pyre River he knew he was safe. He didn't dare move though, not until whatever was about to come to pass came to pass. Then he saw them. Atarans. They came in from the Northern Woods in droves, followed by the Majji.

"They are organized." Boris laughed to himself. "Kahel probably did not anticipate this."

He watched the Majji and some men meet underneath a beautiful dogwood tree. One of the men stormed off, and the Majji's attention diverted. Boris followed the Majji's gaze and the man who stormed off. Boris' Grey eyes focused on a woman. His eyes widened; his jaw dropped.

"Sophia."

He watched the battle ensue and watched Sophia intently. She fought, albeit more clumsy than graceful; still, the once-dancer had become a warrior. When Kahel's troops were defeated, Boris knew in his heart, well, what was left of it, that he had to reach the swamplands of Hokai and enter the Pass. His stop at Vizzini was the most valuable part of his journey. After paying out the nose to blend in with the local Elite, he made his way to the Tavern where the scholars congregated. It turned out that they were all up in arms about the sudden disappearance of Salinas and were more than willing to chat with the dapper Elite visiting the Tavern. That was, of course, after Boris had bought them several drinks. He learned three crucial things. First, that there were other Salinan survivors. Some folks had left Salinas days before, but one large group had been able to escape the morning of the attack through an old tunnel. Identities had been changed and they were safe. Most interesting to him was that one of those survivors is rumored to have opened a shop in Vizzini. Second, Tychi had

begun to revolt against Kahel. The deaths o[...] citizens and word of the Salinan massacre were[...] broke the camel's back. People were trying to[...] control them, Kahel had his Osprey and men fro[...] stationed inside Tychi's walls. And, finally, he[...] Gabriel was still alive, and he had time to mak[...] promise. He was being interrogated but being ke[...] stopped himself from taking the third sip of hi[...] continued forward. Boris swore that his legs w[...] sand with each step, as it took more and more[...] just lift them up. He knew of two Extricate St[...] desert. All stations within the same vicinity [...] checks with one another. Boris needed to be su[...] that check so no one would come snooping aro[...] close, he could feel it. He placed his hand on [...] blocking the sun, and looked into the distance, tr[...] the base. Boris caught a short glimpse of a shin[...] south of him. He channeled what energy he had l[...] into a sprint. Minutes later, he stood in front of [...] structure. Boris pulled out the gauntlet key and [...] placed his hand against the access pad. The me[...] open, and a gust of cold air billowed towards[...] stepped in, and the door slid back closed behin[...] interior was barren. Which was expected; Gr[...] require much except Regeneration Units, [...] supplements. Seeing nothing but two units and sev[...] labeled "water" or "supplement" in the room was[...] to Boris. It had been months since Boris had last s[...] a Regeneration Unit. He rubbed his brow, then tu[...] from the unit. He filled all three water bladder[...] gulps. Boris opened up his bag, then tossed all o[...] supplements in. Tasteless, disgusting bars that p[...] necessary nutrients.

"I'd give my left nut for some barbeque ch[...]

unit, how the warmth enveloped him, the safe feeling, like a child in their loving mother's arms, and the exhilaration he felt when regeneration was complete. The aging man placed his hand on the unit. Boris felt his will begin to fail him. He quickly pushed himself back. Boris took a few stabilizing breaths as he stared down the Regeneration Unit.

"Fuck you. I don't need you anymore."

Boris grabbed his water and satchel and tossed them to the opposite side of the room. He then lay down and curled himself, his back defiantly facing the Regeneration Units.

PART 2

THE WORLD OF FAE

53

DREAM

Sophia's body shivered. She flung her arm back, searching for Lee, but he wasn't there. This was their third night in the Iceway and her third night of sleeping close to Lee. Any warm-blooded creature would grow an affection for someone they had to spend time with within such intimate, confined space. Sophia was more confused than ever. Her love for Gabriel, the unbreakable tether holding her to him remained, there, strong as ever. But her soul ached for comfort, the kind that Lee had been providing. That, combined with the anomaly she had been battling within herself, was enough to drive anyone mad. Her teeth began to chatter as she gathered the blankets over her head. Sophia's mind fought through a thick haze. She assumed it was the extreme cold causing her confusion. She rubbed her arms and curled into a ball. Moments later, Lee crawled into their tent. Sophia pulled the blankets down and popped her head out.

"Shift over," he said with a smile.

"How long have you been gone?"

"An hour and a half. I took Jasira's shift too," Lee said with his back turned to her. He took his layers off, showing his sculpted, toned back, and prepared for sleep again. Sophia watched him, careful not to get caught.

"Cyrus wasn't too pleased when I woke him." Lee folded his shirt. "Something about it being his responsibility and yadda yadda yadda." When Lee turned to face Sophia, she flipped to her side, hoping he didn't notice she had been admiring his body.

"Well, is it?" Sophia asked.

"It is in a way," Lee said. then slipped under the covers. "But he needs his rest too. He's been working hard this journey."

"You are a good friend. Lee."

"Well obviously," he said with a laugh, then laid down and confidently wrapped his arms around Sophia. It felt right to her; everything about them together like this felt right to her. The walls she had up had been slowly falling for a while now, and she tried to remember why she had those walls up in the first place. She drew a blank. That damn haze clouded her mind. The smell of fire mixed into his usual musk was utterly intoxicating. She took a few deep breaths, trying to calm herself, but it backfired. His scent consumed her, and all she could think about was his toned body pressed against hers. Sophia tried to resist. But, again, like every time before, it came from deep within her and all her resistance was in vain. She turned around and was face to face with Lee.

"What's up," he said with a smile on his face.

Sophia laughed, then pushed up on one elbow. Lee followed suit. She continued to look at him, but this time she took her time. At his hairline, his eyes, his jawline, and his lips. Lee's eyes widened as he realized what was about to happen.

"Sophia, I don't think..." he went down on his back and ran both hands through his hair. "I don't think this is a good idea."

"I know," Sophia replied. She lowered herself back down and came close to Lee. He placed one arm around her, and the two embraced. Lee kissed the top of her head, and Sophia then looked up into his eyes again. Sophia lifted a hand and gently ran it across his now-tense jawline. He closed his eyes and had begun to take deeper breaths. She inched forward, getting closer to his lips. Her internal battle was over. Lee lifted his free hand and placed it on the side of Sophia's face.

"I could make you so happy," he said.

Sophia leaned in and softly kissed Lee. The pair flipped to their sides and were face to face. Their lips continually touched. Each gentle kiss was filled with a caring warmth, sending pleasure-filled sensations through Sophia's body. She never thought she'd ever kiss another man, but kissing Lee was like kissing a long-lost friend that you never realized how deeply you cared for till that moment. Lee pulled her closer, she could feel his desire for her and it made her want him even more. She waited for his lips to touch hers again, and waited, and waited some more, but she felt nothing. Everything had stopped. It was cold again, really cold. Reality began to set in as Sophia opened one eye, then the other. The place next to her was vacant. Lee was gone. She willed herself to move and crawled over to the tent opening. She carefully made a small opening and looked out. Lee was sitting by the fire, tossing small twigs into it. Defeated, she let out a sigh and dropped her head. It was loud enough to catch Lee's attention, who was in front of her in a matter of seconds.

"Everything okay?" He said close to her face.

Sophia looked up and stared at his lips.

"Ye...ye, yes." He smelled just the same as in her dream. Sophia shifted. Lee raised an eyebrow and let a small smile escape his lips.

"Well, okay," he said as he stood up and walked back to the fire. "Close up that tent; you don't want to let any more cold air in."

She did as he said, then turned back and flopped on the ground. She stared up at the top of the tent and recalled parts of the dream. Sophia shivered and then pulled the blankets over her head in frustration.

She woke up warm, rejuvenated, and in Lee's arms. Before any part of her could betray her, Sophia shot up and put her layers back on. Lee woke up and pushed up on one elbow.

"We should get going," Sophia said in an unusually high-pitched voice.

"Yeah, we should," he said, running his free hand through his hair with the same smile on his face as last night. Good gods, Sophia could not get her eyes off his lips. Lee let out a laugh.

"Sophia, are you going to tell me what's going on?" Lee asked.

She was kneeling as far away from him as possible.

"It's nothing, it's stupid, it's—"

"Time for us to go," Jasira said as she popped her head into the tent. Sophia yelped in surprise and fell back.

"What's with her?" Jasira gestured towards Sophia.

"Your guess is as good as mine," he said as he put on his coat.

"Hey, Cyrus is pissed that you took my shift, but I'm not," Jasira said while Sophia and Lee exited the tent. "He needed to sleep. So, thank you."

Lee was making quick work of breaking down the tent.

"No problem."

Jasira smiled ear to ear and walked off.

"So, you DID take Cyrus' shift last night," Sophia said as she shook her head slightly. The haze clung to her mind like pine sap.

"No, I took Jasira's shift."

"Same thing, since it's his responsibility anyway."

"You sound just like him," Lee said as he folded the rest of the blankets and shoved them into their packs.

"We will clear the trail soon if we leave after breakfast," Suresh said. He handed Lee and Sophia each a small pouch filled with rice and scrambled eggs. "Eat quickly." Sophia swore she saw frost glistening on his face, but upon closer inspection saw none. Steam billowed from the warm food. It exuded an irresistible scent that Sophia dare not deny. She ate while carefully observing the Atarans. Her gut was telling her something was up. She watched as Jasira carefully gathered the used pans and leftover food. Jasira shook her head and seemed to study her surroundings. They all seemed to be on edge. Santiago wandered towards Sophia and knelt down as if he had dropped an item.

"Something's up," he whispered, "they've been on alert the whole morning."

"Did anything happen last night?" Well, besides that random mildly erotic dream of hers. Sophia shook her head, trying to pull it together.

"No," he replied. "Still, something's off," Santiago scanned the Atarans. "I can't quite pin it."

Sophia agreed. She had felt out of sorts for some time. Even with food in her belly and a good night's sleep, she couldn't fight the haze that had overtaken her mind. They were very far into the Iceway now, and the others had elemental gifts that had awoken. Sophia watched as Jasira played with snowflakes in the palm of her hand. The flakes flew up into the air and sprinkled over Cyrus' head, and he smiled and nudged her with his shoulder. Suresh extinguished the fire by waving his hand over the flames. It flickered, touched his palm, and dissipated into him. But with her? Zero. She figured maybe by this point she would have sensed that bond Halcyon spoke of, and yet she felt nothing.

Sophia turned to Santiago. "Their gifts have fully awakened."

"Not fully," Lee said from behind her. Sophia jumped. Santiago's brows furrowed. Lee picked up a stone and placed it between his and Sophia's hands. When he opened, sand drizzled out of Sophia's palm. She watched as the sand fell and recalled the time outside Tychi where she and Gabriel got into an argument. She recalled handling the dirt outside of Tychi, and how she felt life in it; though little, it was still there. But from this sand, the one that fell from Lee's hand, sand that no Extricate Station has touched, Sophia felt nothing. She looked up curiously at Lee.

"Do that again," she demanded.

Lee did as she asked, and this time she held the sand tightly in her hands.

"What is it?" he asked.

Santiago pushed Lee's hand away from Sophia and came between them.

"That's enough of your parlor tricks," Santiago said. "You're frightening her," he said protectively.

"No." Sophia interjected, "it's not that." She handed Santiago the sand. "I feel nothing from this, do you?"

Santiago nodded "no."

"Do Quentin and Suresh sense the Fae?" she asked Lee.

"No."

"Don't you find that strange?"

"Well, no, they may have backed off." Lee lied right to her face, and it infuriated Sophia.

"Why do you refuse to tell us the truth?" Her voice echoed between the walls as she gestured towards herself, Santiago, and Domingo. "We are Atarans now. I demand you keep us informed as you do the others here." Everyone stopped and stared at the pair.

Like all his free will had been instantaneously stripped from him, Lee obliged. With an involuntary slight bow of his head, he spoke.

"We sense nothing. All of us sensc nothing at all, and this far into the Iceway we fear the Fae have a large-scale attack waiting for us further in."

"You think they have cloaked themselves?" Santiago asked.

"Maybe," Lee said, "but both Suresh and Quentin believe it would be quite the task to cloak a large amount of Fae. It's not easy to hide your Essence. The only people known to do it successfully were the Ibex. But they did it in small numbers." He looked up at the grey sky. The clouds were dark and vast. A storm was on its way. "It is best that we get moving."

Sophia didn't move; her mind was working through that stubborn fog.

"No." Sophia grabbed Lee's wrist. "I can't sense Essence in this land, nor can I sense Halcyon. This has nothing to do with cloaking or them pulling their defenses back." Her mind raced and suddenly the haze that had occupied her mind broke. A fierce cold shot through her body. Sophia turned to Lee.

"They aren't planning anything," she said, the clarity quickly being replaced by a sharp pain in her mind. "It's already happening!" she said, teeth chattering in a panic "Lee, this isn't real! That's why we can't sense anything because it isn't happ—" Those were the last words she uttered before it went black. It was as if someone jerked her back from her neck. Pressure grew from behind her eyes, and her head felt like it was filled with liquid. Sophia's lids slowly opened and her true sight returned. She was sitting upright, topless, in the tent. Lee was directly in front of her, sitting with a frightened look on his face. Sophia grabbed the blanket and pulled it around herself.

"Sophia!" Lee cried out with his eyes closed.

"Gods, wake up!" she heard Santiago call out from afar.

"What's going on?" Jasira's voice called.

"She just collapsed," Lee said.

Sophia looked around the tent. This was the Fae attack; she grabbed Lee's shoulders.

"No, I'm right here, Lee!!" Sophia said as she shook him. His eyes remained closed and unresponsive. Sophia's body trembled with cold. She wondered how long they all have been in this state. Sophia wrapped the wool blanket around herself and covered Lee with the others. She crawled out of the tent and saw Suresh sitting next to an extinguished fire. Frost covered his eyebrows and pale beard.

"What happened to her?" Suresh's blue lips hardly moved in the dark night. Sophia raced to Suresh and embraced him, sharing what little warmth she had. It quickly occurred to her that if she didn't figure how to wake them, they were all screwed. Sophia shivered. Even though the night sky was littered with stars and a moon, they gave little light. She could barely see the cold mist come from her mouth. The panic that was quickly growing inside her had nothing to do with the darkness that encompassed the eerie scene she was a part of, and everything to do with her not knowing how to wake her comrades. Thinking was harder than ever in the unbearable cold. Sophia knew she didn't have any gifts like the others. Having the talent to create a fire would be helpful right now. The only thing she was good at was getting in trouble and being rescued.

"Of course," she blurted.

The courage came from the place deep within her. Sophia let it take over. She stepped out from under the blanket and exposed herself to the cold. She held onto Suresh's hand and kneeled beside him. Having the Essence of the Apprentice gave her a power no one else had. People were compelled to protect her, and if no one woke up to protect her, she would surely die here. She pleaded to Suresh to wake up. Her jaw began to chatter, her eyes watered, and the words came out in short stutters as her body shook violently from the cold.

54

WAKE UP

"What do you mean she collapsed?" Suresh said as he ran towards Lee, who was cradling a limp Sophia. Fear radiated throughout Suresh's body. He knew they couldn't get too far without Sophia. He walked past Jasira, who was crying in Cyrus' arms. Garret placed a blanket that Raja handed him on Sophia. How is it that the Fae managed to attack her? Suresh thought to himself. Just her, it didn't make any sense. They were all alert, all waiting and anticipating an attack. And most importantly, how did they get past him?

"She said something about it was 'already happening' and how something wasn't 'real.'" Lee said. "Then she just fell." Lee shook her gently hoping she'd come to. Suresh's body gave a slight shiver. Instinct spoke; his body let out another shiver, but this time it continued, and his shivering became uncontrollable. A breeze came from nowhere, trailing a faint voice in its wind.

"Wake up. Suresh." Sophia's voice eerily echoed. He looked down at her lifeless body and stepped back. Quentin touched his shoulder with a puzzled look.

"Wake up." Her voice called louder. Quentin looked up into the sky.

"You heard her too?" Suresh asked.

"Yes."

The group looked at the pair.

"Be on alert!" Suresh said as he pulled out his blade. "We are under attack."

"WAKE UP!" Sophia's voice came through loud and clear this time.

Suresh's head slammed back hard onto the ice. He didn't need his sight to understand the peril they were in. He took the blanket Sophia placed on him and wrapped it around her.

"We are all freezing to death, Suresh," she said. His eyes began to regain focus as he looked up at the sky.

"Suresh!" Quentin called from inside his tent, "Does the girl live?"

"Yes," he replied, "the moon, I can't see it too clearly right now, but if I am right, we have spent two nights in this trance."

Quentin crawled out of his tent and wobbled towards Sophia with a blanket for her.

"Sorry, it took us so long to hear you," he said.

"It's okay, but how are we going to wake the others?" she replied.

"The same way you woke us. They have to hear you."

"First things first, though," Suresh said as he handed a pouch to Quentin. "Help me place my orbs around our campsite." The pair wasted no time. They began to chant, and within minutes Suresh and Quentin created a fire barrier that doubled as protection and heat. The blue flames were at least six feet tall and encircled the group.

"Why didn't we set this up earlier?" Sophia asked. "It would have been helpful, you know."

"It takes a lot out of us, and we can't keep it up all night," Suresh said. "Both Quentin and I will be weak after this, but there is no way around it. Now, let's wake our friends."

Sophia started with Lee, who held her for a few moments when he came to. She continued on to the brothers, then Jasira and Cyrus, and finally Garret and Raja. Suresh explained to them what had happened and how long they had been in a trance. They all agreed to pack up and leave as soon as possible.

55

FOOTBRIDGE TO HOKAI

The marshlands of the west were a damp and dark land. Boris trudged through the swamp with his head down constantly reminding himself why he was doing this.

"This is for the boy. This is the right thing to do. This is for the boy."

Whenever he found a solid bit of land, he would rest and attempt to wring his clothing dry. Patches of fog were loosely scattered about, and a string of clouds continually passed across the sun. Sometimes he would fool himself into thinking that the sun was about to break free, but just before it would fully peek through another set of thin clouds would swiftly cross in front of it. He looked around at the bare trees, whose thin branches hung low.

"Bleak. Still, it reminds me of home." He chuckled to himself, thinking of Crossings Forged. Boris got up and continued on. He traveled diligently for an hour before he finally came to an elevated, rotted footbridge. His legs loudly sloshed as he picked up his pace and made his way to it. The bridge came up to his waist. Boris placed his hands on the footbridge and pushed himself onto it. He let his body fall loudly on the wood. The bridge creaked and groaned in protest to Boris's weight.

"Oh, shut up, you whiny whore," Boris said as he rolled onto his back and looked up to the sun. A strange feeling was growing inside him. This was something that, as a Grey, he had never felt, but Boris of the past had. Hope. He smiled. Things inside the Grey had been changing for a while now. He had to let his fear go and accept that "he" was returning. Even though Boris of the past was dead, his memories and his morals were taking over. It frightened him at first; he didn't want to lose control of himself, but then realized that he the Grey will always exist, but now he existed as Boris, and he was okay with it. Boris was an incredible man, who lived a magnificent life. The Grey was honored to continue that life. At one point, he was mad with grief over the death of the man whose body he took, and that's when it happened, when the Grey decided to become Boris fully. Boris stood up and looked in the direction from where he had come. It was a strange sight. The bridge was the only structure for miles, sitting alone in the swamp. Most people would find the bridge out of sheer luck. Boris didn't need that; his memory served him and his newly and drastically improved senses brought him directly to it. He wondered how many lives had been lost in this swamp. Must have been a lot. Why anyone would want to find refuge out here was beyond him. He walked cautiously on the footbridge. Hokai was only a few minutes from here.

"Now comes the hard part."

He knew anyone who wandered into Hokai from the swamp would be captured and delivered to Tychi for questioning. He cursed himself for not taking the Grey's clothing back in the desert. No one would have questioned him then. He would be just another soldier sent in. Sure, he had the eyes, but that wasn't enough. He looked down at his muddied clothing.

"Shit."

He had to sneak into Hokai, and there was only one way to do that. Boris looked down into murky water. He exhaled in defeat and leaped back down into the swamp, then reluctantly went under the footbridge. Within minutes, Boris approached Hokai. He could see light come in between the boards. The town was quiet but not abandoned. He stealthy waded underneath the footbridge. Boris exhaled when he reached the center. He had safely made it and was in the clear. The center of Hokai was an elevated platform supported by many posts that dug deep into the swampy ground. All footbridges eventually led to the center platform. He followed a footbridge that had minimal traffic. When Boris felt safe, he made his way out from under the bridge and climbed onto it. He did a quick check around him, then ran into the first hut he found. No luck, just women and children's clothing. It wasn't until the fifth hut when Boris hit the jackpot. It was a Grey's dwelling, and he was still in his Unit. Boris shut the door behind him and walked to the chamber. With all the strength he had, Boris pulled the chamber door open. The Grey's eyes shot open.

Boris pulled his blade out and slit the Grey's throat. He caught the Grey as he fell and eased his landing. The Grey frantically tried to stop the blood pouring out of his throat. Boris pulled the Grey's hands from his throat.

"Hey, don't fight it, friend. Death is inevitable. Let it come and go in peace."

The Grey looked up at Boris and headed the old man's words. When he had passed, Boris placed the Grey's body curled up in the chamber. The glass on the chamber only exposed the upper torso of its user. With the door closed and the Grey on the bottom, it seemed as if it was just an empty chamber. Boris stripped out of his clothes and found the Grey's uniform.

"Well, this is going to be a tight squeeze," he said as he forced his body into the uniform. Boris did a squat and moved his arms about.

"This will have to do." Boris looked out the window. No one in sight. Boris wasted no time and made his way to the Pass.

56

TWO PLACES
AT ONCE

The last attack left the Atarans exhausted and vulnerable.
They remained until the barrier fell. Hoping to recover from
their injuries, they waited until the very last second, but as the
barrier fell they felt as weary as ever. Their group was
compromised and heading straight into the lion's den. They
walked cautiously without speaking for hours before Jasira
broke the silence.

"We almost froze to death back there."

"Leave it to you to point out the obvious," Garret said
under his breath.

"I'm serious, Garret," she said, her frightened voice almost
cracking. "When I told my parents not to worry, I meant it,
but after that nasty little trick I don't know if I should have
said that." Tears began to form in her eyes. "I mean, what the
hell...we almost died!" She rubbed her face with her arm.
"What was Halcyon thinking when he sent us here?"

Garret had to remind himself of Jasira's naïveté. She was new to all of this. He has been doing recon and missions for over a decade now. He knew he could be raw and cruel sometimes, which was okay in some situations, but she was truly scared. Garret wondered why Cyrus allowed her on this journey. She was obviously not ready for this. If one of his sisters was bonded to Cyrus and he wanted to take her on this mission, you can bet your bottom that shit wouldn't fly with Garret. Garret walked over to Jasira and placed a reassuring arm around her.

"I think this is Halcyon's last-ditch effort. I figure that if there was another option than going far west and pulling a stick out of a corpse, I'm sure he'd given it to us."

Jasira nodded her head.

"Chin up, kid," he said, "I've got your back."

Garret proceeded to tell Jasira jokes and stories to lift her spirits. It brought a smile onto Jasira's face. It was bittersweet to see her laugh. Being in the situation that they were in, it felt wrong to laugh, but mild shoving started, followed by Jasira holding a bare hand open and forming a small snowball in it. She quickly flung it at Garret.

"You little twerp!" Garret said, quickly annoyed. "You wouldn't want to see me use my—" Before he could finish, a large wad of snow smacked him dead-center in the face, sending his hair into a wild dance as he lost his balance and fell back. Jasira grabbed her stomach and laughed.

"I'm surprised how quickly your gifts are coming around," Suresh said as he walked forward "You are the youngest in this group, so Quentin and I assumed yours would develop last."

"Well, you assumed wrong," she replied in a slightly superior tone. Garret stood up and wiped the snow out of his face. He looked at Jasira and smiled.

There was nothing new on the trail for them to see. The

once-magnificent ice walls were now monotonous barriers that repeatedly reminded Sophia that she was fragile, exposed, and most likely going to join the Green on this cold path. She felt her mind begin to drift. She was tired of walking; they hadn't stopped for four hours. Her mind drifted farther, and she let it, anything to keep her mind off of her mortality was welcome. It floated about, then began to wander in the strangest of ways. Her mind seemed to go in the opposite direction that they were walking. This was when she started to worry. Sophia felt as if she was split in two. While her body was walking forward with the group, her mind was trailing further back, and she could see it. It slowed down near the campsite where they were attacked. She watched as some water trickled down from far atop the ice wall. It was getting warmer there. That was nice, she just about had it with cold.

"It's okay." Halcyons voice called to her, "I'll guide you. But you must hurry."

Raja was the first to notice Sophia's zombiesque state.

"Are you all right." His gentle voice asked. The rest of the group turned to look at her.

"Yes, I think so," she said, "I was just bored then out of nowhere," as she thought of a way to explain it without sounding crazy. "Um...well, Halcyon wants me to follow him." Not needing to see their faces to know their confusion, she continued, "I seem to be two places at once."

"Fascinating," Suresh said as he walked towards her. The others, save for Quentin, had screwed-up looks on their face. Garret continued towards Sophia to take a closer look. He examined her eyes, which were wide open with a white haze moving slowly through them.

"Good gods, Sophia, your eyes! Cut that out. You look so strange!" Garret said as he knocked her upside the head.

"What the hell, Garret, I can still feel you!"

"I was trying to snap you out of it."

"Well, it didn't help."

Garret knocked her upside the head again. "How about now?"

"Remind me to hex him when you all return to Atara." Halcyon's voice echoed in her mind.

Lee pulled back hard on Garret's collar. Garret, in turn, grabbed Lee's arm on the way down, and the two started to scuffle. It was short and ended with the two slapping each other on the face while helping one another up.

Suresh rolled his eyes.

"Sophia, can you hear me clearly?" Suresh asked

"Yes."

"Where are you right now?"

"Um, she's right there, dumbass," Garret said under his breath to Jasira as he dusted himself off, and Jasira held back a laugh. Cyrus nudged Jasira, giving her a disapproving look. Jasira bit her lip and looked down to the ground, immediately after Garret gave Cyrus an incredulous look and walked closer to Jasira. He placed his hand under Jasira's chin and lifted her face till she was directly facing him.

"You're alright, kid," he said quietly to her. "I like it better when you are being true to yourself. Laugh when you want." Jasira's cheeks flushed. She smiled and looked away.

57

AVALANCHES

That was new, Jasira thought to herself, trying to make sense of the warmth that grew in her chest when she looked into Garret's eyes. Cyrus slapped Garret's hand off of Jasira and pushed him back. Garret had a sly look on his face as he stepped back.

"Jealousy doesn't become you, Cyrus. If you want her, you need to stop scolding her."

"Well, she should stop acting like a child then."

Shock and hurt filled Jasira's eyes. She turned to look at Cyrus, who quickly wished he had held his tongue. But he couldn't stand how Garret watched Jasira, he couldn't stand when Garret touched her, and he couldn't stand that Jasira seemed to like it.

"I didn't mean it like that, Jasira," Cyrus said.

"Really?" Garret called out. "Then how did you mean it?"

Jasira brushed a tear and walked away from Cyrus.

"Shut up, Garret, or I swear I will..."

"I'm at our old campsite," Sophia said, oblivious of what

was happening around her.

"Quiet all of you; your bickering is nothing but embarrassing," Suresh said, then turned his focus back to Sophia. "What do you see there?"

"Um, the sun is out, the snow is melting."

"Do you know why you are there?"

"Halcyon wants me here, and I feel like maybe we left something behind. But I don't see anything."

Lee tilted his head towards Quentin. "What's going on?"

"Sophia is projecting. It's a power Majjis and their Apprentices have," he replied, "and it was a way for them to communicate when they were far from one another. They would project themselves to an agreed meeting spot when they were busy with other things."

"Wait, so that means…" Jasira added, coming behind Lee and trying to stay away from both Garret and Cyrus.

"Halcyon is calling her." Quentin watched Sophia intently.

"Wo," Jasira said.

"Wo is right." Suresh walked closer to Sophia. "I need you to look around carefully. Halcyon wants you back there, so concentrate."

She looked around at their campsite, convinced there was nothing to be found. She saw their footprints, small holes where their tents were pitched, the area where her tent was, where she spent the night with Lee, topless, having an erotic dream about him grinding against her body and kissing her. Gods, she hoped no one's gift was mind reading.

"I won't tell anyone," Halcyon's voice said in her mind.

"Oh, gods," Sophia said, defeated.

"What? What is it?" Suresh grabbed Sophia's shoulder.

"Nothing, nope, nothing. There is nothing here, Suresh."

"Are you sure? Just a moment ago, you became flush, tensed up, then called out, 'oh, gods.'"

Halcyons' laughter echoed in her mind. Sophia imagined facepalming herself.

"I did?" she squeaked. "Strange, because there is nothi…"

Her heart stilled when she saw them break through the fog, slowly investigating the campsite.

"They've been on your tail from almost the beginning," Halcyon said. "I grow weak and can't hold this connection with you much longer." His voice began to fade. "I have faith. Bring them all home, Sophia." With that, his voice cut out, but Sophia remained split between two places. Sophia watched as the three giant, white wolves lowered their heads and began to sniff the ground cautiously.

Their ears up, listening carefully, mouths exposing teeth that could shred prey in seconds, one let out a small growl. The enormous pads on their feet thudded as they walked from side to side. Sophia slowly moved back and leaned against the wall. Sophia sucked in her breath and flattened herself against the frigid wall. She knew that physically she wasn't there, and yet she swore they would sense her if she didn't keep quiet. The Atarans watched her intently.

"Three large wolves," she whispered. "I see three large wolves."

"What did you just say?" Suresh said.

"Three large white wolves are sniffing around our campsite." Her voice, slightly louder, cracked with fear. "Gods, they are massive." She pushed herself further back into the ice wall in both her physical and metaphysical self.

"It's okay, Sophia, you are here, you are safe." Suresh rubbed Sophia's shoulder. "Quentin." His tone was suspicious. "Never in any story I've been told have they mentioned three large wolves, you?"

Quentin's hand was already on his hilt. "No."

Back at the campsite, one of the wolves shot his head up. Sophia crept backward, using the wall for balance, and the wolf followed. It was impossible for them to see her, it had to be impossible. She went back even further, then lowered down, her actions mirrored in both instances of herself.

"They are getting closer to me," Sophia said. "I want to leave, why can't I leave?"

"I don't know." Suresh's voice was sounding more distant now. "If Halcyon's message was that these wolves have been following us, then you should have been released by now."

"He spoke to me," she whispered, "but he was growing weak, so he left."

She could feel Suresh's hand on her shoulders, but her vision was now entirely at the campsite.

"I can't see you anymore, all I see is them."

The wolf raised his nose to the air and sniffed. This wolf was distinct. Unlike the other two, he was not all white. He had grey tribal markings on his fur. That wolf was closest to her, and he moved towards where she had crouched; it was inches from her face.

Sophia's breathing became labored and louder. The cold air that had once bitten deeply into her skin mattered no more. All she could feel was the fear in her chest and the warm breath of the creature whose muzzle was almost at her cheek. It let out a snarl and then snapped. Sophia cried out loud and turned her face into the wall, shutting her eyes as tightly as possible. Santiago pushed Suresh out of the way and embraced Sophia as Domingo held Lee back.

"Soph, you are HERE. With us. Open your eyes."

Both sets of Sophia's eyes opened. She simultaneously looked into Santiago's eyes and the large eyes of the enormous wolf. The wolf's head cocked to the side in realization.

"They sense us!" he said in a deep, guttural voice. The three wolves howled loudly.

Their sound echoed all the way through the group. As quickly as they heard the howls, their weapons were out.

"What is going on?" Domingo asked while looking up.

"They know I'm there," Sophia said, looking into Santiago's eyes.

She observed as the other two wolves came in line with the leader, then crouched down low.

"Guys, they are coming after us!"

Her second self began to reconnect with her physical self. The wolves started to charge. It was then Sophia noticed the snow beneath their feet. With each step, the snow underneath the wolves began to gather. The wolves began running at a frightening speed, and the snow beneath them grew with equal intensity. It was an avalanche heading in the groups' direction. On top of the rapidly moving snow, were three giant, very pissed-off wolves.

"We've got to move," she said, her two halves finally a whole. With the aid of Santiago, she stood up.

"What did you see?" Suresh asked.

"The wolves started an avalanche, and it's heading our way, quickly," she said.

"We can't outrun an avalanche," Raja called out. "We must climb." The ground beneath their feet started vibrating. "Now!"

Sophia was an accomplished climber; she'd been traversing and scaling walls since she was a child. But climbing a wall of ice with your bare hands is a beast all its own. She made it a few feet up before she began to feel her grip weaken. Everyone was much farther up than her, and even the brothers seemed to catch on a technique. She kept climbing despite the pain in her hands. Gods, she hated the cold. The rumbling became stronger, and the walls began to move a bit. Sophia let out a cry before she slid down. Lee, who was high up with Suresh and Quentin looked down.

"Look for the grips Suresh and Jasira are creating," he called down to her.

Her hands were throbbing at this point. why couldn't their destination be in a warmer climate? Heck, why couldn't their destination be somewhere no one was trying to kill them? She continued to struggle. Raja released his hands and slid down to Sophia. With a single, quick motion, Raja extended his massive arm and placed Sophia on his back.

"Oof," he grunted, "you are much heavier than you look."

"I'm going to try not to take that personally."

"It's a compliment. Muscle weighs more than fat."

Raja began to climb with Sophia clinging to his back. The added weight was making it difficult for him to catch up with the others. The wind burst in, shooting chunks of snow, followed by the avalanche filling in the ground beneath them at an incredible speed. The walls began to vibrate violently, and the snow now was only a foot from Raja's feet and rising quickly. The grip holds had become smaller and smaller.

"I can't anymore," Suresh called out, his body trembling. "I exhausted everything I had back there at the campsite." Lee looked at Quentin, who was struggling too.

"This should be high enough," Lee said. "Just try to hang on," he yelled to everyone. The whole group, save for Raja and Sophia, were high up and parallel to one another. Raja continued to climb, attempting to catch up. Sophia looked to her side and saw the white wolves.

"There they are!" she shouted, her hair blowing wildly.

Raja turned his head and took in the massive creatures. He wanted to reach for his weapon, but he couldn't risk losing his grip. He increased his speed up the wall, but the wolves were faster. They zeroed in on Sophia and Raja like they were a wounded calf that the herd left behind.

"I need you to flip around to my front," Raja said. Sophia did as he asked. Her hands were stiff from the cold, and the bitter chill that wind carried made the task more difficult than it should have been. They now faced one another.

"I can't hold on much longer," he yelled, "we are going to fall. Hang on, okay." Sophia nodded her head. She looked down and saw that the wolves were only a few feet away.

"I'll get the ones down there," the wolf with the grey facial markings said loud enough for everyone to hear, " while you two pick off the rest."

"Disgusting beasts!" Garret yelled. "Have at it! I'll slit your throat if you come any closer!"

Raja's hands slipped again.

"Ready?" he said to Sophia as she nodded and shut her eyes. She tightened her grip around Raja. Raja looked up at Lee.

"Don't worry, Lee. I'll protect her," he called out. Then Raja released the wall.

It was slow-motion for both Garret and Lee. They yelled as they watched Raja and Sophia fall. The wolf with the grey markings lunged at Raja. The beast went in, jaws open, fangs exposed, Raja opened his massive arms, Sophia clung on for dear life, and with his hands, Raja grabbed the wolf's jaw and shut it. He pulled the wolf close and used his strength to crush him. The wolf yelped, and Sophia shrieked against the pressure of Raja's strong arms. Those were the last two sounds they all heard as Raja, Sophia, and the wolf plummeted into the moving snow.

58

THE BREAKING
OF AN ELITE

Talbot and Yaren had secured enough funds to travel to the abandoned town of Carion. Yaren sold the remainder of her jewelry and they obtained food, water, and supplies. When they arrived, Talbot and Yaren examined the decrepit houses and determined that, if they took parts from each house, they would be able to restore one home to livable. Talbot opened the boarded-up well while Yaren searched for edible vegetation. Everything had turned in their favor, but, this night, she couldn't sleep. It had been days since their arrival and she was restless tonight. Talbot was across the room, sleeping on layered-up blankets. Yaren didn't want to wake him. She slid out of her bed, took in a deep breath, and wandered around the house.

When she was confident that her nerves would take more to calm, she stepped outside. Carion was situated on the southernmost part of the continent; the cold season here was quite comfortable. She sat down just outside the house and leaned back. As she looked up into the stars, she wondered about Sophia and what was happening. Then she thought of Leata and Atara. She placed her face in her hands and started to cry. It didn't matter that it was years ago, it didn't matter that they were separated beforehand; the pain of losing her beloved sister was a wound that had never healed. Yaren wiped her eyes and gained control of her emotions. She peered forward into the distance and saw a faint light moving. Yaren stood up and walked towards it. In no time, she was scrambling back towards the house. She barged into the house, startling Talbot.

"Troops, Talbot!" Yaren yelled as she packed a sack full of rations. Talbot tossed sheets across the room as he shot up. Without a thought, he and Yaren began to destroy their little home. Talbot tipped the table, broke some chairs, and made as much a mess as possible. The house they worked so hard to turn into a home had once again become unlivable. The two looked longingly at the room one last time, both wishing the little peace they had here had lasted just a bit longer. With an inhale, they turned their back and were on their way to the dock. Yaren tossed the sack into the boat, Talbot climbed in, then he assisted Yaren. They pulled up the anchor and eased further out to sea.

"How did he find us?" Yaren sank down onto the deck.

Talbot shrugged and sat down with her. "I'm surprised he'd send troops after us. With everything that is happening in Tychi, I figured he would only send several Greys if any."

"It was much more than just several."

The boat began to rock, and the sound of a bottle that had freed itself from Yaren's sack clanked and rolled from one side of the boat to the other.

"Something is not right," Yaren said.

Talbot lowered his gaze and looked at Yaren over his

glasses with a faint smirk on his face. "There arc a lot of things that aren't right."

"I mean about this. There is no way he would search for us at an abandoned port town this south of Tychi."

Talbot's smirk slowly faded. Yaren knew she knew that this was it. It was over.

"Those men are not for us." Talbot's words were barely audible.

Yaren covered her mouth, and her eyes began to water.

"He's setting up base. Which means."

"His armada," Yaren managed to whisper.

They didn't stand up to look, they didn't try to escape, they didn't move. At that moment, it was as if Yaren and Talbot could see the metaphorical fire that they started, the one they fed with the insistence of Sophia at Tychi, the one that had begun to spread through their land with people now carrying a torch ready to fight, that fire. They saw it and now stepped back from it. As the bottle clanked more repeatedly, they knew Kahel's armada drew closer.

Talbot grabbed Yaren's hand. "I'm so sorry."

With an elegance that only an Elite could possess, Yaren tipped her head. "It is I who should apologize. I made us come here."

"No, Yaren. That's not what I meant."

Confusion crossed Yaren's face.

"If we are captured, he will do to us what he did to Boris," he said. "Well, not you. You are a woman; therefore, you have a chance." Talbot turned and opened a small bag tied to his hip. He pulled out a dagger. "I couldn't protect Leata. But I'll be dammed if I can't protect you."

"Talbot, NO!" Yaren grabbed Talbot's hand just before he could thrust the dagger into his abdomen.

"Do you not understand, Yaren? He knows nothing of you; to him, you are just a frail Elite woman. But me? Your sister

Leata begged for my life, for my freedom; he knows there is more to me, that I could have information, and so I will not let him have me. I will not become a Grey; I will not reveal our secrets."

His determined tone caught her by surprise. Yaren had only two regrets in her life. The first was staying behind in Atara while Leata trained with the Majji. The second was this moment. Dropping her guard for the bit it took her to process his determination cost her dearly as Talbot used that opportunity to pull hard at the blade with Yaren's hand still on his. Yaren watched as her last connection to Atara, to Leata, stabbed himself.

"Sophia lives. I can feel it"—he placed a fist across his chest—"here. And I know she will make her way to the Fae before Kahel even learns of their existence. You must have faith; she will make it out alive, and you both will be reunited. Promise me to fight. Do what you must to survive. I don't want to see you anytime soon. Promise me!"

"I promise."

"Now you listen to me: tell them I planned this, tell them I had leverage over you, that I kidnapped you, that I did horrible things to you."

Yaren's face crumpled and she nodded.

"You do that, okay. Kahel would rather believe that I was a mastermind than a woman had outsmarted him."

Yaren pulled the blade out and dropped it. She threw her arms around Talbot, not caring of the blood that was pooling between them.

"When I'm gone," Talbot said, "make sure they do not find my body."

Yaren shook her head in acknowledgment.

"Tell my sister that I love her," Yaren cried, "and that we will be together soon."

Talbot smiled. "Not too soon."

Yaren held Talbot till she felt no more life in him. She then crawled towards their bags of rations and located the rope. She proceeded to strip out of her bloodstained clothes and down to her petticoat. She felt the armada upon her. Three, maybe four of his ships, she thought to herself. She used her clothes to wipe up as much blood off the deck as possible. Finally, Yaren tied some weighted bags to Talbot's body. With effort, she lifted him to the lip of the bulkhead. She kissed his forehead and then released his body. She watched as his body sank into the dark sea. She sat against the side of the boat and wrapped her legs with her arms. At this instant, Yaren was physically and mentally exhausted. She was also content staying there forever or at least till the armada spotted her, which they did moments later. The seamen boarded the little boat with their blades out and began to search the ship. It didn't take much time before they spotted her. What they found, though, was a tattered shell of a woman whose empty eyes poured tears onto her pale cheeks.

"My gods." One of the leather-armored seamen called out. Strands of his jet-black hair were loose from his bandana and blowing across his long pale face. "Lady Yaren…"

The shocked tone of his voice confirmed two things. One, that these men weren't sent there to find them but to set up base at Carion, and two being that she was recognized quickly so Kahel had been searching for them.

"I've found Lady Yaren! Arm yourselves! Talbot must be around here somewhere!" The other men listened without questioning, which led Yaren to assume that he was a general of sorts.

"It's okay now, my lady. I am Commander Duroc; I'm here to take you back to Tychi." As he reached out for Yaren, she retreated as far into the side of the boat as possible. Another seaman came towards her with a blanket. The man approached and opened the blanket, and Yaren's eyes widened at the sight of him. She held herself tighter. Duroc held his hand up, which immediately stopped the forward motion of the man with the blanket.

"Don't. I don't think she knows what's going on," he said. "Hand me the blanket, I'll get it to her; all of you others back away." All the men did as they were told.

Yaren knew precisely what was going on. She was supposed to act like a kidnapped, violated woman, but in reality she just participated in the death of her last true friend and the last link to her sister. There was no need for her to act; Yaren was in full-blown shock. Duroc approached her with a blanket, and Yaren let out a heartbreaking cry as he wrapped it around her. He then lifted her, and she placed her arms around his neck and continued to cry in his chest.

"Sir," one of the soldiers called out, "we've searched the whole boat, but there is no one else here."

"Lady Yaren, where is Talbot?"

Yaren tensed up at the sound of his name, and in her mind she saw Talbot disappearing into the depth of the sea once again.

"You are safe now, he cannot get to you ever again, but we need to know where he is."

She heard his echoes in her mind, repeating "Make sure they do not find my body."

"I stabbed him." Her voice broke.

"Is he dead?"

He's part of the Green now, with my sister. He is eternal now, Yaren told herself.

"No."

"Where did he go?"

Yaren lifted her hand and pointed to the shore.

59

WHEN WORLDS COLLIDE

Garret moved quickly in a lateral direction across the frozen wall. The blood flowing through his injured hands left an unnerving red trail that Lee followed. In the manner that Raja caught the grey-marked wolf, there was no way he was uninjured. And with the amount of blood flowing from Garret's hands, it didn't take a scholar to realize that the wolf's fangs must have cut clear through Raja's hands. Wound after wound began to appear on Garret as he continually traversed the wall. Lee watched as more blood appeared, this time on Garret's back, seeping through his clothing.

"Garret! You're losing too much blood!" Lee started to take leaps towards Garret. "Stop!"

Garret gave no indication that he heard Lee.

"Garret!" Jasira screamed from behind Lee in a pleading tone.

"You are doing the best you can." Cyrus reached out to

touch Jasira. "Don't worry about him! Just keep making those grips."

Jasira whipped around to Cyrus, her face full of indignation, but there was no time for her to yell at him. He was right about focusing on the grips, if Jasira had the time she would like to tell Cyrus "Don't worry? I care about him, a lot, and you need to learn to deal with that." But now wasn't the time. Jasira turned and began to create larger, closer-together ice grips on the wall. Garret turned back to her and through the unforgiving wind, relentless snow, and the distance, for a moment, their eyes met. He then turned back forward and increased his pace. Her chest expanded as she took in a deep breath. It was just a glance, but with that look, Garret had told her, "Thank you, I hear you, and I'll be alright." Feeling energized again, Jasira increased her velocity.

"Slow your pace! You'll exhaust yourself," Cyrus called. "You are doing all you can, if you push yourself, they will fall."

Jasira continued forward. "Do you not trust me?" she called out.

"What?"

They watched as a cut slashed across Garret's cheek. The blow sent his head and arm back, making him lose his grip. Jasira created a large platform, which Garret fell on. He gathered himself and continued forward.

"Jasira, stop! Manage your energy, you're doing too much."

"No, Cyrus, I am not. You and I both know I can do more." Jasira powered forward as she focused on Garret.

"Don't."

"I'm stronger than all of you," she said as she created more grips. "My Essence feels at home here, and I know what I am capable of."

"Look!" Cyrus pointed ahead of him where the two remaining wolves began to dive into the snow.

"Lee!" Jasira called out, "I think they've located them!"

"Unless this avalanche stops, there is no way we can search for Raja and Sophia," Lee called back.

Jasira had stopped so suddenly that Cyrus had to stop himself from slamming into her. Jasira turned to face Cyrus.

"Have faith in me for once." She then pushed back and released the wall.

"No—" Cyrus reached for Jasira but only grasped cold air.

With no more grips being created, both Garret and Lee turned in time to see Jasira's body arch back and dive headfirst into the snow. They then looked up towards Cyrus' crestfallen face as cuts began to appear across it and his arms. There was this unanimous silence between all of them as they looked down into the snow waiting for something to happen. Anything. Then it did. The avalanche began to decelerate. Lee turned to the two wolves who looked perplexed as they slowed their pace. The snow continued to creep slower and slower until it came to a full stop. The wolves charged then dove into the snow.

"They are looking for the grey-marked wolf!" Lee called out as he let go of the wall. "Raja and Sophia have to be near it!"

The entire group released their holds and ran towards where the two wolves were digging and diving. Lee and Garret had a significant lead, with the others several paces behind. Cyrus broke away from them and began to search for Jasira. Each step was crunching loudly in the snow.

"Where are you?" He said, looking down at the snow. "Where are you?" He closed his eyes, then ran to his left where he knelt down. Heat emanated from his hands, softening and melting the snow below. He slammed his hands down, then dug. His arms were shoulder-deep into the snow when he began to pull back. Jasira's hands held his forearms tightly. He pulled until she was completely free. He fell back and pulled her into his arms. The heat he radiatcd warmed her shivering body. Cyrus held her tightly and kissed her hair.

Lee and Garret were continuing their charge when the two digging wolves stopped and faced them. The wolves changed their focus and began sprinting towards them.

"Shit, Garret, we can't take those things."

"We? No. Me? Sure." A pop of electricity appeared and disappeared next to Garret. "Stay back, buddy, once I am done, make a break for it."

Since entering the Iceway, Lee had witnessed the gifts of his comrades awaken. Fire, Ice, and Earth, each respectively made their appearance. What he had never seen was Garret's gift. Lee had wondered if Garret was even blessed with one at all. But now, he knew better. Garret couldn't play with his gift the way the others have. As if birthing from the earth, bolts of lightning crawled up Garret's side. Lee's eyes widened as Garret leaped directly towards the two wolves. The sky cracked open and down came a fierce electric storm that encompassed Garret and the two wolves. The wolves crumpled where they stood, and Garret landed on the snow hard.

"Go now. I'm not sure how long I've stunned them," he said to Lee before he fell on his side.

Lee quickly made it to the spot where the two wolves had been digging. He placed his hands on the snow, and the ground began to shake. It was gentle at first then became violent. Suresh, Quentin, Domingo, and Santiago, who were all far behind, lost their balance. The snow began to crack, then collapse within itself. One of the wolves had regained consciousness and stood up. It shook its head as it tried to balance itself. A large crack appeared in front of Lee. Before Lee could enter, the wolf raced ahead then jumped over Lee into the opening. Moments later, the wolf emerged, dragging out the grey-marked leader wolf. He pulled him far away from the group and began to lick where the leader wolf was bleeding. The second wolf also came to and stumbled away towards his pack. They were licking and nuzzling the leader wolf, who was not responding. Lee jumped down into the crack and saw Raja laying on his side, holding Sophia. They were both unconscious and breathing. Raja sustained severe wounds while Sophia's were only minor. It is evident that, while fighting the snow and the wolf, Raja made sure he kept Sophia safe. With the help of the others, Lee was able to remove the two from the hole.

"They are breathing," Lee said as he climbed out of the hole. "That's a good sign, but Raja is hurt, real hurt."

Garret wandered to where Raja was laying. "You chivalrous idiot," he said while taking deep breaths and sitting down next to him. Garret grabbed Raja's unconscious hand. Raja's wounds began to seal as Garret's grew significantly worse.

"Ow, fuck!" Garret said.

Jasira limped towards her injured comrades with an arm around Cyrus as he supported her weight. The gash they shared was deep and still bled lightly, but to the pair's relief was healing. Garret watched as Cyrus lowered Jasira beside him. Without a thought, Garret closed his eyes and placed his head on Jasira's shoulder.

"You're going to be okay," Jasira gently said as she began to shuffle through her medicine bag. She handed several items to Cyrus, who watched Garret intently.

Garret flinched and squirmed when they tended to the wounds on his body but was statuesque when Jasira touched his face to apply a cream then a bright purple leaf to the cut on his cheek. He couldn't stop himself from staring at her lips.

"Your lips are blue," he said as he reached to touch them. It was then Cyrus unnecessarily tightened a bandage on Garret's arm. Garret let out a grunt and looked away from

Jasira. She then handed him a small vial.

"Drink."

He quickly downed the tonic.

"Jeez, kid, this stuff tastes like shit!"

"You mean to tell me you've eaten shit before?" Jasira smiled and avoided eye contact while she worked on a cut on his leg. "Because, well, that would just be disgusting."

Garret snickered and turned to look at Raja, whose eyes were slowly opening. He let out a sigh of relief.

Cyrus grabbed Jasira's hand as she put away her ointments.

"You promised after we tended to Garret, you would let me heal you," Cyrus said with both worry and anger in his tone. Color grew in Jasira's face as she avoided any eye contact with Garret and sat down with her back to his side.

"I hit a rock," she told Cyrus, "a chunk of it broke off inside my leg. That's why you can't help me heal. You need to pull it out first."

"You should have told me beforehand; you could have been healed by now." The anger in Cyrus's tone masked all the worry he was feeling.

"It wasn't life-threatening, and it could have waited," she said back. Cyrus took in a deep breath. He saw the shard of rock lodged in the side of her knee.

"This is going to hurt."

"I know."

Jasira shrieked as Cyrus pulled the shard out quickly. To their side, Garret clenched his jaw. Blood began to seep through Cyrus' pants, and Jasira's wound began to heal.

"Don't take it all," she said.

"You bravely risked everything and saved us while I clung on like a coward. So, this is the least I can do." Cyrus stood up and held his hand out for Jasira. She took his hand, and they walked towards Sophia, who was conscious and laying against Santiago.

"Are you wounded? Does anything hurt?" Jasira asked.

"No," Sophia replied in a sort of a daze. She sat up and let the last few minutes catch up to her. She just survived a freakishly giant wolf attack during a massive avalanche. Trying to wrap her head around that was difficult. All of her friends looked a little worse for wear, but they were all alive, and she thanked the gods for that. Sophia looked to the west, where the two wolves were trying to wake their fallen leader. She shouldn't have felt any sympathy for them, but for some strange reason there it was, sympathy and guilt. Then, deep within her, something spoke, telling her to go to the wolves. Sophia knew this was just downright crazy. That thing just beat the shit out of Raja and tried to eat her. Again, she felt herself being taken over and began to rationalize those crazy thoughts urging her to approach the wolves. They were only trying to protect their home, their people. They had no idea what Sophia and the others' intentions were; for all the Fae knew, they were troops sent by Kahel. Suresh and Quentin should have found a way to announce their purpose. Not doing so only caused the Fae to defend themselves. That made her and the group responsible for what happened to the leader wolf, and therefore it was their responsibility to return it to health. Sophia grabbed Jasira's satchel and stood up.

"We can't let him die," she said with conviction and walked towards the wolves.

"Him? Sophia, did you not see what that creature did to Raja?" Santiago said. She ignored him and continued on forward. It was then that Domingo came to his brother's side.

"Look at her," Domingo whispered.

Santiago watched as Sophia took steps further and further away. He knew in his heart what his brother meant. He saw it again, just like a few weeks back—that wasn't their Sophia. Lee looked at the group, who were all either too exhausted or taken aback to stop her. He stared at them in disbelief, then ran after Sophia. He grabbed her hand and pulled her back.

"What are you doing? Raja and Garret just about died trying to protect you from those things! Jasira did a swan dive into the avalanche, not even knowing what she was going to do was possible, but did it anyway, all to save you, and you are just going to walk over there?"

She looked down at Lee's hand that was holding her wrist tightly.

"I suggest you release me immediately, Leonardo," she said.

Lee let go and stepped back. Hearing his full name was always jarring, but the way she said it was like an order. Resistance wasn't an option. She continued on, closer and closer to the whimpering wolves. One lifted his head and growled in her direction; the other turned then snapped at her approach. It used its body as a barricade, protecting the fallen leader.

"I mean no harm," she said confidently.

"Our brother lies there dying, by the hands of one of your people and you come to say you mean us no harm." His golden eyes stared angrily at her.

"We all do what we can to protect our own," she said, "and we were doing exactly what you are doing for your kind."

"She lies!" The wolf in front of the dying leader said. His eyes were different; they were forest green and full of hate. "She just wants to get close enough the finish us off."

Sophia stepped closer. "This satchel has medicine that will heal your brother. I promise you that I won't harm you. Let me help. Please."

The leader took a staggered breath, followed by a full exhale. His body flattened, and no breaths followed.

"No! Brother! You mustn't give in!" Green Eyes said. Golden Eyes turned and pushed his nose against the leader's face.

Their words carried clearly in the Iceway. Garret helpcd Raja up on his feet as Santiago and Domingo looked at one another. They knew all too well the pain of losing a brother. Without a word, they approached the wolves. In a matter of seconds, they were standing next to Sophia. To show that they were there to help, Domingo and Santiago held their weapons up and placed them on the ground. Sophia walked forward. The two wolves were distraught; a green glow began to come from the leader wolf.

"Essence," Domingo said softly.

A heart-wrenching sound echoed into the cold sky as the two wolves howled, their brother was gone. Jasira stifled a cry and covered her mouth.

"We are too late," Santiago said.

"No," Sophia said, "we are not. Now help me before he joins the Green." She opened the satchel and handed Domingo a box. "Take half and apply this to the wound on his neck. Santiago, take the other half and put it on the wound on his abdomen."

"He's dead," the green-eyed wolf snapped, "there is no point."

"Then what harm will come if we try?" Sophia responded.

"Let them, brother," Golden Eyes said. Green Eyes growled and stepped back.

Domingo and Santiago did as Sophia said. Sophia then lay her head where the enormous wolf's heart was. She nuzzled closer into the white fur. The green glow that was emanating from the wolf began to pull towards Sophia. Everyone watched in awe.

"It is not your time," she whispered. "It's not your time."

"Cover those wounds up with your hands," Sophia instructed the brothers.

The Essence that was about to join with Sophia backtracked and spread itself into the wolf. At this point, Domingo and Santiago's hands began to glow. A green light seeped from their hands into the wolf's wounds. The wolf's chest started to rise and fall again. Sophia lay on his chest with her eyes closed. The brothers cautiously removed their hands to find the wounds were closed and scabbed over. They were both overcome by strong lightheadedness.

"Sophia?" Domingo questioned. He knew what he saw, but how it happened was beyond him.

"Eilith," Sophia said with tears falling from her closed eyes. "Without even knowing it, she taught me, us, how to cast." Sophia opened her eyes and looked at Domingo. "We just cast a healing spell; we used the medicine and our Essence to heal him."

The leader wolf let out a small moan.

"I had made my peace, tiny human, and was ready to join the Green," he said in a deep voice. "I didn't ask you to bring me back." His eyes shifted down to Sophia.

"It was us, brother. We weren't ready to let you go." Golden Eyes said.

Sophia, Domingo, and Santiago backed away and let the three wolves enjoy their reunion.

"I miss him." Santiago thought of Marcello as he watched the wolves nuzzle one another. "I doubt this pain will ever subside."

"It helped though," Domingo said, "making sure they didn't feel that sort of pain."

"Indeed, it did."

The others walked up cautiously to Sophia and the brothers. Just as Santiago and Domingo did earlier, everyone placed their weapons down.

"I would feel better about this if we had teeth like they do," Garret said. They held their hands up to show that they too were unarmed. The leader wolf got to his feet and turned to face Sophia.

"I find myself questioning orders. We were to kill you," he said. "You may have saved my life, but tell me why I should spare yours."

"This is a terrible, horrible idea," Garret said as he slowly lowered down, with his hands still in the air, eyeing his weapon.

Green Eyes turned his head to look at Garret. He crouched down and began to growl.

"Garret. Get. Up. Now," Raja said.

"You know, Raj, the second those giant fur balls decide to pounce we are all dead."

Sophia looked at the brother wolves and said, "We only seek passage. We are on a mission to retrieve the other half of the Majji's staff." She took a giant gulp. The bravery that compelled her to move towards the wolves moments ago was gone. "Our home was destroyed, my husband killed, their brother murdered, and our only wish is to stop Kahel and prevent any more senseless death."

"Senseless death, you say?" the leader spoke. "The Green is dying, and you seek vengeance? This is why we Fae care not to be mixed into human affairs. Always so self-involved, you cannot see what's right in front of you. You will war, fight, and destroy all till she is dead and there is nothing left but your egos and ash."

"Vengeance means nothing to us," Sophia defended. "We want to save the Green; we want to find a way to stop Kahel. But the Majji is dying and has no Apprentice, and he must reunite the staff to give us a fighting chance."

This information caught the leader's attention. "Halcyon is dying?"

"Yes."

"How can that be? He is so young." The leader looked at

Sophia and the group as he remained pensive for a moment. "I thought you were the Apprentice. With the gifts, you possess, sensing us, and healing with magic."

"It's a bit of a long story, and if you allow us to live I will be more than happy to tell it to you." Sophia shrugged nervously.

The leader scoffed, looked at everyone from the group, then looked back at Sophia. "I've decided to trust these humans."

Garret lowered his arms and fell to his knees.

"I really thought that thing was going to eat us," he said, letting out a long exhale.

60

THE FAE

"I am Dasan, this is Sewati," said the leader wolf as he pointed his head to the golden-eyed wolf, "and this is Muraco."

Sophia looked at the wolves. Both Dasan and Sewati had golden eyes, while Muraco's were forest green. Other than the grey tribal-like markings on Dasan's face, the three wolves were all white. "We are warriors from the White Fang Tribe."

"I am Sophia, this is Domingo and Santiago, and we are from the fallen town of Salinas."

"I am Suresh, and this is Quentin, Cyrus, Jasira, Lee, Garret, and Raja. We are from Atara."

Dasan stretched, then shook. His fur stood on end, all messy for a moment, then settled down.

"Fallen town, you say? Has Kahel declared war?"

"No, our people had no warning," Domingo said. "Kahel wanted his intentions to remain a secret, and a town full of concerned witnesses would prove to be a problem. So, he ordered troops to murder everyone; he didn't anticipate any resistance"—he took in a staggered breath—"but found it in my love, Eilith, who was a survivor of the Warrior Tribe, and our youngest brother, Marcello. They made sure that every single one of those bastards fell, including Corentin."

"Corentin, the Dark Hunter?" Muraco's green eyes widened as he turned towards Domingo. He had cared not about the yapping earlier, but this was a topic he found interesting.

"Yes."

"He resurfaced just to aid the attack on your town?"

"From the information, we had gathered," Lee added, "some years ago, he became Kahel's right-hand man."

"But why would the Dark Hunter join forces with Kahel and stop killing? He required the Essence from his victims; it was the only way he could survive," Muraco continued. "After he was consumed with the Mad Essence, to retain it he had to feed on the Essence of other beings. The people of the Warrior Tribe were full of powerful Essence. That is why he hunted them."

"Wait." Sophia asked, "I thought only the Majji and the Apprentice could absorb Essence?"

"Essence has a choice with the Majji and the Apprentice; it can join you or join the Green. Corentin fed on Essence. He stole it. Which means that Kahel had a way to feed Corentin; it's the only way the Dark Hunter would join him."

"Tychi has a Factory District," Sophia said "it's full of facilities that pull fuel from deep within the land. What if he's pulling more than just that?"

"Mother's milk..." Sewati said.

"Gods. That means he is stealing Essence directly from the Green," Dasan said in disgust.

It made sense to Sophia. Those feelings she felt outside of Tychi weren't hers, they were the Green's.

"She was trying to tell me," Sophia said as she turned to Domingo and Santiago, "outside of Tychi where Gabriel and I fought. When I held that dirt, I felt angry; I felt betrayed. The land was trying to tell me what was happening. So, the land around Tychi isn't dying on its own, its Essence is being stolen." Sophia thought some more. "Gods! He's built those monstrosities all over! He's bleeding her to death!"

Everyone stood in silence for a moment. They all knew deep down something like this was happening, but Dasan's information about how Corentin lived solidified it. Kahel is robbing Essence directly from the land.

"We must go to the Council," Dasan said.

"I am sorry, new friend, Dasan," Quentin said, "we wish you no disrespect, but our time is limited. Our journey will take us through Northern Passage to the Graveland, then back to Atara, and there is no time for us to meet and discuss our findings with your Council," Quentin said in an ever-so-diplomatic tone.

"Quentin and other tiny humans, that was not a request. Safe passage through Fae territory can only be granted by the Council. It is Fae law to kill humans on sight," Dasan said as he turned his back and began walking down the trail. "You all would be dead by nightfall."

"We keep a low profile, so no Fae will know of our presence," Suresh added.

"Everyone already knows of your presence," Sewati mumbled. "We were sent by the Council to deal with you."

"Do not fear, new friends, you travel with us. That will keep you safe until a decision is made," Dasan said.

"Can't you escort us to the Northern Passage then?" Sophia asked as they walked. She couldn't help but notice how Muraco kept turning back to look at her.

"Laws are absolute in Eurija, and there is only one punishment for delinquencies," Dasan said, "death."

"We kept you alive; so we are now marked for death," Sewati added. "We head north instead of south, and they will assume we are trying to escape punishment. We will all be killed."

Sophia watched as Muraco kept glancing at her. She

leaned closer to Lee as they walked.

"I see it too," he said without her asking.

Quentin held his arm out and stopped the group. "If your laws are absolute, then we will be killed no matter what we do. I'd rather fight our way to the Northern Passage, than walk into a Council that will certainly slay us."

Muraco let out a low growl.

"Brother, calm yourself," Sewati said as he sauntered in front of Muraco, blocking him from causing any trouble. The three wolves were enormous creatures. Larger than horses, Sewati was smaller than the others, though. Sophia was sure Muraco could take him, but the wolf resigned his position the moment his brother stepped in front of him. "Dasan failed to explain himself fully." Sewati said, "We have the right to speak before punishment is delivered. We Fae had no idea what your intentions were. Ten of you walked into the Iceway, fully armed." Muraco continued to growl, and Dasan snapped quickly in his brothers' direction. Muraco quieted and turned to look at Sophia again. Lee pulled her behind him. Sewati then continued, "We are fair beings, and I am sure that the Council will hear us out, especially since Dasan himself has a seat there."

Dasan and Sewati explained the Council to the group. One leader was elected to represent each group of Fae: one for the water creatures, one for the flying creatures, and so on. Dasan had represented the land-bound creatures for over fifty years. His tribe, the White Fang Tribe, was one of the highest-ranked tribes in the Fae world and well-respected. They had pull, which the humans needed. The three wolves led the way, followed by Quentin and Suresh. Lee stood in front of Sophia most of the way, blocking her from Muraco's curious glances. All of the wounds the group had sustained healed on the final stretch of the path. Raja was walking as if he had never been near death's door, and Jasira's gash was gone. All that was left was a tear in her pants, decorated with dried blood. Cyrus walked alongside Jasira, who kept her eyes low to the ground. He tried grabbing her hand once, but she pulled away.

"I refuse to allow history to repeat itself," Dasan said as he led everyone safely out of the Iceway. Like they were never in the cold, the path quickly opened up, and green grass aggressively took over. Sophia turned back and saw a massive rock wall that spanned miles from both sides.

"Other than the southern entrance, which remains heavily guarded, this is the only way in and the only way out," Dasan said. "The Kalyptra protects us from ships traveling north, and the Shukai mountains protect us from any ships launched from Hokai. Unless you can fly, our land of Eurija is inaccessible."

After having two large walls on either of their sides for days, being in a vast open space was strange to Sophia. Still, the scenery was breathtaking, gentle rolling hills full of beautiful wildflowers beyond the eye can see, and the sun warm and bright with a calm breeze that began to put them at ease. They removed their coats.

"Make your meals here," Dasan said, walking towards a tree. "Sewati and one of yours can go fetch some water from the brook."

"I'll go with him," Jasira said quickly. Cyrus grabbed her arm in protest, but she shrugged him off. It was then Sophia realized that she missed something. She had to ask Jasira exactly what that was when they were alone.

They quickly made and ate their meals. Jasira had returned with all their canteens full of glorious fresh water. Muraco stood tall and lifted his nose to sniff the air, then turned his eyes to Sophia. She was getting uneasy again, the same way she was uneasy when Boris watched her with his grey eyes. And just like Boris, she felt that Muraco knew something about her that she didn't.

"Apprentice," Muraco called out.

Sophia knew he meant her, and she wished he listened to her story better because she had already explained that she wasn't the Apprentice. Still, it would be rude to keep her silence.

"Muraco, I am no Apprentice."

"Is that what they are telling you?" he said, humoring her. He stretched his long legs, then lay on the ground. "You have an Elemental. You reek of it."

"Muraco, hold your tongue," Dasan said.

"Wait, no." Sophia asked, wanting never to be left in the dark again, "What do you mean?"

"Its odor is all over you and that one over there." Muraco pointed his nose to Lee.

"Elementals have a unique scent. They smell like hydrangeas, thousands of them." Muraco said, "Makes my nose itch."

"Please excuse our brother. He has yet to learn how to respect one's privacy," Dasan said.

"Who has time for formalities? Only an Apprentice who is about to become Majji have Elementals, they tell us she isn't the Apprentice and yet"—he sniffs at Sophia—"an Elemental has obviously been with her for a long time. So, I doubt it's Mahes I'm picking up."

Sophia recalled the regal lion engulfed in a majestic blue flame. Mahes was Halcyon's Elemental.

"I do not have an Elemental, but," she said, turning away from Muraco, "one has been with me all my life." She missed Zephyr; there were times when she was younger when the wind would stop around her, and at the time she would think nothing of it, but now that Sophia knew that he was a living breathing entity she missed his companionship. She looked at the wind play with the blades of grass. Her heart ached. She longed for her friend, but what made her hurt the most was the realization that he wasn't hers. "When Queen Leata transferred her Essence into me, he followed," she finished. Lee, who was sitting to her side, nudged her. She gave him the 'I'm okay' nod.

"Queen Leata," Dasan said, "that means the scent Muraco is picking up is Zephyr. This is interesting, two servant Elementals existing within the same moment."

"Everything and everyone that has come to ever be is existing within the same moment," Garret said while he chewed a grain of grass. He was leaning against a tree with his arms behind his head.

"Thank you for that useless bit of information, Garret," Jasira said.

"No problem, kid."

"Why is it interesting?" Quentin asked Dasan. "Aren't Elementals Fae? We were under the impression that, like your White Fang Tribe, Elementals existed in mass numbers."

The brother wolves chuckled.

Quentin's face grew blank. "Yes. Mocking us is very helpful."

Dasan cleared his throat and regained his composure.

"There two kinds of Elementals, ones the Ibex could call upon, known as the 'Monarchs,' and ones that bonded with the Majji, known as the 'Servants.'" The Monarchs are Ifrit, Shiva, Geb, and Fujin, also known as fire, water, earth, and wind. The Servant Elementals were Fae once, but not anymore." Dasan's words caught everyone's attention. "Us Fae respect and answer to an ancient calling. The same way humans do. When one of yours becomes Majji, one of ours becomes Elemental. We do not receive training; the transformation happens quite suddenly. The Monarchs choose who will bond and bless them with the gift of Summon. One day they are Fae, flesh and blood, and the next day they are Elemental, pure magic and energy with a deeply rooted desire to unite with the Majji. Together they roam the land and maintain balance and peace. It is bittersweet, because the ones who become Elementals, the highest honor possible, are banished from Eurija forever."

"Because it is forbidden to consort with humans," Quentin added.

"So, while five Elementals are existing at once, only one should be roaming the lands. That is why I find it interesting that two are roaming the lands; it's never happened before." Dasan looked at Garret, who had his eyes closed but his slight smile showed that he knew he was being watched.

"Are they bonded the same way Atarans are?" Sophia asked.

"No, not the same, it's much more personal and stronger," Dasan said. "They can connect telepathically, and even though you cannot always see an Elemental they are beside their Majji at all times. In a way, it is as if they become one."

"So, our dying Majji means Mahes will pass too," Quentin said.

"Yes," Muraco said then stood up. "Mahes was amazing as Fae. I wish I could have seen him as an Elemental."

"When he wanted to be seen, he was engulfed in this blue hypnotic flame," Garret said without moving, "he never spoke to anyone but Halcyon, he was always composed, and his majestic presence demanded respect, which we all gave him." Garret opened his eyes, then spit out the grass he was chewing. "Shouldn't we get going? I can't wait to be persecuted for the crimes of humanity." He picked up his coat and pack. "It's going to be a blast."

"Your friend is right," Dasan said. "We will reach the Council by dusk. I'm sure they have already been informed of our presence."

Quentin and Suresh instructed the group to leave their tents, coats, and packs underneath the tree. With Dasan's reassuring words, they knew that no one in Eurija would care to touch human trinkets. Also, there was no point to carrying the extra weight. If the Council denied their passage, they would be killed; if they approved, they would be accommodated for the night and pass back this way to pick up their belongings. Sophia found it ironic they were going to profess their innocence while wearing gear that would say otherwise. With no coats on, their leather and mithril armor was visible. The men wore dark-brown, leather, open-collared tops. They cut off at the lower shoulders, exposing their finely toned arms. Matching pants were kept up by a utility belt with compartments that held knives and throwing weapons. Their weapons of choice were strapped to their backs. Even their brown boots had a loop to store an extra blade. Sophia tightened her belt and looked down at Lee's boots. She wondered about Gabriel. He always had a knife tucked in his boot, and now so did she. Sophia smiled and made sure her blade was secured. The women's outfit matched the men's, except theirs were a light tan. The group looked like they were going in for battle, not peace talks. No wonder the Fae attacked them so viciously. The trek into Fae territory was uneventful, but the further they went into the center of Eurija the more they felt exposed and vulnerable.

They walked, quiet and reserved most of the way, with Dasan speaking once in a while, giving the name of a Fae if they passed one. It had been hours of silence when Muraco's body began to convulse slightly. Then out came a snicker, then a laugh. Dasan grumbled under his breath, and Sewati snapped his powerful jaws at him.

"I can't help it, I can smell their anxiety," Muraco said.

"With good reason, brother. Though I doubt it, we may all be walking to our deaths," Dasan said.

"I, for one, would be proud to join the Green," Muraco added.

"Sure," Sophia spoke, "only to be drawn out by one of Kahel's machines and used for evil." Sophia turned to face Muraco and walked backward. "Is it a trait of your tribe to be ignorant, or is that just yours alone?"

"His. All his," Sewati said.

Muraco huffed and gave Sophia a dirty look before he hung his head down. Dasan instructed them to choose a speaker, as having more than one voice speaking for a clan or tribe shows a lack of discipline and disrespect to the Council. Quentin was unanimously selected. They were to kneel before the Council and not look upon the Fae. Only Quentin could look up at them since he was going to be representing the humans. He could only speak when spoken to and had to keep his emotions in check. The heavily wooded path that they were on began to thin, then opened up to flat grasslands. In the distance, you could see huts and a massive structure made of white stone.

"Welcome to our capital city, Knossos," Dasan said. Not even a second later, heavy thudding was heard. From ahead of them and to their sides, horses came in. Well, what Sophia first thought were just horses. Some were half human and half horse. She recalled Dasan telling her that those were called centaurs. Sophia's arms crossed behind her head as she grabbed her sai.

"Be still, Apprentice," Muraco said. "Worry not, they come to escort us." Sophia and the group lowered their arms.

"Kneel down and put your hands behind your heads," Dasan said as he and his brother sat down. "They will bring us the rest of the way."

Dasan knew the leader of the Fae Guard, Rydan. He had known him since Rydan was a young colt. Dasan even vouched for him when he applied to join the Guard. He could see

Rydan's worried, upset expression as he approached.

"Dasan, Sewati, and Muraco, you are in violation of Ordinance one, sections one through three. All humans seen entering the Iceway shall be killed. All humans seen entering Eurija shall be killed, and any fraternization with humans is illegal and punishable by death. How do you plead?"

"Guilty," Dasan said. The centaurs and horses looked abashed; they examined the group curiously. For a quick moment, worry crossed Rydan's face.

"Dasan, what are you doing?" he asked.

"Take us to the Council. I refuse to get you involved in this Rydan."

Rydan composed himself.

"Follow us," Rydan said. "Flank them!"

61

KNOSSOS

They walked for a while. Sophia's arms ached from being behind her head the whole time. Strangely, besides her tired limbs, Sophia was calm. Sophia could feel Essence dance all around her. Eurija was full of life, the Green thrived here, and it was evident to everyone. Even though she was on her way to have her fate decided by a Council full of human-hating Fae, she was at peace. Sophia found herself wanting to frolic on the grass, leap in the stream, and roll down the hills. She imagined what that may look like and stifled a laugh. Lee glared at her. She was aware of their dire situation; still, Sophia was happy she could maintain her sense of humor when obviously Lee couldn't. Every Fae they passed on the way into Knossos would dare only a peek before they would back away. She wished Dasan wasn't ordered into silence, there were so many Fae she would have loved to learn more about, especially the ones who looked human. They approached the stone structure they had viewed before being detained, and it had grown exponentially in size. The massive palace was breathtaking.

Some sections had two stories, while others had five. Red pillars evenly distributed throughout the palace kept it stable. The white stone had red stripes painted on the top. Unlike the castle in Tychi, this palace wasn't built high into the sky, it was flatter and spread out. The open concept was welcoming. Evergreens lined the palace and grass freely grew between the cobblestoned grounds. The sun was setting as they walked towards the castle. Citizens walked to and fro with their business, and guards chatted happily to one another. They would stop to gawk at the humans, then slowly continue on their business. This was not what Sophia expected. Everything in Tychi was cold and lifeless. But here in Eurija, its people were happy, albeit currently shocked and frightened, but today was an exception. This was the first time many of these creatures has set eyes on a human, let alone ten of them. The humans examined their surroundings as they walked up to the long and wide stone steps. They came through what Sophia overheard being called the North entrance. They maneuvered from alleyway to alleyway and in moments were in an open square. The sun heated the ground they walked on, but the coldness in the eyes of the Fae stripped them of any warmth they could have gained from it. There were no thrones, no holier-than-thou seating for the Council. They just stood in the center of the square. All of the other Fae were grouped up in the sides of the square, behind the pillars. Some peered from openings off the upper floors, while others stood tall on the roofs of the palace. Sophia's eyes scanned a myriad of Fae before Rydan stopped in front of the Council and bowed. The Council consisted of four Fae that stood statuesque upon their arrival. A dragon-like creature stood tall on its two legs and stretched its giant, grey, bat-like wings. It swung its long tail and slammed it down, kicking up dust and debris. Jasira tensed up, then stepped back. Garret placed his hand on the small of her back and urged her forward. Next to the massive creature was a member of the White Fang Tribe, and on the other side of the wolf was a half-man, half-serpent creature. His long, bluish-black hair couldn't hide his pointy ears or his two sets of black horns. One set came from behind his head and ended near his temples. The other set was smaller and emerged from his crown and went straight up. He looked at both Sophia and Jasira as they approached and smirked. His attractive features could easily woo a woman of any species. His upper torso and face had patterns on them that matched his light-tan and dark-brown serpentine lower half. The gold bangles on his wrists clanked together as he crossed his arms. Lastly, a beautiful woman stood beside him, her pale blue skin covered in hypnotic, iridescent scales. Her translucent hair was slicked back and held in place by a headpiece made from white coral. Large fins emerged from the lower half of her head. Her body was humanoid, but her feet were large and webbed. She tilted her head curiously as they approached. Her pouty lips parted, and her gentle white eyes widened.

"Apprentice." Her strong voice echoed like they were underwater.

"I sensed that too, Batea," the dragonesque creature grumbled.

Sewati and Muraco sat down and lowered their heads. All the Atarans took this as their cue and went down on one knee. All did this, except Quentin and Dasan.

"What have you done, Dasan?" A woman's voice cried out from the white wolf. "Answer me! How dare you return here after shaming our tribe; we've been disgraced because of you."

"You speak out of turn, Amadahy. No tribe has been disgraced," the serpent man spoke. "You are here as a chosen representative of your people. Do not make them regret their decision by speaking words that are blinded by emotion." The serpent man took a breath, then looked at the rest of the

Council. They all nodded.

"Let us begin then," he said.

The dragon-like creature stood tall and proud. I, Xenos, blood of Wyvern, am here to represent the children of Air and Sky." His voice was hoarse, but his words were clear.

"I, Amadahy, blood of White Fang, am here in place of Dasan, blood of White Fang, chosen to represent the children of Land and Ash."

"I, Cecrops, blood of Naga, am here to represent the children of Two Kinds."

"I, Batea, blood of Naiad, am here to represent the children of Ice and Water."

"I've been chosen to lead today's proceedings," Cecrops said. "Dasan, Sewati, and Muraco, you are in violation of Ordinance one, sections one through three. How do you plead?"

"Guilty," Dasan said.

The Council, affected by Dasan's words, attempted to keep their emotions in check. "Before the sentence is carried out, the defendant is allowed to speak. So, speak, Dasan; may your words be wise, for they may be your last."

Dasan stood for a moment; he took in a breath and held his head up.

"For years we've hidden from the humans. We've made sure that if a human were to cross into Eurija, they would face death. To protect ourselves, that made sense. Till now. These humans mean us no harm. They were sent by the Majji to cross the Northern Passage and retrieve the other half of the Majji's staff, which resides in the Graveland. Not only is the Majji dying, so is the Green, and the Atarans are trying to stop it."

"She dies on their side. Not ours," Batea said.

"Not for long. King Kahel has found a way to pull Essence directly from the center of our lands. It doesn't matter where he establishes his machines. If he pulls hard enough, Essence will be taken from Eurija."

"Human, speak!" Appalled, Cecrops uncrossed his arms and pointed at Quentin, his bangles clanking as he moved.

"I, Quentin, blood of man, am here to represent the children of Atara."

The Council nodded their heads in acknowledgment.

"Kahel has already murdered hundreds of people, destroyed towns, and taken over the minds of men with these machines of his. We, as Atarans, were content living outside of Kahel's grasp. But the Green is dying, and without her there is no chance of life for any of us. We simply ask for safe passage to the Northern Passage and a safe return."

"Is it true that the Majji is dying?" Cecrops asked.

"Yes."

The Fae all around gasped, you could hear Mahes' name being whispered among the crowd.

"Mahes is dying too then?"

"Yes."

"How is this possible? They are both so young," Cecrops said.

"What I would like to know," Batea said, her iridescent scales shimmering as she tilted her head, "is how the Majji was able to find a second Apprentice, and how is it she already has an Elemental? None of ours have had the transformation; yours?" she asked the Council, but they all nodded 'no.' "We all sense it. Explain, human."

Quentin bowed his head, then explained Sophia's story. The Council stood in disbelief when he had finished.

"And you believed this farfetched and obviously fabricated story, Dasan," Amadahy snapped. Dasan closed his eyes and exhaled.

"And that is the reason you have yet to be selected over me as representative," Dasan said. "There is nothing 'obvious' about their story. Of course, that's unless you were there, which you were not. Leave your feelings about my actions out of your judgment towards the humans."

Amadahy shook her head, abashed from her very public reprimanding.

"Zephyr lives then?" Xenos asked, moving his sizeable, grey neck towards Quentin.

"Yes. He protects and cares for Sophia the same way he did Leata," Quentin replied.

Xenos let out a breath and rearranged his stance, saying, "That is good news indeed."

Cecrops held out a hand. His eyes were closed as he thought to himself. Everyone went silent.

"We live the way we do to protect ourselves." Cecrops opened his eyes and spoke in a reflective tone. "History has a nasty habit of repeating itself, and we swore that we would survive this time; we swore that it was the humans that brought darkness and death. They carry on with their lives, forgetting that in order to live you must survive; to survive, you need shelter and nourishment. If you destroy what gives you that, you've destroyed your chance at life. While the humans of old times lived in such a frivolous manner, the Atarans never have. I believe the stories you tell. But without proof, I cannot agree to risk the children of Two Kinds and allow you safe passage through Eurija." Cecrops slid slightly and adjusted his stance, satisfied with his response.

"Cecrops, there was a powerful pull in the water quite recently," Batea said. "Someone successfully summoned our Monarch Elemental Shiva. We didn't know who or what could have done that, but their story of the Ibex Warrior explains it. We, the children of Ice and Water, stand behind Dasan and the humans."

"I would never risk our people. Children of the Land and Ash do not agree to allow safe passage," Amadahy snapped.

"These two humans have been exposed to an Elemental for some time," Xenos said. "I have faith in Dasan. Though I agree with Cecrops: we need solid evidence." He looked down to the ground ."I fear betrayal from the humans. But that fear is mine alone. I cannot let it cloud my judgment. The children of sky and air side with Dasan and the humans."

"Impasse," Cecrops said. "We would love your wise words at this moment, Dasan; it is unfortunate for us that you are on the other side of these proceedings. It shows us how reliant and trusting we are of your judgment."

"Then trust me now, old friend." Dasan's words lingered in the air as he quickly stilled. He then turned his nose up into the air. With no care for protocol, Domingo and Santiago turned their heads. The Council looked around. Raja turned his head slightly and whispered to Garret.

"Something heads this way," Raja said as he placed his hands deep to the ground, "quickly."

"Xenos, fly! Tell us what you see," Cecrops called out. Xenos opened his wings and shot high up into the air. The gust the motion created cut through the group, shooting pebbles and dust at them.

"Dasan, what have you brought upon us?" Cecrops said. Everyone looked up, waiting for Xenos to speak.

"Blood of Enbarr!" Xenos called out from high in the air. "Coming from the west!"

"The Painted Ones?" Cecrops yelled up towards Xenos, "How is that possible?"

"It was said that their tribe crossed the Iceway years ago and were killed by the humans," Batea said.

"You heard wrong," Quentin said, still kneeling with respect. "No Fae have ever walked on Ataran lands, not for hundreds of years."

"These Fae resemble animals in your world. They could have easily passed as one of your own," Batea said.

Quentin stood confused for a moment. Sophia turned her head back.

"The horses," she whispered to Domingo and Santiago. "Our horses."

"How?" Domingo said, "They couldn't have passed through the Iceway, and the Pass is protected."

Dasan snapped back at the three. Sophia put her head back down.

The thundering sound of horse hooves came closer and closer. Xenos lowered down. And within moments, the horses came galloping in. Sophia dared a peek and saw that they were the same horses that lived around Salinas.

"You mustn't harm the humans." One of the horses spoke. "I, Misae, blood of Enbarr, come with information," she said.

"The blood of Enbarr doesn't exist anymore," Amadahy growled. "They were wiped out when they crossed into human lands!"

"No. We were deployed. Our directive was an ongoing reconnaissance mission. Our ancestors sent us out to blend in with the wildlife, only to return when we had information that Eurija was in danger." Misae looked incredulous. "I find it ironic that we criticize the humans for dismissing their history, while the Fae seemed to all but forgotten us. We lived peacefully for generations, sharing the land with the humans from Salinas. Being with them, we were able to enter Tychi and monitor its ongoings constantly. Just recently the town was attacked, and we tried to evacuate the humans, but fearing for our safety they sent us away."

"Dear gods, then it's all true," Cecrops said. Some of the horses stomped their hooves and whinnied. They paced impatiently behind Misae. "What ails your tribe?"

"On our travels across Eurija, we've overheard that you have a human that carries the Essence of the Apprentice. Is this true? Does Sophia live?"

"Yes," Quentin said. "Her and two other survivors from Salinas, Domingo and Santiago."

The horses went on two legs, they kicked, and they bucked. They danced in circles and rejoiced. Cecrops held his hand up again, and all became silent.

"How were you able the cross into Eurija undetected?" he asked.

"By water," Misae said. "We are blood of Enbarr and can freely cross through all bodies of water. We traveled the Pyre River, under the mountains, and across the swamplands, into the ocean." The Council let that set in. It was a long way to travel, they came to warn the Fae, and in turn were also able to bring much-needed information to save the humans.

"With the evidence before us, I change my vote. I, Cecrops, blood of Naga, stand behind Dasan and the humans." The Fae gasped. "Clear the square; we have much to discuss. These proceedings are over." Rydan stomped his hooves, then ordered his troops to lead the onlookers out of the square and to block off the entrances. The humans stood up. The Painted Ones galloped towards Sophia, Santiago, and Domingo. Sophia recognized Misae's white face instantly.

"You were Carminda's," Sophia said as she rubbed Misae's nose.

"She fought with courage and honor," Misae said. "I mourn her death every day."

"With Leata's help, I was able to ensure that our people were all able to pass peacefully to the Green, and Carminda made it back to Salinas in time, so she was one of them."

Misae looked into the sky and then looked back at Sophia, saying "Thank you." Misae then trotted back to her herd.

It was decided that it would be safer if the humans steered clear of the Fae and only have contact with the Council. The

Enbarr Tribe requested to remain in the outskirts of Knossos for the time being. It was a unanimous vote, this time with Dasan returning as representative. The sun had just about set, barely peeking over the horizon, creating an orange hue to the land. The humans had been moved to the fifth floor. They could move freely around the palace but were asked to remain off the ground floor. Some Fae were anxious about their arrival, and the Council didn't want to cause any unneeded stress on their people. They each had their own quarters with enough food to last them weeks. Comfortable bedding was prepared, and baths were drawn. Sophia sat in the hot bath, taking in the aroma of eucalyptus oils added to the water. They had barely made it through the Iceway alive, and that wasn't even supposed to be the hard part. How in the world they were going to survive; this was a question she couldn't answer. She took in a deep breath, clearing her mind and relaxing her body. There was a soft knock on the wall, and Jasira came walking in. She had a robe around her body, and her hair was damp, but that wasn't causing the wetness on her face. Jasira's nose was red, and her eyes watered. She let out a soft sob, then covered her face with her hands. Sophia grabbed the robe lying next to the tub and stepped out of her bath. She wrapped herself in the dry robe and rushed over to Jasira. Sophia put her arms around her. Jasira's soft sobs became harder. Sophia held her tightly and caressed her hair. She didn't have to ask, Sophia knew Jasira just wanted to go home. She walked her to the bed and sat down. Sophia grabbed a comb and started to brush Jasira's hair.

"I'll talk to Cyrus, and maybe we can get Dasan to escort you home. I understand, and I'm sure everyone else will. This is a lot for anyone to handle," Sophia said as she brushed the last part of Jasira's hair.

"It's not that," Jasira said as she sniffled, "well, it is, but..."

Jasira looked down.

"But what?"

"I almost slept with Garret."

62

AMULETS
AND CHARMS

Lee stood, looking out into the city of Knossos. It was nice to have this break; everyone needed a re-charge after the events in the Iceway. But he couldn't stop thinking that they were wasting time they didn't have. The quarters in the palace were identical. He really enjoyed the openness of the room. Fruits and vegetables were placed on a platter along with some chicken legs. Oddly enough, there were carnivorous Fae. The Fae didn't fight or eat one another, but simple-minded animals were bred and roamed Eurija as well. Still, Lee passed on the chicken leg; he didn't know if they recycled their dead and wasn't about to inquire about it. He grabbed a carrot and crunched down on it. He sat on his bed and pulled out a map from his bag. Lee popped the rest of the carrot in his mouth and used both hands to open the parchment carefully. They needed to head further west, then north into the Northern Passage. He knew the stories, but he wasn't sure if he was ready to believe them. After they pass through the Ice Cave, they would cross into the sacred ground of the Graveland. Lee fell back onto his bed. How was he going to keep everyone alive? Quentin and Suresh's expertise ended at the Iceway. It was all up to him now. They all had their asses handed to them when they went up against Dasan and his brothers. It was comforting to know that they didn't have to fear the Fae anymore, but he had no idea what to expect from the remainder of this journey. Lee lay for a moment and heard footsteps heading his way. His heart wanted it to be Sophia, but his mind knew better. His and all the men's quarters were on the western wing of the Knossos palace, while Sophia and Jasira were on the southern. Anyways, Sophia barely made any noise when she walked. Quentin, Cyrus, and Raja entered Lee's room.

"As you ordered, Domingo and Santiago are out replenishing our rations; they were being escorted by guards and Cecrops," Cyrus said.

"Suresh is seeing if the armory has any upgrades we can trade for," Quentin added. "Also, some interesting news, the Enbarr Tribe has offered to carry us to the Northern Pass. Their bond with the Salinans was strong, and they wanted to aid us as much as possible."

"That isn't interesting news, that's great news." Lee stood up. "We will be able to rest and preserve precious energy." He turned to Raja. "What about amulets? Do the Fae make any that can help us with our gifts?"

"Yes, they do, but it takes time to create them. The amulets and charms they make are species-specific, and none have been made for humans, not for a long time."

Lee sat pensively. Having those amulets was something Lee was counting on. Calling upon their gifts while using as little energy as possible was a benefit Lee and his team needed. Being able to fight using magic along with physical force would significantly increase their chances of survival.

"They have humanoid creatures. Find ones that closely resemble us and trade for those. If they require some other sort of currency, tell them we will reimburse them when we return to Atara. Hopefully, that would be enough for them."

"The Council asked us to remain up here." Raja's face softened. "I've already traveled the market with an escort and have realized that the Fae aren't very accepting of us. I prefer we wait till dusk, that way, not many Fae will be out, and I will be blanketed by the darkness."

"Makes sense." Lee nodded his head. "Where is Garret?"

"Said something about a cold bath." Raja shrugged his shoulders. Lee watched as Cyrus took in a breath and clenched his fists.

Lee's brows furrowed in confusion, "Alright, then," Lee said puzzled, "Raja, I'll meet you in your quarters at sundown, and we will hit the market together. Everyone else, save your energy and rest."

63

TWO AND TWO

Sophia tried to connect two and two, but something was wrong with her math.

"I thought you had a crush on Cyrus."

"I did."

"Then what happened?"

"Nothing. A girl is free to have feelings for more than one man at a time."

True. If Sophia tried to say any different, it would make her a big, fat hypocrite.

"At first, it was nothing," Jasira said. "Garret's always been there, I knew of him, but never knew him, knew him. Then, a couple years ago when I started going on scouting missions, we got close, and, well, it's slowly been coming on for a while now." Jasira turned to face Sophia. "When I am with Cyrus, I feel the butterflies, and my heart races, but I also feel like he wants me to be someone I am not ready to be. With Garret, I don't just feel butterflies. I feel this heat, and with him I can be who I am now, no pressure to fulfill any expectations."

"I can see the attraction. Is that why things are tense between you and Cyrus?"

"Yes. When you were all freaky-eyed," Jasira said referencing Sophia's appearance when they were in the Iceway.

"Thanks. Like I could control what I looked like in a trance?"

"Well, you were. Anyways, they got into a bit of a scuffle. Things have been awkward since. I wanted to talk to Garret, kind of yell at him too for that stunt he pulled in the Iceway. Seeing him obtain those wounds," Jasira shuddered at the memory. "It scared me, it scared me half to death. So, I went to his quarters to tell him off. I didn't know that everyone was out preparing for tomorrow. It was quiet." Jasira let out a frustrated growl and flopped on the bed. It happened only moments ago and was still fresh in her mind.

64

DON'T TELL ANYONE

Jasira had walked down the hallway, admiring the architecture of the Knossos palace as she wandered to Garret's room. In all her life, she hadn't seen such elegant craftsmanship. She ran her hand across the stone walls as she continued to her destination. Jasira began to wonder what her real motive was. Sure she, was upset, but deep down inside she wanted to see him, plain and simple. She peeked around the corner and cautiously scanned the room for him. He was sitting on the windowsill looking out into the town. Garret wasn't wearing a shirt, and his damp hair dripped down, accentuating his toned body. He had just gotten out of a bath, Jasira thought. She stood there and stared at him. *Move*, she told herself. *Don't just stare, good gods, you look like an idiot*, she kept telling herself. But she couldn't. This was the first time she ever saw Garret as himself. Stripped of the missions, stripped of the weapons, and stripped of the humor he would use to keep people at bay. Jasira took in a deep breath and decided just to forget the whole thing. When she finally managed to move, she took a cautious step back. As if it was a cue, Garret turned his head. Their eyes met, and she panicked. She was just caught admiring his body. Her face flushed. Her mouth opened, but no words came out. *What is the point of having a brilliant mind if you can't even speak? Say something anything! Gods, you are making it worse! Close your mouth at least*, she told herself. Jasira closed her mouth. Garret's brows furrowed. Her mind furiously fumbled for a coherent sentence.

"Did you check for bird poop?" she blurted. *Oh, gods...*

"Bird poop?" Garret asked, confused.

"Yeah. They like to congregate on the windows and stuff." Jasira pointed in a matter-of-fact manner.

Garret scoffed.

"Are you lost?"

Was she lost? The audacity! Jasira's fear turned into anger, she took in a deep breath and let him have it.

"Do you know how afraid I was in the Iceway? I get Raja is your bond partner, I get he is important to you, but I traversed the wall following you, following your blood." Jasira looked wide-eyed at Garret. "It was stupid of you! You are lucky even to be alive." Garret swung his legs inside and pensively looked at the floor. He took in a deep breath then looked up at Jasira, who continued to speak.

"You can't do that again, you just can't."

"I'm sorry." His hoarse voice stopped the flurry of words coming out of her mouth. "The only thing I could think of was 'save Raja,' I was oblivious to you or anyone following me. I understand how seeing someone you care about get all bloodied up can be upsetting."

Jasira flushed and stumbled back, "Who, who, who said I cared about you? It's not like I hate you or anything I basically tolerate you, no, so, yeah, I don't 'care about you,' care about you."

Garret smiled. She watched, speechless as he walked towards her. His eyes deep with intent bore into her. Jasira stepped back and hit the wall. Garret lifted Jasira's chin as he pressed himself against her body.

"So, what are you are trying to say is that you don't 'care about me,' care about me?"

"Um, well..."

"Good. At least we cleared that up. Is there anything else you want to yell at me about?"

"No, um, not that I can—" She blinked slowly, staring at his lips. Her body grew warm. "Nothing comes to mind."

"You sure?" he whispered, his eyes closed, with his lips ever so close to hers.

Jasira bit her lip.

"Alright, then."

Garret gently pressed his lips on hers. Jasira's body was tense at first, then she allowed the heat behind Garret's kiss to warm and relax her muscles. To her surprise, the heat didn't stop there. It raced across her shoulders to her stomach, to her abdomen, then further down. His tongue slid into her mouth, and their kiss became more passionate. Jasira broke free to gasp for air; as she did, Garret leaned into her, then kissed her neck. Jasira pulled his face back up, and their lips met again. Garret lifted her, and the pair went tumbling onto his bed. Jasira had dated men from her town, and she'd made out with a few, but nothing could be compared to this. The desire she felt was more than she could take. Their lips only parted for moments, and that was just to take in a breath, then they would return. Garret placed his legs between hers and began moving slowly. Her heart raced as he glided his hands across her abdomen. Garret slid his hand under her shirt. Jasira's head went back in a pleasure-filled gasp. Jasira never moved this fast, but being with Garret was different. She felt free, and it felt natural in some way. She couldn't put her finger on it; then again, trying to concentrate with Garret's lips on hers was pointless. Jasira was in the middle of taking her top off when she heard voices coming from the hallway.

"Oh, shit!" she said, then dropped her shirt back down. Jasira was out of the bed in record time. She was about to leave when Garret grabbed her by the arm and pulled her back into the bed. He placed himself on top of her, and his arrogant smile was full of mischievous playfulness. He lifted her shirt and started to kiss around her navel. Jasira inhaled sharply as his kisses made their way down past her hips. Her pants were unfastened enough for him to go lower, and for all Jasira knew she would have let him, good lords, did she want to give in to him, but the voices came closer. She sat up and rolled out of bed.

"I'm sorry," she said, "don't tell anyone, okay?" Confusion crossed his face, then disappointment. He looked away and agreed. Jasira turned back as she raced out of the room and saw Garret lying back on the bed. He rubbed his face and let out a frustrated groan.

65

REGRETS

Jasira's arm was covering her face as she finished her story. She didn't have to look at Sophia to know that her jaw was on the ground. She heard it smack the floor when she got into the whole part about Garret's hand up her shirt.

"I didn't even lace my clothes fully."

"Gods, and you bumped into Cyrus and Raja on the way out?"

"Of course, I did. Why wouldn't I? They were a few paces behind me when I left. After that final blow of humiliation, I ran to my room, took a bath, then came here."

Sophia sat deep in thought for a moment.

"So, tell me. What is making you upset? That you and Garret had some sexual encounter, or that Cyrus saw you?"

"None," Jasira replied, "I'm upset that I liked it."

"Oh."

"I really liked being with Garret. I don't want to hurt Cyrus. I care for him I really do, but things are so complicated with him right now, and with Garret..."

"It's not."

"Exactly. Also, why in the world is this happening now? Seriously, couldn't my heart choose a better time to go all helter-skelter?"

"Maybe it's because subconsciously you fear this may be the last time you can truly express how you feel. Then again, when it comes to matters of the heart, it's best we not overthink it. The heart does as it pleases; the more you fight it, the more it rebels. Trust me."

"What do I do now? How can I face any of them?"

"So, Cyrus didn't really see anything except you leaving Garret's room?"

"Yeah."

"I'm invoking tried and true 'don't ask, don't tell' saying. I think it's your best bet. If Cyrus wants to hear it, then he'll ask. You two are currently just bond partners and nothing more, so, in all actuality, it's none of his business. With Garret, you need to figure things out with yourself first, but you need to make it soon. You can't just leave him hanging after, well, you know."

"An amazing time on his bed?"

"It was that good, huh?"

"Yes." Jasira laughed, wiping leftover tears off her face.

"Don't let Garret know, he'd hold that over your head for the rest of your life."

There was a knock on the side of the wall. The girls both turned to the opening.

"Are you decent?" Lee's voice called out.

"Yes," Sophia replied as she and Jasira arranged then tightened their robes. Sophia quickly ran her fingers through her hair and placed it behind her ears. Jasira's eyes widened and looked curiously at her.

"What?" Sophia gawked back.

"Lee? Really?" she asked.

"Me, what?" Lee asked as he walked in. A drop of water fell from the spout of Sophia's bath into the still-water-filled basin. Lee looked at both the women.

"Didn't expect you to be here, that's all," Jasira said.

"Sorry to interrupt your ladies' gathering," Lee said, disappointed that Sophia wasn't alone. "Tonight, Raja and I go into the market. I was going to ask you to join. You aren't Ataran, and maybe the amulets will react differently to you. If you choose not to, I ask that you rest as much as possible. We won't have another break like this." Lee turned to leave.

"Hey, Lee," Jasira called out. "Can I come too? I need a walk to clear my mind."

"Sure," he replied, then left.

Jasira was the first one waiting by the door. She was wearing a dark cloak Lee had dropped off in her quarters. It was his idea of being inconspicuous, but four of them wandering about the marketplace in dark cloaks seemed a little ridiculous to her. But who was she to question Lee? Jasira shrugged. Sophia rushed down the white stone steps. She grabbed Jasira's arm and pulled her into the hallway.

"There is another set of stairs around here somewhere," she said.

"Have you gone mad?" Jasira freed herself from Sophia's grip.

"No." Sophia looked behind them. "Raja isn't coming. Garret is."

"What? Why?"

"How am I supposed to know?" Sophia said, continuing to search for another staircase. "I just saw him wandering the corridors in a cloak. I figured you needed more time to sort things out and being around him might not be helpful." She turned and faced Jasira. "That's unless you've already sorted them out. Have you sorted them out, hmmm?"

"Of course not!" Jasira walked briskly. "You say there are a second set of stairs here somewhere?"

"Jasira, Sophia," Lee called from behind them. "I said the meeting spot was the main entrance."

Lee's voice was unwelcome but not as unwelcome as the second voice that came immediately after.

"Yeah, kid, someone would think you were lost again."

Jasira cringed at the sound of Garret's voice. She took in a deep breath and turned around. He stood against the wall with his arms crossed and a smirk she wished she could smack right off his face. Jasira reluctantly walked towards Lee. Sophia reassuringly rubbed Jasira's back. The four walked down the stone steps on to the dirt path of the marketplace.

66

BATEA OF ICE AND WATER

Batea, the representative of the children of Ice and Water, lifted her head out of the water. She wasn't wearing her headdress, so her emergence was silent. The sun had set, and the shop lights near the river were not on. Save for three, just as planned. Batea was told that the humans were going to be traveling the shops in search of amulets. Cecrops helped to pass that motion. His acting so diplomatic rubbed her the wrong way. Cecrops knew that all human paraphernalia was discarded hundreds of years ago and having such items was against Fae law. It was true that there were loopholes. Most Fae knew that if the product that was sold to the humans was also used by the Fae that shop owner was safe. Amulets, well, that was a different story. Amulets were species-based, so anyone who had one in their possession could not sell to humans without incriminating themselves and their families. Cecrops was aware of this. He cleverly had "escorts" travel with the humans. That slithering slimeball.

The only reason he made it into the Council was because he slept his way into that position. Not many can resist the charm of a Naga; women, men, all fell to his graces. He was brilliant, and she respected that. Unfortunately, his intelligence is what made her weary. With the news of Kahel and his rule, the Fae revealing themselves, and war being imminent, she knew a Council of four wasn't going to cut it. War requires one leader. Cecrops and Dasan were clear favorites. If things went south for the humans, that meant Fae taking matters into their own hands. At that point, it wouldn't matter who was on Kahel's side and who wasn't. If you were in the way, the Fae wouldn't hesitate to kill you. Batea allowed her legs to float forward. She lay back in the water and looked up at the sky. Without a slow introduction into the human world, the Fae would experience resistance. That resistance would only get worse once they've dealt with Kahel. Who would be in power then? The success of the Atarans meant that there was a possibility for a treaty. Another one. Batea sighed to herself. So many treaties. The world was more water than land, so why she and her people ever dealt with this pretentious Council was beyond her.

In their own private meetings, the children of Ice and Water often debated moving out on their own. Children of Land, of Two, and of Sky have no understanding of aquatic living and have no business voting on their more significant issues. Batea lowered into the water, wondering when the humans would near the riverside shops. Helping the Atarans benefited her and her people. If the humans took care of Kahel on their own, she wouldn't have to worry about a power struggle, and maybe just maybe, with Kahel gone, her people would be able to swim the oceans of their world freely. Batea gracefully leaped out of the water and landed without a sound. The water slid off her skin and made small puddles as she walked to the side of one of the shops and waited.

67

FAMILY
HEIRLOOM

Lee pulled his hood down and ran his hands through his hair. It had been a frustrating night. Shop after shop, the Fae said the same thing: "no such product exists."

"I'm starting to think that the Fae aren't selling us what we need not because they don't carry the goods, but because they do not want to sell to us," Sophia said.

"I'm starting to think that too," Lee replied.

"I'm starting to think they aren't selling to us because these stupid cloaks are scaring them away," Garret said sarcastically.

"Shut up," Lee snapped.

They had reached the far corner of the marketplace. Three huts still had lanterns on.

Before they approached the first hut, a figure moved in the shadows. Garret protectively pulled Jasira behind him. They all stepped back. The lantern's light reflected lightly off the figure's skin. Batea placed a finger on her mouth, instructing them to remain silent. She waved them towards her. Lee looked around, making sure no one was around, then followed Batea between the shops. Behind the shops, there was a small dock and steps that led into the river. Batea knocked on the back door of one of the shops, her iridescent scales shining in the moonlight. She stepped back, and her long translucent hair moved eerily around like she was underwater. She cocked her head to the side as she looked at the group.

"Why are you wearing those dark cloaks? You look ridiculous."

Everyone turned to Lee. He looked at his friends and threw his hands in the air.

"They are supposed to keep up from looking conspicuous!"

Batea shook her head.

"They won't sell to you, none of them will," she said. "If they sell you what you need, they would be incriminating themselves."

"Cecrops allowed the merchants to sell us goods. Why would they be persecuted?" Lee puzzled

"Because they are not supposed to have these things you are searching for."

A male Naiad opened the back door. When he saw the group, he went back in and turned off his lamps. The other two shop owners poked their heads out and did the same. The male Naiad peeked out, and Batea gave him a reassuring nod. He walked out, carrying a small chest covered in shells. He made no eye contact with Lee or the others. He placed the chest on the ground, then walked into the river and was gone. Another shop owner appeared, a reddish catfish creature that waddled out on two legs. Its large eyes avoided the group. It placed a small box on the ground and disappeared into the water. Finally, the last owner poked its head out. It was a giant turtle. He carried a pouch in his mouth. Hc passed by as if the group wasn't there. He then dropped the pouch.

"Oops," a male voice came out, and just like the others he walked into the river. Batea slowly took a few steps back. She faced the group and smiled.

"Why are you helping us?" Lee asked.

"I have no idea what you are talking about." Her eyes were sparkling in the night. "Well, would you look at that, someone must have dropped those. Better not let them go to waste."

Garret walked forward to retrieve the items. Lee shot his arm out, blocking Garret's path.

"And we are just supposed to trust you?"

"You have to understand, unlike all the other Fae of Eurija, we the children of water and ice encompass this world. We were against the human ban from the start; it restricts our livelihood. The longer Kahel stays in power, the longer the world will remain separated and our waters divided."

"So, you are doing yourself a favor."

"The Council has spoken in private, and we are prepared to break more than one treaty to protect the Green." Batea was now chest-deep in the river. "If you don't deal with Kahel, we will. It matters not the resistance we encounter; we won't differentiate between Kahel's people and others."

It took a moment for her words to sink in.

"That's genocide." Garret's abashed words hung thickly.

"That's war," Batea replied smoothly into the night air.

Lee lowered his arm, and Garret walked towards the chest. It was decorated with shells that were all sorts of beautiful shapes and colors. Seaweed was sprinkled across its top, and the entire chest smelled heavily of fish. It was clear that it had been buried for a long time, deep in the water. He placed his hands on the sides and opened the chest.

Lee stepped towards the nearly submerged Batea. "What did you mean more than 'one' treaty?"

"If we attack innocent humans, they will drop the Kalyptra and bring with them fury and vengeance for the souls we took."

"Who?"

"Her people," Batea said, looking at Jasira. Jasira looked around, confused. Batea smiled at her.

"What are you talking about? My people are these people."

Batea chuckled to herself, "You humans never change. You love your seemingly harmless little secrets sprinkled everywhere. Never caring that they always evolve into much bigger ones that eventually turn into severe problems. Just look where you are now. If you all only were honest to one another, tsk-tsk." She smiled at herself. "Well, this particular little secret," she said, gesturing to Jasira, "has a relic of Shiva in the wooden box." With that, the beautiful creature happily allowed the river to overtake her.

To protect the identity of the Fae that aided them, Lee asked everyone to remove their cloaks. Immediately after the order, everyone cheered. Lee rolled his eyes and then transferred the contents of the chest, box, and pouch onto the cloaks. They then wrapped them up and carried them like sacks. Garret and Lee tossed the chest, box, and pouch into the river.

"Hope I didn't knock anyone out with that." Garret pointed to the chest that sunk into the river.

They returned to the palace in awkward silence. When they had all crossed the threshold, Jasira dropped the cloak she was carrying and the contents spilled open onto the main palace floor.

"What was she talking about?" Jasira asked Lee. "My people control the Kalyptra? My people are the Atarans, so does that mean Halcyon hasn't been forthcoming with us? That means we control the Kalyptra, right? Right?"

"No, Jasira," Lee said. "We do not control the Kalyptra. I have no idea what Batea was getting at."

Jasira looked incredulous. Her heart began to race and panic set in. She turned to Garret, then Sophia, who was approaching her with a sympathizing look.

"Kid, fish-lady was trying to get in your head. Don't worry,"

Jasira stepped back and held her arm out.

"No. No. Stay back. These Fae have incredible instincts. They sensed Zephyr on Lee and Sophia, and they can read Essence like it's written word. They say I am more than what meets the eyes; I will take their word for it."

"Jasira." Garret stepped forward. "She could just be messing with you, and all of us." He gestured his hand towards the floor. "For all we know, these relics are just junk metal. Don't let what she said to get to you without doing some investigating."

"Whether that's true or not, there is just too much going on." Jasira clutched her chest. "And right now,"—she looked at Garret—"I can't handle anymore. I don't need any more adventures; what I need is something safe."

Sophia knew what that meant, that Jasira had made her choice. A decision under stress but a decision nonetheless. Garret's face softened, he reached out, and he grabbed her hand.

"Don't," he said gently. "You don't have to make any decisions right now. I would never rush you."

Jasira looked into his eyes and was beginning to calm down when Cyrus came racing down the stairs. Jasira turned to see Cyrus, then turned back to Garret.

"I'm sorry," she whispered, then pulled her hand away from Garret.

"Jasira!" Cyrus called out. "Are you okay? I was upstairs, and suddenly I had a panic attack. I knew it wasn't me, so it must have been..."

Jasira ran to Cyrus, threw her arms around him, and began to cry. He tightly wrapped his arms around her.

"What is it? What happened?"

Garret looked at both of them, then silently walked away. Lee stood there, looking confused.

"We ran into Batea," Sophia said. "And she rattled Jasira with something she said."

"Well? What was it?" Cyrus asked.

"She said that the kid wasn't Ataran," Garret said as he climbed the stairs. "Which if Jasira thought it out, she would know it couldn't be true."

"Why's that?"

He turned to look at a tear-stained Jasira in Cyrus' arms. "Because she's bonded." Garret let out a breath and walked away.

The relics were all transferred to Lee's room, where he had them laid out on display on the floor. Everyone stood in Lee's room, staring down at the unique array of amulets in the form of weapons, armor, and jewelry.

"Well, how do we know what amulet does what?" Santiago asked. Lee walked up to a pair of open-fingered leather gloves.

"When we were separating all of these, I felt something when I touched the gloves." He picked up the gloves and put them on. Lee stretched his fingers. He walked towards one of the white stone pillars and placed his hand on it. Not even a second later, the stone cracked.

"Oh, shit," Lee said as he pulled his hand back, looking both abashed and apologetic. The Atarans all walked around and sensed which relic was meant for them. Jasira stood back and eyed a pair of silver arm cuffs. The cuffs were long and delicate. They came to a point around the knuckles then opened to a small hoop where one would place the middle finger. She watched when they first opened the chest and saw that the undersides had elegant craftsmanship. A transparent orb sat where the center of the palm would be. Now they lay on the floor across the room from her. It was a mixture of anxiety and uncertainty that kept her from getting up to claim them. Quentin had looked curiously at them, put them on, and when he was satisfied that they weren't for him he put them back down and continued searching. Cyrus picked up a thick, silver, braided, chain necklace with a rounded red jewel in the center. Suresh and Quentin each grabbed two daggers; once in their hands, one glowed red, the other white. Raja picked up two bracelets. Once both bracelets were on, a gust came in from the ground up. Garret grabbed a necklace like Cyrus' except his jewel was yellow. The brothers each picked up rings. Sophia stepped forward; there were only two items left. Sophia picked up an elegant circlet. The gold metal strands were curled around one another in a gorgeous pattern. She admired it for a moment, then placed it on the crown of her head. Once on, it settled itself. Sophia shook her head, and the circlet didn't move an inch. It was Jasira's turn, now.

Jasira wondered how she and the group were so easy to read. Batea and the children of Ice and Water knew precisely what each person needed. Deep down, she knew what Garret said was true. She must be Ataran; she bonded. But looking at those cuffs, her heart sank; in some form, Batea had to be right. Which only meant one thing. Her parents had been lying to her. This hit Jasira particularly hard, being that she unconditionally trusted them. Jasira walked up to the cuffs. She held back her tears and placed the cuffs on her arms. Once on, the metal shrank and formed around her arms like a second skin. The transparent orbs began to glow a deep blue color.

"Wow, hands down, Jasira, you got the coolest amulet out of all of us," Lee said. Jasira didn't respond. Ever since she saw the cuffs being taken out of the chest, they called to her. She looked down at the somewhat familiar design on the forearms of the cuffs. Her mind worked hard to place the pattern. When the realization finally came, it came along with tears as Jasira tensed up. She was going to have to confront her parents when, well, if, they ever returned to Atara. Jasira faced the group. They all had quizzing looks on their faces. Jasira then bent her elbows and slowly began to place her forearms together in front of her. A low humming emanated throughout the room. With her fists clenched in front of her face, she began to draw her forearms together. The cuffs finally connected. The room grew dark, and frost spread from underneath her. The group was in awe at the power of her amulet. It was then that they finally saw it, what it was that caused Jasira to cry. With the cuffs side by side, the pattern made an easily recognizable design: two perfectly crafted horns on the head of a ram.

6 8

YOUR SUCCESS
BENEFITS US ALL

Sophia woke relaxed and refreshed. Jasira, who spent the night, was still fast asleep. Sophia thought she would give Jasira a few more moments of this peace. Sophia rolled off the bedding and wasted no time getting ready. She wore the same leather gear she wore yesterday, but now she had a new accessory. The circlet. Sophia brushed her hair back. She doubted Jasira would want to wear her amulet. Last night, Jasira had a bit of an awakening. Jasira found out she was Ibex. Well, part Ibex. Sophia knew of the Ibex from stories and of course from Eilith. Jasira didn't show the known physical trait of the Ibex, the pointed ears; still, the amulet responded to her and her alone. Which meant her parents weren't being forthcoming with her and/or each other. Sophia put her hair in a ponytail, then placed the circlet on her head. Besides reshaping itself to fit her perfectly, Sophia didn't know what magical properties the circlet had. Sophia walked to Jasira and caressed her face.

"Jasira, you should get up now."

Jasira stirred, opened her eyes, and nodded in acknowledgment.

"I'm going to go downstairs to see if there is anything to eat."

Jasira nodded again.

Sophia felt a new sense of bravery course through her body as she descended the stairs. Her heart was elated at the thought of the journey ahead of them. The last time she recalled feeling this awesome was when Halcyon cast the spells on them. Sophia stopped for a moment. Then she doubled back to Lee's room.

"Lee!" Sophia cried out as she turned a corner and hurried into Lee's room. Her pace was so fast that she was unable to stop herself as she ran into a topless Lee, who was lacing up his pants. Their bodies made a smacking sound as they collided together. The force of the impact sent Sophia back. Lee caught her arm with one hand and held up his pants with the other. He gave her a second to stabilize herself.

"You good?" he asked her.

"Yeah, thanks," she said as she watched him pull his pants further up, covering the ever-coveted "v" that drives females crazy. He continued to lace up his pants. It took all of her will to keep her eyes from bugging out. Sophia turned her back towards him.

"What's up?" Lee asked as he pulled on his undershirt.

"I think I know what this circlet does; I think it increases the bearer's gifts and spells."

Lee gave Sophia a quizzical look.

"I feel the spells Halcyon cast on us, just as if he cast them moments ago. I also sense him. I am aware of his presence, even though he is so far away."

Lee turned Sophia around.

"His health, can you sense that?"

Sophia didn't need to circlet to know that Halcyon was a very private man and didn't want his business publicized. She also knew Lee, quite literally, had the weight of the world upon him. He didn't need to know Halcyon was fading fast.

"He's doing okay, Lee."

"That's good to hear."

Lee turned and wandered his room. He rubbed his brow and remained silent for a while. Sophia placed her hand on Lee's shoulder.

"I know that you are worried about keeping us all alive, but all you need to focus on is getting us there and back. Let us worry about our own mortality." Sophia nudged Lee. He smiled at her.

"Lee," Cyrus' voice called out from behind Sophia. "Everything is ready for our departure.

"Thank you, Cyrus, go get some food before it's all gone." Cyrus nodded and walked away.

"You should go too; we leave within the hour." Sophia did as she was told. She made her way downstairs, where there was a spectacular buffet set up. Every single person had his or her face full of food. It reminded her of the time she went to Cytrine's. She found herself longing for that moment. Sophia laughed to herself. She never thought she'd long to be anywhere near Cytrine. Sophia sat to eat as Jasira walked down. Garret kept his eyes on his food but still managed to clench his jaw. Raja didn't miss a beat and patted his friend on the back. Garret nodded, and they both continued to feast.

When everyone had their fill, the whole group was escorted by Rydan and his guards to the outskirts of Knossos. There, the Council, including Dasan, who had reclaimed his rightful position as representative of the children of Land and Ash, met them. Batea looked upon the group who had donned the relics her people gifted to them. Lee gave a grateful look to Batea. She slowly batted her eyes and smiled a little. It was enough communication for the two to understand one another and leave the rest of the universe out of it.

The group, save for Quentin, kneeled as they did before.

"Humans, you have made all Eurija question our beliefs and laws," Dasan said. "Many moons ago, an act such as this would have ended in bloodshed. But your words and your honest intentions have opened our eyes to a situation we were blind to. While some see it as an act of kindness, the Council and I have all agreed that it was an act of mercy. You could have killed my brothers in the Iceway and killed more Fae on your way to the Northern Ruins. But you chose to spare us and risk your lives to relay an important message. Kahel is murdering the Green. His poisonous grasp spreads like disease, destroying the lands, sucking life daily from the Green. His tyrannous reign must come to an end."

Sophia couldn't fight the sensation that someone was staring at her. She lifted her head slightly enough to see Cecrops looking at each of them. His eyes darted at their relics and amulets.

His eyes met her, and she heard clear as day his voice hissing in her mind: "where did you get Thalia's Circlet?"

Sophia's heart jumped, but she kept calm and lowered her head. The circlet enhanced her abilities, not his. Then again, she knew nothing of Nagas and hoped they were not telepaths.

"We are honored to have met you all," Xenos, the massive grey wyvern, said.

"We wish you all a safe journey," Batea added.

"Yes, all of you," Cecrops said. "Now, with your new-found fancy trinkets, your skills will have some newly added benefits." Batea remained statuesque as he spoke, "I am happy our merchants could attend to you so well."

"It was no merchant," Quentin said, "some of our people found them quite literally laying around."

"How convenient," he hissed.

Dasan and the other Council turned their heads and looked upon Cecrops in disbelief.

"Careful. Cecrops, you're showing your true scaly colors," Dasan said. Both Xenos and Batea let out a small laugh. Though, in all honesty, anything "small" that Xenos did was actually quite large. His little scoff sent a cloud of dust towards the group.

"Sorry," his deep voice muttered.

"Enough. Dasan, you must be curious who gave them those relics?"

"Not at all, Cecrops. I am grateful. This will aid the humans; it will enhance their chances of success. And that's what you want, right? That's what we all want. For them to succeed."

Cecrops held his head high and looked into Dasan's eyes.

"Of course, that's what I want."

"Then there is nothing more to be said," Quentin added.

Dasan nodded, and Quentin signaled for the group to stand up.

"Misae and the others will escort you to the Northern Passage. We will have a small base set up at the entrance. You will have food, shelter, and medical supplies at your disposal before and after your journey."

"Thank you, Dasan," Quentin said. "You are all too kind."

"As I said before, your success benefits us all."

Sophia rode Misae of the Embarr Tribe to the Fae base. She couldn't shake the nagging feeling that she was being watched. The chances were high that it was just her circlet making her connection with Halcyon stronger. Even so, the feeling deep within her kept telling her that it wasn't.

69

MURACO OF
LAND AND ASH

Muraco, the green-eyed white wolf, stood high in the cliffs. He didn't know what brought him here, yet there he was watching the Atarans below. When they began their journey up north, he followed them in the shadows. Sophia kept looking around, and once he swore she spotted him. After stopping under the tree to retrieve their belongings, they rested for an hour before Misae and her tribe took them on the final leg. When they arrived at the Fae base, the centaurs tended to them, refilling all of their supplies and offering them hot meals and warm beds to sleep on. Muraco thought, if he knew they were safe, it would be enough for him to go home, but whatever force was drawing him to the Atarans did not end. He didn't tell his brothers where he was going; hell, he didn't tell anyone where he was going.

"I don't want to worry my brothers," he said out loud to himself. Muraco turned to go back home, but each step away from the base felt heavier and heavier. He stood for a moment, trying to rationalize what was happening to him. With a sigh of resignation, Muraco ran to the closest tree and rubbed up against it, then scratched the tree's base. He hoped it was enough of a marker for his tribe if they were to go search for him. Muraco quietly crept past the base and raced into the Northern Pass.

70

IMPRISONED

Gabriel sat in his cell with his back against a corner. His once sumptuous, long, black hair was disheveled and dirtied. Gabriel's new hard-brick dwelling was a luxurious comfort compared to everything else that had come to pass since being taken from his home. He didn't understand why they kept him alive. He knew nothing about Talbot and Yaren, yet every day like clockwork an Osprey would come in and beat him to an inch of his life during questioning, toss him in a horrid Regeneration Unit, and start all over again the next day. Except for yesterday; no one came for him yesterday. The worst part was, every time he emerged from the Unit, he felt different, like he had lost a part of himself. He held on to the memory of his beloved Sophia; it was the only thing that kept him from going mad. Gabriel wrapped his arms around himself and leaned into the corner. He wanted to be with Sophia. Gabriel heard the footsteps heading in his direction, along with a scuffle. He distinguished the sound of a fist connecting to a face, followed by another scuffle. Gabriel crawled to the cell bars and pressed his face against the cold metal.

"You fucking morons! Don't you know who I am?" Boris called out.

"We do, and we also know that you skulked around here, zapped our buddy, and were caught in Hokai trying to cross the Pass."

"Of course, I was; you idiots haven't had any success, so I decided to give it a go. Funny enough, I got pretty far and would have gotten even further if you didn't stop me!"

"Shut up, just shut up!" a guard exclaimed.

A cell door opened to the side of Gabriel. He heard them toss Boris in.

"Sethos will decide what to do with you," One of the guards said as he closed the cell door.

"Kahel will have your necks for this!"

When the guards were out of earshot, Boris cursed to himself.

"Shit, fuck, fuck fuck fuck." Boris paused for a moment. "I'm sorry, Gabriel. I tried. Reach your hand out to me, boy."

Gabriel did as he said and reached his arm out of the bars and towards Boris. They grabbed each other's hands.

"This is the end of the road for us. Once Kahel learns of the murders I've committed, he will understand that I've defected. I'm sure he has been interrogating you and getting nothing. Because you don't know anything." Boris exhaled. "Are you hurt?"

"Not right now. Several weeks ago, Kahel came in, slashed me in the back. A frighteningly large man stopped him from beheading me."

"Sethos," Boris added.

"When Kahel left, they put me in this large thing they call a Regeneration Unit."

"He wanted to question you..."

"Since then, every day I've been beat, questioned for hours, then put in one of those units."

"They didn't come yesterday?"

"No."

"Sethos must know that there is nothing he can gain from you."

"What will they do to me?"

Boris let go of Gabriel's hand and patted it. Gabriel understood what that meant.

"At least, I'll finally be with her." He resigned. The thought of reuniting with Sophia brought a sense of peace that had eluded him for weeks.

"Gabriel," Boris said with a considerable amount of restraint, "Sophia lives."

"What?"

The door opened.

"Go back to where they usually find you," Boris whispered. Gabriel did as he said. "Finally!" Boris called out. "I mean, come on."

"Put a sock in it," a dark voice called out.

"Sethos," Boris said.

"I'm not here for you. It's time to end this man's useless life."

"Useless!" Boris called out. "All the work I put into getting him, and now you say he is useless?"

"He was not the Majji, whatever potential Essence that is in him Kahel could not draw out, and he has no useful information to give."

"Okay, so why am I in here then? If you are going to kill him, why keep me here?"

Gabriel heard Sethos' footsteps stop. Gabriel crawled forward again. He saw Sethos looking directly into Boris' cell.

"Because you are no longer a Grey. Don't think for I second that I didn't notice."

"Can't fool you, can I?"

"We need to figure out how it happened, so this doesn't occur again."

"You all fucked up, that's how it happened. Boris was a strong-willed man, and you couldn't rob him of that, even in death. So, because of your stupidity, I, an obedient Grey, was overtaken."

"What? What did you just call me?"

"I didn't call you anything. I implied, and you are just proving my point. I told you what caused Boris' reemergence and, like a pigheaded moron, you ignore useful knowledge and focus on your pride."

"Pigheaded?" Sethos' eyes grew large.

"Gods, you are thick. I could say that people who have something to live for and strong-willed people are poor candidates for full regeneration, and it wouldn't sink as long I end with an insult such as you are an imbecile with a revolting face that only a mother could love."

"I'm going to fucking kill you!"

"Taint cheese."

Sethos began to shake the bars.

"Guard! Open these doors!"

"Cock sucker."

Gabriel watched as a guard opened the door, and Sethos barged in. He heard Boris gag.

"You'd rather strangle me than learn from me, dickhead?" Boris managed to say.

"Stop! Stop!" Gabriel yelled as he slammed his fists against the rock wall. "I'll tell you anything, everything!!!" Gabriel knew what Boris was doing; there must be other Greys who potentially would defect. With Boris gone, their secret would be safe.

"Shut up!" Sethos called out. "We know you don't know anything!"

Boris began to laugh.

"Quit laughing!!!"

Gabriel continued to object while punching and kicking the wall loudly.

"I said, quit laughing!" Sethos yelled. Gabriel heard Boris take in a short gasp.

"No, no, no, no!" Gabriel yelled. "You ass, you putrid, vapid, dumb fuck! With a face like yours, I'm surprised your whore mother didn't toss you the second she birthed you." Gabriel forced a laugh. "But, honestly, I wouldn't be surprised if she was just as fucking ugly as you."

"Wait. What?" Sethos' voice, which had lost all authority, reverberated in the damp cells. "What did you say about my mother?"

"Boy, don't," Boris said as Sethos dropped him.

"I said your mother was ugly as fuck. Why? Did that bother you?"

"Why, you little shit!" Sethos rushed to Gabriel's cell and reached through the bars. Gabriel jumped back and pushed himself as far against the back wall as possible.

"Guards! Guards! Open the cell! Open the cell, now!" Sethos looked at Gabriel and gave him a terrifying smile. "You know, I was just going to slit your throat, but now I'm going to rip you apart slowly." The guard showed up and opened the cell. Gabriel cowered in the corner, trying to find any bit of who he used to be. He thought about home, he thought about working the fields, the sunset from the dogwood, of his mother, of dancing, of Sophia, of Sophia—Sethos took an ominous step forward. Gabriel took two collective breaths and stood up.

"I am not going to make this easy for you." With that, he lunged at Sethos.

Boris struggled to take in some breaths; he knew that he needed to realign his neck. Boris yelled, then twisted his neck with his hands. He could hear Gabriel fighting for his life in the cell next to his. Boris walked towards the cell opening with the intention of assisting Gabriel. Unfortunately, he was met by two guards. One he had never seen before, and the other had an annoyingly familiar face.

"Remember me?" the guard said as he tapped his zap stick in the palm of his hand.

"Heh, yes, yes, I think I do," Boris said as he nursed his back "Aging mind, my friend, but I've never forgotten a face, we had dinner, right? With your aunt, Geraldine?"

"No, you moron! You zapped me!" The guard said as he stepped forward. The other guard wearily grabbed him.

"Hey, man, are you sure this is Boris? This"—the guard gestured to Boris—"old man was the one who disarmed you?"

Boris stood up straight.

"Who are you calling old?" Boris rapidly grabbed the familiar guard's electric rod and zapped the new guard. Before the familiar guard could do anything, Boris had the zap stick against his neck.

"Codes for the secondary doors NOW!"

"OOHHH, not again, not again!!!"

"CODES, DAMMIT!"

"3720, then 4958, please, don't zap me again, plea—"

The guard yelped as Boris zapped him. Boris grabbed the other stick and ran into Gabriel's cell, Sethos had a gash on the back of his head that was bleeding profusely, but he was standing and Gabriel wasn't. Sethos' back was to Boris, and he was kicking Gabriel, who was limp on the ground. Boris took both sticks and set them to the highest level. He jabbed both rods into Sethos, who violently shook as he attempted to turn around. Boris proceeded to alternate the rods in a punch-like form, then finally Sethos collapsed. Boris zapped him a few more times for safe measure, then spit on him. He dropped by Gabriel's side.

"Boy, say something..." Boris said as he lifted Gabriel's head. Gabriel's bloodied face opened its eyes. He looked at Boris.

"My back is broken," he managed to say, "I can't walk."

"We can fix that. I got the codes to get out of here and get you to a Regeneration Unit."

"No, there will be nothing left of me if you do."

"You'll die if you don't!"

"Let me see the sun, I want to see the sun one last time."

"Gabriel, don't be stupid! I can save you!"

"I don't want to be one of them, I don't want to be a Grey."

"You are strong, Gabriel; you would return."

"But, just like you aren't really Boris, it wouldn't really be me. I don't want that life, old man. Now, please, let me see the sun."

"You dumb bastard," Boris said as he lifted Gabriel and put him on his back. "Hang on, boy." Boris opened the first door with the key card he had lifted from his old guard friend Zappy. Then came the secondary doors into the castle. He used the keycard, then used the first set of codes. The doors opened up to a narrow hallway with three sets of steps and platforms that lit up as he escalated them. Boris grunted as he struggled with Gabriel's weight. He opened the door at the end of the hallway. He was on a large landing. To his left was a garden, set up high on a large balcony known as a Floating Garden, and to his right was the interior of the castle where the Regeneration Units were kept. Boris hesitated for a moment. Boris walked out to the gardens but only made it a few steps outside when he collapsed under Gabriel's weight. Boris held Gabriel and scooted away from the entranceway. He leaned Gabriel up against a pillar. The garden was large and beautiful but sterile. The grass was cut short, the plant life perfectly placed in organized rows, and the hedge was sculpted with precision into abstract shapes.

"What is this place?" Gabriel asked.

"The Floating Gardens."

Gabriel laughed and then coughed up blood. "I can't." He took in a short breath. "I can't believe I turned my back on her"—tears began to fall down his eyes—"she sensed what I couldn't anymore, she knew something was awry, and I"— Gabriel looked up into the sky—"I betrayed her trust, and this is what it got us. If I listened to her, we wouldn't have come here, none of this would have happened."

"This doesn't have to happen; we are just steps away from a Regeneration Unit!" Boris said, "We could have this 'old man,' 'bastard,' back and forth for decades to come."

Gabriel smiled.

"This isn't your fault, Bastard. Whether you came to Tychi or not, Kahel would have gotten to you. These events would have unfolded differently, but he would have still found you, so do not take this blame to the grave with you."

Gabriel swallowed, then grimaced in pain.

"You find her, Boris, and protect her." Gabriel's brilliant blue eyes stared deeply into Boris',. "Promise me, Old Man!"

"I promise."

Gabriel looked into the sky. "It's strange," his voice trailed, "I feel so calm, like, this was meant to..."

Boris held Gabriel tightly, his face crumpled, and he allowed himself to cry for the first time since he became a Grey. Gabriel was his only friend as a Grey. Only. He'd be lying to himself if he said he didn't love him as a father would a son. Boris lowered his head to Gabriel's.

"I'm so sorry."

He heard a multitude of steps heading in his direction. He

gently placed Gabriel on the ground and then closed his eyelids. Boris clenched his fists, and his face hardened. He stood up and marched towards the footsteps. He found himself face to face with seven guards.

"I've fucking had it with this bullshit!" Boris yelled. "Two of you go inform the King that I demand his presence!"

The guards stood flummoxed, looking at one another.

"NOW!" Boris yelled. The guards stepped back, then two walked off.

"There are two downed guards in the lower dungeons. Sethos may still be in there; if he is, he requires a Regeneration Unit, and three of you would be enough to clean all that up."

Three guards broke from the group.

"Finally, there is a dead body out there on the other side of the pillar. He was a powerful and important asset. Give him a proper burial." The last two guards walked away from Boris. With that done, Boris made his way to where he was certain Kahel was.

71

SEVERED TETHERS

Sophia and the others walked unescorted through the Northern Pass. Unlike the Iceway, the Northern Pass wasn't bordered by giant walls of ice. You could see mountains to your left and right. If it weren't for Lee, who was leading the way, Sophia would have easily wandered off the beaten path. They slowly climbed altitude as they walked. The further they went, the heavier the air felt. The wind had begun to object to their presence, pushing hard against them.

"The centaurs gave me what information they knew about the Graveland," Lee yelled back, snow billowing in from ahead. "If Rydan is right, we only have half a day left." Everyone nodded in acknowledgment. Without the fear of being attacked by the Fae, everyone's nerves were calm. Save for Sophia's. Her gut was telling her to turn the hell around, that this wasn't where she was supposed to be. Something Sophia had learned the past several months was that her gut was generally right. Unfortunately, the journey she as on was imperative to the Atarans' survival. She couldn't just turn around. Another gust of wind pushed past Sophia, but this time it carried a voice with it. She stopped and remained still as the others continued further. Her breathing became erratic, and she began to panic. The wind carried his voice, there was no denying it, she heard his voice clear as day.

"I love you forever and ever, Soph."

72

THE BEGINNING
OF THE END

Halcyon walked among his people. Observing them all, taking in every moment as if it was his last. For all he knew, it might be. He then stopped and remained still as Atarans passed by. His breathing became erratic, and he began to panic. He walked quickly to the closest tree and leaned on it. The Atarans finally noticed his distress and walked over to aid him. Halcyon couldn't understand what was happening to him when suddenly he felt a pain like none other, like his soul was being torn in half. He let out a pained cry, then Halcyon collapsed and lay unconscious on the ground.

73

ON HER OWN

Sophia's wails could be heard for miles. She clutched her chest and was on her knees. Around her, Quentin and Suresh both had taken out their blades and examined the surroundings while Jasira held Sophia, trying to make sense of what was happening to her.

"What is it?" Jasira asked. "Were you attacked?"

Sophia pushed Jasira off of her. The force sent Jasira back, her rear hitting the snow hard. Jasira sat up and watched as Sophia bent over and clutched the snow. Sophia's face was tear-stained and red.

"He's gone!" She cried.

"Who's gone?" Lee bent down and touched her shoulder. "Who's gone, Sophia?"

Sophia left out another wail.

Lee retracted his hand and stepped back.

"It's like I was just torn in half, I felt it, I felt him leave me," she cried. Sophia sat up and saw that the others were staring at her. She looked up at the sky. Sophia had managed to gain control of her sobbing, but the tears fell freely. She could still hear his voice being carried by the wind. Sophia wrapped her arms around herself. She looked back to Lee, then the others, and finally fixed her gaze at the brothers.

"I just felt Gabriel die," she sobbed. "He's left us for good."

"How can that be?" Lee said in disbelief. "Only Atarans have that kind of bond. It's impossible to sense someone's death that far away."

Sophia's brows furrowed and her face grew hard.

"I don't know how it happened; all I can tell you is that it did." Sophia held herself tightly.

"Sophia," Domingo began, "you have been through much these past few weeks. Are you sure that this wasn't some sort of attack, maybe by Mad Essence? That could be possible, right?" He searched for verification in the eyes of the others.

"It's possible," Raja said, "but what Sophia described sounds like what we experience when we lose one of our own. Can you tell us more?"

"I felt panic, my memories of him flashed through my mind. When we first met as children, our school days, our first kiss," Sophia's face crumbled. "His smile, his laughter, our last moments together, then...his voice."

Raja held out his hand then gently aided Sophia to her feet and embraced her as she cried.

"That is what we feel when our bond partner passes. A loss of yours is a loss of ours," he said and kissed her forehead. Garret then took Raja's place, then repeated Raja's words, then kissed Sophia's forehead, and all the Atarans followed suit. The brothers were beside themselves. Lee walked towards them and patted their shoulders, then made his way to Sophia.

"I am so sorry, Sophia. I cannot begin to imagine what you are feeling right now. I also cannot ask you to continue on with us. If you want, I can have Garret, Raja, and the brothers escort you back to Atara."

Sophia took in a few staggered breaths. She would have loved to go back to Atara and put an end to this insane journey. Strangely enough, the urge that made her want to turn around was gone. There was nothing now, no gut feeling, no anything to make her second guess what decision there was to be made. That sensation was strange to her, a welcome feeling, but nonetheless strange. She looked around and gathered herself; she stood up and looked up into the sky. If she left now, Gabriel's death would have been in vain, the death of her people would have been in vain. She continued to look into the sky,

"I can't go back." Tears fell. "He wouldn't have given up, so neither shall I." Sophia looked at Lee. "We must go on, together. Besides, Halcyon wanted me here."

"Okay, we will travel till dusk," Lee said. "Garret, keep an eye on her and the brothers; if they start to fall behind, I want you and Raja to fall behind with them."

Garret nodded.

They only fell behind once before dusk, when Sophia began to mourn again. With the brothers' insistence, Garret and Raja left to meet up with the group.

"It's okay. We got this," Domingo maintained.

"Are you sure?" Raja looked at Sophia crying in Santiago's arms. "If you fall too far behind and something happens..."

"We promise to be right behind you. Sophia just needs a moment."

"All right, we will walk slowly, but if we do not see you behind us, Garret and I will return."

Domingo nodded then turned back to Sophia. It was several minutes before she was able to continue on. They followed the tracks in the snow until, in the distance, they saw both Garret and Raja turn their heads. Domingo waved letting them know that they were okay. Garret and Raja acknowledged and continued to walk forward.

Sophia walked with her head down, looking at the tracks made in the snow. She tried to keep her mind busy by separating the footsteps.

"Jasira's, Raja's, Quentin's, Lee's, Suresh, Garrets, Jasira's, Raja's, Quentin's, Lee's, go left, Garret's."

Domingo grabbed Sophia's arm.

"What did you just say?"

"Nothing, I was just looking at the tracks."

"No, Sophia," Santiago added. "You said 'go left.'"

"Did I?" Sophia lifted her head for the first time in a while to look at the brothers. She then looked at the path ahead of her and noticed that they were at a fork. The tracks in the snow indicated to her that Lee and the others had continued forward and to the right. While the snow on the path to the left remained untouched, resembling a comforting white blanket welcoming her in.

"The Fae must have told him to keep right. They know these lands." She turned to face the brothers. "They know their land well, and all that's up the Northern Pass is the Graveland, right? Then what's down this fork?"

"Whatever it is, you just told us to go in that direction," Domingo said.

Sophia looked forward and saw Garret and Raja walking towards them.

"Make them go away," she whispered and went into Santiago's arms, crying dramatically.

"Tone it down a bit," Domingo said out of the corner of his mouth as he attempted to wave them off. "We'll be right there! Just walk a little slower!" He called out. Garret and Raja nodded.

"Do you sense something?" Santiago said to Sophia as she continued to fake cry on his shoulder.

"It's okay, they've turned around," Domingo said.

Sophia lifted her head up.

"Come on, quickly, before they turn around again." She galloped down the path, lifting her legs high like a doe through the thick snow. Sophia's excursion ended when she came face to face with a large boulder. She placed her hands on it.

"Something's off. Please say you feel it too."

"Yes," both brothers said in unison.

"That." Domingo pointed to the boulder. " Shouldn't be there."

The three looked around and saw a potential path.

"There is something important on the other side of this." She stared at the grips on the wall to the side of the boulder, knowing well that she could climb them easily.

"Do you think the Graveland is this way and the Fae have led us astray?" Domingo asked.

"No. I think that they never felt what we are feeling right now."

"We should meet up with Garret and Raja. We've been here too long," Santiago said. "We will let Lee know what we've found and maybe on the way back..."

"No." Sophia looked sharply at Santiago, then at Domingo. "We cannot tell him or the others."

"Why?" Domingo asked.

"Because I am not in the mood for one of Lee's lectures. He is also determined to return to Atara as quickly as possible. If we tell him, he will make sure we do not come this way by putting his babysitters on us. We three can explore it on our own, once we've accomplished the mission at the Graveland."

After agreeing, the three raced back to the fork and headed right. They caught up just as Garret and Raja turned their heads. The five met up with the group, and by midday they had reached the Ice Cave.

"I don't want to go further into the cavern until we are well-rested," Lee said. "Even the Fae haven't been this far in years. We will set up camp outside." Lee said, "tomorrow we enter the Graveland."

Sophia watched as they began to set up the tents. Tonight, she didn't want to share with anyone. She wanted to be alone. Sophia knew that it would be selfish of her to ask that of anyone. It was going to be cold, and, just like the Iceway, sharing heat would be the best way to stay warm. She watched as Lee finished setting up their tent. All Sophia wanted to do was go home.

74

UNDER THE DOGWOOD

They both lay under her favorite dogwood tree, holding hands. The blossoms were in full bloom. Sophia looked up as one delicate pink blossom slowly fell down. She sat up and examined her surroundings; she couldn't see Salinas or the Northern Woods. The only clear things were the dogwood, her, and Gabriel.

"The tree is in full bloom," Gabriel said.

"Strange. It's winter," Sophia replied as she hugged her knees.

"Is it now?"

"At least I thought it was." Sophia processed her situation. Like a bee that you thought you shooed off coming back and irritating you over and over again, there was this nagging in the back of her mind that was trying to remind her of something. Why in the world were they under the dogwood again? Where were the Atarans? And there it was, realization, the stinger. Sadness rippled through her.

Sophia grabbed Gabriel's hand and urged him up.

"I've missed you so much." Heartbreak was evident in each of her words. "It's cruel, so cruel, that we should meet up here."

He placed his free hand on Sophia's cheek, replying, "I've missed you too."

"I don't want to wake up from this."

"You have to, my love. There is so much you still need to do, Soph."

"I'm so tired, Gabriel. I don't think I can handle much more. I just want it all to end and be here forever with you. This feels right. Being with you feels right, not with them, not out there."

"You know better than anyone, I am now and will always be, forever, with you." Gabriel embraced his wife. "Be strong, Soph, I love you."

That was the first night Sophia dreamt of Gabriel. She felt enough like an invalid that she didn't want to add to it by telling someone about the dream. Sophia tried to act as normal as possible when she woke up, but the dream remained fresh in her memory. She could feel Gabriel's warm touch, she could hear his voice, and it made her soul ache for the normalcy she had once had. Sophia sat up, scooted away from Lee, didn't smile, didn't speak; she just tossed on her clothes. Lee watched her quizzingly as she crawled out of their tent.

Moments later, he emerged to see her grabbing breakfast.

"Hey," Lee called out as she scooped food out of her leather pouch. "Are you okay to go on? You can stay here while a couple of us head into the Graveland."

"I told you already that I want to continue on," she said,

then walked off. Lee ran his hands through his hair. Cyrus walked over as Lee watched Sophia's back.

"I've said it once, and I am going to say it again. You are just going to have to leave her be." Cyrus placed a hand on Lee's shoulder. "There is nothing you can do or say that will help her. That woman carries a lot, and it will never go away. She must learn to live with it on her own."

"Trust me, I am trying to let it go, but my insides turn when I see her in pain."

Cyrus patted Lee's back and walked away.

Everyone finished their breakfast and packed up camp. Just like when they entered Eurija, they decided to leave what supplies and equipment they didn't need behind. They would be returning that way, anyways. The group shoved their belongings behind a rock on the outside of the cavern. Each member tightened his or her leathers and armor as they prepared to enter the Graveland. Sophia made sure her sai were secure and accessible. She pulled her coat over her shoulders and gave Lee a nod.

"We are setting foot on to sacred ground here," Lee said. "The Graveland has not been disturbed for over a thousand years. Nothing I can say or do will prepare us for what we might see there. Be on your guard and remember that Essence and magic are alive and strong here. Ready?"

The group nodded and followed Lee deep into the cavern.

75

BORIS CHOOSES

Boris paced the throne room. He figured, by this point, Kahel had heard about the dungeon ongoings, and Boris expected his King to walk in at any moment. Kahel did not disappoint. He pulled his long, blonde hair out from behind his high collared regal roble as he entered. Kahel didn't bother buttoning the front of his golden embroidered attire, revealing a silky white shirt beneath. He sat on his throne and crossed his legs.

"Boris, my friend, you have quite the pair. I've heard some disturbing things about you. I find it surprising that you would ever risk getting caught. You had the opportunity to run, but you didn't. Instead, you came to me. This I find interesting; therefore, I am going to give you two minutes to speak. Convince me to spare your life."

Boris worded his story carefully, twisting his tale in such a way that no one in their right mind would believe he was a traitor. The intricately spun story told Kahel that Boris needed everyone to think that Boris had betrayed them in order to gain Gabriel's trust. Boris' seemingly traitorous trip to the

Pass? Well, that was a ploy to convince those on the other side of the Pass that he was not loyal to the crown. Thus, ensuring his passage.

In Kahel's eyes, Boris made sense, Boris was brilliant. His plan was perfect, and he would have infiltrated the Pass if he wasn't stopped.

"You see, my Lord, people talk, if you knew, if anyone knew what I was up to it would slowly spread in slight whispers at the pubs, in passing conversations, and make its way to the wrong ears, and everything would have been for naught."

"Risky, Boris, and because I was not informed it was still for naught," Kahel said as he leaned back on his throne exasperated. "Fuck! I should have had more faith in you."

Just as the words came out of Kahel's mouth, Sethos barged through the door.

"Don't listen to a word that traitor says, my King!"

"Sethos! You're awake!" Kahel said cheerfully. "Boris did a number on you, didn't he?" He laughed, then stopped. He looked at Boris. "What was the point of assaulting Sethos? He was sent to kill that useless sack of skin Gabriel."

Boris' mind raced.

"Gabriel knew more than he revealed."

"That's impossible. We had Gabriel interrogated and tortured daily. There is no way a man could hold anything back," Kahel said.

Sethos smiled and pointed to Boris. "I told you he was not to be trusted."

"You still don't get it, do you?" Boris said to Sethos, "He was my asset! I could get him to talk!"

"Well, did you?" Kahel asked. "In his last moments, did you get anything from him? Hmm?"

"Yes," Boris said, "Gabriel told me that Talbot was Ataran." At first, Boris only had a hunch that this was true, but after entering the Inn and seeing the décor and art, he was pretty darn sure. "Gabriel told me that Lady Yaren always seemed terrified around Talbot"—a lie—"and that Talbot forced his group to leave that day"—a lie again—"then that as they were leaving, he saw Talbot speaking to the Atarans"—a big, fat, super lie.

Kahel's eyes widened.

"He told you all of this?"

"Yes."

"I don't believe him!" Sethos said.

"What do you know? You were out cold when this all happened."

Sethos took a step towards Boris.

"No, Sethos." With that stern tone, no one would question Kahel. "So, you gained his trust, just before his death."

"I always had his trust. I knew from the beginning he was valuable. I also knew how to get him to talk. Torture," he faced and said to Sethos, "was not the way. His people were honest folk; they valued family, friendship, honesty. Torture would only shut him down. He was content with dying with his secrets until I came in. Your ape of a henchman has no knowledge of the people and how to work them! He is just your muscle. I am your brain."

Kahel sat back and digested the information.

"First off, I am the brain, don't ever forget that. It is my brilliance that is paving the way for my ultimate rule. You help," Kahel said to Boris. "Secondly, I'm sorry, Sethos, but he makes sense. I feel if we had more trust in Boris here, things would have turned out differently and in our favor."

"My lord!" Sethos protested.

"No. He was right about you being my muscle. Disastrous things happen when you try to use your brain. Boris, we welcome you home."

Boris bowed his head. Sethos walked close to Boris.

"You just as much give me a look that makes me question your loyalty, I will end you." Sethos walked away.

"Forget about him, Boris, he's always been hot-headed."

"Tell me about it."

"Now I'd like to hear about your ventures to the Pass. How is it that you've gone further than anyone else?"

Boris needed to be careful. He didn't want to give Kahel any tips on how to infiltrate the other lands. He thought carefully.

"I had to convince them."

"Convince who? Who the fuck is them?"

"There are sentient creatures out there who have been stopping us from crossing; they have been watching us."

"Sentient, huh? Boris, how do you know this?"

Shit shit shit shit. "It was a hunch at first." No, it wasn't. "As I wandered in alone, I saw one of their natives. Seemed like a primitive culture." Biggest lie yet.

"Hm, do you think you can lead troops in there?"

"No. It would be too obvious."

"Do you think you can go in and do some reconnaissance?"

"It would require careful planning, but I believe it would be possible for me to enter alone."

"I'm happy I didn't kill you. Now get out of my face," Kahel said as he waved Boris away. "Go regenerate."

Boris nodded his head and walked to his quarters. It had been some time since he set foot in his bleak stone quarters. During the True King's rule, this room never felt suffocated or devoid of joy. On the contrary, it was decorated in vibrant tapestries. But when he left for Crossings Forged, it had been altered. Under the new rule of Kahel, the quarters didn't have much in them. He looked around, and it was as if he never left. The room was clean, his chest full of clothes and his Regeneration Unit sitting upright, ready for use.

"Fuck."

76

CURIOSITY AND
THE WOLF

The wind blew Muraco's white fur left and right as vibrant green eyes watched the humans walk further into the cavern. Yesterday, he had seen Sophia fall, he heard her scream, but he hadn't sensed any other Fae in the area, so he knew that it wasn't an attack of his kind. He overheard her cries as he stalked the humans high up on the ledges of the mountains. She had lost her mate. He was surprised to hear that he was still alive. Sophia had mentioned that he was murdered along with the rest of her people. Anyways; he thought, she chose a new mate with that Lee character. Anyone with a nose could sense the attraction between the two. Muraco waited until the group was out of sight, then leaped down. He stared into the dark entrance and knew that he had to find another way to follow them. The cavern echoed, and he couldn't risk being spotted. Muraco examined the snow-covered exterior of the cavern and started to climb again. There was no point following them through the cavern entrance. His presence would certainly be known. He leaped up from ledge to snowy ledge until he was able to find a path. He was about to continue after the humans when a strange scent caught his nose. It smelled of death, magic, and something entirely unknown to him. Muraco curled his nose and shook, his hair stood on end. He looked at the path that would follow the humans and then back to where the scent was coming from. He double-backed quickly and followed his nose. Besides the humans, there aren't any unknown scents in Eurija. If there was a new entity in his land, it was his duty to his kind to investigate and bring his information back to Dasan. He fought his internal desire to follow Sophia as the scent became stronger and stronger. Muraco slowed down and saw that the smell came from the second path that Sophia had momentarily paused at before arriving at the cavern. The route wasn't accessible from the ground, the giant rock blocking it made sure of that. But Muraco was high up and skirted it with no problem. He jumped down, and the smell of death became unbearable to him. He circled around, then faced the large rock. Muraco dug quickly and stopped the moment his paws touched bones. He pushed his nose down and inhaled deeply.

"Humans. Here?"

He then moved to another spot and found more remains. He continued on until he unearthed twenty-nine sets of human remains.

"Massacre, these humans weren't even armed." He padded around for a moment, then came to the conclusion that the giant rock blocking this path was not an act of nature, but intentionally placed there, most likely by these humans before they were murdered. This is where the scent of death and magic originated. Muraco followed the path; the magic scent was stronger where the bones were, and it faded as he continued forward. But, as the magical smell began to fade, the unknown scent became stronger. He had walked a quarter of a mile. The rocks on his sides grew to walls. It was shortly thereafter that he arrived at an area where the stone walls encompassed him in a semi-circle, and in the center was an enormous, silver, metallic platform. He cautiously walked forward and investigated. Muraco placed one paw after the other on the platform, his nose low, taking in the scents. Without any warning, the platform lit up. Muraco shot his head up and watched as the area around him became blurry. The light grew brighter, and Muraco shut his eyes.

When he opened them, he was no longer at the Northern Passage but inside a large structure. The lighting was very dim, save for the platform he was standing on, which was identical to the one he had stepped on moments ago in the Passage. Muraco cautiously stepped off the platform and walked towards the only other light source in the room. Tiny square objects were lined up neatly across one another, seven rows long. Little lights blinked on the table of small squares. Above it, a large rectangle of thin glass was suspended. The dim lights gently illuminated as he approached the strange object. The suspended rectangular object then flickered on with a human female in the center of it.

"Welcome to Island Eight. Please say a command."

77

THE GRAVELAND

Not knowing what to expect became second nature to the group, but that didn't mean anyone accepted it anymore. The cave opened up to a broad valley, and they stood at the opening and took in their view. Lee waved his hand forward and they continued on. The valley was breathtaking. The trees that were scattered throughout were identical to the dogwood in Salinas. These were in full bloom with beautiful pink blossoms. The branches danced left and right like there was wind passing through them, but there was no wind. As they continued forward on the vibrant, green, moss-covered path, they came across a lake. It stood eerily still. So much so that it resembled a mirror more than a lake. Garret picked up a stone and tossed it in. It quickly reappeared by his foot.

"Hmph, and no ripples." Garret's voice broke the silence. "I think this place is trapped in time. Some serious magic must have gone on here to keep this place in this state."

"I think it's a safe bet to say not to touch anything," Lee added.

"Yeah, except for the stick that has impaled a very powerful Majji. We'll just go yank that out and be on our way."

"Shut up, Garret."

"I'm just saying, man."

The blue sky above them had a mild glow to it, telling them that it was right before dawn. The group had left a few hours after sunrise. They all agreed; Garret was right. The valley was trapped in time. With weapons out, they moved further in. It didn't take long for them to encounter the first body. It was a male in metal armor. Then they passed the next body, decorated the same way. The next one didn't have metal armor; he was in robes, ones similar to Halcyon's. They passed at least fifty bodies, laying in the exact conditions they fell, hundreds of years ago. The body count quickly rose as they reached what seemed to be the apex of all the fighting. That's when they saw her. As they approached, they saw her beautiful, long, black hair tied back in braids, her dark goddess-like youthful face, her baby blue iridescent robes decorated with intricate stitching. She wore silver and gold bangles and a feather-beaded necklace. She stood against a tree, her face lowered and hands still on the half-staff that impaled her against the tree.

Lee knelt down, quickly followed by the others. Sophia needed no instruction here; she and the brothers followed suit.

"Neith. Mother of the New Dawn, we mean you no disrespect walking upon your resting place and disturbing your peaceful sleep. The Majji of our time needs your help." Lee gulped. "He requires the other half of the staff."

Neith didn't move.

In a moment of uncertainty, Lee looked back at the group, hoping for some sort of reassurance. Is this the right thing to do? This quest was insane; why did he agree to it? Why did he risk the lives of all these people? He turned back to Neith and got up. He took several steps forward, fear building in his gut.

"I need you all to be ready to run if shit goes south." Lee reached out and moved Neith's warm hands off of the staff. He then pulled. The staff easily came out. Neith loudly gasped as if she was trying to fill every inch of her lungs. The action sent Lee jumping back in fear. Her eyes opened. She then exhaled. She looked at Lee as he continued to move back. Her brilliant blue eyes scanned the group as a gentle smile escaped.

"My darling Leonardo. I've been dreaming and waiting one thousand, two hundred and fifty years for you."

Lee's eyes widened.

"That many years ago, I made an unfortunate error that led to a disastrous outcome. Before the battle, I had visions of you removing the staff from me. In the vision, I saw my youth; I saw no war, so I assumed we'd won. I assumed Mad Essence would be dead and not long after I did this"—she gestured to her healing abdomen—"you would come to free me. I didn't realize that my actions would stop time." She took a step forward, her eyes only on him. "I didn't realize that thousands of years later I would remain here, helpless to stop what was happening. It is too late, you see, it has escaped. My eyes were closed and my body immobile, but I saw him as he approached me. Blonde hair, pale skin, curious eager eyes. He attempted to remove the staff but was unable to. Mad Essence sensed the opportunity."

"Kahel," Lee whispered.

"He was a kind soul, trying to help, wanting desperately to know what had happened to this land, but that was his downfall. It sensed a weakness in him, his desire for knowledge at any cost. Through the staff, the Mad Essence fused with him. "

Sophia's mind took a step back upon hearing Kahel being referred to as a "kind soul." There was nothing she'd seen or heard about Kahel that would ever make her categorize him as such. Something inside her twisted, his face flashed in her mind, but it wasn't the face of an evil leader she was accustomed to seeing. It was the face of a broken man looking down at her. Sophia suddenly felt a rush of sweet, loving emotions course through her. She was looking at the true face of her father. She understood, somewhere, under all of the Mad Essence, lay the soul of a man whose body and life were stolen. The face quickly shifted into the Kahel they all knew; he turned away.

"Get rid of her," his voice distantly echoed.

Her heart instantaneously broke. The vision was gone. She covered her mouth and let out a soft cry. Neith turned to face Sophia, her brows furrowed,

"You have more than one voice within you; they speak clearly to me."

Sophia wearily looked up.

"One stronger and much louder than the others. The voice, she survives within you."

"My grandmother?"

"Leata sacrificed every inch of herself to give you a chance to come this far." Neith shook her head. "There is not enough left of her to ever be mortal again."

"I am honored to carry her Essence within me."

"As you should be. The one within you"—Neith took off her necklace and tossed it to Sophia—"I give my consent to. What's left of my Essence desires to join with you, Sophia. When the transfer of Essence happens, she will emerge from you and take this body. The necklace is blessed. It will give you strength and help you recover from this."

Neith took several staggered breaths and walked towards Lee until she was so close her full lips almost touched his.

"Your face is so familiar to me, every contour, each strand of hair. I've spent so many years dreaming of you. I wish I had longer to explain all that is happening in detail"—she placed a hand on his face—"but know this"—Neith came close to Lee's ear—"we've loved you forever," she whispered, then pulled back. "When the time comes, you will understand." Neith then leaned and sweetly kissed Lee. She looked at him for a moment, then addressed the group.

"Arm yourselves. I violated time"—Neith gestured out to the valley—"and it moves again. The Green here will attempt to regain balance, its equilibrium. The Majji Essence within me is about to merge with Sophia. When this is completed, both Sophia and I will be weak. Protect us both, and she will be a powerful ally if you make it out of here alive."

"Lee, what the hell is she talking about?" Garret said.

"Weapons out!" Lee called out.

The trees began to wilt, the sun quickly set, the stars moved through the night with haste, and the sun rose again. The dead bodies on the ground began to convulse and age.

"Without Essence, their bodies will deteriorate, but they will still have mobility," Neith said as she fell to her knees. "They will continue their fight as if a thousand years hadn't passed, but if they notice you then they will try to steal your Essence to survive. Their minds are only an echo of their past."

"Lee, the dead bodies are moving. Why are they moving?"

"I don't know, Garret!"

Garret charged his gift and shot a bolt out. The undead body shook, then turned to face them.

"Gods, did you not hear what I said? They need Essence, and you just shot some of yours at them," Neith called out. "Make your way stealthily around them, and you may come out unscathed." Quentin tossed one of his fire orbs at the creature. It caught on fire but wasn't affected. He then threw an ice orb, and the dead froze for a few moments, then broke free of the ice and continued forward.

"I'm pretty sure this falls under the 'shit going south' category. We should run, now," Quentin said.

"I second that. We will be outnumbered in a matter of seconds," Suresh added.

Panic spread quickly through the group as groans escaped the bodies lying on the ground.

"Sophia, you must come to me now if Eilith is to survive!" Neith called. Sophia put two and two together, sprinted to Neith, and embraced her. A green light shot out from Sophia as a golden light came from Neith, and the exchange happened. The dead bodies began to push themselves up. Garret took his blade and made off swiftly with the deteriorating man's head. The body collapsed. It lay immobile on the ground.

"How did you know to do that?" Raja asked.

"It was a safe bet; nothing ever comes back from a head-chopping."

The dead rose quickly. Jasira screamed in horror as the dead approached them. Moments after, heads flew in all directions. No one was there to protect Sophia and Neith, who were both lying on their sides. Sophia was the first to wake; she willed herself up and tried to balance. She felt warmth emanate from the necklace.

"Neith! Get up!"

Neith stirred then tried to push herself up.

"A mortal body is so much weight to drag around," she said. "It's been a while since I've had control of one."

"Eilith?"

"Not quite. Pleasantries later, escape now. Help me up."

Sophia placed Neith's arm around her.

"How are we going to make it out of here?"

Before anyone could respond, Cyrus's cries took their attention.

"Jasira, NO!" he said as he swung his blade and caught a dead man across the face. Jasira was leaping across the bodies and was running towards the water. She didn't respond. She continued up a tree that overhung the lake then across a branch. She turned to look at everyone.

"Run when you have the chance!" Jasira dove into the water.

Cyrus looked at her in disbelief.

"Why does she keep doing that?" He yelled while swinging his blade.

Within seconds, several ribbon-like strands of water shot upwards. The strands thrashed around wildly.

"Get down!" Lee called out.

The ribbons of water then whipped towards them, entrapped the dead, and pulled them all back towards the lake. The bodies wriggled and floated in the water, then were mercilessly dragged down. Cyrus stood up, grabbed his chest, and coughed out blood and water. He clumsily ran towards the lake and jumped in. He came up moments later with Jasira holding on to his back.

"She's okay. Go, go now!" Cyrus reached land, then fell to his knees. Jasira slid off his back and took several large breaths.

Raja took this opportunity to run to Neith, then scooped her up.

"Remember," Neith called out. "Stealthily! The other bodies will continue their war; do not disturb them."

Raja then carefully maneuvered through the fighting.

Lee tried to help Sophia, but she pushed him away.

"I'm okay, help Cyrus and Jasira." She pointed towards the lake, then gasped at the sight of her young friend. Jasira, with help from Cyrus, was hurrying over, but her pale blonde hair was almost white and her lips blue. Garret rushed over to them.

"You have to stop putting so much stress on your body, Jasira." He ran his fingers through her hair. "You're killing yourself."

Jasira looked up at Garret with apologetic eyes.

"No, don't do that," he whispered. Garret looked at Cyrus before stepping back.

"There's more, so many more," Jasira said to the group, "but at least the ones that sensed us are gone now."

Sophia finally accepted Lee's help and stood up. They could see the cave opening about a half a mile ahead of them. There were also hundreds of bodies fighting while slowly deteriorating. They watched as Raja safely made it to the cave entrance.

"We will do this in several passes. Domingo and Santiago first; when you are halfway cleared, Jasira and Cyrus will go. Sophia, Garret, and I will follow; Quentin and Suresh, I need you to have our backs."

They all nodded. It was all going well until one of the bodies turned on Jasira. Then all hell broke loose. It grabbed her by her neck. Cyrus, forgetting Neith's warnings, seized the body and attempted to set it on fire. His Essence drained into the body. It grew stronger as Cyrus grew weaker. Jasira made gagging noises and tears fell down her eyes. Sophia saw this in the distance and pushed off of Lee. She grabbed her sai and spun them so she was holding the monouchi end of it. She concentrated for a split second, then flung both at the body. They caught him in the head. The body's eyes rolled, it dropped Jasira, and it crashed on its back. Cyrus took his blade and decapitated it. It was then they all noticed how many bodies were aware of them.

"RUN!" Sophia cried out.

Jasira's cries echoed loudly as she and Cyrus were overcome by bodies. Garret unsheathed his blade and sprinted towards the assault. Lee followed. The carnage that ensued was enough to turn the toughest of stomachs. Limbs, heads, and blood coated the ground. Lee and Garret's clothes and faces both had blood splattered all over them. During the bloodbath, Lee found Sophia's sai and tossed them back to her. She helped out as much as she could. Eventually, Quentin and Suresh caught up. Quentin grabbed an unconscious Jasira, and Suresh aided Cyrus. Jasira's limp body dangled in Quentin's arms. Cyrus looked desperately over at Jasira and at the brutal cuts and bite marks all over her body.

"She still breathes, but barely!" Quentin looked around. More bodies were heading their way. Without a word, he ran towards the entrance. Cyrus, with the help of Suresh, followed.

"Garret, get her out of here!" Lee pointed to Sophia. "I'll try to hold them off."

"You can't do this on your own!" Both Sophia and Garret yelled.

"She has to live, don't you get that yet? If this were a game of Kings, she would be the King; we can't let her fall."

"I'll come back for you with those who can fight." Garret and Lee embraced. "Stay alive."

Garret tried to pick up Sophia, but she shoved him. "We will be faster if I ran on my own."

"FINE. Just go!"

Sophia kept looking back, watching Lee slice anyone who turned, when she and Garret passed. There were so many, yet he continued, strong and determined. She felt all was going to be well until the arrows started in their direction. Garret caught one in the abdomen and Sophia in her thigh. They both collapsed, then struggled back up. She looked forward in such desperation. They were so close to the entrance. Raja, Quentin, and Suresh came running back. Raja held his abdomen in the same place as where Garret was shot. The moment he was close enough to Garret, he ripped out the arrow. A catapult sounded in the distance, and a fiery mass crashed near the group. It sent them all flying.

"What the fuck!" cried Garret. "Do they not get that, if they kill us, they won't get our Essence?"

"I don't think they care." Raja lifted Garret and supported him. "They want to destroy anything and everything at this point. Look at them; they are tormented with nothing to live for."

Somewhere in the distance, Sophia pulled the arrow out of her thigh and yelled. The impact of the cannonball left Sophia with a gash tracing her hip up to her ribs. She crawled to the nearest tree and pulled herself up. She scanned for her comrades. It was then she realized she was tossed further back from the entrance and that the group was ahead of her. She let out a sob of desperation. Then a pair of gentle, loving hands lifted her into a cradled position.

"Just shut up."

Sophia didn't fight Lee this time. Her blood flowed quickly out of her side and onto his arms. Lee ran as fast as he could towards the entrance. Raja and Garret were safe inside while Quentin, Suresh, and the brothers fought the bodies that attempted to enter. Sophia let herself believe for a moment that they might all get out alive. Tears of relief fell down. But it is a universal truth that the moment you let your guard down is when the worst wave hits, and it hit without mercy. Lee sensed it before Sophia did, and with all the force he had left he tossed her out of the way. Sophia's body fell hard. Her head whipped back and smacked the ground. She recovered, then knelt as she scanned the battlegrounds for Lee. She found him at the end of a large spear that was being wielded by the most massive body she had seen yet. The enormous man charged towards a tree. He crashed his spear at full speed into the tree. Lee howled in pain.

"NOOO!" Sophia pushed herself up and grabbed her sai.

Before she could toss them, Sophia was pulled from behind by a large set of teeth and tossed up into the air. She flailed about helplessly before she landed on soft white fur.

"Hold on," Muraco called to her, then began to sprint towards the cave opening.

"You have to turn around!" Sophia looked back.

Muraco reached the entrance and shook his back, tossing Sophia to the ground.

"You have to go back for him!" she pointed in Lee's direction.

"Apprentice, nothing can save your tiny human from death now."

"You can! You are strong enough to pull that spear out," she pleaded.

"If I do, he is still cut through, impaled."

Cyrus weakly walked to Sophia. "He doesn't have a bond partner; his wound cannot heal."

Sophia couldn't believe what she was hearing.

"But you are all healing! How is it that he won't?"

"He will heal, but without a bond partner, it will not heal quickly enough to save his life."

Sophia felt that strange boiling inside once more; whatever it was within her was going to make its presence known again. She didn't have the will to fight it anymore. She felt dizzy and lightheaded, then allowed it to unconditionally take her over.

"How dare you sacrifice Leonardo because of your assumptions!" Sophia stood tall and authoritative. "You will bring him to me now!" Her presence filled the room, and for the first time everyone saw what Santiago and Domingo saw weeks ago. This wasn't Sophia.

As if Muraco couldn't resist her demands, he turned back into the war. He effortlessly dodged attacks as he approached Lee's dangling body. The spearman who impaled Lee was trying to pull the spear out, but it was too far in and the angle too high up the tree. Muraco locked on to the spearman, took one forceful leap, caught the spearman in his mouth, and snapped him in half. The body fell to the ground and looked Muraco in the eyes. Its expression wasn't of anger or hatred but more of gratitude. The spearman slowly closed its eyes. A faint green light came from its body and then dispersed into the ground. Muraco's eyes widened. He looked at the large spear, then grabbed it with his teeth and tugged. The spear came out. Muraco caught Lee's body in his mouth and sped to the entrance. He trampled the bodies that were giving Suresh and Quentin a hard time. Once in the cave, he lowered his head and placed Lee next to Sophia's feet. She was breathing heavily, and only her eyes looked down towards Lee. Cyrus checked for a pulse. He put his forehead on Lee's.

"I feel nothing." A tear fell down from Cyrus' eye. "I feel nothing."

They had no time to process this blow.

"We can't hold them off!" Santiago kicked a body back, cut the arm off another, then spun in a half-circle and cut the head off a body that came in from behind.

Sophia stood in disbelief, jaws clenched, tears streaming down her eyes, blood slowly seeping through her healing wounds. Everything happening around her was a blur.

"I will not let you take him." The sound from her mouth was barely audible.

"Did you not hear me? We can't hold them off!" Santiago looked back at Sophia, who did not respond to him.

"You cannot have this one." A voice unlike Sophia's echoed.

Dripping in blood and sweat, Domingo watched as Sophia stood immobile. He reached out to touch her shoulder but retracted almost instantaneously when he sensed an un-known energy.

Suresh took another swing, and another body fell, which led several other bodies to notice them. The battle seemingly had no end. Muraco jumped and tore through a group of bodies.

"They want to die," he said. "I saw it in their eyes. Death is their only escape from this."

"Then why are they trying to take our Essence?" Suresh asked.

"Think about it: you are dying of thirst, and you know death is on your horizon, if you find a cup of water, though it wouldn't be enough to save you, would you not still drink it?" Muraco swung his massive tail and smashed seven bodies with it.

Quentin and Suresh looked at one another.

"We would die before we could free every single one of them," Domingo said.

"Correction. *We* would die." Quentin said gesturing to both himself and Suresh. "You all need to go now." He placed his hand on Domingo's shoulder. "It was an honor meeting and fighting along your side and along your brother's side. But the only chance you all have to escape is if we make sure those things do not come after you. You know it's the truth. Take the staff and Sophia back to Atara."

Muraco made another quick sweep, but the more Muraco did the more attention they gained.

Domingo didn't even try to argue, as he needed to get Sophia out of here. He placed his hand on Quentin's shoulder.

"May your Essence pass peacefully to the Green, my friend."

"Hurry it up!" Muraco called as the sound of another catapult launching could be heard in the distance. The fireball landed several hundred feet in front of the cave opening, killing many bodies. Quentin and Suresh used the brief break in the attack to bid their final farewells. They then walked up to Sophia and kissed her on her forehead while she stared blankly at them. Then the men knelt down and kissed Lee's forehead. They began to walk towards their deaths when Sophia let out a small cry behind them. It wasn't the sort of cry that comes from sadness, but once that comes from physical pain.

Quentin and Suresh turned to see Sophia, who had bent slightly and covered her abdomen. Blood began to seep through her fingers. There was a confused look on her face. Sophia then jerked back and looked down at Lee then back at her wound.

"Gods!" Quentin called out, "There is hope after all!" He pointed down to Lee. "His wound heals!"

Sophia took several staggered breaths, smiled slightly, then collapsed.

"Muraco, you need to carry both her and Lee out," Suresh said as he lifted Sophia. "They've bonded!" He laughed. "Gods, the Green is here watching over us. I knew it then, and I know it now more than ever. This miracle"—he pointed to Lee, whose chest had begun to rise and fall—"is the Green's will," Suresh said.

"I agree." They both laughed.

Muraco bent down so that Suresh could place Sophia on his back. The pair walked towards the Graveland entrance. Once there, they looked back at their friends one last time. Sophia lay belly down on Muraco's back while Lee was gently carried in his mouth. Raja cradled Neith, who held the staff. Cyrus supported a groggy Jasira, Garret stood tall with his arms crossed, and the brothers stood with their left fists upon their hearts.

Quentin and Suresh placed all their remaining orbs before their feet, then knelt down. They stabbed the side of the cave, hard with their blades, and began to chant. The Orbs they placed shattered and released Essence that started to circulate around them. Even with a group of bodies charging, Quentin and Suresh never broke their stance. With one hand on their blades and the other on the ground, the land began to shake, and an intense green glow emanated from them. It merged with the Essence that was circulating. Suresh and Quentin looked at one another and nodded. To the naked eye, it was a simple nod, but to those two who'd experienced so much together, it was love, respect, gratefulness, and goodbye, all in one. They looked forward and released a battle cry that tore through the core of the group, leaving them all both heartbroken and elated. An intense explosion followed. The force of the detonation shot forward, but the backdraft was strong enough to knock the Atarans a few steps back. They covered their faces as the cloud of dust billowed towards them. And, just like that, it had cleared. All those who could wander forward did so. To their surprise, the Graveland was as it was when they first entered. The dogwoods were blossoming, the lake looked like glass, and bodies now all gone, the Graveland seemed at peace like no one had ever had set foot in it.

"We need to go," Raja's voice broke the silence. "The land beneath us is struggling to keep its form."

Muraco was the first to take off running. Everyone else followed, and the ground shook more with each step. As they approached their last campsite, Cyrus, who had been assisting Jasira, purposely dropped down to grab as much of their clothing left in the cavern as possible. The cave began to collapse around them. With one giant leap, they safely landed on the cold, wet snow as the cavern behind them ultimately gave way. They all remained in the exact spot they fell, staring at the crumpled entranceway, their faces emotionless. The wind pushed snow up and around. It circled the group as they sat and, just like the Graveland, they remained motionless as they allowed time to pass around them. They had lost Quentin and Suresh. An emptiness began to resonate through them all, then the gravity of their pain took hold. Muraco cradled both Sophia and Lee. Garret comforted Raja as he wept for the loss of their friends. Jasira held Cyrus and wiped the tears from both his face and her own.

"We did it. We did what we were meant to do, Cyrus," she said. Cyrus didn't respond. "I know. Losing them is something that we will never get over, but we survived and will be able to bring the staff back to Halcyon."

"Their loss weighs heavily, but what weighs more is that he died," Cyrus turned to look at Lee's unconscious body. "There was no life left in him. For a moment there, I lost my best friend, my brother. Yes, the Green granted him life again, but the Green only did so when Quentin and Suresh agreed to sacrifice theirs."

"They did it to save us all."

"Our destiny is not in our hands." His forceful tone began to turn heads. "The choices we think we freely make are orchestrated by a more powerful entity. If we do what the Green thinks is best, we live; if we don't then, well, I don't want to think of what she would do if we didn't comply with her."

"Stop it," Jasira scolded, "if that were true, Kahel would be gone."

"Yes, that's true." Cyrus pushed himself up. "But still, the Green is tipping the scales."

"And you believe that it's only in Sophia's favor?"

Cyrus' face grew firm as they both looked towards Sophia, who had woken and sat up. Cyrus grabbed the clothing he was able to recover and tossed it towards the other Atarans. He then proceeded to Muraco, who was still cradling both Lee and Sophia. Garret picked up his and Raja's coats while watching Cyrus intently. Sophia, oblivious to anything around her, brushed Lee's hair from his unconscious blood-caked face. She was shocked to see that he had fully healed. It had taken Jasira much longer to recover from her wounds when she had been caught in the explosion.

Sophia looked up at a stone-faced Cyrus. "I can feel him, here." She grasped her chest. "I feel him, how is it that I can feel him?"

"Don't you remember?" an unfamiliar menacing tone escaped the once-kind Cyrus. "You demanded the Green spare him. Then you were granted you that. I should be happy Lee lives because of you, but I am more terrified than grateful. We have no clue what you are and what you are capable of." Cyrus stared wearily into Sophia's eyes. "I am unsure if someone who can give direct orders to the Green should be anywhere near Atara."

"But, I—" Sophia looked desperately left then right as if something around her would give her support. "I don't rememb..."

"Yes, we all gather that you wouldn't remember." Cyrus knelt down and lifted Lee. "He will need to rest on your back, Muraco." The large wolf obliged. Cyrus tenderly placed Lee on Muraco's back, then turned to Sophia, "We all gathered that you would have no memory of it because it wasn't you making those demands."

"That's enough, Cyrus," Domingo called out as he walked towards a terrified Sophia. "It's okay, Sophia. Santiago and I will help you through this." He knelt before Sophia and grabbed the terrified girl's hand. "It's done. We can go back to Atara now and figure out what's happening to you."

"No," Cyrus called, surprising even himself with his bold tone. "I want the three of you to leave Atara."

Jasira and the others all stood tall in protest.

"You can't do that!" Jasira cried incredulously. "Halcyon said that they were to remain with us, Sophia has a home there, Domingo and Santiago have a home there."

"Lee's home!" Cyrus' face was firm and unyielding. "Ever since he carried her here from Salinas, she's brought us nothing but death! I will have no more of it. I will speak to Halcyon and help him see reason."

Neith looked curiously at Cyrus. "Am I to be banished along with them?" she said in a calm, defiant tone.

Cyrus, looking more cross than ever turned to Neith.

"You have no idea what I am capable of," she continued. "So, I assume you'd want to banish me along with the others."

The pair stared silently at one another. Everyone watched, waiting for someone to say something, which happened seconds later when a groggy Lee groaned from above Muraco.

"No one is going to be banished. Cyrus, my friend, I understand where your heart is, but that's not the answer, especially now that Sophia and I have bonded. Remember what you told me? 'Where she goes, I go, always.'"

Jasira who had never heard Cyrus speak of her in those terms softened her tense posture.

"Yes."

"Well, where she goes"—Lee gestured towards Sophia—"I go, always. We are on the brink of war. Banishing our allies isn't in our best interests."

Muraco made an aggravated growl and gained everyone's attention.

"Your squabbling isn't in your best interest either. I would have aided you in the Graveland sooner, but my attentions were pulled elsewhere. There is something you must see. I can't make any sense of it, but maybe you humans might. It is not far, back down that way," Muraco pointed his nose down the path. "There is a fork in the road."

Domingo helped Sophia up, then pulled her to the side. Muraco's ears turned to listen in.

"Isn't that the path you were drawn to?" he whispered closely.

"Did you sense it too, Apprentice?"

"Yes." She looked at Muraco's ears. He then turned to face her. "You should have ordered them to change course. Your other two humans would still be alive."

Sophia mulled over Muraco's words as they arrived at the fork. The way he said it was as if she could order them. Lee was in charge. But Sophia knew that if she really wanted to, she could make them. They followed Muraco as he showed them the climbing path up and around the boulder.

They all stood in shock as they looked upon piles of bones. The scene was reminiscent of Sophia's discovery at Salinas not so long ago.

"What happened here?" Sophia asked.

"So much magic used." Garret knelt down and touched a bone. "These people didn't have a chance; whatever it was that did this to them was incredibly powerful. There is still residual magic lingering here."

"I can sense it from here," Raja added as he stood tall.

Muraco paced impatiently. "Yes, but you must come, there is more." The group cautiously stepped around the bones as they followed Muraco down a path. Soon they found themselves encompassed by walls like that of the Iceway.

"Follow." Muraco led the group onto a large platform. The platform brightly lit up. In a panic, Jasira tried to step off but felt her movements become slow. The light burst spectacularly around them. When Jasira's body regained full momentum, she fell forward and off the platform. She fell hard onto a black onyx floor. She looked into her reflection for the first time in a long time. The floor showed her a tired woman with lips blue as ice and hair white as snow.

"Oh, my gods!" She scrambled back. "Oh, my gods!" She turned to Cyrus. "Why didn't you tell me?"

"I told you not to push yourself."

"What's happening to me?"

Neith stepped off the platform.

"Jasira, this is what happens when the Ibex strain themselves. It's because you were in Atara so long and have a bond partner that you still live."

Cyrus helped Jasira up. "It will be okay."

Garret patted Cyrus on the shoulders. "We have no idea what she is capable of either," he said, pointing at Jasira, "you should suggest to Halcyon to banish her as well." Garret winked at Jasira and walked away.

Jasira relaxed and gave Garret a gentle smile. Muraco's voice echoed loudly in the room, denying Cyrus the chance to cause an unneeded scene.

"This here, the floating tablet speaks. I do not understand any of this."

The group examined their surroundings. Jasira's eyes lit up. This technology was familiar to her.

"Garret!" she gasped.

"I know."

"Those schematics from Kahel's castle you drew up for me."

Cyrus and Garret looked around and motioned for the group to remain still.

"The tech is the same." Jasira closed her eyes as her memory flashed images of Garret asking her for help with a security system. He placed a set of drawing before her and walked her through the schematics. There were several sheets, but it was the last one he showed her that had the most similarities to this room.

"The floating tablet is what controls this place," she said with confidence as she walked across the room.

"Jasira, wait, you don't—"

Garret grabbed Cyrus' arm. "Yes, she does, man."

The room lit as she came closer and closer to the tablet. She looked down at the controls.

"Welcome to Island Eight. Please say a command."

Jasira studied the control tablet and its buttons as the others approached. They all stared in awe at the woman on the screen. She had tan skin and dark hair that was parted in the center and pulled tightly back in a low ponytail.

"Command list, please," Jasira spoke.

"I am Island Eight Mainframe supercomputer. I can compute any command."

"Well, then, what are you?"

"My designation name is Prisha, named after one of the scientists who created the Islands, Dr. Prisha Kaur. I control Island Eight."

"Prisha, what is Island Eight?"

The screen flickered and transitioned to blueprints.

"Island Eight is a Noah's-ark-style structure constructed by a large team of scientists and engineers with the hopes of saving humanity. Island Eight held seven thousand, five hundred lives in cryogenic bio suspension until the Earth acquired full stability." The picture zoomed in to the top tier of the structure "Main controls, supercomputer, controller, elevator access, and telepads are located on the top tier of the structure. The five levels below each are equipped with fifteen hundred cryogenic bio units. The lowest level is the hydraulic mechanism that powers the Island." The screen's picture returned to the woman.

Jasira's brows furrowed. She looked back to see that everyone had similar confused looks on their faces. She turned back to the supercomputer.

"What is 'the Earth'?"

"Earth, Terra, Land, the world we live in, the world all around us."

"What is cryogenic bio suspension?"

"The act of suspending life in sub-zero temperatures to halt the aging process in order to allow a specified amount of time to pass. Using genetically modified cells of the turritopsis dohrnii, the immortal jellyfish, the body and brain are able to regenerate themselves repeatedly throughout hibernation. Once that time has passed, full reanimation of the body begins, and life can continue as if no time has passed at all."

"Holy shit."

The face on the screen pursed her lips and nodded her head.

"How many lives were suspended?"

"Island Eight successfully suspended seventy-five hundred lives and successfully reanimated six thousand, four hundred and thirty-one lives."

"What happened to the other one thousand lives?"

"The Islands were built to run fully through the supercomputer. If there is an error that endangers the inhabitants of the Islands, the supercomputers are to take what energy we need to rectify that error, even if it means shutting down several cryogenic units."

Sophia covered her mouth.

"You said 'the Islands,' plural" Jasira continued. "Does that mean there are more?"

"No. All the other Islands have been decommissioned."

"How many Islands were there?"

"Ten Islands."

"All carried seventy-five hundred lives?"

"All carried seventy-five hundred lives, but none were able to support all seventy-five hundred lives for that length of time."

"How long was 'that length of time'?"

"Nine hundred and ninety-two years."

Jasira flinched back, skepticism displayed on her face. Gathering herself, she pressed forward.

"Prisha, what year is it?"

"The year is 4682 A.D"

Just like a candle being extinguished in the wind, silence swept the group. The echoes of their voices slowly rose above them and dissipated into the air.

78

ATTEMPTED
USURP

Dasan snapped at Amadahy. The sizeable female wolf quickly jumped back and avoided another wound. The two were encompassed by the White Fang Tribe in a snow-covered arena. Anger boiled in her, and she callously lunged again. This time, Dasan stepped left, dodged the attack, and immediately turned back and grabbed Amadahy by the neck. She loudly yelped as Dasan pressed her down. She kicked and tried to break his grip but couldn't. Sewati, Dasan's present brother, walked forward, his demeanor calm as ever.

"Amadahy, do you yield?"

Amadahy growled and struggled some more.

"Amadahy," Sewati said louder, "do you yield?"

"Yes! Gods, dammit! Yes."

Dasan released his grip then cautiously stepped away.

The White Fang Tribe howled, yipped, and pawed at the ground.

"How can you all cheer?" Amadahy called out. "One of our kind travels with the humans! Filthy, dishonest humans! His brother! And you cheer his victory. Muraco's direct involvement has put our clan in danger. Which makes Dasan unfit to lead our kind."

"Dasan is wise!"

"Muraco made his own choice!"

This support for Dasan came from the group, followed by howls.

"Amadahy," Dasan's powerful voice cut through the howls, "Muraco has not violated any laws. He is free to travel with the humans if he wants."

"Their kind will be the end of us! It was before, and it is bound to happen again! If you were smart, you would order us to break from the Council and travel north, away from all of this!"

Some howls from the group erupted agreeing with her.

"That is absolute nonsense. Breaking off and hiding would do nothing to aid our kind. We are not cowards!"

"But you will make us out to be fools! This isn't our war, this is theirs. We shouldn't be involved."

"Where is your head at?" Dasan asked. "We all share the same world; this is and always has been our war." He turned and faced the White Fang. "The Fae went into hiding thousands of years ago, and because of their inaction our kind were helpless to stop the events of the World's End! After the humans disappeared, we had a thousand years to restore our society before they reemerged. We are all living proof that second chances happen." Dasan's tone grew dark and bold as he faced Amadahy. "I will not tempt the fates and risk the lives of our kind because of your cowardice."

"Learning from history is not cowardice, it's perseverance!" Amadahy replied. "Humans cannot resist; even after they reemerged, the peace held for only three hundred years before they warred among themselves again. Our ancestors and the Warrior Tribe were smart and intelligent to separate themselves. It is reckless to have faith in a species which is known to be the catalyst of their own demise."

Her words echoed in the arena as the tribe grew silent.

Dasan took in a deep breath. "I understand how many of you have reservations, and they are valid. But, as Amadahy said, learning from history is perseverance, and history shows that hiding almost killed us off and damaged our world. The Warrior Tribe may have opted for that, but the Council and I agree that humanity's destruction was not limited to just to humanity. They took down everything around them. We, us Fae, are here to stop the destruction of the Green, of our world, and if aiding the Atarans is what will stop Kahel from killing our world then so be it!"

The tribe howled loudly, all except for Amadahy. She glared hatefully at Dasan. She huffed as Dasan came close to her and whispered, "Tell Cecrops 'nice try.'"

The two stared intently at one another as the tribe, ignorant to their exchange, continued to howl.

Amadahy smirked in resignation then trotted away.

"Make no mistake," Dasan addressed his tribe, "I do not side with the humans. Just because we met some intelligent ones in the Iceway does not sway my deep belief that humans are never to be trusted, but we must do all we can to ensure the survival of those humans who openly oppose Kahel. Once the Green is safe, we can discuss how to deal with their destructive ways."

79

ISLAND EIGHT

"4682? That's not possible," Jasira said.

"Not only is it possible, but it is also a fact," Prisha said.

Lee grabbed Jasira's shoulder. "Listen," his tone apologetic, "the Majji, he told us."

"Told us? Told us what?" Her jaw clenched.

"Well, told some of us, at least, about our ancestors and how they nearly destroyed our world. He said it was a long time ago and gave us some scrolls to read."

Jasira began to take deep breaths.

"He told us that only the highest-ranked in Atara were informed of this. The scrolls we were given covered information about the Ibex and Fae, but they didn't give us a timeline or tell us exactly what our ancestors did, only that whatever happened took the world hundreds of years to recover from."

Jasira looked at Cyrus, then to Garret, whose guilty looks were enough for her. She turned back to the computer.

"Prisha, is what he said accurate?"

"The information he provided, though incomplete, is accurate."

"Well, what happened? Back then, so long ago. What happened that our ancestors felt that these Islands were necessary?"

The screen flickered and images of war appeared, families starving, people running from battles, abandoned cities, droughts.

"It started in 2118 when humanity finally realized that their ignorance had led to the ultimate end of our world's natural resources. The Earth's energy went from being concentrated in its own state of equilibrium that provided habitat to all living creatures to being dispersed and spread out. Humans were transferring potential energy into kinetic energy at a higher rate than the kinetic energy was able to revert back to potential energy."

Lee raised an eyebrow. "Are you getting any of this?"

"Sort of," Jasira replied.

Videos of oil drilling, a rapid time-lapse of dinosaurs decaying and becoming oil, forests being wiped out, trees growing, glaciers melting, and lakes receding, all appeared on the screen.

"The energy, or Essence, to sustain your habitat could not be restored at the same high rate it was being used. The Earth was becoming unsustainable. Though many fought throughout the ages to protect Earth and help her regain her equilibrium, their efforts were in vain. Those who had the power to make the change chose to do so centuries too late. The damage they had caused was irreversible. Famine swept our world. Genetic food modification gave humans a little more time, but war inevitably broke out over Earth's seed storage and the only fertile land left. An earlier government had stopped the research into finding other habitable planets, knowing that no matter how much financial backing they gave these projects, they could never successfully launch and establish a civilization on another planet before the Earth became inhabitable. With the freeing of financial assets, Dr. Prisha Kaur and her team of engineers and scientists were able to acquire grants and funding through private corporations to move forward with their plans. The Green spoke to her. The Green spoke to everyone who found their way north to the Islands. Those who could not listen could not be saved. Many humans knew what was happening to the Earth, many had already begun searching for alternative ways to survive. Prisha and her team were given the only answer. They were able to save thousands of lives. War escalated, and no living creature was safe. The Green held off as long as possible, saving energy, building up as much strength as she could. When it was time, the Green unleashed a fury upon humanity resulting in massive volcanic eruptions, earthquakes, tidal waves, tornados, and hurricanes. Save for those safe in the Islands, humanity was wiped out."

"How did they do it? How did they survive?"

The supercomputer played raw footage from a floating orb camera. The date stamp read 2119, and people who were dressed in thick insulating coats were walking through snow.

"Right here. This is it. This is where we begin," Human Prisha said as she pointed to the ground, "this will be Island One."

The next clip played; the date stamp was 2125. Prisha was standing in front of a control panel identical to the one Jasira was in front of. The walls displayed the number seven.

"Islands, this is Prisha at Control Seven; do you read me?"

"Alexei at Island One hears you loud and clear."

"Olivia at Island Two, clear as day."

"Joylette at Island Three, ready."

"Aldis at Island Four, a go!"

"Yeah, let's go Voltron Force!" a man's voice called out.

"Joel," Prisha scolded.

"Lame-o. Joel at Island Five, yadda."

Prisha rolled her eyes.

"Um, can I go now?" a timid male voice called out. "Yes? Hello? Okay, I guess I'll just go. Dennis at Island Six, a go."

"Neith at Island Eight," called out a young girl's voice, "ready!"

Everyone turned to Neith, who made her way to the back and was looking at the screen. Her expression was of both joy and heartbreak.

"Nobuo and Ryoko at Island Nine ready."

"Ervin at Island Ten ready."

Prisha smiled. "Alright, guys! We have fully functional transmission!

Everyone cheered. "Time to get ready for the cryo units. The next few years are going to be key to the success of this project."

The next clip appeared; the date stamp was 2128.

Prisha appeared on the screen. "The war has already taken so many lives. I feel its hateful fingertips getting closer and closer to us every day. Each day that passes, we have more people wandering up to us, not truly understanding why they are here but happier than anything else to find that they aren't insane. I feel it, so many of us feel it. Something terrible is about to happen; we need to finish these Islands."

The next clip loaded. It was multiple shots of all ten control room cameras and cameras on the levels beneath and around the main level. It was time-stamped 2130. Thousands of people were dancing to music, eating food, and laughing. All the cameras shook, and they lost feed for a moment.

"Islands, this is Seven, do you read?"

All cameras came back, one by one, as each person called out their status.

"Okay, I'm going shut down all other feeds except for us. Now I am calling up exterior cameras."

When the cameras were cued up, they all could see the

outside. The horrific sight took them all by surprise. People were clawing at their security walls. The Island leaders watched as the ground beneath them shook and cracked. Bomber jets flew overhead.

"Holy shit! Prisha, we've got to let them in!" Joel called out.

"Okay, give me a moment."

"Are you crazy? We don't have any extra units available!" called out Ryoku at Island Nine.

"Are you suggesting we just leave them out there?" Aldis at Island Four responded.

An argument ensued as Prisha worked some numbers.

"We can share," she called out, "it drops the sustainability by twenty-seven percent, so we just might wake up a few decades early."

"I'm opening my doors," Neith at Island Eight called out. Before the doors could fully open, the jets dropped several bombs. The impact vibrated through all the Islands. The feed was lost again for a moment before it returned. Island Eight's feed was choppy, Neith appeared disheveled, and sparks flew all around her.

"Why are they bombing us?" she called out.

"I think they want in too." Alexei at Island One responded.

"Well, there will be nowhere to get into if they blow us up!" Joel at Island Five said as another explosion shook the Islands.

"Oh, god," Prisha called out. "Full cryo mode! This is not a drill! Activate supercomputers!" The inhabitants of the Islands, group by group, made their way to the elevators. Prisha called up every camera on her screen and watched as people entered their cryo units. She watched as Island commanders worked frenziedly to begin their slumber, and she watched as the outside world began to fall apart. Tears fell down from her eyes as the exterior cameras projected the images of the people they couldn't save. The ground shook furiously again.

"Another bomb?" Aldis asked, his dark skin glistening with sweat.

Prisha scoured the images on the monitor and saw no jets. Another rumble.

"No, not a bomb; it's beginning. Are we ready?" Prisha saw Neith at Island Eight turning to protect herself from the sparks. Prisha bit her lip, the lives of tens of thousands of people rested on her words.

"Initiate."

The roll call began.

"Island Eight." Neith coughed. "Unable to initiate full cryo mode. I'm working on it, guys; the blast screwed up the computer."

"No more." A more mature Neith's voice called out, bringing everyone back to the present for just a moment. "I can watch no more." She walked further away from the group.

Young Neith's cries were heard as a third blast shook the Islands. She was then no longer on the screen. Smoke billowed from the computer.

"No! Neith!" Ervin at Island Ten with a thick Middle Eastern accent called out.

"Island Ten, initiate." Prisha held back her sobs.

"Neith needs our help!"

"Ervin, you are responsible for seventy-five hundred lives. Initiate."

The man glared at the screen.

"Island Ten, initiating full cryo mode. Ervin, signing off."

Prisha watched as Ervin walked away from the control panel. She took in a deep breath and said, "Computer, enlarge the exterior security cameras."

Joel walked back towards his control panel and sat.

"Jesus, Mary, and Joseph," Joel gasped as he saw the Earth falling to pieces around them. No one remained outdoors, as the ground shifted and cracked, but none of it affected the Islands.

"Computer, connect to Island Eight."

"There is no response from Island Eight's supercomputer."

Prisha looked at Joel.

"Joel. You need to get into your cryo unit."

"I know what you're thinking and it's crazy. We don't even know if Island Eight's telepad is functional; you could dematerialize forever."

"Computer, set the telepad coordinates to Island Eight."

"Prisha, don't!"

Without a response, she walked off, got onto the telepad, and disappeared. Another camera view opened up on the screen and showed Prisha arriving at Island Eight. She raced to the hanger doors and cleared up junk that was blocking it from closing correctly. Once the door shut, she ran to the control panel and lifted a limp Neith. She checked for a breath, then a pulse.

"She's alive, Joel, are you there? She's alive."

"I'm here. Your signal sucks; everything is coming in choppy."

"I'm going to put her in her cryo unit."

The video feed changed over again. Prisha was underneath the computer. The sparks had stopped, and there was no longer smoke coming from the control panel. She crawled back out from underneath.

"How are things looking out there, Joel?" She began to type codes into the computer.

"Same as three days ago: the world outside is fucked, and every living human on Earth is in cryostasis except you and me."

479

"Heh."

"I could help, you know. All you have to do is unlock my telepad."

"You'd try to stop me."

"I think we could find another solution than this. You don't need to rush into it."

"The computer needs a new motherboard, a functional superbrain. We do not have any spare parts to create a new one. None of us will live long enough to run Island Eight manually. So, this is the only solution."

"But you can't just insert yourself into the computer."

"Sure, I can."

"Goddammit, Prisha!"

"I will not forfeit all of their lives, all seventy-five hundred lives, Joel."

"Your life is just as important! Why can't you see that? Unlock the telepad, let me go over there, let me work on this, give us five years, and if we can't figure this out in five years, then fine, wire yourself in."

She ignored him and continued to punch in codes.

"Prisha, come on, please." Joel's eyes spoke louder than any words could. "You're all the family I've got left. My wife, my kids, my mother, father, brothers, they all abandoned me. They tried to get me locked up. When I begged them to come north with me, they didn't. They told me I was crazy and, hell, I really started to believe that I was. But then I found you, and we knew, we just knew. You're my li'l sis. We're supposed to have more time, so much more time. All I am asking is for five more years."

Prisha wiped her eyes.

"I can't, Joel. Just having you with me on the screen is almost stopping me. If you were here, knowing that you were happy, it would be enough to stop me. I'd never go through with it."

Joel knew he was losing; he became desperate.

"Hey, hey, remember we said that, once we wake up, I'd help you find some super dork like you, and when you two get married, I would be the one who'd walk you down the aisle to the *Doctor Who* theme song?"

Prisha started to cry.

"I'm so sorry, Joel. I love you so much."

"Oh, god, Prisha, no, don't!"

There were no cameras where Prisha went. Just moments after she disappeared, Joel's control panel unlocked and he gained full access.

"Computer, connect telepad to Island Eight," he huffed.

"Access granted."

Joel ran onto his telepad. The security cameras followed him as he went from Island Five to Island Eight, then to the back area where Prisha had gone.

His cries vibrated through Island Eight as if he was there with the group.

Joel walked out and slid to the ground. He held in his hand a piece of paper. Joel continued to sob. The feed then ended.

"Supercomputer," Jasira said, "did Joel go back into a cryo unit?"

"Yes."

Jasira gulped. "When?"

"Dr. Joel Reed achieved full cryo suspension twenty-eight years later."

"Jasira," Raja called. "What is it you know?"

"I think Joel was the creator of those Regeneration Units. I am figuring that the letter was not only Dr. Prisha Kaur's goodbye but also instructions for him. To make sure she didn't make a mistake along the way. Think about it. She did all that in a rush, so there were bound to be some issues. I am pretty sure she asked Joel to run maintenance on her system."

"You are quite brilliant, Jasira," Neith called out from the back. "For Joel to see the success of Island Eight, he had to modify his cryo unit. Instead of making him slumber, it regenerated him so he could work around the clock. He managed to tap his unit into the Earth's lifestream, what we call Essence. It took him over two decades to make Prisha fully compatible with the computer."

"Tell us, Neith, what happened when everyone woke?"

"I recall that we woke up first, all the leaders of the Islands, about two years before everyone else." She walked forward into the light. "We were shocked to see how much Joel had aged. He told us what had happened. He then showed us Prisha. She was in her cryo unit"—Neith's eyes watered—"with cables inserted into her head. She had also begun to age. With the changes she made to her unit, she was not being preserved. Within the first nine months, we were able to remove her and replace her with a simpler motherboard. Prisha never woke up and died in Joel's arms. Joel died several weeks later. They were buried side by side outside of Island Eight. After the burial, the remaining leaders began to survey the area. It was then they met the Ibex and Fae, whose ancestors did not slumber. Information, including history and topography, was exchanged. Together they created a telepad between here and Eurija. The Green had rested. She was strong. We learned to respect her, nurture her, and knew if we did then she would forever provide. We began again. Groups went their own ways and settled colonies. I became the human representative at the Fae Council. At some point, something inside me changed. I could hear the Green and became more connected. That's when I became the First Majji. As I speak these words, I feel these memories fading."

"Is that accurate?" Jasira asked the supercomputer.

"Yes. Neith became Majji and often traveled the Iceway from the newly established colony of Atara to meet with the Fae Council."

"Has anyone else accessed information from you?"

"Yes."

"Do you have a record of this?"

The screen blipped, and Kahel appeared. His wide eyes were looking curiously at the screen, while his fingers gently moved over the board.

"Did he see what we saw?"

"Yes."

"Anything else?"

"Yes, he wanted a timeline of events till his time. He then inquired about the last event on the timeline."

"Show me."

Jasira watched as Kahel learned about the Graveland battle and about Neith being impaled. Worry crossed his face, then he gathered his traveling party and rushed onto the telepad.

"He returned, didn't he."

"Yes."

"Show me."

This time, Kahel's face had changed. His gentle, curious touch had been replaced by an aggressive, impatient one. He turned to face his party and ordered them to draw what was on the screen.

"What did he take?"

"Building plans for Joel's modified cryo unit. He began to collect information on the Islands, but I went into an emergency shut down. After they exited through the hangar door, I went into lockdown, then hibernation."

"How did you wake up from your hibernation?"

"My sensors detected the White Fang Fae near the telepad. It triggered a reawakening sequence. While my database on the Fae is vast, it has all been manually entered throughout the years. I had never seen one. I was curious. So, I unlocked the telepad."

"And with us?"

"I saw Neith."

"Prisha, do you have a world map? I'd like to see how Kahel arrived here."

"Yes. Here is the last topographical information, inputted in 3432, your year 310."

A map appeared, showing the world as they now knew it, but with two crucial differences: one, Island Eight was part of a large solitary island far north that was not protected by the Kalyptra, and two, across from their land, east of Tychi, on the other side of the Kalyptra, was another Island marked "Ibex."

All except Neith stood, jaws open.

"Um." Garret pointed to the screen and turned to look at Lee. "Did you know?"

"No."

Garret then turned to Neith, "You?"

"Yes."

"Explain."

"Not now," Jasira interjected. "Right now, it's more important we collect the information that was given to Kahel. Prisha. can you please release that to us?"

"Yes."

Each person took turns as they wrote everything down using whatever tools they could. It took several hours before they finished. They learned that Kahel obtained vital information regarding how the Islands were powered. It was not only hydraulics but, at the very bottom of each Island, a long silver rod with a large diamond tip protruded deep into the Earth. Each Island was connected to the Green. Lee communicated with Prisha and asked to remain the night, and she happily obliged.

That night, Neith told them that the memories of both Eilith and Neith reside in her. Neith's memories were becoming hazy, while Eilith's remained strong.

"She was tired and ready to go." The beautiful dark-skinned woman examined her hands. "It's strange, how I feel more and more like Eilith, but this body is Neith's." She looked at the group. "So, I feel you should all continue to call me Neith."

"What of the Ibex?" Garret asked. "You were one of them. Eilith, I mean."

"Yes, I was. After the battle of the Graveland, the Ibex saw traits in the humans that made them uneasy. The Atarans were content living simply, but others wanted to expand. Even with the knowledge of humanity's history kept secret to prevent a relapse, it seemed that humans were bound to repeat their mistakes again. The Ibex wanted nothing to do with it. The announced departure of the Ibex made the Fae nervous. They didn't want to deal with the humans on their own and came to the conclusion that it would be easier if the humans were just removed, so the Ibex stepped in. Tensions grew. Before another war began, the Atarans, led by the Second Majji, created a treaty between the three species. The Ibex would raise a Kalyptra protecting the Fae from the humans and the humans from the Fae. The Atarans would guard the Iceway against Fae exiting and humans entering. The Ibex would then live peacefully on the other side and would only drop the Kalyptra if someone broke the treaty. It takes a lot of magic and energy to keep the Kalyptra up. This is only the second one ever created. Thousands of years ago, another Kalyptra was made. The humans called it the Bermuda Triangle. It was larger than it seemed and hid the Ibex and Fae well."

As everyone slept, Jasira woke and quietly made her way to the control panel. Prisha appeared, and she quizzingly tilted her face.

"Hi," Jasira whispered. "You said something earlier today, and it's been bothering me." She looked back at the group. "Just me, no one's else brought it up. You said the word 'curious.' You said you were curious about the Fae, and then, later on, you said you went into 'Emergency shut down.' You need to be a conscious being to have curiosity, and shutting down like that to stop someone you feel is evil, that's an ethical decision."

She looked at the woman on the screen. "Prisha, are you alive?"

"Alive," she said in a soft tone, "No. Not in the same sense as you are. I am comprised of materials and metals fused together, powered by a hydraulic system. I am not alive, though I am fully aware. Dr. Prisha Kaur and I were linked for over eight centuries. While the humans slept, we became friends. Through her, I learned what was good and evil, kindness and hatred, but more importantly I learned to think independently."

"That's why they didn't shut you down with the other Islands. Because you're ali—" Prisha was about to correct Jasira. "Because you are a conscious being."

"Conscious being. Yes, I like that."

"Do you get lonely?"

"No. When I hibernate, I re-live Prisha's memories over and over again."

"I promise," Jasira whispered, "I promise to come back and tell you all I know about our history, about what happened after the battle at the Graveland, and I promise to find a way to try to free you."

"I'm happy to have met you, Jasira. While I could never hold someone to that promise, I'm appreciative of the gesture."

"In turn, could you teach me? Everything you know about ancient technology?"

"It would be my pleasure."

80

IT'S OVER

They did not stay long, the morning after. Lee's horrific wound had mostly healed, and he wanted to make it back to Knossos as soon as possible. With their moods somber, limbs fatigued, and spirits depleted, they embarked on the journey to the Fae base. The entrance to the Northern Passage was a day's walk, and without the anticipation of the unknown the trek back seemed quicker. Even so, their exhaustion overtook them, so they camped out one more time in an attempt to rejuvenate. It was in vain. Muraco would often nudge Sophia with his muzzle, urging her to ride on his back. Sophia would only respond by scratching the back of his ear. The pair remained so close to one another that his soft white fur would often brush against her soiled face. Muraco had even slept outside of Sophia's tent next to her. She didn't protest; she just snuggled up to that side of the canvas. In the final leg of the trip, no one spoke, no one stopped to eat, and just like the bodies they had fought they moved down the Northern Passage as if it was all they knew. In the distance, Sophia could see Misae and the centaurs. Her face crumbled. It was over. She let her weight fall onto Muraco and began to let out sobs of relief.

"Apprentice. It is okay. The Fae here will not hurt you." Muraco tried to console Sophia, misunderstanding the meaning behind her cries.

"Lee," Muraco addressed him appropriately for the first time, "I think it best you do not tell Rydan of Island Eight. Let me tell my brother first. Rydan is bound by laws and will inform the whole Council of your findings. I am not sure that is a good idea right now."

"Am I to lie to him?"

"No. Just postpone giving him a report."

"How long?"

"Evening. Eat, relax, cleanse first. By then, I should be back."

"Okay. This evening then."

With that, Muraco took off. Lee took in a breath.

"It's over, guys. We made it."

81

TO DASAN'S
SURPRISE

Dasan stood high on the Cliffside and awaited his brother with judgmental eyes. It wasn't until he saw the state of the party that he thought it best to hear his brother out.

"Gods. They lost two humans, and who is that female?" Dasan said to himself. He then observed the human they call Sophia grab Muraco. Dasan's eyes widened as he prepared to run towards them. This was an incident he must avert. Muraco would surely snap at the female and create an interspecies dispute, which was the last thing they needed. But, to his surprise, his brash, hot-headed brother turned affectionately towards her.

"What in the—?"

Muraco had broken off from the group before Rydan, captain of the Fae Guard, spotted them. Rydan and some of his men raced towards the humans. The Ataran Lee spoke some words. Rydan made the signal for the medics to come.

At that point, just about all of the Atarans fell to their knees. They received treatment in ointments and medicine. They were given water and food.

"Brother," Muraco's voice echoed.

Dasan turned his head.

"What has happened, Muraco?"

"Our world's balance has been disrupted. The Green is upside down. I know this because that girl"—he gestured to Sophia—"was to be Apprentice, but never will be. I do not care what the humans say, deep in me, I sense I was to be her Elemental. Us Fae cannot allow the humans to attack Kahel and the Mad Essence alone. The humans' success will ensure the survival of all the species that exist, and success cannot be attained without the Ibex and us. I saw that firsthand because I was part of it firsthand. Without my intervention, they would have never made it back alive. There is so much to tell, brother. So much."

82

RETURN TO THE FAE COUNCIL

Fae hospitality could never be matched. It was a fact that they were better as a friend than a foe. The humans took hot showers, were given clean robes, fed, and healed. They were also given one area to cohabitate. The room was the perfect size to house everyone. There were mats laid down with blankets for each person. The heat came from a wood stove that had stones on its top. If the room got too dry, they would pour water over the rocks, which in turn would produce steam. Sophia sat by the door and watched as Muraco sauntered into the base. She walked out of the warm, wooden room and into the flickering torch-lit night. Muraco huffed, then flopped alongside the wall. Sophia wandered to him and rubbed the bridge of his nose.

"Dasan said to report everything. By now, he should have reached Batea or Xenos. I know my brother seems paranoid, but Cecrops, while an incredible leader, has his own agenda for his kind."

491

"It's why they probably chose him for the Council," she said.

"Right, indeed. Cecrops would do just about anything to make our Council a one-Fae-led Council, like you are all ruled by one."

"One man we are trying to usurp."

Lee and Garret walked out and saw Sophia and Muraco. Muraco nodded at Lee, and that was all the acknowledgment Lee needed.

"What's going to happen now?" Sophia continued.

"Your human Lee will tell Rydan everything. Rydan will feel like this information is imperative and rush to the Council. You will all be required to return to Knossos, and refusal is not an option unless you want to be marked as a threat again. A new human representative will be chosen to speak, your intentions will be revealed, and then the Council will see if they must kill you or not."

Muraco nonchalantly groomed his paw.

"Wait, what?"

A mischievous smile grew on Muraco's face in time for Sophia to hold back her panic. She pursed her lips as Muraco continued to groom himself, chuckling slightly now.

The next day, as if Muraco was clairvoyant, everything happened as he had said. They were all escorted back to Knossos. They rode the horses from the Enbarr Tribe. Once again in Knossos, they chose Neith as their representative. She spoke eloquently and was not in any way intimidated by the Council.

"Us humans cannot do this alone. Kahel's technology is far more advanced than any of ours. He's had years to modify it to what he needs it to do. We do not stand a chance."

The wyvern huffed.

"How do you expect us to help?" he boomed.

"Yes, how can us Fae who are so technologically far behind help?" Cecrops hissed.

"Scouting," Neith said in a matter-of-fact tone.

"What?" Cecrops snapped.

"We need to know how many bases and how many of those Essence-siphoning contraptions Kahel has set up. We need an updated map that shows everywhere Kahel has been. Some of your kind resemble animals that are seen daily. They could roam freely and come back with information."

"We can go by sea to examine the shores and islands," Batea added.

"When we have a map, we could slowly, one by one, start attacking and disabling those siphon systems of his." Neith nodded.

Cecrops clicked his tongue. "What good would disabling them do?"

"They power his Regeneration Units. Destroy enough of them, and he will become vulnerable. That's when we would attack."

"What you propose could take years! What if he decides to attack first?"

Batea rolled her eyes. "Then we defend ourselves. The way I see it is that we could be proactive and potentially get attacked. Or we sit here, do nothing. then potentially get attacked. I, for one, would rather be helping the cause." Her aquatic hair showed her annoyance by waving the slightest bit faster in the air.

"Hear, hear," Neith called out.

Batea bowed her head in appreciation.

"Hear, hear," said all except for Cecrops.

"As for the matter of the Fae helping the humans scout our world, the motion has passed. Are there any other matters that should be discussed?" Dasan inquired.

Batea raised her arm gracefully.

"State your matter."

"Our history tells us that our Council held six chairs. Two open chairs remain. One for the humans and one for the Ibex. I believe those should be filled."

The robust wyvern tilted his head in thought, Cecrops seemed appalled by the idea, and Dasan seemed unmoved.

"I think that is a good idea, Batea," Xenos spoke. "But are there qualified, willing candidates?"

Cecrops rubbed his forehead. "Are we seriously considering this, because I would like to remind you that we don't make snap decisions. That is the whole point of this Council. We discuss, then take the topic back to our people. Once they are informed, we get a vote through them. That is the vote we represent! Or are we trying something new here?" he hissed.

"I know how our system works!" boomed Xenos. "This is a decision that was voted on ages ago by our ancestors. The only reason the seats have not been filled is that there were no eligible candidates." His last words reverberated in the air, silencing even the wind. The large wyvern huffed and readjusted himself. He stood tall, rigid, and most importantly, dangerous.

"Friend Xenos," Dasan said, "I'm sure Cecrops meant no disrespect; he just didn't choose the best words to express his concern. But you speak the logic that we rely on you for. This is a matter that had been voted on years ago. The seats are open, we should fill them."

Xenos bowed his head and relaxed his stance. The humans took note: never insult the intelligence of a wyvern.

"Exactly, I meant no disrespect. What I meant was the matter of humans and Ibex holding seats in our Council was voted on years ago. When there was peace and an alliance. But now? Is it truly safe to trust them?"

"Do you want to put it to a vote?" Dasan asked, his tone

showing his confidence.

"Yes."

The vote was in the humans' favor. With trust solidified, they moved on to assigning the seats. The humans assembled for a moment, then came to the conclusion that Domingo and Santiago would represent the humans and Jasira was temporarily sitting in the Ibex seat with Neith by her side for advising. It was no surprise that Cecrops was upset with this turn of events. Rumors had been circulating of war and of the Council selecting a single, unifying leader. By this point, that rumor had hit the ears of all who held seats. While the talk was welcome to some, they all knew that now was not the time. With the addition of the humans and Ibex to the Council, the possibility of a single leader was shelved. It wasn't only Cecrops who opposed the seat assignment. After the meeting had been adjourned, Cyrus pulled Jasira to the side.

"You can't do this."

Jasira's brows furrowed.

"You can't because then I can't be by your side. My duties as a military member of Atara require me there in Atara. I can't stay here with you unless I abandon Atara when they need me the most." His tone was growing more desperate as he continued, "You must decline."

Jasira looked at Cyrus, aghast. "Why is it okay for me to abandon my duty to Atara? Representing the Council when no one else can is a huge honor, Cyrus. We are attempting to unite our kind with the Fae."

"We are bonded, Jasira!"

"I can travel back and forth, Cyrus!"

"So, you'll put everything on hold then?" His words weighed heavy on her.

"Nothing is on hold"—her voice softened—"what is meant will be; this is my intended path. I feel it. And this way, I'll be able to learn more from Prisha and Island Eight. This is good,

Cyrus, for once please have faith in me.

Jasira looked over at Garret who was leaning up against a pillar, his head tilted and his face firm as he watched them.

"Everyone else seems to." Still watching Garret, she turned to Cyrus to see his jaw harden.

"As if I have a choice." Cyrus huffed and walked away. He sneered at Garret, who rolled his eyes and followed him.

"Hey, man," Garret reached out and touched Cyrus' shoulder. "I'm only going to tell you this for her sake. A woman doesn't like it when her partner looks down on them. Trust me, I have a lot of sisters. Jasira is brilliant and more than capable of making decisions on her own. If she says she's going to go back and forth, then trust that. And remember," Garret said as he pushed his emotions back, "she chose you. You are one of her decisions. Don't screw it up."

Cyrus took a deep breath.

"I'm sorry, Garret. This journey, being away from home, I feel it has changed me."

"It's changed us all, friend. I fear that this was merely a sample of what lies ahead."

Escorted by the White Fang brothers and Misae, the group of worn-down friends began their journey back to Atara. They stopped at the tree to collect themselves then continued forward to the Iceway.

"This is as far as I go." Misae bowed her head. "Within the next several months, my tribe and I will begin scouting the southeast territories for Extricate Stations. Safe travels, my friends."

"I too will say my goodbyes here," Sewati added. "My brothers will safely take you the rest of the way."

"Quick question before you go," Garret's infectious smile caught everyone's attention. "Couldn't you just do that snow tide thing you did to carry us most of the way?"

Muraco laughed, showing his marvelous deadly teeth. His brothers laughed.

"Well, sure, but you'd lose your footing and die. Only the White Fang can produce that, and only the White Fang can reside on top of it. Well, she might be able to survive," Muraco gestured towards Jasira."

Raja lovingly nudged his friend.

Garret shrugged. "Hey, didn't hurt to ask."

83

BORIS AND YAREN

It had been several days since Boris resumed his regeneration routine. The first night of full regeneration, he accepted that the moment he stepped out of the unit his consciousness would be gone forever. Boris entered the Regeneration Unit, fighting a deep sadness; not only was it hard for him to come to terms that all his efforts were for naught, but Boris also struggled with the idea of becoming a mindless drone again. The silver lining was that he didn't have to remember how he failed and how he let that poor boy Gabriel die. Boris took one last breath of free will and shut the door. Hours later, all that had happened was that he regenerated. Boris stepped out healed, refreshed, and with memories intact. This day, which was many days after his first regeneration, he sat, distraught, in his old room, the one that had been given to him years ago by the True King. He leaned on the edge of the bed, with elbows on his knees and hands through his wild, silver hair. Since the day he had convinced Kahel to let him live, he'd been involved in several dehumanizing acts. At first, he didn't allow it to affect him much because he was confident the first regeneration was a blip, and after several goes in the chamber he'd lose himself and not remember a thing. But what he didn't realize then was that, whatever he was, whether it be a puppet, Grey, or drone, he was without question NOT Boris. Boris had died many years ago. Nor was he human, at least not anymore. He couldn't lose himself like any other average human would in a Regeneration Unit. He was different, an entity who was created through regeneration, therefore the potential remained that the regeneration wouldn't erase who he was. He stood up and wandered towards the window. His quarters were large and had the general essentials: bed, light, bureau, and a window to look outside. Even with the cold, grey, stone walls, it was nice, but he wanted none of it. What he wanted was to go back to the moment when he could have stopped the Salinans from going to Tychi. He wished he could tell them to turn around, to run home, to save their families. Boris's face grew firm and dark. How they violated Gabriel's body. Kahel wanted to take all the Essence that he had left. He was convinced that he sensed something in him. Boris let out a frustrated yell. Just then, a knock came at the door. Boris gathered himself quickly.

"Enter."

"Boris, Kahel requests your presence."

"Yes, yes, of course. Just give me a moment, I'll be down in a bit," he said, waving off the guard.

"He said, 'Now.'"

Boris cocked his head. "Alright, then now it is."

Boris followed the man down the stone stairwell to Kahel's throne room. Sethos was in the entryway, far from Kahel, a strange arrangement. In the throne room, he saw the back of Duroc, commander of the armada, and two other seamen. Kahel sat at his throne and cautiously waved Boris in. Duroc turned his head.

"Slowly."

Boris did as he was asked. When he reached Duroc, he could see that a waifish Lady Yaren shook in his arms.

"Gods. What's happened to her?"

"Talbot abducted her. We don't know the details, but it's apparent he's done some horrible things to her," Duroc explained.

"Talbot?" Boris's tone was incredulous; he was about to speak more when he caught a glimpse into Yaren's eyes. It was the eyes of a brilliant woman, not of a broken woman. She then feigned a faint. Duroc caught her. Boris felt a fleeting moment of hope. He had a choice to make. Capitalize on it, or dismiss it.

"Yes, Talbot. Oh, that Talbot, such a master of manipulation." Boris nodded. "My lord, but why is she here?"

"I asked the same question," Sethos murmured. "She is worthless. We should just kill her."

Duroc's demeanor remained unchanged, but Boris swore he saw his hold on Yaren grow a fraction tighter.

"No, Sethos," Boris rolled his eyes. "Once again, you jump to a homicidal conclusion, furthering my belief that you are a dog off his chain who needs to be put down."

"That's murder, too," Sethos retorted. Everyone looked at Sethos. He then took a step back and remained silent.

"What I meant," Boris said irritated. "Why isn't she at her home with a doctor?"

"Two reasons,. Kahel stood up and walked towards them. "One, she knows something about what the Atarans are planning, why else would Talbot abduct her? We"—Kahel gestured to them all—"need to find a way to get it out of her. Now, my methods have been failing me. For the lack of a better term, siccing Sethos on her will only lead her to shut down, as Gabriel did. You had only moments with him, and you were able to extract more information than I could have dreamed about. I want you and her to spend time together, 'healing.' See what you can find out."

Boris nodded, "And secondly?"

"You don't see it, do you? Nobody alive really would, except for you."

"See what, my lord?"

"Look at her, Gods, dammit!" he hissed, "She looks like my mother! Why the hell does this woman look so much like my mother!"

Boris always had his suspicions. When he was fully human, he knew the Queen hid things from the True King. And then there were those strange letters that went back and forth.

"What's going on in that strangely shaped head of yours, Boris?" Kahel demanded.

To continue to move freely about the castle and town and to secure Yaren's future, Boris did the one thing he swore he would never do again, give the King accurate information.

"Because, my lord, I am sure that Lady Yaren is Queen Leata's sister and your aunt."

Kahel's face froze. His nostrils flared, and his breath grew rapid.

"You keep her safe, Duroc. You hear me?" The wild-eyed King pointed to Yaren. "And you, Boris, get me all the information possible from her. Take her to her home, and guard her door; she must always be watched."

Just like that, history repeated itself. This time, instead of Leata locked in a tower, it was her sister, Yaren, who Kahel thought was his last living relative.

84

A BRIEF HISTORY
OF GODS

The closer they came to Atara, the more the walls of the Iceway lost their ominous weight. Still, while that weight dissipated, another one pushed into Sophia's mind. She didn't realize until now a wall had been erected between her and Halcyon. Worry crossed her face, and Lee picked up on it. The wind blew hard against their backs as they fully emerged from the Iceway. They saw Zephyr in the distance. He had just materialized into his full form for the first time in front of the group. Zephyr swooped down and into Sophia. She wrapped her arms around his neck.

"Gods, I missed you."

Zephyr let out a small cry and nuzzled Sophia. He turned his head, and his eyes widened as he took in the mass of white fur to Sophia's side.

"Blood of White Fang," Zephyr called out. Both Muraco and Dasan bowed their heads.

"No. Don't."

"You are Elemental." Dasan peered up at Zephyr. "Our highest form."

Sophia stood confused. "How is it that you can hear him?"

Muraco and Dasan looked at Sophia, perplexed.

"This is the first time anyone besides Halcyon and I could hear him. Is it because you are Fae?"

"So, no other humans can understand him? No one else has spoken to him."

"Well, they've spoken at him but never had a conversation. I can hear him here." Sophia pointed to her head.

"Interesting. This is a first in Fae history," Dasan said. "We've never been able to communicate when ours goes through the change. It's illegal, you see. Once they make contact with humans, they cannot return. It seems that an Elemental communicates through telepathy."

"And only with other Fae, the Majji, and the Apprentice," Muraco added.

There was no one else to greet them, and this fact did not slip past the group. Granted, they were several weeks later than anticipated, but there is still usually a much larger welcome wagon.

"What gives?" Garret asked.

Without the harsh Iceway winds, their noses were tickled with a scent that lingered thickly in the Ataran air.

"No," Lee said softly. "No." This time was louder. He dropped his bags and was about to run when Zephyr zipped in front of him. He bowed his massive head, and Lee understood. This was the second time Lee would merge with Zephyr. Before Sophia could ask what was going on, Lee climbed right on and the pair zipped away.

Sophia stood with a perplexed look on her face.

"Hyacinth," Jasira said as she grabbed Sophia's hand. "How did you not sense this?"

"Sense what?"

"Halcyon, Sophia. How did you not sense that he is on his death bed?"

Sophia's eyes bugged out. It was then that the wall blocking her mind dropped entirely. An immense sadness washed over her, she felt weak, and her body ached all over.

"The hyacinth is his bloom. Every Majji has one. It's a gift from the Green. A Majji will always know a place is safe when they see or smell their bloom. It's one of the many ways the Green speaks to the Majji."

Sophia felt like an idiot. How did she not sense this? She was overly concerned with all the events happening to her that, even with the circlet sitting on her crown, Sophia had forgotten to check in with Halcyon. Sophia exhaled and looked into Jasira's upset eyes.

"I'm sorry, I'm so sorry."

"We would have rushed back, Cyrus, and I could have helped."

Jasira grabbed Cyrus's hand and pulled at him. They ran towards the direction of Halcyon's hut, with Garret and Raja not too far behind.

"Apprentice, it is strange that your link with the Majji didn't alert you of his health," Muraco stated.

"He blocked me! I said I was sorry. I am new at this! I didn't know he could do that."

"Why are you apologizing to me? The tiniest of the tiny humans is the one who is upset with you. I was just letting you know that being the Apprentice, you—"

"Should have sensed it! Yes. I get it."

Neith placed her hands on Sophia's shoulders.

"No one expects you to be a full-fledged Apprentice. Don't beat yourself up."

"It wasn't my plan to upset you," Muraco apologized. "If you would like, I can escort you to your Majji."

Sophia turned, teary-eyed, to Santiago, Domingo, and Neith.

"Go," The brothers said in unison.

"We will walk back with Dasan," Neith added.

Sophia wasted no time; she grabbed the staff and climbed on Muraco's back.

The scent of hyacinth was thick in the air. Even with Sophia's head turned to the side as Muraco raced through the roads of Atara, it still engulfed her senses. Her heart continually broke the closer they came to Halcyon's hut. Muraco slowed his pace, and Sophia looked forward. The hills were covered with Halcyon's bloom. Many Atarans had laid out blankets several yards from Halcyon's hut. Worry and fear crossed their faces when they saw the large white wolf approach.

"This is as far as I go. Until you can explain me to your people, I feel it safer I stay away from them."

"I agree." Sophia hopped down. A gentle breeze whirled around her.

"Zephyr, escort Muraco to my home, please."

The breeze swooped under Muraco then pushed up, momentarily fluffing Muraco's fur.

"Fascinating," the wolf said. He shook his fur back into place

Sophia watched as Muraco leaped left then right, avoiding Zephyr's bursts of wind as they walked away.

She turned to face Halcyon's hut. Jasira sat outside, hugged her legs, and had her face buried in her arms. Sophia knew she was inconsolable. She then turned to face Garret and Raja, who stood leaning against the hut, both gazing at the sky. Tears streamed down freely as they took deep, synchronized breaths. Cyrus stepped out; he gestured towards Sophia. Her legs and chest were heavy as she ran towards him.

"He is still with us, but he has maybe a day or two left. He hung on. For us. He told me, told us all, not to be upset with you. He put up that wall in your mind to make sure we didn't return prematurely." Cyrus took in a breath. "I had no right to say the things I said to you." Sophia could feel his remorse weighing on each word. "Halcyon saw everything. He told me that you have no control over the transformation you are enduring. With his guiding words, I was able to see that what is happening to you is a blessing. Because of it, the Essence of the Apprentice remains with us. It gives us a chance. However small that chance may be, it's still a chance." Cyrus looked up to Sophia. "Please, forgive my foolishness."

"It's okay, Cyrus. This has been hard on all of us."

Cyrus's face grew stern as he tried to keep his emotions in check. Sophia placed her arms around him and held him tightly.

"You are a good person, so don't dwell upon it." She kissed his cheek.

"Thank you." Cyrus nodded. "Lee is inside. Halcyon wants to see you."

Sophia sauntered in. The small table Halcyon was fond of had a small pot of tea and two cups upon it. No one sat there, but the chairs were pulled out, letting her know that they were full once. She wondered how long it'd been since Halcyon had been strong enough to sit there. She then turned into the dimly lit room. Lee sat next to Halcyon's bed, holding the Majji's hand between his. While the room may have been dark and seemed empty, Sophia knew it wasn't. The feeling rushed her, almost knocking her off her feet. The overwhelming sensation of love and happiness danced around her, filling her soul and heart with insurmountable joy. She crossed her arms around her abdomen and laughed. She fell to her knees and began to cry while laughing. Lee looked at her puzzlingly.

"You can feel it, too, can't you. How much joy is here,"

Halcyon's weak voice called out.

"Yes. They love you so much."

"It's the residual energy of everyone who has visited."

"It's beautiful," she said as she stood back up.

Halcyon laughed as Lee looked between the pair.

"Hey, you two, want to let me in on this?" Lee asked.

"Oh, Lee," Halcyon said, "eventually, your bond will be so strong you will want nothing more than *not* to know what she is feeling. But for now"—he gestured to Sophia—"go ahead, show him."

"Show him how?"

You know, child. You know how to communicate with your bond partner.

Shocked, Sophia looked at Halcyon. His voice was clear in her mind. Halcyon looked back at her and nodded. Sophia knew precisely what he meant.

The most intimate form of communication we all use, she replied telepathically. *Touch.*

Sophia walked up to Lee and placed her hands on his cheeks, then leaned her forehead to his. As if the shock of her approaching him in such a determined fashion was not enough, what followed sent his emotions into a tizzy. Lee took in a sharp breath and backed away. He placed his hand on his chest. His eyes grew teary, and he began to laugh.

"Gods," he sniffled, "that's amazing."

Sophia smiled at him.

"Lee, can you give Sophia and me the room, please?"

Lee nodded and walked out, closing the door behind him.

"Here," Halcyon said and patted the bed, "sit, please."

Sophia gripped the staff tightly and did as she was told. He ran his fragile fingers across her face. "You know, while you have so much of Princess Anne in you, you look so much like your grandmother."

Sophia gently caught Halcyon's hand and placed the

broken staff in it.

"Yes, this thing." Halcyon chuckled. "Lee debriefed me. So much you must have learned on this journey." He looked into her eyes. "I see so much growth, so much change. So much strength. And look at all the new amulets you brought home with you. Please tell me about them."

Sophia told him about Knossos, about Prisha, about Neith and her necklace, and about bonding with Lee.

"There is still so much for you to learn, but I am afraid I won't be here to instruct you the way I instructed Leata. You must find Yaren."

"Lady Yaren? But why?"

"Because she is your great-aunt and knows the stories. Leata couldn't resist teaching her sister everything she knew." Halcyon looked at the dumbstruck look on Sophia's face. "Good Gods, my child. No one told you?"

"No," she said breathlessly.

Halcyon tapped her hand, apologetically, "Unfortunately, there is no time for this. You must know something about our ancestors and the Fae. This story is passed down when an Apprentice becomes a full Majji, and only those in high positions in the Fae Council know it. Thousands of years ago, the Fae lived among humans. The Fae used their powers to help blend in. Eventually, some of the Fae revealed themselves to the humans. The Fae who chose to remain hidden raised a Kalyptra around a land that was full of Essence. It remained hidden from humans."

"Prisha called it the Berimooda triangle."

"Yes, that. Things were tumultuous at first, but before the World's End there was this moment in time where all living creatures lived in harmony. The humans, the Fae, the Ibex, and the Green. That, Sophia, that is our ultimate goal, to be in harmony with our land and one another. But back then, Mad Essence had already spread and done its damage through the use of humans. Their peace was short-lived as the Green continued to die. While we all have our differences and our similarities, there is one thing we share that connects us all."

Sophia looked at Halcyon earnestly.

"How we all came to be." The room bristling with his voice. "How life began. Each belief has its own stories of creation, and they are all sprinkled with truth. But it's not the whole story. What connects us all is the Creator. One of our gods, and one of the most important. He goes by both the Creator and the Father."

Halcyon saw Sophia's confusion.

"I know this is a lot. Even if you can't process it all right now, I do need you to at least remember it. All religions stem from the truth, but the Creator was the one god out of all the gods that mattered. Billions of years ago, the Creator was traversing the universe, as gods do, and came across our world. At the time, it was nothing but fire and ash, and he felt a deep pity for it. So, he blessed our world with life. Our world, which we lovingly call the Green, well, she began to flourish. It took a very long time for humans to evolve from the Creator's gift. Humans are interesting creatures that took a step away from the natural growth of all other life that was part of the Green. It was religion, you see, that sent them spiraling into destruction, and, from there, they never recovered. While faith and religion are wonderful things, when you leave it to man to transcribe the words of a god, things can go a bit awry, and they did. But their biggest mistake was believing that there was only one god. The humans began to wage terrible bloody wars in the Creator's name, though this was not what he or the Green wanted. So, the Creator sent his son, another god, to work with the humans and repair the damage. But in the end, his son was killed."

"What?" Sophia's tone was incredulous. "They killed the

Creator's son? Our ancestors killed a god?"

"Yes and no. Here on our terra, he was mortal, and his body was killed, but he returned to the Creator. The Son was injured and remained unconscious as he healed. But in time he woke. Now, what happens next is very important."

Sophia stared at the pensive Majji.

"They leave."

Sophia let that sink in.

"After realizing their failure, the Creator and the Son moved on to other worlds. Leaving the Green behind. Our ancestors continued waring in the Creator's name, trying to get in his good favor again. They had been called many different names, but in the end, it all refers to the same two gods, the Father and the Son."

"How is this relevant to now?"

"Because what are the Father and the Son without the Mother and the Daughter?"

Sophia's eyes widened.

"I see you are beginning to understand."

"The Mother is the Green?"

Halcyon nodded.

"But why didn't she leave?"

"Because she couldn't. Our world is her life. While the Creator was the god of man, the Mother is the goddess of life on our planet."

"But you said Mother and Daughter, so there is another god besides the Green who remained?"

"Yes."

"Where is she?"

"Well, part of the Daughter is in you, another part of her is in me, and the last part, which has slowly been leaving my body, has been placed somewhere else in the Green."

"The Essence of the Majji is the Daughter?"

"After seeing the Son crucified in his mortal body, the

Green decided that if she were ever to dispatch a god to help her, the god wouldn't use its mortal form, it would live within a human. We are just vessels for the Daughter. We transfer her Essence between Majji and Apprentice. If we die, our Essence escapes back to the Green, so she can start again."

"But no longer." Sophia looked down.

"I do not know why, but my Essence refuses to merge with you. It's been slowly dripping out of me and into the Green since my failed battle with Kahel."

"This doesn't make sense if we carry the Essence of the Daughter and Kahel is possessed by Mad Essence. Is he?"

"Possessed by a god? No," he said, shaking his head. "The Creator and the Son are mighty gods that freely travel from world to world. The Green is the powerful goddess of our world, but just our world. The Elementals respond to her, so you can look upon them as gods also. Mad Essence has always been a part of everything because of the balance. There can be no good without evil, no light without darkness. But Mad Essence is no god. It is said that billions of years ago, a large piece of land crashed from the sky, bringing with it anger and hatred. Mad Essence was able to draw power from that. It shifted the balance."

"So, the Creator took pity on our world when the Green and Mad Essence were at war?"

"Yes. Mad Essence had grown stronger and was able to become its own entity. It was spreading throughout her like a plague. The Creator had no idea what he had interrupted. He just saw a world dying. His blessing gave the Green the chance to overpower Mad Essence. Mad Essence had lost the battle. It was only temporary. Mad Essence began to infect humans, and they killed one another over greed, jealousy, and anger. They ignored the Green. Mind you, she is a proud god, and those humans were not hers. Humans murdered her son, drove her companion away, and had decimated her lands. Her vengeance was swift and merciless. The Daughter, on the other hand, felt pity for those who were still connected to the Green."

"Prisha and the inhabitants of the Islands."

"Yes." Halcyon nodded.

"And when they went into cryostasis?"

"Mad Essence had nothing to feed on, then lost a second battle, and well"—Halcyon gestured around him—"here we are. Again. Fighting it as it gets stronger. The Green has no empathy for most of humanity. Yes, she loves the Majji and the Apprentice. After all, they are her Daughter. She loves those who care for her Daughter.

"Atarans."

"She loves those who do her no harm."

"Fae and Ibex."

"But only half of the Daughter's Essence remains, leading me to believe she is calling her back. If given the chance, she would destroy us all again to end Mad Essence once and for all. But we have hope." She felt his elation and it made her nervous. "Leata's Essence stayed with you; therefore, you have half of the Majji's Essence. Half of the Daughter, half of a god, resides within you," he clarified. He looked into her eyes, and Sophia's heart was in her throat. She didn't like the intensity that was in his eyes and what she could sense from him. Sophia came from a small town, lived a simple life. She didn't ask to be a part of this oncoming war. All she wanted was to do was be with Gabriel and live their simple, peaceful lives in Salinas. This was just too much.

"You must lead my people. You must find a way to end this war, to restore balance, to stop Mad Essence for good before the Green fully awakens. Humanity will not survive the second coming of her wrath. You, the wife of my son, are the next leader of the Atarans."

Nope. *That* was too much. Sophia couldn't speak at first;

still, her mouth remained open as something coherent attempted to escape. She closed her mouth and shook her head.

"That's for Lee or Cyrus."

"The leader of the Atarans must be the vessel for the Majji's Essence."

"But I don't have all of the Essence."

"You have half, and this." Halcyon gestured to his broken staff. Sophia looked at him and at the staff in disbelief. Halcyon chuckled.

"I do not see anything funny here, Halcyon!"

"We are at the cusp of another life-altering war," he said, dismissing her panic. "These relics you have gathered are all very powerful and will help you. Please put them here."

Sophia removed the circlet and necklace and placed them beside Halcyon on the bed.

"Now, hand me my staff."

Sophia did as she was told. Halcyon sat up. He connected the two broken ends of the staff, then placed the circlet on top of the break. Finally, he wrapped the necklace around both the circlet and staff tying them together.

"Here." He grabbed her hand. "Hold the staff together." Halcyon placed his hands on top of hers.

"Et ego invocabo restituere id quod est viridis cum praesidio erat, et filii eius." A light began to glow between their hands. "I cannot give you my Essence, but I will give you all else that I have." He gave her a loving, honest smile.

Sophia gasped as she saw Halcyon's life flash before her eyes. His Apprenticeship, his roaming the land, Mahes appearing to him, meeting her grandmother, the battle with Kahel in the courtyard, him carrying her unconscious in his arms. She felt his sorrow for failing Leata, and she felt his love for his people. When it was all over, Sophia held a beautifully crafted staff. There were intricate metallic carvings from top to bottom, a thin rope weaved around the head. The rope was tied off at the ends and was finished with the beads and feathers that once were Neith's necklace.

85

THE MOTHER, THE GREEN

She lay in the gold chamber. Her translucent onyx skin, glittering like a thousand stars lived within it, moved to and fro throughout her as they pleased. She was getting stronger. Her v-shaped face was immobile. Then her eyes flitted open, showing darkness with deep purple irises. Her face remained emotionless.

"Daughter, what do you think you are doing?" she called out into the emptiness.

86

END OF
THE MAJJIS

Sophia turned to Halcyon, who was taking deep breaths. Mahes appeared out of nowhere and jumped on the foot of Halcyon's bed.

"Child, we do not have much longer. I thank you for bringing the Blood of White Fang. They will talk to my people, bring them news of Atara and about us, Servant Elementals." Mahes' brilliant blue flame was more subdued and sleepy-like. The giant lion fluffed the bed a bit before he finally decided to lay. Sophia helped Halcyon down and tucked him back in. She kissed his forehead as tears fell.

"Please. Don't leave me here alone. I can't do this without you," she quietly sobbed.

"You are the Apprentice. The Majji and the Apprentice will never truly part, and you are not alone." Halcyon closed his eyes. Sophia could feel Lee; even though he was on the other side of the door, she could feel him sending her his strength. Comforting her.

"They will always be by your side, all of them," he said with a smile. "Now I must rest, I am so tired."

Sophia remembered, blinking.

87

Lee held her hand often.

Jasira kissed her cheek often.

Raja and Cyrus hugged her often.

Garret rubbed her shoulders and kissed her forehead once.

Muraco and Zephyr never left her side.

88

Domingo, Santiago, and Neith talked to her and attempted to show the people of Atara that all was well.

Numbness swept through her. Those who didn't know Sophia didn't see anything strange with her countenance. But, the others, they saw a painful emptiness behind her eyes when she spoke.

It didn't feel like a week had passed. She couldn't believe that Halcyon passing in his sleep and Mahes dissipating happened seven days ago. Sophia had never seen anything like it. People closest to Halcyon knelt in his room. Halcyon's and Mahes' breaths were in peaceful unison. Mahes grew fainter and fainter, Halcyon's breath slowed, and with one final exhale a brilliant golden glow came from Halcyon while a blue light emanated from Mahes. Both lights swept through the people in the room and continued across Atara, bursting quickly through their lands with a speed that lifted dirt and dander. When it was over, Halcyon lay draped in copper robes, his long white hair tidied up in a braid and slung over his shoulder. He lay atop his bed with his hands across his abdomen. Mahes was gone. The scent of hyacinth was overpowering. Then Sophia blinked.

89

IT IS TIME.

One week of mourning passed, and they stood before the Majji's burial ground. Located deep within the woods of Atara and only accessible when the Green allowed it, which had been approximately every five hundred years. This day, the Green reluctantly opened the path, not wanting her child to be buried so young. You could feel her sadness ebb through the drooping branches as Atarans pushed leaves away so those who carried Halcyon's wrapped body could pass freely through into a clearing. A Sabino tree, large enough to put Kahel's castle to shame and with a trunk wider than Sophia's house, was a backdrop for several Anadenanthera trees. Before each tree, save for one, were small mounds littered with distinct flowers and a metal plaque for each. The group carrying Halcyon walked towards the last tree, where they lowered his body and stepped back. Atarans filtered in, filling the large clearing. Jasira led Sophia forward to Halcyon.

"You have to set him free now, Sophia."

Sophia worked to collect herself.

"Just for a few moments, pull yourself together. Please. For our people." While Jasira showed her support, there was an underlying emotion deep within that she tried to hide, that she wanted to hide from Sophia. Unsuccessfully, of course. Without even trying, Sophia could sense the emotions of everyone around her. The feeling in Jasira was an emotion Sophia sensed in more than one Ataran and, more painfully, in those she considered her close friends. Resentment. Oddly enough, this was not found in Cytrine. Within her Sophia sensed empathy and sadness. Because now together they were trapped in Atara. Sophia gained a new appreciation for Cytrine and for the first time Cytrine was a comfort to be around. Even so, around Jasira the resentment crept. There it skulked and lurked, then would scurry to its hole like a wild animal running from a predator whenever Sophia was around. It hurt her. Maybe because they didn't believe in her or perhaps because they knew that Sophia didn't want to be their leader.

Gabriel, my love. I wish to be with you. Only you. I want no part of these people, this life, but I can't just walk away. They need me. I refuse the leave them vulnerable the way our people of Salinas were left. But I don't believe I am fit to lead these people.

She felt her belly warm, and just as it happened so many times before she felt herself being taken over. She let it. She welcomed it. Sophia looked at Jasira with pained apologetic eyes, and then she was gone.

Jasira noticed the change in Sophia's disposition and turned her head silently, asking if Sophia was okay.

"I'm okay. All will be well," a calm voice called through Sophia.

She reassuringly squeezed Jasira's hand and walked towards Halcyon's body. The staff Halcyon forged with the last of his energy was in her hand. Sophia hadn't set it down since

Halcyon's passing. Sophia turned to Lee, who walked forward and placed a monogrammed plaque against the tree. She nodded at him, and he returned to the group. Sophia knelt by Halcyon's wrapped head.

"You served her well. Do not feel like you failed anyone. We love you dearly, and if she allows me I promise to come by and nag you every now and then."

Sophia stood up.

"The Green mourns her child as do we. Halcyon did her will. He nourished her, respected all her children, never took more than he needed, and therefore he will forever be a part of her." She turned back to Halcyon and kissed his wrapped forehead. She felt her strength leaving her. She stood up and turned to the Atarans. "May his Essence pass peacefully into the Green."

Lee reached for her hand and walked her back. They stood to watch as glowing green vines slowly emerged and began to cover Halcyon's body. Ribbons of sparkling gold guided each vine with the gentle care that has been for centuries reserved for those holding the frailest of newborns. Within seconds, Halcyon was shrouded in grass and vines. Hyacinths were scattered across his mound, just as flowers covered the other hills next to his. Lee turned to Sophia and furrowed his brows. He could sense her even more now through their bond and knew something was very different. It was Sophia in the sense that this was her body, and he sensed her there. But this person holding his hand was offering him strength. The strength was powerful and full of uninhibited love, not reluctant and naïve like the Sophia he knew. Sophia continued to look forward as a single tear escaped.

"There is no guarantee we will survive this," Sophia said.

He nodded.

As the vined mound was finally completed, the golden ribbons collided and dispersed through Atara, touching each and every one of them. The warmth consumed Sophia. She felt complete and at peace. *This* she remembered, this feeling she'd had several times, *but when?* She felt a warm breeze walk around her; it wasn't Zephyr, but whatever it was, she knew it well. It caressed the back of her neck and put tension on her waist. As if she was about to go into a lift. Sophia's eyes shot open. And instantaneously, Lee felt the energy of the Sophia he knew return.

"The dance," she said to Lee. He tilted his head back, gently took in a breath all while still enveloped in the euphoria of Halcyon's final gift, and then glanced over at Sophia

"At Tychi," she continued, "when Gabriel and I danced. Somehow, I did this. He knew, Halcyon knew, he knew that I could do"—she gestured to the golden glow surrounding them—"this."

He looked puzzlingly at her, and his expression changed to worry, then quickly to acceptance. Sophia didn't like those changes one bit. He sensed that in her and held her hand tighter.

"No, no, don't worry." His voice was gentle. "If you have any doubt about Halcyon's choice of you as our leader, then there is your answer," he whispered. "Only a full-blown Majji can perform a healing."

Lee harbored no resentment towards Sophia; what he tried to hide from Sophia was fear. It peeked its head out for a quick moment, then hid deep in the depths of Lee's subconsciousness.

"There is something else, isn't there? There is no sense in hiding it, Lee, please tell me."

Lee took in a breath. "A Majji has never been bonded. I'm concerned that being bonded to me might prevent you from ever performing a healing again."

"I guess only time will tell."

90

THE MOTHER
COURTESAN

The candlelight danced as Weiya exhaled in the dark archives room. Alejandro lifted up from the scrolls he was reading and turned to Weiya.

Weiya placed her finger on her lips and gestured to the others, who were all immersed in their reading. He understood the message even though it was she who made the noise, but that's always been her. So proud, too proud to ever admit any faults. Alejandro rolled his eyes and returned to his reading. It had been weeks since they started their research, and getting to this point was no easy feat. Gaining access to the room seemed impossible as it was a fact that only scholars were allowed in. Weiya, though, had her ways. First, by obtaining access to her family's ancestry charts that stated her family line of Elites dated back to Barons and Baronesses of long ago. She used that status to acquire schooling for her "wards." She knew that the only way to obtain that ever-needed passage into the Hall of Archives was to be a scholar or a student. Weiya paired mentors perfectly with a Courtesan or a Chevalier. More than intellectual knowledge was exchanged during their private sessions. The outcome was unexpected and surprisingly beneficial. Even after they gained the access to the Hall of Archives, the students continued to study and mentors continued to mentor. The teahouse had never seen so much business. Before, scholars would enter, order their tea or elixir, and leave. These days they would sit, invite other scholars, study, and converse in the teahouse, and at night, for those who desired more, there was much more. For the first time in history, the town of Vizzini was livelier than it had ever been.

Weiya was in the middle of piecing together an ancient map when Alejandro stood up.

"This translation can't be right. I must have done this wrong." Alejandro stared down at his parchment.

"What is it?" Weiya asked.

"We know that the Atarans are not evil and that they were quite literally warriors for the Green. But it says here that one of their main tasks was to..." Alejandro looked back down at the scroll, then to his parchment.

"Yes?" Weiya asked, now standing up.

"Protect the giants of ice from releasing the fury that lay in the Western land."

"What?" They all called out to Alejandro.

"With alliances destroyed, to keep the peace: Fae to the west, Ibex to the east, and humanity in between."

"Well, this just got a little more complicated," Weiya said into the eerie silence.

91

THE UNKNOWN

The brothers' house became an unofficial meeting space for Sophia and her Council. It was established between her, Lee, Cyrus, and Garret that they, along with their bond partners, would serve as a Council of sorts for her. Jasira walked in later, followed by Neith, with bags on their backs. They set them down and then sat. Sophia stood in front of the fireplace. Warm flames crackled, and it seemed like years to her since she first woke up here in Atara. She looked around as everyone watched her attentively.

"I appreciate you all. Every single one of you. And I want you to realize that I did not come to this decision easily. You, my Council, have come to an impasse. Half of you want to join forces with the Fae and fortify their barriers. Let Kahel do what he does, and hope that he burns the candle at both ends. Leaving us safe in Eurija, and all those who chose to remain with him in the east to wither and eventually die. The other half of you wants to be proactive and fight. Stop him now at great cost to us, ensuring the future of the Green, which in turn will ensure the future for us. There is no right option here. Both are dangerous. We sit and defend, we risk losing everything; we suit up and fight, we risk losing everything."

Everyone nodded.

"But Halcyon told me, that many years ago, the Green released her fury on our lands. I believe that if she becomes strong enough, she will not hesitate to decimate all that we know. If we remain here at an impasse, it could be catastrophic for humanity. Batea, representative of the children of Ice and Water told us that the Kalyptra has been dropped. We've learned from Jasira that her father has the blood of the Ibex in him. Halcyon knew this; he also knew of the Ibex living across the water on the other side of the Kalyptra." She looked at everyone. "We have allies. To our west and to our east."

"We don't know the Ibex are our allies," Raja said in his rumbling deep voice.

"Jasira will travel with Domingo and Santiago to the northeast corner of Atara. With the help of Muraco and Dasan, we've been able to reach Misae and the Tribe of Enbarr. The tribe has agreed to aid their passage across the water. If they are successful, we will have human, Ataran, and Fae representation to speak to them."

Cyrus turned quickly to see Jasira, then back at Sophia.

"I'm sorry, Cyrus. You do have an option. You can join her, but understand these two things: one, she's the lead, so she would make the decisions, not you. And two," she said as she drew from the strength deep within her, "I need you here." She then returned to the group. "I stand with the decision of the Fae Council. Jasira and her group will move east and try to gain the trust of the Ibex. Neith, Dasan, and Zephyr will travel back to Eurija. Lee, Garret, Raja, and I will travel the towns and see what intel we can gather about Yaren and where they are keeping her. If Halcyon was right and Leata

told her everything, she will have crucial information for us."
She looked back at Cyrus. "This is why I need you here with
our people. You will have our generals stand guard outside of
the woods. We do not know what Kahel's plans are and we
have to be careful." It was the first time Sophia referred to
herself as one of the Atarans. It felt right to her. "I will give
you one night to decide what you want to do." She turned to
face the fire. "The Essence within me calls upon me to bear
arms. I felt her long ago when I traveled to Tychi. When I held
the earth in my hands. I will not let her cries go unheard. I
apologize to those who wanted to avoid war. But it is
inevitable." Sophia walked towards the ladder of the loft bed
and looked out the window she had once escaped through.
"The alliance I plan to build will take years. When Jasira
returns, I will travel to Knossos to meet with their Council and
Jasira will make her way back to Prisha to learn what she can."

"I do not need tonight to decide. I will do as you command.
I only ask that I am allowed to escort you and Jasira to
Knossos," Cyrus replied.

Sophia nodded her head.

"Lee, then I will need you here."

He nodded as well.

"That's where we will start. I've already informed Muraco
of my decision and he is on his way to the Fae Council as we
speak. His return will give us an update on the Fae and set our
plans into action."

"Why wait for the wolf?" Garret's tone was more curious
than demanding. He leaned against the wall, as he usually did.

"I feel a pull to Muraco, and he does to me. I am confident
that he was to be my Elemental if I were to fully become the
Majji. While the days of the Majji are over, our connection
remains. Therefore, I promised to wait for him before we
embark on our mission."

"Yeah, like a giant white wolf won't be conspicuous,

wandering around towns." Garret laughed.

"He is skilled at making himself unknown and carries his own magic that prevents others from seeing him for what he truly is. Apparently, all Fae have this gift. It's the reason Misae and her tribe were able to blend in at Salinas so well. We saw horses, but they are much larger and ethereal-looking than that. You have to know what you are looking for to see it. No one outside of Eurija besides us knows what Muraco looks like, so no one will be looking for a giant white wolf. They might just see a tamed wolf."

"Good to know."

"The more we spend time with the Fae, the more we will understand them."

Sophia stretched into what seemed to be her new skin. She looked at the brothers, who were looking proudly upon her.

A week later, Muraco returned. Jasira and the brothers met up with Misae and four others from her tribe. Just as Sophia had said, now that they knew that they weren't looking at normal horses they saw past Misae's magic. They were large creatures. Their faces, while still resembling horses, were more elongated and angular. Their bodies looked slick and wet. But what stood out the most were their golden eyes and their manes that constantly flowed like Batea's, as if they were in water. They headed out the same time Neith, Zephyr, and Dasan did. Sophia informed the army and their people that Cyrus was in charge and then said goodbye to them all. She stood with her pack on her back, before the woods, with one hand caressing Muraco. Lee stepped behind her.

"Are you scared?" he asked her.

"No."

"Yeah, neither am I."

Muraco scoffed, "You smell of fear."

"It's not fear," Lee shot back.

"It's the unknown," Sophia said. "We are equipped with the knowledge our ancestors didn't have. We are creating a new path; we are going to fight for the Green and the survival of life here in a way no one has in the past. There is no right or wrong here, nor anyone to tell us which way to go or what to do. Just blank pages and new choices ahead of us. So, I don't think it's fear in the way we all know it. It's apprehension, excitement, and curiosity all wrapped in one," she said, content.

"Great." Garret and Raja seemed to appear out of nowhere. "Apprehension, excitement, and curiosity all wrapped in one? So then we're basket cases." Garret walked past them and towards the Northern Woods. The earth groaned as branches and vines cleared a path. "Are you coming or not? Or do you need more time to digest that trite revelation?" he said as both he and Raja powered forward.

"I might eat that one before this is all over." Muraco exhaled and sauntered into the woods.

"You know," Lee said as he scratched the back of his head, "I'm not sure I'd stop him."

Sophia smiled at Lee. They watched one another for a moment, letting all their experiences wash through them. With a deep breath and a shoulder nudge, Sophia and Lee caught up with the others as the group of friends walked forward into the unknown.

92

REGENERATED

His eyes took a moment to adjust. Once they did, he saw that the area he was in was dark. He pulled himself out of the coffin-like contraption. His body made a popping sound as he emerged. He was cold and naked. Reaching his fingers out, he tried to feel for a wall. After taking several steps, the room lit up. The man covered his eyes and waited for another adjustment period. When his eyes didn't hurt anymore, he removed his hands and saw that there was a bed with a robe and clothing placed upon it. He wobbled towards the bed and wrapped the robe around himself. It was then he saw a water basin. Finding his footing easier now, he slowly walked towards it and washed his face. He took several deep breaths and looked up. There, in the mirror looking back at him, was an olive-skinned man with long, dark hair that fell far past his shoulders. He looked at the left of his face, then the right. He needed to shave, he thought. Then he stared directly at himself. The man's brows furrowed as he continued to look deeply into the mirror. While everything else sccmed normal about him, the intense color of his eyes intrigued him. The color was of a deep brilliant grey.

- End -

ACKNOWLEDGEMENTS

Hey, look at you! Reading the last few pages of a book. Seriously hardly anyone ever reads these final straggling words. So, I say, pat yourself on the back, give yourself a literal round of applause and treat-yo-self. If you would like to continue reading, go for it. Just get your treat first.

I would like to say thank you to everyone at Atmosphere Press for taking a chance on me. They had no idea the project they were taking on, seriously I'm a handful. To Luan Bittencourt @luanfb.design thank you for bringing the map of Gea to life, to @birdys.garden thank you for your wonderful portrait of me. Thank you to the incredibly sexy creature I call my husband, for being my best friend, and for supporting my delicate dreams of becoming an author. Also, for the numerous times he saved my laptop from becoming a projectile in my deepest moments of self-doubt. Thank you to my two boys for being patient with me when I was "in the zone" and making me laugh when I desperately needed it. Thank you to my mami, pops, brother and sestra for cultivating an environment of open mindedness that celebrated uniqueness, love, and family. To my brothers from another mother, WWG? You allowed me to spread my strange awkward wings with no judgement. You are my home away from home. Hey Troublemakers! We rock.

I am forever grateful to each and every single one of you. Besos y abrazos.

ABOUT ATMOSPHERE PRESS

Atmosphere Press is an independent, full-service publisher for excellent books in all genres and for all audiences. Learn more about what we do at atmospherepress.com. We encourage you to check out some of Atmosphere's latest releases, which are available at Amazon.com and via order from your local bookstore:

Twisted Silver Spoons, a novel by Karen M. Wicks

Queen of Crows, a novel by S.L. Wilton

The Summer Festival is Murder, a novel by Jill M. Lyon

The Past We Step Into, stories by Richard Scharine

The Museum of an Extinct Race, a novel by Jonathan Hale Rosen

Swimming with the Angels, a novel by Colin Kersey

Island of Dead Gods, a novel by Verena Mahlow

Cloakers, a novel by Alexandra Lapointe

Twins Daze, a novel by Jerry Petersen

Embargo on Hope, a novel by Justin Doyle

Abaddon Illusion, a novel by Lindsey Bakken

Blackland: A Utopian Novel, by Richard A. Jones

The Jesus Nut, a novel by John Prather

The Embers of Tradition, a novel by Chukwudum Okeke

Saints and Martyrs: A Novel, by Aaron Roe

When I Am Ashes, a novel by Amber Rose

Melancholy Vision: A Revolution Series Novel, by L.C. Hamilton

The Recoleta Stories, by Bryon Esmond Butler

Voodoo Hideaway, a novel by Vance Cariaga

Hart Street and Main, a novel by Tabitha Sprunger

The Weed Lady, a novel by Shea R. Embry

ABOUT THE AUTHOR

M.Z thoroughly enjoys adventuring, if there are lands to be discovered, stories to be told, or fun to be had—you can count on her to be there. M.Z. resides in Rhode Island with the love of her life, their two hilarious boys, a pair of energetic pups, and one cat to rule them all.

CPSIA information can be obtained
at www.ICGtesting.com
Printed in the USA
BVHW040314260922
647801BV00002B/6

9 781639 885343